Far Beyond the Pale

A NOVEL

Daren Dean

Fiction Southeast Press
Baton Rouge, LA

Publisher/printed in the United States of America

FIRST EDITION

ISBN-13: 978-0692347621

Fiction Southeast Press
Baton Rouge, LA

Cover photo: Notley Hawkins

Fiction Southeast.org

For Cassie, Claira, Finn & Mom

I marked all kindred powers the heart finds fair through death to love moonclouds from child to youth from youth to arduous man from lethargy to fever of the heart from faithful life to dream dowered days even as a child of sorrow that we give the dead boat that draws dark water of night like a burning sword across our souls look in my face my name is might have been I am also called no more too late farewell

-Frank Stanford, *The Battlefield Where the Moon Says I Love You*

That's not true what I said. It was a damned lie ever word. He's a rogue and a outlaw hisself and you're welcome to shoot him, burn him down in his bed, any damn thing, because he's a traitor to boot and maybe a man steals from greed or murders in anger but he sells his own neighbors out for money and it's few lie that deep in the pit, that far beyond the pale.

 -Cormac McCarthy, *The Orchard Keeper*

Bad Luck Sign

As long as I can remember everyone's always called me Honey Boy. It wasn't Mama who gave me that name, she just mostly called me "Honey." Mama Horne used to take care of me when I was little and Mama worked late at the tavern, and as soon as she saw us pull into her driveway she'd quick-walk all bowlegged out to us with her arms stretched wide, "Where's my Honey Boy at?" My heart jumped every time she called to me. She would wrap me up in her arms, the smell of onions on her hands and lilac perfume in her hair, and coo, "Where is my baby? Where is my Honey Boy?" No matter how young or old a person is, the heart always knows who's calling for true.

When I was almost thirteen, I don't mind telling you, I worshipped my mama the way boys sometimes do. Something inside me rested when we were together even if by then we had already lived in half a dozen states. We had outrun bad men, bad jobs, and flat-out desperate situations. Mama talked sweet to the old Ford, "Aw, come on baby. Just a little bit more now." She leaned in real close so her lips almost touched the dash and practically purred to the damned old thing. Her red lipstick so bright it made her lips look huge. The Ford wasn't listening though, and it died out in front of Roy's gas station just a block from the square, with bad luck and trouble still hanging over our heads.

Despite the sorry state of things a secret smile spread across her face. She was happy to be back home, but I remembered she once said Fairmont was the kind of small town heavy with all its secrets and it was that heaviness that depressed her. She pushed a strand of auburn hair out of her eyes. They were brown with a golden hue around the pupils. She used to wear her hair straight to her waist, but she had cut it off back in San Diego to her shoulder and I thought it looked nice. She had been born a twin, but the other her died at birth. She had two sides to her. There was the Mama I knew, and there was another woman I'd seen rattling around inside those eyes especially when men were around. No matter where we lived, her mind was looking down the interstate for what new dream might appear shimmery in the distance.

I was not happy about moving back. We'd been living with a woman named Beth Ann, a half-assed hippy, and her two towheaded kids in a little house at Ocean Beach. All I had to do was walk a couple of blocks down the street to see the Pacific, or hike along the sand cliffs, where a diver might appear like a sea creature stepping awkwardly toward the beach holding an angry green crab, though it wasn't a pretty beach like the golden stretches of sand in front of the fancy hotels, it still beat looking out your window and see-ing herefords chewing their cud and shitting all day out in a pasture. More often as not, there were bikers leaning on their Harleys at the end of the street talking to a neighbor-hood pot dealer.

Before we even hit the Nevada line, I'd vowed to leave the state of *Misery* forever as soon as I could. I tried to talk Mama out of leaving California by endlessly making fun of *Misery*. I talked about hicks sitting around in their overalls playing banjos; hillbillies drinking moonshine out of jugs like on the signs at the tourist traps down at the Lake of the Ozarks; goobers dry-humping their livestock. Mama finally got tired of it and corrected me much more sharply than usual: "It's pronounced Missour-ah." I heard pride in her voice the way she said it. Now that *she* had decided to come back it was a completely different story. She was sick of working at the local choke and puke, but I wondered how it would be any better back in Hooterville.

A couple of days earlier she fell asleep at a rest area. I unzipped my duffle bag and took out the old-timey pistol and rubbed the pearl handles in awe. It was the one I took from Sonny's glove box. I imagined him scratching his chin, the way he did, and wondering where the pistol went. It made me think of the story, "The Frog King," my fourth grade teacher, read to us once, except Sonny didn't drop the gun in the water and I wasn't a frog. I pretended that I was Billy the Kid, because it was a western-style pistol—and it was loaded.

The way I had it figured Sonny owed it to me for all the times he slapped Mama around and I would have to go sleep on the neighbor's couch. Sonny claimed to be kin to Jesse James, Robert E. Lee, John Wayne, and Steve McQueen. He said all the Vaughns were kin to them too. He dared me to say they weren't. He'd look at me like the sun was in his eyes with a cigarette hanging off his lip all theatrical impersonating James Dean, "There, then, now . . . Honey Boy . . . are you having a good time?" He was an okay guy as far as that goes but he was bad news for Mama just like his brother Vaughn. I guess I didn't hate him all the way. Even if he was a son-of-a-bitch. He could be fun sometimes too like when he would take us over to the Zoo and play frisbee in Balboa Park.

Mama had stopped at Gasper's truck stop to change into a black mini-skirt and dark hose. There were Kenworths and Nationals parked all over the place with their diesel engines rumbling, and the gasping sound of hydraulic brakes. A fat woman in a blue house dress and a skinny old man in jeans and feed cap were giving away Heinz 57 puppies out of a cardboard box near the front door. Mama wore big round sunglasses that made her look like a starlet. Truckers whistled as she wiggled down the hallway toward the restrooms with me. I was proud to be with her, but nobody paid attention to me except. I was invisible. Her hand trailed down to light on my shoulder and she called me her escort. She knew how to make me feel good instead of like a little boy. She was still young, she said.

Mama pulled into Roy's gas station and the power steering moaned like it did every time she turned it sharp and drove over the line causing the bell to ding-ding. She found a way to make her looks work for her. As the gas station attendant started toward us from the garage she gave me a wink and her blinding white smile.

"Lorene? Lorene Kimbrough?" Raffert Clearwater asked. I'd seen him by the garage changing the oil on a cop car, Deputy Sheriff it read beneath the seal, a Plymouth. Rafe had oil all over his blue mechanic's shirt with his first name on the little oval patch. I was hoping he wouldn't see us. I could have cared less about Rafe Clearwater.

"That's me," Mama shook her shoulder at him like Betty Boop.

I remembered Grandma Kimbrough said Rafe wasn't worth a good goddamn, so why didn't Mama ever listen? Grandma seemed all right the last time we visited her at the King's Daughters retirement home in Fairmont. She kept repeating, "Now is the winter of my discontent," but I didn't know what she meant since it was spring when she said it. They let her keep some of her old stuff from home: the big fake leather chair that was Otherdaddy's, an old picture of a man and woman she called Ma and Pap in an oval frame from the dinosaur age, and a dark picture of Jesus praying hard in Gethsemane. I knew all about Jesus and the Bible from Aunt Oleta. Sonny called her a fanatic and a Bible-thumper. When I was little I thought Jesus was one of my great uncles since he held such an honored place on Aunt Oleta's wall.

By the time we were ready to go, Grandma started following us through the place: "Don't leave me babies. Take me with you. I want to go home." Aunt Oleta flashed her mean-eyed look and said, "Hush that up, now. You know we can't take you with us." Grandma grabbed at my arm with what had turned into a claw and I started bawling like a little baby. I didn't want to leave her, but it wasn't up to me. Shit, if I didn't hop to quick enough, I'd get left myself.

"Little girl," Rafe said. "You wouldn't believe just how good it is to see you."

Rafe stuck his big hairy head in the window so his face was inches from Mama's filling the truck with Hai Karate, gasoline, sweat, and beer breath. He leaned back and rested his chin on his forearms crisscrossed over the window. His fingernails had black dirt under them. His fingers left their imprint on the red interior of the driver's side door. His face twisted with a pathetic effort to make an expression that passed for friendly, but it wasn't used to it and nearly cracked from trying. His eyes looked Mama up and down and he wetted his lips with his tongue.

Go away, I said in my mind. *Go away, please.*

"Rafe," Mama laughed, swatting at his arms with the tips of her fingers. "Well, we only got back just this minute. You think you might could take a look at this bucket of bolts?"

"Why sure! Ain't nothing' a Clearwater boy can't take care of."

"Shi-it," I said under my breath.

"Watch the language," Mama said, but not mean. "Don't get yourself all worked up. You know how you get with your asthma when you get all hot and upset."

"Is that your new boyfriend in there with you?"

"Hey Rafe," I said with a half-wave that said, "Kiss my ass."

Rafe got us bottles of Coke and he jury-rigged the truck. He would end up putting in a big yellow button to start it without a key—it was the damndest thing. While he worked with the hood up, he would flex his biceps extra hard because he knew Mama was watching. He spun the nut

around a few times and looked at our air filter with a disgusted expression as a cigarette bounced out of one side of
his face and he squinted his eyes and talked to us through
the smoke. He revved the engine a couple of times, put everything back together, wiped his hands on a red rag and
chucked Mama under the chin like she was a snot-nosed
kid. Then, he gave me a wink like I was in on some private
joke.

Rafe had black hair down to his shoulders. His face
looked like it was eaten up by acid. Mama said his face was
pockmarked from acne but saying it was caused by acid
seemed more dramatic. It made him look mean. His eyebrows kind of grew together too. Mama smiled at me when
he walked into the gas station office. I took it to mean she
thought he was a real hunk because of his muscles and everything. He didn't fool me. He was being nice because he
wanted to get friendly with her. Rafe was only pretending to
like me until he got what he wanted. I'd seen it all before.
She always fell for it too.

Mama wanted a man to love her. I never understood
why my love wasn't enough for her, but I was beginning to
understand there was a different kind of love that she needed from a man. It was wanting that love that made her lose
her head. She left me with Aunt Oleta for a few months at a
time, here and there, in Fairmont when I was a little kid just
so she could chase after one man or another. Just stuck
there with nothing to do all day but watch Aunt Oleta trick
out her bouffant or watch her stories. Aunt Oleta wearing
curlers, spraying half a can of Aqua Net on her Jiffy Pop
hairdo about made me want to vomit. Getting left, even if it
is with family because no one really wants you around is
hurtful. I used to draw pictures of storms with the black
crayon until it was a nub. I gnawed on the red and maroon
crayons until they crumbled. It made me mad to see other
kids with their mamas and daddies at church. It was unfair. I

felt like God had broken the rules. I was getting too old for crayons and believing in fairy tales so I started sneaking cigarettes.

When I used to live with Aunt Oleta, in Sunday school with long braided hair named Ruth played guitar and asked us if we had any song requests. I requested "Slip Sliding Away" but she said we didn't sing those kind of songs in church. I was old enough to know better, but that song made more sense to me at the time than Jesus Loves Me. There was a part of me that still wanted to believe that God really cared about me, but then if he didn't do things to make your life better like see that your Mama meets a nice man, or finds a job making more than minimum wage, or letting you live with your own Mama—then that God was kind of mean if he was all powerful like Brother Pappy said.

A couple of hours later we left the truck on the lot to go out with Rafe for the night. Rafe made us get into his hopped up Mustang and took us down to a freshly blacktopped road just outside of Auxvasse. Locals liked to pronounce it the way strangers passing through for gas did *OX-vase-EE* with emphasis on the OX and the E as a joke. The paved road ended down near an area called Wildwoods where Grandma said she was born in a house, without paint, not much bigger than a chicken coop where winding roads curved in between scrub pines and choked maple trees. It didn't take much for Rafe to convince Mama. She sprayed herself with Jean Nate perfume. I was kicking myself for forgetting my duffle bag in the truck at the gas station.

Rafe won his first race against a guy whose goatee made him look like the Devil. His car, a classic Chevy, painted black with fire on the sides. The Devilman sucked on a skinny cigar like that ol' boy in the western I saw at the drive-in awhile back. The cherry glowed and he flicked the butt out into the road near the yellow center line. It was a cool car, but it wasn't made for dragging like Rafe's Mustang. The Chevy didn't have a chance.

"How did you like that, Chief?" Rafe asked, laughing fit to kill. He had his hands raised up in the air in fists over his head like he won the Indy 500.

We sat in a pink convertible parked on the side of the road with a girl named Lizzie.

Lizzie kept shooting Mama dirty looks. It was clear who she was there to see. She showed off her legs and her boobs too, but she seemed like a real tight-ass to me. She had ash-blond hair. Every so often she tossed her head and swung her hair around throwing honey-gold rays of sunshine in the air. She kept looking at the men and pointing to this one or that one and telling Mama, "What a fox!" or "Don't you think he's a fox?" I about upchucked. Lizzie was one tight-assed mother.

Danny Vaughn had tried to tell Rafe there wasn't any point racing a farmer's work truck. It was red like a fire truck. He even had this white toolbox that reached from one side to the other of the truck bed with an air compressor in the back. Mama screamed as soon as she saw Rafe veer onto the gravel shoulder. Guys were running up to the wreck real fast in their engineer boots and rolled up shirt sleeves. One cowboy's hat fell off behind him as he ran to the wreck. There was smoke coming out of the car so Lizzie was rubbing her hands together like a fly with excitement. "Bitchin'," she kept saying. She was hoping the car would blow up and then I began to like her a little bit. I could see yellow and orange flames leaping into the air. A cloud of blue-black smoke rose up and made it hard to see. I had a coughing fit. Mama used to say I had asthma and just about anything would set it off. Lizzie narrowed her eyes as if I had interrupted her fun on purpose. Just when I thought I could control it a few coughs would sneak out of the fist I held pressed to my lips.

"Shut it up, squirt," Lizzie said to me.

I stopped wheezing.

"I think Rafe's a goner" Danny stuck his head in the window and started laughing like a hyena bathing us with his beer breath.

I felt a surge of hope rise up from my belly and into my chest. Maybe Rafe was killed in the wreck. Mama would have to find someone new, someone better, to get a crush on.

"He really fucked up that Mustang," Danny said. "Hey, Honey Boy. You've grown since the last time I seen you. You won't recognize the boys. They've about grown up on their old man. Y'all staying with Rafe now?"

"Maybe," Mama said with her lips pressed tightly together like she wanted to say it ain't none of your business. "I just got into town. Haven't decided on what I'm doing. I might go on over to Aunt Oleta's."

"We *cain't* stay around here much longer," Lizzie said. "Go check on Rafe for us, hon."

Red lights started flashing behind us. Too many people piled into Lizzie's car. I found myself in my usual position smushed, in the backseat, straddling the hump. Lizzie said I was *riding bitch*.

Rafe came striding down the middle of the highway out of the smoke, flames surging up in into the starry night sky like he was some kind of badass. I figured Mama was weak in the knees now. Then Rafe squeezed into the front seat and took a Ziploc baggy half-full of pot and stuck it in Mama's purse. I started hoping the cops would catch us and throw Rafe in jail, but instead they chased someone else. Rafe said he would report his car stolen tomorrow morning. Besides, he laughed, his cousin Mitch was a cop in Audrain county. People were running back and forth across the narrow stretch of macadam. Cars were trying to turn around. A teenaged girl was hiking up her tube top. I turned to watch the car burn as it grew smaller framed in the rear window like a drive-in movie.

Some by Signs, Others by Whispers

Rafe listened to old songs that had funny words like Hank Williams howling at the moon. Rafe used to make me call him the King too, and then he would gyrate and act the fool. It was nothing like the real thing. If I had to choose between Sonny or Rafe, I guess it was six of one and a half dozen of the other. Sonny was a whole lot bigger than Rafe, meaner too. Mama used to go with Sonny's older brother, Vaughn, a hundred years ago. She wasn't no slut, but she was pretty wild according to Aunt Oleta. Then again, Aunt Oleta's notion of high times was taking her homemade pecan pies down to the community hall for the Kiwanis Club or the Ladies Auxiliary Patriarchs Militant. Sounded like a bunch of whackos to me.

We went busting into Rafe's house by the lake. It was pretty out there. I had seen it before in the daylight so I knew that much. Sonny and Rafe used to be best buds and was always competing for girls, especially Mama. Rafe's place had pine trees growing everywhere. It had a gate you had to get out of your car to open, like one that went out to the pasture. Just about everyone on the estate had a little dock and a boat. Rafe just had a little fishing boat, but everyone else had bright-colored racing boats. Something about him living out here didn't make much sense considering he was brought up by Mad Whiskey Watts down there past the MFA in a rusted mobile home. Something peculiar was going on. A thick fog hovered over the lake like when the preacher at Redeemer Pentecostal said that thing about the spirit of God hovering over the surface of the waters while he stood preaching with one foot in the bonfire on glowing coals.

"Good night, Honey Boy," Mama said. Rafe gave me a pillow and a blanket and pointed me toward the couch. Mama and him started sucking face and clawing at each other's clothes like they was going to eat each other up on the spot. Mama used to talk Rafe down to Sonny, but I guess she forgot all that since we didn't have any place to go. She used to always tell me, "Kids ain't the only ones got to do what they don't want. You do what you can. You do what you got to. Remember that before you go judging."

So I had to listen to them in there jumping around in the bed wearing each other out, and then I finally got some sleep after watching the sickle moon through the window for awhile. The sound of the headboard banging against the wall disgusted me and then to make matters worse I could hear skin slapping against skin. I had a glass on the coffee table in front of me where I lay on the couch and watched the water tremble. It made me want to vomit. I must have caught a shotgun buzz from all the grass they smoked earlier, because I could see the individual particles that made up the blue and pale yellow moonbeams. I knew it wasn't no way for a kid to live, but I had to make the best of it. Nobody ever had to tell me that. I'd been doing it my entire natural life.

The icebox kicked on into its cycle, making a ruckus, so it drowned out their love talk.

"You're awake, man," said Rafe whe he came out of the bedroom with just his jeans on. "I can tell by the way you're breathing. You're awake so there ain't no use in pretending you sneaky son-of-a-bitch."

"What?" I stretched real big then. "I was dreaming."

"About what?" Rafe said looking mean. "What was you dreaming you skinny little shit? I'm suddenly feeling like I'm in the mood to hear your dream. What was you dreaming about? Choking your chicken and then you woke up, and you was?"

"I was dreaming about a talking asshole," I said. "When I woke up, there you were."

Rafe's head turned purple. I thought it would explode. I took a wild roundhouse swing at him as he came my way but he batted my arm away with no problem. To me it felt like my arm was going to come off at the shoulder. He came over and sat on my chest, licked the tip of his fingers and began to slap at my forehead so only his fingertips would make stinging contact and leave little marks like uneven sunburn. Then he began to poke his thick index finger into my chest over and over again. The whole time I could see the cherry of his cigarette burning bright as he puffed. I pretended to be invisible and just watched the cherry. I guess my face must've went blank or something. Then he saw me watching the cigarette so he took it out of his mouth, grabbed my lower jaw with his hand, and made me puff on the filter while he held me down, but I had all but run out of air.

"How you like that hotrod?" Rafe asked. "You ain't so damn smart now are you?" He pulled down the blanket and grabbed my right arm by the wrist. "Now we're going to see what kind of man you are." Rafe held my arm down on the couch and pressed the lit end of his cigarette into my forearm. Tears clouded my vision. It hurt. The humiliation of it hurt more I guess. "Are you going to cry now? Huh? What are you, a little girl? Well, I been in there fucking your Mom all night so I guess I could come in here and give it to you too since you're a little girl."

I wanted to holler at him that I was going to get my pistol and blow his brains out, but I didn't want him to know about it. I had to clamp my jaws shut so I wouldn't blurt it out. I figured him for a sorry bastard, but Mama seemed to like that kind. What was it? She looked pretty when she wanted to so it wasn't a looks thing. She talked all right too. She couldn't cook too good or just didn't want to cook. Maybe if she learned to cook, or I learned to cook, fried chicken with mashed potatoes and chicken gravy with biscuits and salted down corn on the cob smeared with butter she might find somebody with a good job. The service station didn't pay jackshit and everybody knew that. It was a job for ex-cons unless you were the owner.

"Rafe," Mama said from the bedroom. "Leave him alone and come in here. Bring my cigarettes if you don't mind, darling."

Did she know what was going on? Why didn't she do something? She stood there smoking that Viceroy and was giving me a hard look or was thinking seriously about something. She didn't want me ruining things with Rafe since we didn't have no place to go. It's the worst feeling knowing you got no place to go. Rafe brushed past her sort of poking his forearm out to push her out of the way. She looked right through me breathing blue smoke out of her nose as she shut the bedroom door. She didn't seem to notice what he had done to me.

"That boy of yours has got a smart mouth on him," said Rafe's voice through the wall. "Don't he know he's just a woods colt?"

Why don't you just shut up! Your mouth ain't no prayer book!
I felt more alone than ever right then.

I sat down on the couch with my face in my hands and blubbered. I'm not too proud to admit it. Nobody was there to see it. Who would I tell? I held my arm in my hand and felt sorry for myself. Aunt Oleta used to call them pity parties. What if they were? No one else was invited. One day I'd have a jillion dollars and then wouldn't everybody be surprised. I would show them all then. I'd drive by in a red convertible Corvette or a brand new black Cadillac wearing dark sunglasses and not even notice them when I drove through town with Mama in the seat next to me.

A train wailed past; I cried some more.

I wondered again who my daddy was and why he wasn't here to protect me. He was probably big and strong and brave. Did I look like him? Whenever I asked Mama about him she gave me serious looks and sort of swallowed her words down like bitter medicine. I imagined a muscular shadow walking into the living room. Leaning over the couch to ruffle my hair with his warm hand and then going to the bedroom to beat the tar out of Rafe. Then the two of us would go outside where a black stallion with a star on its head was waiting for my Daddy, and a half-wild mustang that liked only me waited for us to saddle up and ride out of town to our hideout where no one would ever find us.

Later on Rafe poked his big head out the door again, his bangs falling down near his bushy eyebrows. "I'm gonna do you a favor, and then you're going to do me one. Hear?"

"You ain't my daddy," I whispered.

Don't you love me?

A man was talking in my head. I didn't say nothing, but I cocked my ear to see if the voice would say anything else. I kept listening for it. *Don't you love me anymore?* The voice whispered so quiet I could just barely hear him like a phantom radio station late at night playing your favorite song and making it through the powerful waves of the local station's signal that mostly blocked everything else out. Listening. Nothing. I can't explain it but a smell flooded into my nose unlike anything I ever smelled before. The best I can explain it, it was like the scent of honeysuckle but soured. The smell went away and I wondered what it meant, if anything. It reminded me of the last time we lived in Fairmont. Aunt Oleta had Mama taking me to church twice a week. Once was more than enough if you asked me. Part of a hymn or a prayer ran through my mind, "a sweet savor."

I felt better telling Rafe off even if he hadn't heard me whispering and choking on my broken-hearted scolding. Mama would never tell me who my daddy was and always made it into a joke. "Ain't I enough for you?" She might ask in a flirty way turning her head at an angle to look at me like I was a little baby.

Whoever my daddy was, I knew for a fact that he wouldn't put up with the kind of goings-on that were the norm these days. Someday I was going to find my daddy. I made up the notion that my daddy had somehow gotten separated from us. Not that he wanted to, but that's the way it happened. It was like a movie where a family is waiting for someone to arrive just as their train is pulling out of the station. Just then the person they were waiting on arrives but the train has picked up speed and it's too late. The steam from the locomotive makes the scene go hazy. The whistle blows in a downhearted tone. There was the outline of my daddy standing on the platform waving pitifully because he just missed us and his pockets were stuffed with cash. At least, that's how I tried to see it. The only other explanation I could see was that he and Mama had fought over money, or about him or her stepping out on the other one. Either way, that would mean it was permanent. I would never get to see my daddy. Mama would never find a real man to settle her down.

The Pistol

Thinking of that pistol made me get up and put on my soured clothes. I washed my face in the bathroom. There was Superman and Archie comic books in on the toilet, but what really got my attention was the Hustler magazine and the naked women. Looking at the women stirred something up in me, but I didn't know exactly what it meant. They were real interesting and, even though I was alone, they made me blush. I found a pad and bandages in the medicine cabinet and wound a piece around my forearm and put some white adhesive tape over it so it would stick.

The hell if I was going to sit around all day and wait for Rafe to wake up and start ordering me to go get him a beer, a flathead screwdriver, or griping at me about a three-quarters wrench. I made some toast with butter and cinnamon. There wasn't much in Rafe's fridge besides hot sauce and beer. I was determined to walk those four or five miles to the gas station and get my duffle bag out of the truck. I closed the front door carefully, and then allowed the screen door to smack shut. The sound made me grin despite the pain in my arm. It was an angry burn like a miniature volcano and the only positive thought that came to mind was that it might make me look tough when school started again.

Outside the sun had already warmed the macadam. The cicadas screeched everywhere among the horseweeds in the ditch going into town on Highway 54. A little black dog, part Lab by the looks of him came up to me blinking his eyelids and beating the ground with his tail. It said *Buddy* in black lettering on the red collar around his neck. When I started walking again Buddy got in front of me with his tail in the air like a battle flag and trotted past the Purina feed store, Modern Farm Equipment Company, the Drive-in, a used car lot with costs written in white on the windshields, and the roller

skating rink where Big John spun the records and worked the
lights. Buddy led me into town, and every once in a while
he'd look back at me to make sure he was doing all right. He
made me feel better. That's what dogs do best.

When we got into town some of the old people sat up in
chairs and swing-
benches on their porches. Kingdom Days Historical Society
was sponsoring a parade according to the banner stretched
between the buildings on the square. Buddy would run into
people's yards and piss on their trees, provoking the geezers
to ask, "Is that your dog, son?" To which I could truthfully
reply, "Nope."

I found the truck and my duffle bag wedged behind the
seat. Buddy tried to hop up in the cab. When I pulled him out
he kind of gave out a yip and old Roy came out of the station
office. He was wearing a John Deere cap and chewing tobacco made his cheek bulge like a gray squirrel. He had the pack
in his hand like he was a starving man stuffing French fries in
his mouth. Didn't even have a chance to notice my pistol as I
slipped it behind the tail of my flannel shirt and down into
the waistband of my jeans.

"What you doing in that truck, boy?" Roy smelled like a
mixture of Old Spice, grease, and sweat.

"Just getting my stuff, sir," I said.

"Don't sir me," he said. "Just call me Roy. People that say
sir too much are generally liars."

"Getting my stuff!" I yelled at the constipated expression
on his face.

"Oh?" Roy looked at me as if to say *I'm wise to you.* "You're
Lorene's boy. Now,
what's that she calls you? Honey Boy? That ain't much of a
name for a young man full of piss and vinegar. What do you
want me to call you? Cause I sure as shit ain't calling you
Honey Boy."

"Everyone started calling me Honey Boy on account of Mama Horne use to keep me with her kids," I had to yell because he didn't act like he could hear very well. "When Mama would pick me up after work Mama Horne used to tell her "He is my Honey Boy," and Mama thought that was funny. It just kind of stuck. Most people call me Kid."

"Say they do?" he pushed up the bill of his cap. "That ain't much better. What's your given name?"

"Nathan," I said.

"Say again?"

"Nathan!"

"What kind of sodie you like, Cracker Jack?" Roy spit tobacco juice on the gravel between his teeth like a pro.

"Dr. Pepper," I said.

"At ten, twelve, and two?"

I didn't know what he meant so I just stood there squinting into the sun rising up smaller and hotter all the time.

"Guess you know it's got prune juice in it?" Roy asked, starting to walk back to the office. "You drink enough of those and they'll give you the shits. C'mon in. I'll give you one of those sodies. Got a surplus on Dr. Pepper, because don't nobody want that much prune juice in their diet. Who is your friend there?"

"Somebody's dog," I said. "He followed me here from Rafe's."

"So y'all stayed out to Rafe's?"

"Yeah," I said, my head down, afraid I was telling too much private stuff about Mama.

"It's all right," Roy said, lifting the lid to the old Coca-Cola freezer and pulling out a sodie and handing it to me. "Rafe and your mama been knowing each other for a long time. He could've almost been your daddy, I reckon. He's supposed to be into work today but I guess he's hung over and won't be here again. It's the same every Saturday. It don't seem to do no good to holler at him. Oh, you don't like him much do you?"

"No," I said. "He did this." I pulled back the taped up pad and showed him my forearm.

"Damn. He's a mean little shit," Roy took hold of my arm. "If I were a little younger I'd take him out behind the barn and teach him some manners. I'm too old for that though, sad to say. Maybe you two will grow on each other. It's been known to happen."

Roy disappeared into the bathroom and came out with a white first aid kit that looked like a small toolbox. He took out a smelly little bottle of "salve" soaked a cotton ball and dabbed it on my forearm. Then, he taped on a bandage that was way too big for the burn. He even gave Buddy a drink of water out of an old hubcap.

"Know who that dog belongs to?" Roy asked.

"No sir."

"He's one of them Vaughn's Hill dogs." Roy wiped his forehead with a red handkerchief. "I tell you that for your own protection. Some of the Vaughn boys catch you with him, they may beat the shit out of you. They just live down off UU. It's your lookout though. He's a good dog. Just don't try to keep him."

"He was pissing in people's yards earlier," I said. "People kept asking me if he was my dog."

"I expect they knew who he belonged to," Roy said. "They were probably trying to figure out who you belonged to. You don't look like a Vaughn. They're big corn-fed sum-bucks! Hey now, wasn't Lorene and you living out in California with Sonny Vaughn?"

"Yep."

"Then you know what I'm talking about," Roy said "Gas prices were high in California I bet?"

"Yep," I said. "We had to wait in real long lines. Sometimes people'd get out and play Frisbee while they was waiting. You probably seen it on the news, huh?"

"People got to be crazy to want to live out there anyway," Roy said. "How did Sonny like sitting in gas lines?"

"Not too well."

Roy kind of snorted, "I expect not. Them Vaughns ain't got much patience." The old man's face went kind of funny like he was remembering something. I thought he was getting ready to tell me too, but I guess it was just one of those things you don't tell. "Do you gotta shit?" he said.

"What?"

"You drank that Dr. Pepper down so fast I was just wondering if you gotta shit now?"

"No sir," I said.

"Then get the hell out of my station," Roy said. "That's all that Dr. Pepper is good for. Boys and dogs make it hotter than hell in here. I've got work to do."

Hellfire

A John Law was eyeing me from his cruiser as I stepped off Route UU and onto the gravel road I thought would be a short cut to Rafe's lakehouse. Sonny taught me to be a good lookout for cops. He used to make me and Mama call shotgun to ride up front. It meant you had to keep your eyes peeled for the heat. Mama usually got to sit up front no matter what, because she's an adult. The squawk box barked out some loud talk. John Law just looked at me his face cold behind his dark sunglasses, but he gave me a nod and pulled onto the road with his cherry tops churning around after a speeding Merc.

Buddy was following me now instead of leading. He was starting to take mincing steps as if he had arthritis. Insects were humming all around. A garter snake slipped from the side of the road and into the ditch. A horsefly was buzzing around me, a big fucker making a humming noise like a dirt bike so I stood still until he landed on my arm and smashed him dead with the flat of my hand. We were beginning to pass fields of soybean and corn. Along the white gravel road were hedge trees, walnut, and cottonwood that the pioneers had planted in the old days to mark their property boundaries from what Sonny used to tell me. He was always talking about coming back to Kingdom County. Up ahead was a broken windmill standing guard over a pond with a bunch of herefords hanging around chewing and looking annoyed.

I only just made it to the first big bend on the county road when I heard a pickup sliding around a dog leg on the gravel road. The closer the truck got, the louder the twang of country music. I knew right then I had to do something with my pistol so I rolled it up in my flannel shirt, dropped down next to the culvert, almost as big as an Ozark cave, and tossed it into the cylinder and hoped we wouldn't get a flash flood. It didn't take but a few seconds to toss my shooter in, but getting back up was a son-of-a-bitch because I had to bear-walk on all fours to get back up on the road.

Three boys were sitting across the front seat of the pickup, far as I could tell. There was a huge white cloud of gravel dust formed up behind them. I was already dreading it—I was going to time it so I could hold my breath when the cloud hit so I wouldn't have to breath it in. A mean looking red headed kid with freckles was driving and he hit his brakes just as he passed me and skidded to a stop. The dust cloud passed over us and I tried to hold my breath. My heart fell into my stomach. I should have known they'd stop.

"Buddy," the red headed kid said. "Get up in here!" The kid put his fingers between his teeth and whistled as he held the door open. Buddy jumped onto his lap from the road, wedged against the steering wheel, until one of the boys threw him down into the floorboard. "What're you doing with our dog?"

"You trying to steal our dog, man?" the dark headed one in the middle said.

"He just been following me is all."

"Oh is that all, you all?" the driver asked with a nasty mocking tone. Punkin was his name. It just popped into my head. I hadn't been gone so long I couldn't remember all three of them: Punkin, TC, and Rusty but they were acting like they hadn't ever seen me before. I was bigger now than I used to be.

"What's your name, kid?"

"Honey Boy," I said, knowing he would laugh.

"Honey Boy," the kid in the middle said. "What kind of name is Honey Boy?" He climbed over the driver's lap jumped down on the gravel road and punched me hard in the stomach. I didn't fall on the ground. I did stagger back and hold my gut. He caught me off my guard or I would have kicked him in the cucumbers. I had been to so many schools that I had the feeling that if I kept my head and played it tough I might be able to get through this.

"I don't know," I groaned. I clutched my stomach with my left hand and bent over at the waist. It was mean of Rusty to do it especially since he had two bigger boys waiting to jump in and help him if I did anything back.

"Where are you from?" Punkin asked.

"We just came back from California." I wheezed some more.

"Who would want to live in California anyway?" Punkin sniffed theatrically.

"We left Sonny there and just came on back."

"Sonny? You know Uncle Sonny?" Rusty said.

"He's practically my step-daddy."

"Would you listen to that little motherfucker? Practically's ass," Punkin said and kind of backhanded the lanky kid next to the passenger door in the midsection. "What do you think about that TC?"

"He's something else," says Rusty. "He's Lorene's whelp. I didn't hit you that hard, did I Honey Boy?"

"No," I said. I made myself stand up straight although my face felt red and hot. My eyes stung with angry tears but I refused to cry. He smiled crookedly at me. "I wasn't ready for it is all, man."

"He's practically our cousin," Punkin said. "I'd say he's about two pounds of Vaughn in a one pound sack. Get your narrow ass in this truck, Honey Boy! I remember you from before you all went out to California. Used to stay out to Mawmaw Vaughn's. We was just fucking with you. Where in the hell is Uncle Sonny? Why ain't he with y'all?"

The driver told me his nickname was Punkin like I didn't now it already and he looked really old like he could have been eighteen. Rusty was closest to my age. The tall quiet one with a hearing aid like a transistor radio that sat in his front

pocket with a thin white cord running to an earpiece was TC.
I wasn't sure how old or young he was. Something about his
hang-dog expression and the one lazy eye made me think of
an old man. I was sitting half on Rusty and half on TC. They
adopted me right on the spot. They started laughing about
how they pretended not to know who I was and Punkin kept
saying, "You should have seen your face." The truck was flying down the road. The windows were down and it was
started to get hot and humid. Punkin refused to slow down
for the occasional oncoming truck and then we would eat the
white dust gravel the trucks stirred up. We had to pull over
once to put Buddy in the pickup bed. Punkin claimed to
know me since I was a seedling. The interior of the truck
smelled like WD-40 and all us sweaty boys. Rusty pulled out a
hardpack of Marlboro Red's, lit a cigarette and stuck it in my
mouth, and he even rolled up the nearly-empty hard pack into my T-shirt sleeve like I was as tough as him.

"Look at these chicken wings he's got," Rusty said. "Flex
your muscle!" I must have blushed since I knew he was kidding me. I flexed it and Rusty pretended to be impressed.

We went to their place first. There was an honest-to-God
flagpole in the front yard with a Confederate flag thrashing in
the humid breeze. Their daddy was Danny Vaughn. Everyone
called Danny the quiet one except when he was pissed or
drunk or drunk and pissed. I overheard a man tell a truck
driver at the Spot once, "Danny Vaughn has a long fuse but
don't get him riled up because he ain't got no quit in him."
Danny's wife, Dorothy, was a tall thin woman with large
hands. Danny called her Dot. She wore house dresses and
could do twice the work of any man, which she needed to do
since it was common knowledge Danny was a drunk. She did
like to watch her shows in the afternoon and once I saw her
take a few tokes off a joint.

They lived at the end of the road on Vaughn's Hill and we
drove to a little house that had bicycles and parts of bikes lay-

ing all over the place. There were red, orange, blue, and black bikes. I saw dirt bikes, town bikes, 3-speeds, and a few 10-speeds. A couple of town bikes had orange flags tied to the back wheel. Rusty went to one and rang the bell on a "old man bike." Punkin hopped on a bike and jumped a mound of dirt especially erected for the purpose of Evel Knievel-like jumps. TC showed me the chopper he made and wanted to sell it to me, but I didn't have any money.

"Where did you get all these?" I asked.

"Some kids gave them to us," Punkin said with a sideways grin.

"I borrowed some from a kid I know," Rusty snickered. "He's got eleventy-seven brothers and sisters."

"Uncle Elston is gonna want to see you, Honey Boy," Punkin said. "Only when you see him make sure you listen to what he says. Don't go running off at the mouth. If he likes you, you don't have nothing to worry about. If he don't like you, he just might kill you."

"Don't you think he'll remember me?" I asked.

"Uncle Elston don't forget nothing" Rusty leaned in close to my face.

"Call him Vaughn," TC said. "He likes everyone to call him Vaughn, plain Vaughn.
"When he passes someday, I think everyone's gonna call me Vaughn."

"Would you listen to that!" Punkin looked surprised. "That's what I call a motor mouth! That's more than TC says in a month of Sundays. I think TC likes you, Honey Boy. He's taken to you awful quick. We ain't trying to scare you. Other than being kind of small, I can tell you're a Vaughn. You're good-looking like one."

"Uncle Vaughn is bad to drink whiskey," Rusty said. "So we might just turn around and leave if he's had too much. He can get mean then."

No one had ever said much about what I looked like before whether good, bad, or otherwise besides Mama. She mainly just wanted me to "look presentable" when we went to eat Sunday dinner at Aunt Oleta's house. She made me take a bath the night before these dinners, wash my hands before we left, and sometimes she would even spit on her finger and try to smooth down my cowlick. I'd endure just about anything for roast beef with carrots, onions, and potatoes. Listening to the sound of Aunt Oleta's hissing pressure cooker was music.

Elston Vaughn was sitting at the dining room table pouring lighter fluid in a silver lighter big as some belt buckles. He was drinking Old Grand-Dad. His head seemed enormous, too big for his body, bigger than I remembered. His hair was dark and wavy, his sideburns flared out along his dark jowls, brown-black eyes. He wasn't so tall, but he had a bit of a beer gut. On his lower right forearm was a tattoo of wings attached to the surname VAUGHN. The muscles in his biceps were as big as softballs. The farmers around Fairmont made me think they could have sprung up out of the clay soil like a cedar tree, but Vaughn was different. He seemed like something wild, not of the earth like a tree but more like a coyote or feral dog. Right away I noticed that the boys kept their eyes off of him because if he thought someone was trying to stare him down he'd make like he might get up and do who knows what. I remembered he would visit Mawmaw Vaughn when we were living out in her old barn that was converted into an apartment. He used to give Mama and me mean looks and holler at Mama a lot, but I could only just barely remember it like in a bad dream.

"You want me to do that for you, Daddy," Vaughn's wife, Arlene said.

"No, I like doing it. I like the smell."

Hellfire, I thought. Smells like hellfire, but I was too afraid to say it.

Vaughn's brother Danny, and cousins, built their homes together even though none of them knew all the details about building houses, they each possessed some piece of the puzzle. Lonny and Corinne knew how to frame up the walls and their kids, Rusty, Win, Colleen, and Lloyd pitched in and between them they made the rest up. Colleen was pretty and could punch harder than any of the boys except for Punkin. Claude and Nan lived in a trailer out near the dump. Claude would come down slowly holding his cane in front of him trying to pretend he didn't need it but plunking down into the ground before he fell over face first. He'd sit in an old metal lawn chair and holler advice from under the pin oak stroking his chin out of habit.

The house had electricity, but there were places where you could see the wires through the sections of wall they forgot to cover with paneling or drywall. They tended to do a half-assed job of it. Danny Vaughn and his boys had a house, but no indoor bathroom but they knew all about outhouses so that's what they had. Punkin said once he got big enough the disgusting job of maintaining the outhouse fell to him. When he started in on the details it liked to turned my stomach. Putting in a bathroom was their summer project.

I remember Sonny would take out a Bicycle card pack while he played solitaire and tell us about how he idolized his older brother Vaughn when they were boys.

"What I found out about Vaughn is," Sonny said holding a card in the air above one of his stacks. "Chiefly he is, was, and always will be . . . a son-of-a-bitch." He looked at me for a six-beat and then grinned the way he did at Mama when he convinced her to leave Misery. "I'd tell him that to his face too, but he don't give a damn."

Vaughn's four year-old little girl, Sugarbaby, was sitting in a chair next to Vaughn. Her hair was bright yellow and her face was dirty. Her lips were bright orange from her last partial glass of Kool-Aid. She was alternating between smashing Brazil nuts with a hammer and trying to use nutcrackers. Intent as she was on cracking those nuts she never even looked up to peek at me. When she managed to crack one she put the meat in a bowl for her daddy. Vaughn would reach over every so often and eat the nuts and wash it down with a swig of Miller beer, yellow like horse piss. Just because it looked like piss, don't mean I don't like it.

"You want a nigger toe?" Vaughn held out a handfull of nuts in the palm of his hand.

I meant to say no, but he handed one to me and I looked at it suspiciously.

Vaughn was studying me without trying. Occasionally he'd give me a look as if he was purposely making me wait. He flipped his lighter open and shut like a cowboy practicing his quick draw. I could smell his stale Old Spice cologne. There were stacks of old of *The Fairmont Sun, St. Louis Post-Dispatch, Kansas City Star, True Detective, Reader's Digest,* and *National Geographic* laying around everywhere—even a battered black leather Bible. When he was ready to deal with me he put the lighter down on top of his pack of Camels. He reached behind him and pulled on a shoulder holster with a .38 in it. Patting the gun after he put it on. "I bet you know the value of self-protection," he said. "If you don't, you ought to learn."

"Yes sir," I said. I knew my manners: my yes sirs, and no sirs, and thank yous and your welcomes. Men loved to be called sir. Don't ask me why. I used it on them whenever I needed to. Women gave me sour looks whenever I said Ma'am so I wasn't sure what to say to them except to say whatever they was wearing made them look pretty even if they was ugly, or thin if they was fat. Sonny had taught me all that old junk.

"Nice and polite," Vaughn opined, taking out a pocket-knife he opened the blade slowly and began to go at the grime under his fingernails. Those fingers were enormous and freckled. Each finger looked like a sausage link. His knuckles were huge as if there weren't but one thing they were good for, cracking skulls. "Polite young men may go far in this world," he said more to himself than me.

"Oww!" Sugarbaby wailed. "Do I have to keep cracking these nuts, Daddy?"

"No," he said. "Don't you got something for Daddy?"

"What Daddy?"

"Where's my sugar?"

"One lump or two?" Sugarbaby asked. He held up two fingers and Sugarbaby kissed him twice on the cheek. She hopped off his lap and picked up her battered Mrs. Beasley doll off the floor and disappeared into the kitchen.

Vaughn took another sip of beer, lit a Camel and had a couple of leisurely puffs. Considered me some more. Every-thing smelled of woodsmoke even though it was warm now and they probably hadn't banked a fire in a couple of months. I could hear the boys playing pool down in the basement. The crack of the balls. Punkin and Rusty were arguing about something, but I couldn't hear them too well. I was wishing I was down there fighting with them too. It was easy to guess what other kids would do, but with grown-ups you never know.

"Why didn't Sonny come back with you?"

"We snuck off," I said, picking at a scab on my elbow.

"Why's that?"

"He was beating' on us and we got tired of it," I said, defi-antly as I dared.

"Fair enough," he said. "Your Mama's shacked up with Rafe Clearwater. You think he's better than Sonny? You think y'all's better off with him?"

"No," I said, holding out my bandaged arm. "He done this to me . . . put his cigarette out on my arm."

"He won't do it again," Vaughn said, matter-of-fact. "You know, your Mama used to come see me some before she grabbed on to Sonny? That Sonny's too handsome for his own good. Other than being kind of mouthy, he ain't bad. You know your mama and me used to be together?"

"I heard about it," I said. "You and Mama."

Blue smoke was swirling around in the room, around his too big head like evil spirits was locked up in the room with us. Something about Vaughn made me want to get out of the little wooden chair and never come back. I could tell he was mean to the bone. Hell,
anyone could.

"You know what I mean when I say, be together?" He held his mouth in a way that made the word cruel bubble up to my lips but I fought against myself and didn't say it. He reminded me of some of the bullies I had met at different schools. Vaughn looked to me to be the kind that could be mean and enjoy every millisecond of somebody else's pain.

"I guess so."

"I reckon you don't," Vaughn said. "But that's okay for now. You tell your mama come by the house for me. You tell her to get shut of Raffert Clearwater, because I aim to scare him off or put his lights out. Don't matter a tinker's damn to me."

"I'll tell her," I said, scooting out of the chair. "But that don't mean much. She don't like to do what people tell her. She's hardheaded. That's what Granny says anyway."

"I guess she is at that" Vaughn laughed, but not like it was funny. "I want your mama and you to come stay with me for a while. Arlene and me be glad to have you, ain't that right, honey?"

"Yes daddy," Arlene said. She had that old-timey Missouri twang in her voice. I saw her face cloud over as she turned to go back into the kitchen.

"Let me tell you what," Vaughn began. I tried to listen real good and then he said it again. "Let me tell you what—" but he never did tell me what. He was having another talk with somebody in his head or that's how I featured it. A glazed look come over him and I could see expressions changing on his face like a Japanese puppet show we saw a film of in school. One puppet had a face long and permanently sad and another face was always happy. The story was a complicated one at best.

Vaughn pushed himself up with his hands on the table. He put a toothpick in his mouth and placed one of his heavy paws on my head to steer me out the door in front of him. It was as if he'd known me his whole life and it felt good and scary at the same time. It was nice to be known after being like a secret everywhere we had been. Like we was under some witness protection program, only not. I suspect we were hiding out from something Mama was afraid of, something inside her head and not out in the world. I knew that much. It choked me up a little to have this powerful person know me, have good will toward me, but I couldn't say how I felt because all the roaming had knocked all the normality out of my actions and manners. We'd been gone for going on three years or so except for Christmas that first year when we came back, so being amongst home people felt kind of funny.

At the doorway, Vaughn unholstered the gun and held the butt of it up to my chest. I just stood there. I wouldn't take it. Kept my eyes on the ground too, because he got mad so easy.

"Don't tell me you're afraid of guns?" he said, his pointing finger in my face as we stepped out into the mudroom with all the work boots, flannel jackets, dirty laundry, and a moaning white freezer.

"No sir," I said.

"Take it then, boy!" Vaughn bellowed.

"I don't want it." I locked my arms against my body and clasped my hands together behind my back. He put his rough hand on the back of my neck and we went out the through the screen door. It whapped shut behind us.

The yard was full of livestock of one kind or another. There were white chickens clucking and strutting around like they was up to something. There were some big smelly pigs in a pen over to one side that like to make me gag. On a old wood fence about fifty paces away were some Coke and beer bottles I figured Vaughn wanted me to try to shoot down. He just kept holding that .38 and I could hear him breathing louder than he had been a minute earlier. The kind of breathing Sonny did when he got mad. I knew what was coming, or thought I did. Just as the boys came busting out the screen door, Vaughn shifted the gun away from me and started shooting chickens. He shot three of them. The blasts echoed around the world and back. I hoped that Buddy dog was under the house because I believe Vaughn might've shot anything in front of him.

"It won't hurt you!" Vaughn shouted at me without looking toward me. TC went over and kind of methodically went to each chicken and violently twisted its head with his bare hands like they was rag dolls. It made me sick to watch, but I could not look away either.

"Does that mean we can stay for dinner?" Rusty asked, a big hopeful smile on his face.

"No, it don't," Vaughn said. "The only girls I need around the house are Arlene and Sugarbaby. TC take those chickens home with you and give 'em to your Mama to cook up."

"Yes sir" TC was already walking home so fast the other boys had to jog to catch up.

"See ya, Honey Boy!" Punkin said over his shoulder. Punkin and TC took the chickens down to their house. When Vaughn wasn't looking, Punkin flipped me off like you do

with your buddies. It was like being abandoned. I didn't know
if I should be afraid of Vaughn or proud he wanted to associ-
ate with me instead of the other boys. They were all older
than me and usually grown-ups like people closer to their age,
especially men. Rusty stayed to watch us like he was watching
a John Wayne picture on Channel 11 out of St. Louis. Rusty
kicked his feet in a rusted out metal lawn chair that was fairly
riddled with bullet holes.

Low and under his breath Vaughn said, "Take this here
gun."

"I don't want to," I said. "I ain't got nothing against guns
or you, but it ain't my gun."

"I'll shoot," Rusty said, a cigarette bobbing in his mouth
made him look like a grown up. Vaughn ignored him.

"What do you mean, boy?"

"I mean," I said. "I got my own gun and that ain't it."

"Where is it then?" he asked. I said if he was willing to
drive I was willing to show him.

"Where y'all going?" Arlene came out of the house.

"Crazy," Vaughn said. "It's a short trip. Want to come?"
We couldn't help laughing.

The peeling bumper sticker on his pickup read: VOTE
NIXON! We slid across the cloth bench seat, Rusty in the
middle, and Vaughn started driving like a maniac on the gravel road. The backend was fish-tailing like a son-of-a-bitch.
Rusty was smiling like he was on a ride at Silver Dollar City.
Me, I was about to piss my Wranglers. On the radio a gal was
singing about walking after midnight which didn't sound like
a good idea for a pretty gal, if she was one. We drove back
down the road and when I said to stop at the culvert we slid
to a stop, Vaughn cussing. There wouldn't have been no
good time to tell him to stop without getting cussed at, I
knew. A bank of dust puffed up from the wheels of the truck.

I wondered if it was a good idea to take him to it but
thought why not. *Why the hell not!* I slid down the embank-

ment, found my shirt and had to bear walk up it again, un-wrapped the pistol and passed it up to Rusty who handed it over the seat to Vaughn. I was breathing heavy like an ob-scene phone caller. He looked it over and his mouth was mumbling something. He motioned for me to get back in.

"Damn, Honey Boy," Rusty said, and promptly receiving a palm to the back of the head from Vaughn. The boy's head snapped forward so his chin rested on his chest for a second. His face turned red.

"Nice pistol you got there," Vaughn said. "Put it in the glove box for now."

I didn't say nothing. I did what he said.

"Except there's only one problem," Vaughn said. "It ain't yours. I gave that pistol to Sonny or he stole it from me. I don't recall which. Then you stole it from him. Kind of funny if you *ast* me."

What could I say? I just sat there like I didn't have a care in the world, but that pistol was something. It made my hands itch just thinking about it sitting in the glove box. I hoped it wouldn't get scratched in there. I didn't know much about firearms in general, but I knew I liked that particular piece. It was heavier than it looked. The pearl handles on it was pretty. I just waited. Thinking nothing. Holding my breath.

"Tell you what," Vaughn said. "I'll make a deal with you. I'll let you buy that gun off me cheap since you got such big balls and all."

"I'm just a kid," I said. "I ain't got no money, man."

"That's all right, MAN," Vaughn said. "I'll keep it for you until you can pay me. Matter of fact, you can work for me. I need a partner. It's hard work. Man's work. Got me?"

I nodded.

Rusty was rubbing the back of his head and sniffing.

"Shut that up, Rusty," Vaughn said. "What are you, a little girl? Maybe we should go back home and you can wear one of Sugarbaby's dresses?"

"Her dresses wouldn't fit me," Rusty said through clenched teeth. He knew it wasn't much of a comeback, but he was afraid to say anthing too smart to Vaughn.

"Her diapers might," Vaughn said. "Don't talk back to me, you little pussy."

We went back to the house for awhile and shot the shit out of every can and bottle on the place with the pistol. Vaughn started hauling his entire arsenal. I had never even heard of some of them before but had I never shot guns before and I was tickled. Playing five dollars on the pinball machine was the closest I had come to it, but that didn't compare. Even hearing the pop when you won free games wasn't close to it, even getting high score wasn't nothing. Vaughn said shooting guns made your dick big. Women liked that, he said. He had about every kind of gun there was out in what he called his armory. It was really just the mudroom. He told me to keep my mouth shut about his guns. He reckoned there were bad characters around who would break into his place and steal his guns if they knew about them. I couldn't imagine the fool who would take on Elston Vaughn.

"Would you ever shoot that Buddy dog?"

"That dog's just a Heinz 57," Rusty piped up. "He ain't good for nothing."

"Why would you ask me that?" Vaughn said. His eyes turned watery and puffy
like the beer was working on him. "You think I'm like that?"

"No," I lied. "I just think that ol' Buddy dog is a good one."

"He can't do nothing but eat, piss, and shit," Vaughn said. "I once traded a good coon dog for a Glock. He was a damn good dog. That Buddy dog is too stupid. He ain't worth nothing. But if you like him I'll keep him around. He's right friendly, ain't he?"

"Yes sir," I said.

"Sometime I'll have to take you out for some real sport. I get some ol' boys together and we ride around drinking beer in the backwoods looking for coyotes. We shoot the shit out of 'em. It's gotta be done or them coyotes will eat up your livestock. Some folks like deer hunting and coon hunting. I like hunting them too, but hell if you leave out some dogfood coons and skunks and all kind of things will come right up to your house as far as that goes. Arlene got to feeding coons. She'd take pictures of them. Them coons love to have their picture taken. But then they started breaking into the house. Came home and one was right on the kitchen table, big as life, eating cereal with his fingers like a hungry-ass kid. I put my foot down then, by God."

I was watching Vaughn real close. Mama says I'm nosy. Just about all the Polaroid's ever taken with me in them show that I'm watching someone else, everyone else. When Vaughn talked it was more to hear himself think. He was talking to me like I was some old man like him, someone he had known his whole life. No matter how friendly he pretended to act I could tell there was something else going on behind his eyes. He was thinking things he wasn't saying to nobody—least of all me.

Arlene came out of the backdoor like she was going to call us in for dinner. Vaughn whipped around with his .38 and pointed it at her. She had a dishtowel over her shoulder. Sugarbaby was on her hip. Vaughn pointed the gun at her head and just let it stay there. The gun looked bigger now. Arlene let Sugarbaby slide off her hip and onto the ground. Arlene's face turned white. Her bottom lip was quivering. She got on her hands and knees and her hair covered her face and she was blubbering real loud. My stomach was doing flip-flops.

"Is dinner ready or something?" Vaughn asked. He lowered the gun to his side.

He just walked past her and went inside to wash up like nothing happened. Arlene was crying and kind of rocking back and forth. I put my hand on one of Arlene's shoulders, but I knew it didn't matter what I said. She didn't even know Sugarbaby and me was there so I tried to take Sugarbaby in to wash hands and eat dinner, but she wouldn't let me take her hand, stepped back and made her hand like it was a gun and pointed it at me. The girl's face was blank. She put her finger to her lips like it was the barrel of a gun and then pointed it at Arlene who was still on her hands and knees in the red clay dirt.

Arlene had cooked ham and beans with yellow cornbread. The blue and white Jiffy box was still sitting empty on the counter. Vaughn and me ate dinner without a word and licked our fingers afterward. The .38 was on the table in front of Vaughn like he thought the law would come breaking in any minute and he would have to shoot his way out. Arlene was still out there just sitting in the yard real quiet-like when Vaughn ran me back over to Rafe's lakehouse in his pickup with a bottle of beer between his legs. He lit another cigarette with his big silver Zippo that had his initials carved into it real fancy, more hellfire.

Every So Often, Something Interesting Happens

Mama was shaking me awake by my foot and smoking. She was always smoking, but she had a sly way of doing it so nobody would call her a chain smoker. She would light one up in the kitchen, take a couple of long drags, and let it burn in the ashtray before going to the living room in the natural progression of things and light another. There wasn't a thing wrong with it, but nobody wanted to be accused of being a chain smoker. I didn't see any difference, but I guess it was like drinking. It's okay to drink, but you don't want to be called an alcoholic.

I peeked at her through slitted eyes. Mama was looking at me suspiciously. She didn't say a word. It was Saturday, and still July, so there wasn't any reason to get up early for school or anything. It was legal for me to be in bed. She didn't normally get up until 11:00 and when she did, she'd ask me if I had made coffee. She worked the dinner shift at the Spot Cafe and as a cocktail waitress at McMillan's Tavern. She petted my hair out on the pillow and called it a mop. She was wearing her blue terrycloth robe.

"We need to cut this mop," Mama said.

"It's just finally at a decent length," I said. "Only dorks have short hair."

I followed her into the kitchen. She poured a cup of coffee from the silver coffee maker, dumped four spoons of sugar with a dash of creamer and stirred it up and took a sip. I heard her throat work it down. I thought about when I was little how she would take me up into her lap and I could smell her warm soapy skin. Now I was too old for that but I missed it anyway. When I was a kid I wanted to spend every minute with her, but it just wasn't possible. Sometimes I'd live with

Grandma Kimbrough or Aunt Oleta while she disappeared for months on end only to show back up and take me with her again.

When she ran off, it about broke my heart every time. She usually explained she was going to get setup somewhere and come back for me when everything was perfect with the man she had chosen to go ramble around the countryside with. Aunt Oleta sighed she was "juneing around."

"Your mother thinks she's too good for us," Aunt Oleta once said looking down over the frames of her pointy glasses at me. "She's got to go traipsing around kingdom come and back. She ought to come home from work and watch her kid. A good mother takes care of her kids."

This one time, she left me at Aunt Oleta's without so much as a word, kiss my ass, or goodbye. I expect it was easier on her that way, but it made me feel like that old sock in your drawer that you can't find the mate for.

It was already hot enough for the box fan, but she said it made too much noise. She liked her quiet time. It charged her batteries up for dealing with people. I hadn't noticed last night, but the TV was missing. It was a big color console one and I'd thought only rich people had TVs like that. I figured Rafe was pawning it. She wasn't in the mood to talk and I knew she wouldn't hear me anyway so I went outside and sat on the wood deck out back.

She saw me looking and hollered through the kitchen window, "The fat man down to the rent-and-own came and got the TV earlier!"

The lakehouse was by far the nicest place we had ever lived. Once we had an apartment above a hardware store; another time, we'd stayed in a poolhouse in the Williamsons (the richest people in Fairmont) backyard where across the street was Dubois Mortuary; we lived in an apartment in a white washed Methodist church on Route JJ. I'd seen more trailer parks, campgrounds, and motels across Colorado, Texas, Mississippi, Arkansas, Tennessee, and North Carolina than I cared to recall so I hoped Rafe and Mama weren't on the outs, not because I liked him, but because I wanted us to settle in a decent place for a change. We lived a little better when she shacked up with someone for awhile.

When Mama was young she'd been in a car accident that hurt her back. I don't know what happened exactly, but it left her with terrible migraines and she would stay in bed for an entire day. She said she was taking a Darvon for the pain in her back after she made me a "girlcheese" sandwich and tomato soup. It made my insides sing to know fMama was making something for me to eat. Why does food always taste better when somebody else makes it? So I came back inside and waited for lunch. She called it "brunch" when she was in a good mood.

The cigarette burn on my arm was still there, but it was getting better. It scared me to think what Rafe might do next to me or Mama. I heard him smacking her around in his bedroom before too. He would get tanked and start beating on her for no earthly reason that I knew of but she would take it before it would ever enter into her head to leave. Sonny had done some beating on her too but he was more apt to chase other women. Mama hated that like poison. Getting cheated on was worse than taking a beating. Just listen to all them records about it if you don't believe me.

Mama brought out a hot bowl of soup and a plate with my girlcheese on it and set it down in front of me on the coffee table. I liked to eat there instead of the kitchen table. Mama didn't care like Charlie Trapp's mama. Mrs. Trapp always went around with hair piled up Pentecostal style. His mama would plumb start foaming at the mouth if you ate anything over the living room carpet. Them Trapps even had an extra living room, Grandma Kimbrough said it was a parlor, that nobody was allowed to actually *live* in. There was clear plastic covers on the sofas.

The Trapps had a nice color console television and Charlie had the whole upstairs to himself. He was one lucky duck and didn't even know it. His daddy sold life, house, and auto insurance. I didn't know too many folks who could afford insurance anyway. I'd asked Mama if she had insurance on me or the truck and she looked at me like I was some kind of nut.

Mama sat down on the couch while I kneeled in front of the coffee table to eat. There was a nice big fireplace in the great room. I didn't care if the TV was gone. Eating in the living room was where I liked to eat. Mama tried to tell me she was having a cup of soup, but I knew it was a Bloody Mary. I knew if she got started drinking I'd have to keep an eye on her. I'd seen her fall dead asleep before with her drink still in her hand. We listened to the country-western station. It blocked out all other stations. If you wanted to hear rock-n-roll you had to drive out of the city limits. Some kind of weird conspiracy. Sonny used to blame it on the government. I snuck a bottle of Rafe's Orange Crush out of the fridge and popped the top on a drawer handle. He was so hateful it made the sodie taste especially sweet.

That Buddy dog was out there too thumping his tail and smiling at me. He yawned and sat next to my foot so I'd pet him real good. I couldn't help wondering what that son-of-a-bitch Rafe was up to. I was sitting on the porch sipping from the bottle when I looked up through the pine trees and saw a black and white car driving slow down the lane toward me. There was no question, but it was making its way toward us because all the homes around the lake had their own private drives. Gravel crunched under the tires and I could tell it was the same John Law I'd seen before.

"Mama!" I slammed my bottle of sodie on the railing. "The cops are here."

Mama went running out. Buddy got excited and raced up to the cop car with her. She stuck her head in the window for a minute and I watched them talking. I could see the officer's head bobbing as he talked to her. She backed up and the officer swung his legs out of his cruiser as he held a clipboard in front of him like a serving tray. He wrote some things down. Mama was shaking her head like she didn't know, didn't understand. He was flirting with his eyes and his smile even though he was younger. Even put his hand on her shoulder like he was comforting her, but I could tell it was because he liked her. Most men did.

I sure hoped the cop wasn't there for me. Maybe I had done wrong and could not remember it. Did someone think I stole Buddy? Then the notion that I could be one of them psychopaths hit me and one of my other personalities had viciously axe-murdered Big Jake at the bowling alley because he hated kids and deserved to be killed in my book.

The police cruiser was backing up out of the driveway as she walked toward the house barefoot. There was a raised up round birthmark I'd seen many times on the sole of her foot about the size and color of a raspberry. She looked like she just woke up from a nightmare. Her eyes stared out like there was nothing in them.

"What was that all about?"

She walked by me like I wasn't even there.

"What did he do? Did they throw him in jail?"

I figured Rafe got pinched for stealing. That was right up his alley in my opinion, but you know what they say about opinions: they're just like assholes, everyone's got one.

"Rafe's dead," Mama said. "Someone shot him up near Blackmore Lake. They've got their suspicions, but they don't know." She came over and hugged me for a minute and whispered in my ear "Oh, Honey Boy." I followed her to the bar in the dining room and she poured some vodka all the way up to the lip of the glass. Mama gulped a sip down and made a face. She went to the back bedroom with the bottle in her other hand and closed the door behind her. I knew what happened or had a pretty good hunch. Our world had gone haywire again.

I stood outside her bedroom door for a second like a fool. I put the palm of my hand flat on the door and thought about knocking. She was always leaving me behind. It was like as soon as she couldn't see me she forgot about my existence. I wanted to make her see me someday. The phone started ringing off the hook for the rest of the day. I'd hear Mama's boozy voice on her side of the door. For some calls she sounded cool and collected but for others she was bawling and hiccupping. I just wanted to be in there with her.

"I don't know what we're going to do," Mama said to someone on the phone.

Mama had to go to work tonight at the tavern, but I knew she wouldn't make it in. I don't know if she was more sad about Rafe or that she was alone again.

The brown paneling on the wall didn't look right to me as it began to stretch and twist at an angle and go dark. Buddy was at my feet one second, and then the next he was not. Rafe hadn't even liked people to wear shoes in his place and now a dog was standing over me breathing his hot breath into my face.

The phone was ringing. Mama must have fallen asleep. I answered the kitchen phone on the wall.

"Hello."

"Johnny Cool?" the voice said. "Guess who this is?"

"I don't. . ." yellow and green spots were dancing in front of my eyes. "I don't know. This Vaughn?"

"Hell yeah it's Vaughn!" he laughed. "I guess you know you owe me big time. Get your ass over here ASAP or I'll knock the Billy Heck out of you. Hang up now."

I went and took five one dollar bills from Mama's tip money out of her purse. I even took her cigarettes which I had never done before, but I needed something to settle my nerves. It was a pretty safe bet that Vaughn had found an excuse to kill Rafe. Normally Vaughn bullied people, but I didn't know about him killing anyone before. He even had my pistol so I didn't know if I needed to bring some protection or not. I went to Rafe's gun cabinet but all he had was two deer rifles, an old musket that must have been an antique, and a pocket knife longer than my hand with two blades in it. There was a seven point buck on the wall looking down at me with its sad eyes glittering, reflecting the light like I was its killer. I put that Dallas special in my back pocket. I made a bologna and cheese sandwich with ketchup and went out the back door.

"My coon dogs all give out," Vaughn said. "Just look at them. Look like they done give up the ghost, don't they? Don't let them fool you. Once they get onto something like a coon or a pole cat, they'd rather die than give it up." Two hounds were half under the front porch. One dog's head stuck out in the sunlight and the only movement it made was an eye-twitch when a green fly landed on the dog's face. The air was rank with the smell of dog.

"Cops came out," I said. "Out to the lakehouse."

"Oh," Vaughn said. "I was out coon hunting and hadn't heard nothing about it." He smiled and sipped out of a midget Coke bottle. "Want one?"

"No," I said, but I did want one. "Someone killed Rafe out to Blackmore's Lake last night."

"That's a damn shame." Vaughn tossed his empty bottle in the back of his pickup. "He should've been coon hunting with me and the boys last night. He'd probably be alive today." He looked at the pack of cigarettes folded up in my shirtsleeve. "Kind of young for that, ain't you? My Daddy would've tanned my hide for smoking when I was your age."

"I'm old enough," I said. "What else am I supposed to do?"

"I guess you are at that," Vaughn said. "You plumb tickle my ass, kid. The way you talk to me. You know, I ought to just go over and talk to your mama myself and make sure she's doing all right."

"I don't know," I said.

"Why the hell not?" Vaughn's face got all mottled red. He looked like a devil when his temper flared up.

"I mean," I said. "I guess you can do whatever you want."

"When I look in your eyes," Vaughn said, towering over me "You know what I see?"

I shook my head no.

"I see a boy who got crazy on his mind," Vaughn growled. "I swear but you're going to end up in the funny farm someday. Mark my words now." His face loomed up at mine, turning a beet color and huffy. He blew up like a hot air balloon and I went down like a shrinky-dink. Then, slowly, he deflated himself and became regular sized again. He smiled and it was so hideous I almost fainted, but I grabbed onto a piece of mind and stayed on my feet.

Vaughn dropped me off in town in front of the picture show. He called it the Opry House. I walked around the square and talked to some boys sitting on the brick wall around the courthouse. Boys my age who weren't old enough to drive or just didn't have cars. A black boy was telling how the police in town hated niggers and was always harassing them. Another boy told him not to hang out on the square and they probably would leave him alone, but the boy said he didn't have nothing else to do but go home and get beat up by his daddy. He thought he was better off with the police in the long run. When I started walking off the square I began to count my steps: one, two and one, two between each square of sidewalk. Then I tried to stop but I couldn't. *If you have less than forty steps to the next block, but more than twenty-five to that driveway your mama will meet the man of her dreams.* I tried to turn my mind off but it just wouldn't shut up. *All you have to do is walk twice with both feet in each section of sidewalk and you will find out who your daddy is.* I wondered sometimes if that voice was the devil, me, or just my mind talking out loud.

Dance with the Devil
in the Pale Moonshine

The truck was creeping along the gravel road with the headlights off. I was sitting on the window with a flashlight in hand shining it up front. The only thing we had seen so far was a possum staring at us with its eyes like rubies glowing in the light. The night was buzzing with insects and peep frogs. Moths were already dive-bombing the flashlight. It was warm and the moon was partially hidden by clouds. I'd heard about a meteor shower tonight, but it would probably be too cloudy to see it. The radio started talking about the mysterious death of Rafe Clearwater until Vaughn clicked it off.

"I got news for them," Vaughn said. "They ain't never going to find him."

A rustling sound in the weeds caused me to shine my light on a girl coming up out of the ditch. Behind her past the tree line was a birght white light from a utility pole beaming a silhouette of a two-story farmhouse. The rusted out hull of a Studebaker sat in the front yard on blocks. The girl was real pretty with dark hair past her shoulders wearing jeans and boots and a gray Missouri Tigers sweatshirt despite the warmth of the night. I twisted out of the window and let her in the truck to slide over next to Vaughn. He gave her a kiss right on the lips even though she couldn't have been more than sixteen or seventeen tops. He wedged his big hand between her legs and the seat, up near her crotch.

"She's sweet, huh?" Vaughn asked. I nodded. She had a real pretty face, although somewhat big-boned but I don't think that would've bothered anybody. The only thing that marred her beauty was a scar across her cheekbone and another up on her forehead that she covered up with makeup so it was tough to say how badly her face had been damaged.

"She had a farm accident on a crazy horse that ran her into a barbed-wire fence. Cheryl, this here is Honey Boy."

"Hi,"she said and gripped my hand real hard so that the bones popped. "Call me Cheryl."

"Go ahead," Vaughn said. "Give him a kiss. He's my right hand man."

Before I could say anything Cheryl pressed her lips against mine. Her tongue pushed through my lips and began moving around like she was looking for gum. A jolt of electricity went through my veins and the taste of strawberry-flavored gum in my mouth. I could feel my face blushing so I was glad for the dark. She turned me loose and pushed me away like she had done her duty, proud to do it too. I could see a turquoise ring on her pinky.

"He's real pretty," Cheryl said. "But he's just a kid. Is he old enough to run with us? You sure he can handle it?"

"Damn straight," Vaughn said to her. "Y'all ain't never going to forget tonight."

We drove for the better part of forty-five minutes. Vaughn had a wad of Big Chief tucked down between his cheek and gums. He started off sipping at the can of beer between his legs then, gulped it down, and tossed the it at a mailbox.

"Beer," Vaughn reached his hand over the top of the seat.

I opened the cooler on the floorboard and stuck my head down in the ice and retrieved a cold one for Vaughn.

Cheryl had her back to me the whole time and was rubbing her hand up and down Vaughn's leg so I thought she might rub clean through his jeans. He seemed to know every gravel road in the state and we only drove across blacktop roads every now and again. The night air felt nice but Cheryl kept complaining about being cold so Vaughn made me roll the window up. I started smoking one of Mama's Viceroys, really concentrating on it too since I didn't have anything else to do. They was about to make me sick the way they was all over one another. Vaughn being married to Arlene and all, I knew it wasn't right.

When I was a little kid Aunt Oleta and Grandma Kimbrough used to tell me Jesus was looking down on me and crying whenever I did something they couldn't abide. After I got that lecture I said, "Jesus wept," and Grandma Kimbrough threatened to box my ears. Aunt Oleta said I was a little heathen. I tried to tell her I was just quoting the Good Book. Jesus wept is the shortest verse in the whole entire Bible according to Miss Vernie in Sunday school, but Aunt Oleta wasn't buying it.

The next day I stepped on a nail in the garage and had to get a tetanus shot at the hospital so I gathered it was bad luck to say sacrilege. Then Grandma got sent to King's Daughters. It wasn't enough for God for me to suffer, but he had to make sure Grandma suffered too. That's how God appears to work so it's best not to fight it when you break one of his rules. Jesus couldn't be none too happy about this Vaughn-Cheryl situation. I knew somebody better look out, man!

We stopped at Cox's Corner convenience store just outside Fairmont. Fairmont was the seat of Callaway County and its claim to fame was the fact that Winston Churchill had given his famous Iron Curtain speech there. They were proud people and it made me nervous messing around in a town like that because them people were known to take the law into their own hands, but Vaughn wasn't worried despite the fact that Cox's faced Highway F. He got out under the lights with his crowbar, yanked at the front door and be damned if it didn't pop open on the third try. The place had been robbed a hundred times over the years and several of its employees and a couple of customers had lost their lives there so I guess that's why he thought it'd be safe to take it down. Folks always wanted to believe it was strangers that done those wild things.

He strutted out like the cock of the walk with a cardboard box full of supplies. He was in no particular hurry. Even had Cheryl and me get out and look at the rum, vodka, Jose Cuervo, black label Jack Dannys, Pabst Blue Ribbon, Coke, candy bars, a gallon of Central Dairy milk, Backer's potato chips, cartons of Marlboros, Lucky Strikes, and Camels even a 12-gauge the proprietor probably used for protection. Vaughn made six trips, opened up his tool box behind the cab and loaded up right there in the parking lot as if he were shopping at Cooper's grocery store. A big rig rumbled by on the blacktop hissing at us like it was cautioning us to be quiet: *watch out.* Vaughn would probably buy cigarettes and a RC Cola there the next time he was in the area. We drove off like Cox's was open and we were on a daytrip to see the capital at Jeff City. Soon we were on another gravel road driving passed a Baptist Church and a cemetery. I felt funny from my crotch to my stomach. I didn't want to go to Juvi.

"Here it is," Vaughn said. "No flashlight. I know this place."

A dog was barking a couple of miles away. Vaughn told me and Cheryl to take a blanket and go up the road around the bend and keep watch on the bluff overlooking the gravel road to where it met up with Route NN. Cheryl carried the blanket and we walked up the road a ways until we came to the foot of the bluff. I tried to find the best angle to go up. We slid around on the rocks in the ditch for a second.

I walked stooped over up the steep incline first and found an old fallen tree to grab onto, turned back and held my hand out for Cheryl. She pulled herself up and grabbed the root of a willow that was hanging out of the ground and helped me up. She tossed the blanket over the lip of the embankment and I pushed her up and she disappeared for a minute into the nightfall. Finally her hand came down but I mostly pulled myself up. She did jumping jacks and waved, her breasts bobbed heavily up and down, so Vaughn would see her sil-

houette against the night sky and know we were in position.
Cheryl was bigger than me but that didn't bother me either.
She could be my girlfriend if she ever got tired of Vaughn. He
whistled Bob White at us despite the fact that hearing them
calling at night might be a dead giveaway.

From our vantage point it was easy to watch both ways.
We could see Vaughn going to where the hogs were pinned
and it made me think it went against everything I had ever
learned from watching cowboy and army movies on TV
about waiting for the moon to go behind the clouds first.
Vaughn picked up a big hog that must have weighed 275
pounds easy, but he carried it only a straining a little. I started
to head back down then, but Cheryl patted the blanket next
to her so I sat down and put my hand on hers like it was an
accident. She smiled, her eyes turned sidewards. Kissed me.
Rubbed her hand over my crotch, through my jeans, until I
thought my head might explode. She took my hand and put it
on her titty like it was the most natural thing to do. Her saliva
tasted like bubble gum; a little bit sweet and sour.

Vaughn put his second hog in the back of the pickup. He
opened another beer and tossed it back. He Bob-Whited us
again. We hopped up off the dirty blanket, Cheryl snatched it
up as we made our way down the bluff. Going down was a
whole lot easier than coming up. I stared at her ass as she
made her way down. I did not want to but I could not stop
myself. Aunt Oleta said I was a bad boy and I can't lie and say
I'm not. I saw something trailing a white line against the black
sky out of the corner of my eye.

"Did you see that?"

"What?" Cheryl asked turning to look up at me. She
pushed some stray hair over her ear prettily.

"Falling stars," I said. We stood there like statues for a
minute and saw two more until we heard *Get the hell down here*
instead of Bob White.

We got back into the truck and Cheryl was smiling at me. Her eyes glistened with excitement. She tugged on Vaughn's arm, but he needed it for shifting. He messed with the clutch for a second, grinding gears, cursed, and we took off. It was like being Bonnie and Clyde of the hog world, but I wasn't sure who that made me unless it was like the camera man or something.

"Teach that sumbuck to mean-mouth me," Vaughn muttered and laughed. He brought out a tiny squat medicine bottle, opened the top, put it up to his nose and inhaled deeply. Cheryl took it and did the same thing and smiled funny. Her eyes went cross-eyed like she was drunk. She gave it to me and I did the same thing. For a split-second I thought I was going to die. My brain felt like it expanded and was going to explode. I fell over, my head bumped the window.

"That's rush," Vaughn said. "You like that shit?"

"I don't know," I said. "Let me try it again."

"Ha ha," Vaughn laughed. "Let me try it again. That's a good one."

"You still got it in your hand," Cheryl said.

Vaughn reached out with his big hand and turned her face toward him. With the other hand, he placed a folded over wad of cash and slide it into her hand. She smiled and they started making out. He stuck his fat tongue in her mouth like a lizard hunting insects. I guess she needed the money real bad. She was fresh and young and there was a wildness to Vaughn, part werewolf and tough purple ironweed. Watching them kiss made me feel gross and jealous at the same time. I wanted to kiss her again, but I knew she'd only done it to make him happy. I felt like a jerk just being apart of the whole nasty business of the night. I couldn't help but feel more alive than ever at the same time. I knew she was playing the part so he could say he helped the kid get a little, but I didn't hold nothing against her. A girl with a smile like hers made you want to do anything to make her happy.

There we were only a mile south of 54 on a gravel road with several *hugacious* grumbling hogs in the back when we came over a rise and noticed a station wagon, one of them woodies, off in the ditch, in an area of the road where four roads came together and the ditches on all sides were steep. The station wagon was in the ditch nose first and all the doors were open. The dome light lit up the wagon like it was a UFO just landed. We all got quiet and Vaughn slowed down to see if there were any bodies lying around the accident.

I got out and kind of hopped into the backseat. Jammed between the front and back was a blue plastic cooler full of Budweiser, but there was no sign of people. It hadn't been abandoned like this for long though. I grabbed three beers and went back to the truck and handed them out to Vaughn and Cheryl.

"Nobody there," I said. "Probably just teenagers out driving the roads and got stuck is all. They probably went to get somebody to help pull 'em out."

Then we were off again. Vaughn worried because of the hogs. The night was getting away from us. His leg doing a quick jig: up and down, up and down, up and down. I knew he was close to yelling. The sounds of the night lessening, beginning to get quieter. The wind whipped into the windows. I had to shift one of the triangular side windows so air wouldn't push into my face and make it hard to catch my breath. As we turned off Route O and onto Route UU a red light began to flash behind us. Vaughn cussed and slammed the steering wheel with his fists.

"Reach into the glove compartment and give me the gun," Vaughn said. I handed my gun out to him. I hoped he didn't kill nobody with my pistol, least of all a cop. I was too surprised to notice what kind of cop was after us, but Vaughn kept saying something about the goddamn highway patrol had it in for him. Vaughn kept driving but not too fast just smooth and steady as you please. He laughed under his breath. No highway patrol was man enough to get the best of him, or so he said. From the shoulder, the spotlights were shining into the cab of the truck and in the rearview mirror I could see the patrol car, a Plymouth Grand Fury, and my face which looked so plainly guilty even I could see it.

"Good evening Elston," the Highway Patrolman said. "Corporal Royce Stafford. How are you folks this evening?"

"Fine," Vaughn said.

The name Stafford was familiar to me. I'd heard many of the barflies who came into McMillan's say Royce Stafford was this and Royce Stafford was that. Mainly they didn't like him because he was apt to knock your head in as give you a ticket. Vaughn and I both noticed that a flashlight was the only weapon he had in his hand and I saw a smile cross our side of his face which scared the blood out of my veins. Corporal Stafford did not look so confident, nor so cocksure, as he had just a second before walking up on us.

"You all in a hurry?," Corporal Stafford began. "You had to be driving at least seventy. As you know, the speed limit is fifty-five now. Whose hogs you got back there?"

"Mine."

"Whose kids are those with you?"

"Mine too," Vaughn said, trying to hand his drivers license out the window.

"Elston . . . now that won't be necessary . . . what I'm going to ask . . ."

Vaughn showed Corporal Stafford my pistol. It was such a beautiful piece that I found myself just looking at it. Stafford looked at it too and the words stopped coming out of his mouth. His face was angular and it reminded me of the brutal intelligence of an eagle
and other birds of prey had, like they would pluck your eyeballs out and not think nothing about it. Stafford's hands reached for the pistol on his belt and then flew up over his

head. He just stood there for a moment. Under the spotlight from the patrol car, Vaughn's breath became ragged and his neck was turning a dark plum color whereas the patrolman's was going so white that with his hands in the air I thought he could fly off into the night like a ghost. Corporal Stafford backed up into the road in a semi-circle, kept on up until he was standing within an arm's length of his cruiser.

"Put that up," Corporal Stafford shouted. "I'm going to let you off with a warning but next time you and me is going to butt heads."

"You better go talk to Judge Hollings over in Jeff City," Vaughn said, "before you go threatening me. He's a good ol' boy if you get my meaning and you just might find yourself back on the farm in Howard County where you was hatched, Royce."

I couldn't see Stafford's reaction, but I watched in the side mirror as the Plymouth backed up, and the patrol car did a U-turn and disappeared in a hurry, bobbing brake lights and all. And that's how things were in Kingdom County. Even the law gave Vaughn a wide berth.

Vaughn ground his gears, killed the engine, cursed and re-started it. He turned the radio on and I be damned if there wasn't an old rock 'n' roll song about a fella singing how he fought the law, but the law won. Vaughn snapped off the radio, pulled over, got out of the car and took a piss in the ditch. It was a long one too. Cheryl and me exchanged a look and even though we had just been scared shitless earlier, we started laughing. Vaughn whipped his head around like he was mad. He hopped up and down, zipped up, and smiled like he allowed something about that night might be funny after all.

One thing was for sure, everyone in Kingdom County was afraid of Elston Vaughn. I figured the deputy sheriff, even the sheriff, and people who lived in Fairmont feared Vaughn. I knew I was scared of him, but I never counted on the highway patrol being scared of him too. Being with him made me feel feared too. I never felt so strong in all my natural life. He told us Royce Stafford was the only lawman in Missouri he respected by reputation and in person. It was high praise coming from Vaughn.

"You keep the pistol," Vaughn said. "You earned it tonight. I want you to keep it on you all the time when you're with me. I don't care how hot it is, you wear a shirt or jacket to hide it. Someday someone's going to get the jump on me, and if you're with me, you're going to be there to watch my back. You will sure as hell be the angel of death."

"Yes sir," I said. It was my pistol now for keeps. Nobody would try to take it from neither, because Vaughn would have their ass. He made sure I had a couple of boxes of bullets so I could practice. Even Mama wouldn't object if Vaughn said, or so I reasoned to myself. Cheryl reached across me and touched it, stroked it, and mooned over it with me.

"Don't it make you feel powerful," Cheryl purred in my ear. "Just holding it in your hands?"

Exiles

Raffert's people kicked us out of the lakehouse but Mama seemed to take it all in her stride. I guess she tried to put Rafe somewhere in the back of her mind like he never existed so it couldn't hurt her. The Clearwater people wouldn't soon do us any favors, because they held Mama responsible the way people do when the person they ought to be mad at was much too scary for them to face.

"Because of you," Red Clearwater said, "Rafe is dead. And over your skinny piece of ass. What was he thinking? And you got that bastard kid on top of it. It just don't make sense. I want you out of here, today." I could smell the sweat mingled with English Leather and alcohol wafting off him into the house as the early evening sun slipped down the tree line on the other side of the lake. He turned away in his paint-stained clothes and spit off the porch before he got into his Beater.

"I'll get you," I growled under my breath. "You don't know who you're messing with, man."

We packed up our clothes in paper grocery sacks and garbage bags. We used to have suitcases but Mama had given Sonny one and sold the others for a few bucks out in California. She never thought about the future one minute. Mama stole Rafe's cooler and stopped at the Country Mart and bought ham, cheese, a gallon of Central Dairy milk, a six-pack of Schlitz, and those little greenish-tinted bottles of Coke. In the newspaper rack the Fairmont Sun's headline read: BODY OF LOCAL MAN FOUND IN BLACKMORE'S LAKE.

I told Mama Vaughn wanted us to move in with him but she didn't get all upset like I thought. She just unsnapped her little cloth cigarette holder, calmly took out a cigarette and smoked in the darkened kitchen of our new place in a shitty little trailer a couple of miles northwest of Fairmont on HH.

A couple of kids, a little boy and a girl, were playing on our silver propane tank riding it like it was a pregnant horse. She told me to stay away from Vaughn. I hadn't showed her the pistol and wasn't about to anytime soon either. Like Vaughn always said, "What she don't know won't hurt her."

I told her I was hungry and she fixed biscuits and gravy. I was tired of having the same thing for three days in a row for dinner and couldn't we mix it up, but she said people in Africa were starving. She stuck her tongue out at me when I said I wouldn't mind sending them some sausage gravy.

She worked all the time. Her eyes were tired. She was worn slick. I wished I could save her from working all the time. I told her I might get a paper route. Mama said once you get started working, you never stopped.

"Do I look like my daddy?" I asked her out of the blue.

"Some," she said, vaguely, pushing her bangs out of her face.

It made me think about the times when Mama was between jobs and we would get hungry. I didn't do without much. It wasn't real poverty because most mornings there was cereal, but sometimes with water instead of milk. I'd go several afternoons with peanut butter sandwiches for lunch. I loved peanut butter so that was okay or I'd take saltines and pour on the ketchup. It was times like those I wished I had an older brother. I wondered who my real daddy was. Where was he? Did he ever think about me? And couldn't he send us some fried chicken and mashed potatoes and gravy with a side of green beans with a slice of bacon in it for extra flavor? Karo syrup was real cheap so I'd have it over bread or toast or sometimes just sugar poured over a slice of white bread. Other times I would go visit neighbor kids at supper time and their parents would invite me to eat with them.

Times when Mama worked at the Spot, she'd just up and take me down there and Harry Lee would make me French toast or anything I wanted. I wondered how many more

choke and pukes she was going to have to work before something good happened so she wouldn't have to do it anymore.
Everyone said Harry Lee was queer. He was pale with dark
black hair and his hair was already receding although he was
still in his twenties.

We went out to Kingdom Gardens Cemetery where the
Clearwaters were having a graveside service. Mama parked
the truck on the other side of the graveyard under an oak
tree. She took me by the hand for courage I guess and off we
walked toward Rafe's people. My brown clip-on tie at my
throat was choking. I never liked Rafe and it bothered me a
little to think it, but honest-to-God I didn't want to be there
at that minute. Mama held her arms away from her body for
balance as she walked over the loose gravel like she was doing
a high wire act for the circus. All the friends and family were
standing around uncomfortably in their Sunday clothes like
they didn't know if they should cry or if they were waiting
for a fight to break out. We made our way toward the casket,
all the Clearwaters looking at us like we carnival freaks, her
hand squeezing mine for all she was worth. Red put his hand
on the minister's shoulder for a second and then marched
toward us like he meant to cold-cock Mama.

"Lorene, you ain't appreciated here" Red's lips were tightly shut as if hiding his teeth. His face was sunburnt since the
time we had seen him at the house.

"I just wanted—"

"We know what you wanted," Red growled. "You best go
on." He looked over his shoulder at the bunch watching us.
"If it weren't for you and Elston Vaughn, Rafe would still be .
. . Mama don't want you here. Nobody does. I've got a news
flash for you since you're the only one don't know, but
Vaughn has same as put his brand on you. How many more
good men you figure to get killed?"

"So you're just going to run us off like we was dogs?"
Mama's eyes were full of tears, but it wasn't because he'd hurt

her feelings. She cried when she was pissed off, but people who didn't know how she was just saw a woman crying. He was probably a sentence away from death without realizing it.

Red looked down at the toes of his boots. They were scuffed to hell. His face was smooth, unlike Rafe's, and he was a good week of chicken and mashed tater dinners heavier than his cousin. He whipped his head away from her and his shoulder-length hair was blown back in the wind making him look like a pirate.

The sky was flooded by white clouds with dark hulls coming in like invaders from outer space. It seemed fitting to me that it rained when somebody died instead of being bright and sunny even if it was Raffert Clearwater. I never had much use for him but he only did what he knew to do. Not much, was all his mama and daddy taught him. One thing I can say about him was he always wore a gold cross on his necklace. The man said he couldn't abide organized religion, as opposed to disorganized religion I guess. Rafe never went to church, but his people were Baptist. He believed in God, but it didn't change his dealings with folks every day. So that made him no better or worse than the rest of us.

"All right then," Mama turned her face to the ground. I could tell she was afraid, but she was trying to be brave. She'd been shacked up with Rafe as they put it and it would have made her look lowdown if she hadn't at least tried to come to the service. At least, they couldn't say she was some kind of whore who never gave a rat's ass about him. A few days later I heard some boys talking about how the men gathered out to old lady Clearwater's to drink the last six-pack of beer Rafe ever bought so they could pretend for a little while he was alive and still crazy as a shithouse rat.

The Twister

One day I was out playing in a hayfield with two girls who seemed to like me an awful lot when I noticed dark blue-black clouds gathering in the west. We didn't pay them much mind. Tempie was pulling on my arm and asking me to swing her. I'd get behind her and reach my arms around her waist and swing her off her feet around in circles. I'd Swing her until I got tired, then, I'd rest a minute and Regina would want me to do the same. The girls never came right out and said it but I knew they liked to feel me against them. They wanted to know who I liked best, but I didn't want to hurt their feelings so I'd just play along with whatever game they had in mind. They both wore daisy chains on their heads like fairy crowns.

I never tried to kiss either of them. I hadn't gotten the hang of kissing. It was enough for me to touch them and smell the Johnson's baby shampoo in their hair. There was a thought in my mind that I would like to take one of them into the woods and do something, but I wasn't sure what. Or, I was, sort of, but I didn't have the guts. I felt terrible guilty about it too but they were both very pretty even if I didn't actually tell either of them. Tempie and Regina gave each other competitive looks, but then it dawned on me that I wasn't really so important in their rivalry. They were more interested in getting me to pick one of them over the other.

Tempie and me would kind of wallow around and lay on each other those July nights in her backyard looking at the Milky Way with her parents right there and I'd think about the softness of her skin and the smell of her dirty-blond hair. Her daddy, she called him "Dad," would come out with his flattop guitar and he'd chord it and sing "Goodnight Irene" to Tempie's mama and she'd start in with the snot-nosed bawling because her name was the same as the song. It was so sappy but they seemed to love each other and I hadn't come across that very often. It was nice. They didn't pay much attention to me.

Tempie's daddy worked for National Brick and drove a shiny red pickup with lots of side panels that held tools and junk. On the door of the truck "Irene" was written in white stenciled cursive letters. Tempie and me were at an age when her parents didn't think we should have such strong boy-girl feelings, but it was still awkward enough between us that we never even kissed. She wore white-yellow barrettes in her hair made to look like spring flowers.

We ran through a yellow field of flowers and weeds, the sunlight blinding, until we came to the twisted creekbed. I waited for Tempie and Regina to catch up and we followed the cracked dry lines in the creek. A lizard was sunning itself on a rock. I chased it around and caught the little dragon and showed it off to the girls who squealed with a mixture of pretend gross-out and delight. They each reached out and touched the lizard's head. Dragonflies were buzzing around the few dank puddles of mud like helicopter fighter pilots. The humid air suddenly felt cooler on my skin. I found an arrowhead and just as I started to show it off to the girls a gust of wind blowing dust and twigs took my breath away.

We hadn't noticed the thunderhead coming on like the damn Horsemen of the Apocalypse until the gusting wind hit us full in the face. The clouds fell over us like a giant pulled a curtain closed on a rod. It was that fast. The sky was on our heads with low flying, rumbling, black clouds. A particular bank of clouds like the Devil's anvil was floating above as if it was looking for the three of us personally—I kept expecting to see the funnel cloud snake down to the ground and start scribbling in the dirt. I saw a narrow jag of lightning in the West. The electricity energized my insides even though it was a bad situation. Those summer heat lightning storms made me feel alive, but this was going to get a little more wild.

The girls ran on either side of me holding my hands until I couldn't keep my balance and ran ahead of them. We followed the creek out until we came to the old city cemetery and found ourselves at the Stillman mausoleums. The Stillmans were the *la-ti-da* important family in Fairmont. They owned the half of town that was worth a damn including the bank. It made sense their kin who had passed would live in mansions for the dead too. The mausoleums sat on the hill like some kind of beacon and I knew they were shaded by huge pin oaks, but first we had to scramble up the narrow dog trot. When I reached the top I watched the girls making their way up the trail with their arms up and away from their bodies for balance as if they were in a high wire act until they were at the top with me. We squeezed inside one of the mausoleums just as the winds were nearly bending small trees over and threw ourselves down on the cool floor.

"I'm scared," Tempie whimpered.

"It's going to be all right," I said. The truth was I didn't know for sure.

Mama was at work and I hoped she was okay. I was afraid the wind would blow the mausoleums down like dominoes and crush us inside. The three of us sat on the floor and held hands while we waited for the twister that we figured was on its way. I remembered the lighter I'd swiped from Rafe; I flicked my Bic, and Tempie's face was bright red and tears were welling up in her eyes. Her large doe eyes seemed to darken and then lighten up the more upset she was. The flame reflected in them. I had the strangest urge, seeing her so upset, to taste her tears. I knew nothing I could say would help. I got my hand loose from hers and touched the corner of her eye and brought some of her salty tears to my tongue. It made her laugh, but then we could hear the sound of metal careening against something solid.

"I wish I was home with Mommy," Regina said like a little girl. She fought to get her hair out of her face and mouth.

Tempie tossed her head and straightened her hair all in a single gesture I'd seen older girls make. There was something stirring about seeing her do it just as my lighter got so hot I had to let go and set it down in front of us so I wouldn't lose it until it cooled. The image of her face in such a pose in the light of the little flame burned into my imagination like a camera flash and it was one of the moments I knew I'd never forget. Tempie grabbed my hand and I felt the adrenaline really coursing through my veins, the sound of the ocean, even more powerful than the fear of the tornado.

Tempie prayed for us since she had been to the Assemblies of God summer camp back in June.

"Dear Lord," Tempie began, "we are just kids, so like Jonah in the belly of the whale, please save us from the tornado. We know that since your Son died on the cross and that we are yours and you know the number of hairs on our heads. We know you won't let that dumb old Devil get us so we BIND him up in the name of Jesus. Take away this spirit of fear and give us the peace that passeth all understanding. Thank you Lord, in Jesus' name we pray. Amen."

There was a muttering that sounded like spirits talking to each other in the darkness.

"What's that noise?" Regina whispered. "It sounds like ghosts."

I would have been plumb terrified hearing it in the dark, but I knew it was Tempie talking on tongues. They did it at Aunt Oleta's church all the time. It actually made me feel safer hearing her pray that way.

"It's the language of the Holy Ghost," I said.

"Oh," Regina said. A minute later she said, "Please save us God. Amen."

When she was finished praying Tempie moved closer to me and slipped her hand in my mine.

"Do you believe in God?" Tempie asked.

"I think I do," I said. "I think He turns his back on people who aren't in His will like David's son Absalom. Problem is, how do you know if you're in His will or not? Some Bible people, like Job, thought they were and then nothing but bad things happened to them and that was on a bet between God and the Devil."

"I believe in God," Tempie said.

"I believe in Him too," I said. "I know He exists and all but I think He probably has more important things to do than to listen to me crying about stuff if that makes any sense."

From where the door was cracked I could feel the wind licking around and into the mausoleum. The span of sky I could see had turned the hazy yellowish color it gets when a tornado is on its way. The wind had died down. I peeked out the door. Outside the sun was as bright as before and the wind was calm. Most of the clouds had passed over us and we felt lucky. We looked at each other and made up reasons to laugh. The underpinning from a nearby trailer park floating on the oily surface of the lagoon made us giggle with relief for some reason.

Tempie and Regina both wanted to get home because their people would be worried about them. Tempie hugged me but Regina hung back. They walked down the cemetery lane to the street instead of going back up the creek way.

When I went home the phone started ringing and it was Mama making sure I was okay. She said while the storm was brewing people had just sat in the red leatherette booths calmly drinking coffee, eating pecan pie, and watched the funnel cloud through the large fly-specked window panes like it was no big deal. The Spot didn't have a basement so there wasn't anything else for them to do.

Little Glow Worm

Mama told me to stay away from Vaughn so I did my best for awhile. I wanted her to be happy. Not long after that the phone seemed to be ringing all the time. She'd answer the phone but nobody would say anything. It wasn't hard to figure out. Sometimes she'd answer and say hello and just keep the receiver to her ear. Other times she would start cussing into it, saying all the words in the book, using the kind of words she warned me not to say. Mama would say, "Honey Boy, take the phone off the hook." We listened to the rock 'n' roll music she liked from when she was a kid.

Mama got the green label Jack down from the top of the fridge. She poured a little Co-Cola in with it "to take the sting out."

When she was really down she'd take out an old record with a red label in the middle, it was heavier than the others because it was so old. She was extra careful with that particular record and made sure to Scotch tape a nickel on the arm to make it heavier so the needle wouldn't skip. She would make a big thing out of telling me she was about to play her mama's favorite song. Her mama had died when she was a kid, younger than me. She told me her mama, my grandma, was trying to save her baby at the time, but then she clammed up. Then she went quiet on me for a spell but finally she looked at me, "My grandma had rheumatic fever when she was a girl, Mama said."

The record sounded like a man and woman singing harmony about a little glowing worm leading us to love. The song didn't really make any sense to me. She would pull me close to her on the couch and hug my neck, sometimes giving me sloppy kisses. I didn't even mind the hot alcohol smell of her breath. Things were good between us when she didn't have a man, but those times I could tell she was terrible lonely.

"It seems like last week you were a baby," Mama said. "You were such a serious looking baby. You watched me all the time. And you didn't like to be put down. You wanted me to hold you all the time. Oh, how you cried when I put you down."

"What else when I was little?"

"You would do whatever it took." She smiled from behind her glass. "You would spit up, start in on the screaming fits, just to get me to pick you up. You thought you were so misbused. And, you know, guess I was naturally limber because I'd see other pregnant woman try to get out of those plastic orange chairs at the laundromat with all kinds of trouble. I never had that problem. I guess I was so young I was just naturally limber. Can you believe it? Your Mama was young and skinny once too? But the thing that got me to pick you more often than not was your beautiful smile."

"Mama," I said. "I'm not a baby."

"Well," she said. "You had a beautiful smile and a little dimple on one cheek. It made you irresistible. It still does."

"Shoot."

I wanted to ask her why she'd left me with Aunt Oleta them times, but I stayed quiet about it. Just hoping she would talk more. She hugged my neck to her. I stopped worrying and thinking about things. When she got up to go into the kitchen I snuck a few sips of her mixed drink.

Mama made Jiffy-Pop popcorn during the news with lots of butter and salt. I sat with her on the couch, and she was dead to the world before Channel 13 news with Dick Preston went off the air. *Star Trek* came on. Later, I watched Abbott and Costello in a movie with a mummy. I laughed at Costello pointing to one side and screaming, "Abbott!" I turned to look at Mama. My biggest fear was that she wouldn't wake up. I don't know what made me think such a thing. She was asleep not long after the Captain Kirk's log was said.

As long as we were together I felt like things made sense. Later I got up so as not to wake her and covered her up with the red, white, and blue afghan. "The Star Spangled Banner" was blaring from the television, so I got up and turned it off. I dreaded hearing the announcer say: "This ends another broadcast day. . ."

The phone calls stopped coming so often, maybe only once a week. We heard Cheryl drove her daddy's rig to the auction barn with two hogs in the back. Mama said people were talking about it because she was a young girl who had never been interested in such things before. Talk was going on about her and Vaughn. Everyone knew Vaughn had a bunch of women doing things for him. She came right out and said she was doing it for Vaughn, but everyone already knew she was doing it for him anyway. He'd probably show up and collect the money himself most likely. Vaughn told me he figured to get $275 apiece for them hogs.

I snuck over there to Vaughn's. The coon dogs was barking. Arlene told me Vaughn went to Kansas City to wait for things to cool down. He'd probably be back in a couple to three weeks. Farmers would be mad, wanting to blame somebody for their stolen livestock. She said Vaughn didn't call her when he was gone like this 'cause all the Vaughns shared a party line. A party line ain't secure, but he didn't want to change the tradition. Mawmaw Vaughn, everyone called her Mawmaw—even people who weren't related to her—was the only one on the axle-busting road with her own line. Vaughn knew when to disappear. He had a sixth sense about cops, and a scanner.

Arlene told me Vaughn wanted us, Mama and me, to move in with them. I asked her how she felt about it. She was

washing dishes at the time and she shrugged like she didn't
have much choice.

"You know how Vaughn is when gets his mind set on
something."

Sugarbaby was out back. She would climb up on the top
rung of the gate to the hog lot and ride it all the way until the
bottom stuck in the dirt. She looked to be having a high time
too, but I wondered if that girl wasn't a few bricks shy of a
load. There weren't ever any hogs in the lot, except for those
Vaughn heisted and they didn't stay around long. I wasn't
supposed to talk about it.

TC, Punkin, and Rusty came over and got on the roof and
started yanking off the shingles. I didn't have plans to work,
but to hang out with the boys I took some unsteady steps up
the rickety ladder they had and bounced on it. I could see the
rusty rods in the ladder weren't doing much to hold it together. I got up there anyway and it took most of the afternoon to
throw all the shingles into their daddy's dump truck. Vaughn
had hired the boys damn cheap to do the work, but they
would do just about anything for him.

We took off our shirts while we worked. I got so sunburnt
I was as red as a lobster. When the red started to show later
Punkin would touch my arm to see the whiteness of his
thumbprint. Rusty slapped me on the back real hard and
laughed. Arlene made us two pitchers of iced tea with lemon
and ham salad sandwiches between thick slices of homemade
white bread. At home Mama didn't cook much unless you
counted special occasions like undercooked turkey on
Thanksgiving, so as simple as it was I considered Arlene's
food a real treat.

The next day I fell off the roof and twisted my ankle. TC
wouldn't allow me to come back up after that. He said I was
too young to be up there with them. Rusty sat up on the edge
kicking his feet, dangling off the edge, and gave me the finger
the way you do to one of your running buddies. TC had

worked for a guy doing roofing for the past three summers in a row so he knew all about it and he told Punkin and Rusty what to do. Rusty went around barefoot as much as he could. His feet were stained by blackberries that grew practically in their backyard. TC said they was learning a trade. That Buddy dog palled around with me as we watched the boys put on a new roof over the older part and re-shingle it too.

I guess the thing all of us boys liked about Vaughn was that even though he was a grown man he didn't talk down to us when it was about important subjects like women, sports, and hunting. We were good enough in his mind to give special jobs to us. He was the first grown-up man who took an interest in me as a person apart from my mama or so he made it seem. If I wanted to smoke, he didn't give a shit. If I wanted to cuss, have at it. Most of the time anyway. It depended on his mood. By his standards, Vaughn said I was so lazy I'd stop plowing to fart. Why, to hear him tell it, at my age, he used to chase tail all day and run coons all night. He said he'd had fun chasing coons and made decent money for the skins back in the old days. There were even rumors, not just among us boys, that he had killed an attorney in Jeff City for a state senator, Brydon Van Matre, supposedly just for criticizing him in the Tribune.

I helped Arlene in her garden. Tempie came with me. I stepped through the barbed wire and cut my thumb holding the middle wire up while I pushed the lower wire down with my foot so Tempie could get through. I told her about how Rusty pissed on an electric fence, or so he said, which joined their property. We picked strawberries for Arlene. We ate as many as we picked until we made our stomachs sick. Looking at the little hairs growing out of the skins I wondered who was the first person to decide to eat them but they were so sweet I forgot about the ugly little hairs. We each filled up little orange plastic beach pails with mostly ripe strawberries.

When we brought them in the kitchen, Arlene washed them off in the sink. Tempie tried to get me to come home for dinner with her folks on Linnaean Street, but Arlene looked so lonesome I decided to stay.

Before it got too dark I knocked down the mud dauber nests in the outhouse. The Vaughn clan had recently got around to installing inside toilets for everyone who lived on Vaughn's Hill, but the men and children still used the out-houses in emergency situations. That's how they did everything. If one wanted something they'd talk about it and then they'd all do it together like they were Amish. Everyone came to Vaughn first because he was the boss.

Arlene was cooking meatloaf and some kind of vegetable I tried to ignore. I told her if I could eat meals like hers every day I'd be proud to move in, but then she put her hands under my chin and just looked at me for a minute. Her hands still had flour on them and smelled like onions. She laughed in a thoughtful sort of way but didn't say nothing else.

Sugarbaby was standing on the kitchen chair eating Life cereal out of the box, threatening to step onto the green surface of the Formica table. We ignored her and so decided not to do it. I set the table for the three of us. The boys had gone on home at 5:30 to eat with their daddy and step-mama down in the holler after our mudclod fight. If you get hit with a dry clod of dirt, more clay than mud, it can hurt like the crazy, especially if there's a rock in it. The boys wanted to go cow-tipping later. I was a little worried it might be like a snipe hunt, but TC told me that what they did was to sneak up on sleeping cows and flip them over. It sounded weird to me, but I was up for just about anything to fit in.

My Eyes Are Still Curly and My Hair is Still Blue

Mama was usually asleep until it was time for her to get up and go to work at McMillan's Tavern. She asked me if I'd been eating lately. I couldn't lie. I told her Arlene Vaughn had made dinner for me a couple of times, and it seemed to make Mama mad. She was all dressed up in her short black dress with high heels, her hair stacked up high on her head, but still she was determined to fix something for me even though I wasn't hungry yet. She made me a cheeseburger with mayonnaise and Backer's potato chips and a pitcher of iced tea to wash it down. I told her a beer would sure hit the spot. She smirked at me. Sometimes when she was at work around supper time I would wander over to a neighbor's like nothing, like I was just dropping in on them, and get myself invited to eat with them. Most folks were real good about that.

Mama watched me eat every bite of my burger. She asked me if I wanted another, but I didn't. She rested her hand, the one the cigarette wasn't in, in my hair, and played with the curls. She sang some funny little song she used to sing to me when I was about "Why don't you love me like you used to do?" and I ended like I always did singing "My eyes are still curly and my hair is still blue." She sat down in the chair next to mine wailing that she wasn't a very good mother and started crying with her forehead resting on her arms. I told her she was the best mom a kid could have. When she got all weepy-eyed like that I felt hopeless but good, too, because I knew she cared then. Finally, she went back into the bathroom and fixed her makeup.

"There's a carton of cigarettes on the fridge," Mama said. "I know how many packs is left so you leave them alone, okay, Honey Boy?" I told her I could just go down to Roy's gas station and steal a pack, but she made a face at me and went out to the truck. She was going to the tavern to have a few drinks. She never explained or made excuses about leaving me at home when she went tonkin'. She held up a black dress and a red one. I pointed to the red and it seemed to make her happy. The whole place stank of Aqua Net hairspray; it stung my nose. When she came out of the bedroom she held her hair piled up on top of her head and asked me to zip her up.

"Thank you, sir," she said. "I'm painting the town—don't wait up." But she knew I would stay up until she walked through the door.

"You look pretty," I said from the front porch. Men used to tell her she looked like Natalie Wood when she was younger, but she had been steadily gaining weight over the last year. There was a runner in one of her hose, but I didn't say anything. When she got in the truck she tooted the horn twice and I went back inside before the funnel of dust she'd raise from the gravel could get me. I tried walk-the-dog with my yo-yo, but I wasn't very good at doing any tricks with it. I guess you have to practice that stuff.

In my closet I still had my old toy box. It was just a big cardboard box with old plastic trucks, green John Deere tractors, and mainly Hot Wheels I hadn't brought myself to part with yet. When I dumped all the toys out I found the purple Crown Royal bag. My pistol was in there safe and sound. I'd stowed it away after that last night of hog-thieving. I unloaded it, stuffed it down the front of my jeans like they do in the movies, and practiced my quick draw. Vaughn gave people tough looks like he didn't have a soul, like he was dead on the inside, and I tried to make my face do the same as his. My face didn't do it exactly right, but good enough for a kid.

"You won this one," I said to my reflection. "But I'll be ready for you next time Stafford, by God!"

I didn't know what Mama had against Arlene. Mama said Arlene was a lonely woman who had been beat down by life, and by Vaughn. Her people were from down along the Osage River somewhere around Mokane. Mama said she'd growed up in a house on stilts right beside the river. I'd heard people in Fairmont call them "river rats." Mama didn't tell me to stay away in so many words, but she acted like I had betrayed her somehow. Still, I couldn't wait to go over to Arlene's because she promised to make an angel food cake and use the strawberries Tempie and me had picked to make a sweet topping with.

About that time the phone rang. I answered. Nothing. I listened harder. I could hear the sound of highway traffic in the background. Normally we didn't get these type of calls when Mama wasn't home because Vaughn knew Mama's schedule so well. She had temporarily quit the Spot in a pissed-off moment and was working full time at the tavern, but he didn't know, at least we didn't think he knew. There wasn't any point in saying anything so I just listened wondering if he was going to say boo to me. The sound of a crowd roaring like ball games on television made me wonder if he was outside the stadium, if he was going to see the Royals play. There was the sound of traffic and then a dial tone.

"Hell, yes it's me," I said to myself. "Who'd you think it was?"

I don't know how she had time to get them, but when she came home the next day about half past noon she had a pair of black Chuck Connors for me. I threw my arms around her. I knew a couple of older boys who wore shoes like them. Now maybe they'd quit calling me a "shit-kicker."

A Wonderful Life

Finally Mama decided we should go see Grandma Kimbrough in the nursing home. She was real happy to see us, but she didn't seem to know who we were from minute to minute. Her eyes and expression had a fierceness to them, like a hawk looking for mice in a field, and Aunt Oleta said she knew more than she let on. Grandma knew who Mama was for the most part. Used her front name a good bit: Lorene this and Lorene that. But she was way behind the times. Grandma didn't seem to realize I'd ever been born. The biggest part of her memories stopped in 1964 according to Mama and that was before I was a gleam in my daddy's eye as the saying goes.

The window unit was roaring and the goosebumps stood out on my arm. We didn't have air conditioning at home so it felt like a meat locker in there. It made me realize just how hot it was outside. "It ain't so much the heat as the humidity," was Aunt Oleta's favorite saying that summer.

"Hi Grandma," Mama said. She was hoarse from staying out too late. Grandma Kimbrough was actually my great grandma, but who has time to put great in front of the rest of it? Grandma nodded gravely and it made me think she wasn't quite sure who we were.

I wondered how long it would take Aunt Oleta to say, "Why haven't you come to see me? Don't you love me anymore?" It was her catchphrase like characters on television shows have. Mama was especially susceptible to guilt and Aunt Oleta was good at pouring it on so I guess that's why Mama stayed away most of the time.

"Lorene," Aunt Oleta said "I didn't think you would ever come to see me. Why didn't you come and visit me right

away instead of hanging out with that stinking Rafe Clearwater? Don't you love me anymore?"

Mama looked at me and we both tried not to laugh.

"Honey Boy!" Aunt Oleta said running her fingers
through over my hair. "You've still got your curls. Old wom-
en like me have to get a permanent to get curls like those.
You would have been such a pretty little girl. Ain't it always
the way! The little boys get the curls. You're shooting up just
like corn." She smashed my cheeks together and I figured she
would get all kissy but she
didn't—thank the Lord.

"I ain't no girl," I said with my fists balled up at my side.
Sometimes old women told my mother what a beautiful little
girl she had and I was always a hair's breath away from
punching one of them old broads right in the gut. I hated to
admit it, but it was probably time for a haircut. Cool people
like But short hair was for squares. Cool people like Uncle
Sonny had long hair.

Aunt Oleta turned to trying to slick down Clarence's cowlick. She'd spit on her fingers and then wipe at his head.
Clarence would put up his arms to defend himself, he was
probably a foot and a half taller than her. "DON'T, THANK
YOU," he'd wail like a little kid. She treated him like a baby,
but he was a grown man in his thirties. Aunt Oleta told me
not to call him a re-tard, said to say it nicer, "Clarence is mentally retarded, not a re-tard." Clarence would give me his
serious look, like he was a regular grown-up: "Say retarded—
thank you." Aunt Oleta was big on manners. She taught Clarence to say "please" and "thank you," but he didn't always
know the right time to use those words so to keep Aunt
Oleta off his case he'd just throw in a please or thank you to
cover his bases.

Aunt Oleta had all kinds of plastic green curlers in her
hair. She looked like an alien from outer space to me. She said
was going to the Senior Citizens dance where she liked to jit-

terbug with other old coots. To make matters worse she had masking tape across her forehead to hold her bangs down in a straightline over her penciled-in eyebrows.

"When I was a girl—" Aunt Oleta sat on the end of Grandma's bed trying to work on one of Clarence's black-heads "—my friends and I would go out in public with our curlers still on."

"Where did you go *like that?*" I asked.

"Oh just everywhere," she frowned, catching my tone. "The grocery store or the drugstore."

"WHY?"

"Because," she huffed "you silly thing! It meant you had a hot date that night! Everybody knew you were going out that night if they saw you wearing curlers."

"Do you have a date tonight?"

"You better watch your smart mouth," Aunt Oleta said.

"I just don't think that's the style anymore," I said making a big show of looking at the crazy curlers on her head.

Mama was cutting the corn off the cob with a steak knife for Grandma Kimbrough
on account of her dentures.

"Lorene," Grandma Kimbrough said with her mouth full of corn and mashed potatoes "have you been taking that boy to church?"

"We haven't been for awhile," Mama said. She didn't want to say we never went to church except with Aunt Oleta every once in a blue moon.

"I had thirteen brothers and sisters," Grandma said, food falling out of her mouth and onto her bib. "We didn't have no television to watch. There wasn't no entertainment back then, except church. People believed back then. You had to get to Church early back in them days because if you didn't you had to stand outside and look in through the windows. And when it was harvesting time folks would come in everyday for two or three weeks to thank the Lord for the harvest and His mercy. You don't see that anymore."

"Well," Grandma huffed. "We're living in the end times like the preacher said. It's a godless time. Clarence and I go to church every Sunday morning and night."

"And Wednesday night ser-vice," Clarence said. "After church they have cookies and punch. We thanked God last Wednesday that Aunt Oleta doesn't have to use a red hair rinse like Sister Hawkins because it makes her look like an old woman. Right Mama?"

"Hush that up, Clarence," Aunt Oleta said. "We did no such thing."

"Yes we did!" Clarence got tickled and started laughing. "That's what YOU said! YOU SAID IT! YES YOU DID!" He was squealing in a high pitched voice.

"I SAID. . .HUSH!" Aunt Oleta hollered. "Or you will have to stay home next time you decide to tell everyone my business. Do you understand, mister?"

"Yes," Clarence barely whispered now with his eyes full of tears. "You said it."

"Shush it up."

Someone was listening to Lawrence Welk-type music in the bedroom next door.

"We used to dry apples up on the roof," Grandma said.

"Oh," Mama said to Aunt Oleta. "He's just trying to fun you."

"He can be just plain mean sometimes," Aunt Oleta said. "I gave up my life for taking care of first Odie and then Clarence. Odie had his heart and respiration problems. And then my only baby ends up born retarded. I do and I do for him, but do you think he appreciates it? He just messes and messes and then mean-mouths his mama. It just breaks my heart."

Aunt Oleta liked to heap guilt on folks. Her voice would go up high like a bird and she would talk about how the world did her wrong. Mama said she was melodramatic like the people on the soaps. It was a pitiful thing to witness.

"Clarence loves you." He was slobbering all over his shirtsleeves. "Clarence loves his Mama. Clarence is a bad boy."

Except for Aunt Oleta and Clarence sniffing and bawling, it was quiet. I could hear an old woman calling from the direction of the great room, "Help me. Somebody help me. *C'mooon. Hurry u-pp! C'mooon Hurry u-pp!*"

"Have y'all ever seen *It's a Wonderful Life?*" Grandma her head shook when she talked and her hair was white and puffy as cotton candy at the Kingdom County Fair.

"Is that what you're watching?" Mama asked to interrupt all the squabbling. "Why are they showing it in the summer?"

"It's on channel 11," Grandma said. "Out of St. Louis. The Bijou picture. We get it here if the wind's blowing right."

"Who's that fella?" I asked.

"That's Jimmy Stewart," Grandma said. "I bet you never heard of him?"

"Oh, I know who he is," I said, but I hated it when people talked to me like I was a little kid so I'd pretended I knew what they were talking about even when I didn't.

"I love Jimmy Stewart," Grandma said. Her eyes went dreamy and got real soft and I believed she did love that cat too.

We watched the movie on the little black and white TV on the dresser. She had all of her bedroom furniture in there, but it looked smaller like an antique store in the nursing home. Her furniture didn't fit in with the waxed floors and smell of disinfectant. The worst of it was the smell of old people all around you like it was a disease that was catching.

An old-time song was playing on the radio on her bureau. It sounded kind of cheesy and every so often a bunch of people hollered "Pennsylvania 6-5000!"

She still had the big oval picture of Great Granddad's parents over her bed. The photograph was made when they were

real old and it was dark and their figures were wispy like
ghouls watching over her. Kimbroughs all over the state were
already swearing they would get the picture when she passed.
Some of them seemed more eager to get their hands on that
old picture than passing the time of day with Grandma. It
was sick if you ask me. The retirement home people didn't
even allow Grandma to make sugar cookies no more and the
fact that she didn't have any to offer made her somehow less
than what she had been in my view. She loved making cookies and seeing people eat them.

Grandma Kimbrough had been bowlegged for my entire
life. She looked even more bowlegged than I remembered
and now she had to use an aluminum walker just to go over
to her dresser to get her pillbox. She didn't even know what
day it was so I don't know how the pillbox for every day of
the week helped. Every so often I'd catch her looking at me
suspiciously like she didn't know me from Adam.

"Lorene," Grandma said "who is this handsome young
man with you?"

"Mama, that's Honey Boy, you know."

"That's Honey Boy, Grandma," Clarence snorted. Aunt
Oleta started in on Clarence telling him to respect his elders
until he was wailing. Then she took him outside to give him a
talking to or pray for him. She was awfully religious. She even
called herself a "Jesus freak." I could fully agree with part of
that statement.

Aunt Oleta carried a little Bible with her everywhere. It sat
on a stand next to her orange chair. When commercials came
on she picked up the little black book and sat it on her lap
like it was a little kid she loved. I always ignored it, but now I
took a look at it. It said *Holy Bible* on the front cover. On the
binding it said *King James Version* and *Red Letter Edition* below
it. She saw me sneaking a look at her bible and held it out to
me, opened some of the pages, pushed her glasses up on the
bridge of her nose. I was afraid to touch it. I knew it was the

Lord's book. It had real power to it and that was something I couldn't deny, but I was afraid to put my hands on it. It made me think of them boys, them priests, that reached out to steady the Ark and were killed for it just because it belonged to God. Nary a one of them stories made any sense to me, but I wasn't taking chances.

I looked back at Grandma and she was still looking at me like I was the man from Mars.

My heart fell in my stomach when I knew for sure she didn't recognize me. My throat began to get tight too. I felt like I might start blubbering like some sissified idiot. I touched the back of my hand to my eyes to keep the tears welling up from spilling out. I went over and sat on the arm of the dingy brown recliner to be next to her. Her wrinkled hand slipped into mine and I couldn't help noticing the liver spots, the tremor, and what looked like food under her fingernails. Orange stuff. Carrots. Grandma gawked at me like she expected a kiss so I pecked her cheek. Her skin felt like powder on a chalkboard. Then she turned away and went back to watching the movie. We sat like that watching Jimmy Stewart running around for about ten minutes and I thought how we must look to the aliens who were probably watching like we were under government mind control.

Grandma tugged on my shirt. "Have you all ever seen *It's a Wonderful Life?* It's my favorite movie."

I didn't say nothing. There wasn't any point. She began to rock back and forth and hum to herself. She cocked her head to me all of a sudden and pointed her bony finger in my face.

"Elston! I'm only going to tell you this one time. You better take good care of our baby girl! Don't you be running around on her. She's too good for that!"

I wasn't sure what to say. I looked back at Jimmy Stewart but my mind was trying to make sense of what she had just said. I didn't have much time to ponder before Aunt Oleta and Mama walked back in the room. They laughed at

Grandma who smiled in her confused way back at them. I could not laugh because this reality stabbed at my heart: that time kept passing like a television screen that continually needed its vertical hold adjusted. I guess that when the day came when I started to lose it everyone would think it was funny, too. It just made me feel like crying so I turned my head away so no would see me sitting there in the dust motes coming through the curtains.

The Sugar Booger Express

I was watching *Hee Haw* on TV when Vaughn showed up in a used Ford with a gooseneck trailer hooked on back with two of the sorriest looking cows I'd ever seen. He also had a little Shetland pony separated in his own stall baring his teeth at us and kicking the metal walls. The trailer was big and blue and had a fancy script sign on the side:

THE SUGAR BOOGER EXPRESS

He opened the car door and his big western-booted foot stuck out first and he set it on the ground in a confident way that made me feel good just watching him do it. He demonstrated the electric windows and there were even buttons for adjusting the bucket seats. I got in on the driver side and pushed the button and the seat went down, back, and tilted at an angle like I might be heading up into outer space.

"Come in Houston," I said. "I am in the Moon rover."

Vaughn was holding Sugarbaby when I turned around. They were walking back up to the house. Arlene had her arm around his wide waist. I looked after them and my eyes came to rest on a new western belt he was wearing that had his front name stenciled on it: ELSTON. He was even wearing a bolo tie with a turquoise stone glowing at his neck. He smelled like aftershave and beer.

He yelled back at me to bring in the presents he'd bought for everyone. There was a coat made of rabbit fur for Arlene, it was soft and the hairs were surprisingly long and every shade of rabbit I'd ever seen; the awnry bowlegged pony named Tony for Sugarbaby; a little diamond ring he gave me on the sly for Mama; and a bone-handled knife for filleting fish he gave especially for me in a nice leather sheath. The knife was so sharp that when I put it back in the sheath it cut through the leather and into my thumb so deep I just stood there watching the blood flow like I was hypnotized.

"Gawd!" Arlene said. "Oh my Gawd!" She kept saying. She gave me a tea-stained dish towel to wrap around my hand. Even though it was clean, it smelled sour. "Don't let Honey Boy sit there and bleed to death!"

"Watch your tone with me," Vaughn said. "Don't holler at me. I'll haul off and knock your ass into next week!"

"Elston," Arlene said. "Oh Elston, just look at him." She was jumping up and down like she had to pee and shaking her hand in a jerky motion with her palm down. The whole time she was talking she was backing into the kitchen which was about the only room in the house she was truly comfortable in could claim as her own.

"Shut the hell up!" Vaughn yelled in Arlene's direction. "Sit down on the couch boy, and watch you don't get blood all over!"

"I'm fine," I said. "A little blood never hurt nobody."

"That's right," Vaughn said. "That's right. You hear that, Arlene? The boy knows his shit."

Vaughn told me to go home and come back the next night. Mama's car was gone, but there was a can of Campbell's chicken soup sitting on the counter in a big silver pot with a black handle from earlier that morning. I squeezed the dish towel tight around my hand like Vaughn told me. He'd lectured me on pressure points which degenerated into how he could kill a man in various ways by attacking his vulnerable parts.

I knew Mama was off. I wondered where she was and who she was with. She hadn't even left a note. I thought she might look at the cut on my hand and tell me it would be okay. Just then I heard the train that went by behind our trailer beyond the backyard as it followed the tracks east and over the trestle. Sometimes I thought about jumping on the caboose and waving goodbye to Fairmont. We had done it plenty of times.

I'd jumped on the train and rode it for a few miles with the neighbor boys, but no more than six miles at the most because I would have to walk all the way back from east Jesus. It wouldn't be too hard to do it alone.

It was an old fashioned train with a scoop on the front for gathering up cows that got on the track or so Mama told me. One of my smaller goals in life was to see that once, to see a cow scooped up like it was on a playground slide with all fours in the air with its bell ringing and the whistle blowing.

I ran outside and slammed the trailer door shut hard behind me. There is no more satisfying a sound in all the world than slamming a trailer door shut. It's like trailer doors are made to be slammed. I listened to the train clack on by; as an added bonus this one had a couple of passenger cars. The people stared at me with blank faces like I was an animal exhibit in the zoo and it occurred to me that they must be rich to be riding on a train. Most everyone seemed rich to me. Those train people aren't eating chicken noodle soup and saltine crackers for dinner, I told myself. I took the miniature black velvet box out of my pocket and threw it side-armed at the train.

There wasn't much in the fridge, but I grabbed the last beer and it tasted bitter and cold, good.

Wrongdoers Respect Me

First thing I noticed was the empty trailer, the Sugar Booger, up on blocks in Vaughn's driveway. Vaughn never stayed on an even keel. He was always yelling, puffing himself up, as if he had to prove that he was a big man. It made me embarrassed for him when he acted like a thug, even when there wasn't anybody to see him. I could feel my face flushed red with guilt and maybe even excitement. Seeing him standing with his upper body cocked at an angle and his arms down straight with his elbows sticking out made me want to do the same thing, but I didn't have the size for it.

"Farmers are the biggest chumps in the world," Vaughn said. "Glenn is the worst of them because like my daddy used to say, he's all vines and no taters."

We were zipping down Highway Z passing nothing but fields of gold. There were pastures full of staring cattle looking shell-shocked like they could see themselves in the future as ground chuck in the meat aisle at Kroger USDA certified. Silver metal silos were lined up at intervals along the highway and it made me wonder how many were actually missile silos armed with nuclear warheads aimed at the Soviet Union. The more he talked about how farmers burned his ass the more clearly we were heading out of town into the heart of farmland itself.

"The problem with farmers," Vaughn said. He took out a cigar and began to lick it up and down. He bit off one end, flipped it around and lit it. There was a band around the cigar where his fingers held it like a cig and the emblem on the paper band had some kind of interesting red and gold coat of arms but I couldn't see it too good. "Farmers are lazy," Vaughn said. "They'd rather live off the government check.

Lots of farmers here in Kingdom County get paid *not* too farm, if you can believe that shit. Glenn Starkey is the laziest sod busting son-of-a-bitch I ever seen. He likes to parade around down to Ike's bar like a big man, but his mouth done wrote a check his body can't cash. He thinks buying me a beer is going to get him off scot-free. Well, he don't know . . . he don't know the half of it. His granddaddy used to have the biggest farming operation in the county, but the operative word here is *used*. Glenn's daddy, Raymond Starkey, had to sell most of it because he was a gotdamned drunk. He conveniently leaves that part out. It's one thing to be proud, but stupid is the unforgivable sin."

Vaughn's knuckles were white as he fishtailed onto a dirt road after he goosed the gas. Pea gravel was pinging on the underside of the Ford. My hands itched with wanting to be in the driver's seat messing around with the electric seat adjust buttons. I wanted to adjust the seat more than I wanted to drive. The dust wasn't too bad, but it usually isn't at twilight. It dawned on me that we were heading for that no-good tenant farmer's spread, Glenn Starkey.

I could look at Vaughn's hands all day. They were as leathery and weighty as a catcher's mitt. They were freckled and one had a liver spot squatting on the flesh between his thumb and forefinger. He reached down between his legs to adjust himself and then stretched his hand under the seat and retrieved a paper bag in the shape of a bottle. He took a big swig and I watched his throat work and then he *yippy-yi-yayed*, yanked the bag off and threw it out the window in one quick motion. He was drinking Mad Dog 20/20. Sonny always said only niggers drank that shit. I told it to Mama once to be funny, but she said to say negro.

"You're one nosy son-of-a-bitch," Vaughn said, looking right at me. For one awful moment I thought he was actually seeing me, seeing me all the way down to the bone. "You're always watching people. Why is that? You're studying people, you're studying me, and that means you're smart." He made a clicking noise out of one side of his face and pointed his finger at me and his thumb bowed down like he was shooting me, but in a good way.

"People don't tell me jack," I said. "I got to learn somehow."

"Glenn Starkey is going to be shitting his pants before the night is over." Vaughn laughed. It was that no emotion, no humor, kind of laugh he did that made the blood in my veins go south. "When I get through with him he won't know whether to shit or go blind."

I didn't have the nerve to tell Vaughn I didn't want to sit in the car watching Starkey's house. Vaughn just sat there taking sips of Mad Dog and staring at the house like he had X-ray vision. The Mad Dog smelled like cheap cough syrup. He pushed me in the elbow with his forearm to tell me he thought I should drink some, but I didn't want none of that. But Vaughn was the kind of man who would say you were a pussy and a cornholer if you didn't drink when he says drink, so I drank it.

The porch light came on at the Starkey's farmstead and a skinny woman in a homemade housedress that was part quilt-part robe, came out and looked at us. She hollered something behind her, into the house, in a rough country accent. There was some kind of angry and scared yelling coming from the back of the house that I couldn't understand.

"What do y'all want?" the skinny woman crowed. She had a big nose and her voice could strip varnish off an old pie safe, quaverly and lonesome. Vaughn didn't say nothing. He just stared at her hard for a long while until she went back inside. Frogs and crickets were busy telling stories on one another. I looked over to see Vaughn trying not to bust out laughing at old Mrs. Starkey. He plainly fed off her fear and I realized that he ate fear like most people had to eat food, he craved fear.

I fell asleep for a while; drinking tends to put me to sleep.

It was almost dawn when I awoke. My throat was dry and I had to piss. I was thirsty, but for a glass of cold Central Dairy milk, not Devil juice. Mama once posed for a newspaper ad with a jug of Central Dairy in her lap. The old-fashioned glass-bottle variety. I had a craving for one of them Dolly Madison apple pies and a midget carton of chocolate milk. The frogs and bugs had shut up, but birds were starting in now. A blue jay sounded pissed about something the way they do. The sun wasn't up yet, but the sky was light blue and the stars were invisible again—a peach color flavored the sky.

"You awake, pard?"

"Uh huh," I said.

"I guess I showed him," Vaughn said. "Next time I'll do more than just sit here. Next time I'll burn down the fuckin' place all around him. I don't give a shit." The headlights slashed on as a cat walked across the road and its eyes were creepy green jewels glowing like Kryptonite.

The lights were still burning inside the little shotgun shack—even the porchlight was still on. If Glenn Starkey came from a big time family then the mighty had fallen pretty far to be living in a place like that. The Starkey place was sadder than living in a run-down trailer court like Mama and me. Vaughn spent most of the night telling me all about it: Did I know, he asked, that this was the last 60 acres Ray Starkey ran out of time to drink up before he keeled over dead in Fairmont State Hospital from a life of alcoholism and a history of insanity on his Mama's side?

Old Man Starkey didn't seem to be much of a threat to Vaughn. He was a dried-up bean pole of an old man. But Vaughn had harbored a good deal of hatred for Ray. He'd worked as a mechanic for Raymond Starkey when Ray owned the Chevrolet dealership back in the early '60s and gave it to his son Glenn to run into the ground according to word around town. Since his retirement, Old Man Starkey served as a deacon at Nine Mile Baptist Church. Nine Mile because it was built on Nine Mile Prairie near to Williamsburg. Starkey was a volunteer firefighter, and he was a member of the Independent Order of Odd Fellows. Basically, he was what people meant when they pointed to a pillar of society type— except he wasn't too bright. But his not having much book smarts or everyday walking around brains kind of made everybody in town love him. He was the sort that had those little root beer candies and extra quarters to give to little kids. Vaughn pestering him was like picking a fight with a cripple or kicking a puppy.

"I feel like I been beat with a ten cent mop," Vaughn said as he stretched and accidentally hit the dome light with the heel of his hand.

"I got to piss," I said.

"Well I ain't going to hold it for you," Vaughn said.

"Okey doke," I said.

In the stickery weeds I peed on the smilax, the poison oak, and purple-plumed ironweed. Vaughn came out on my side after I zipped up and the splatter his piss made sounded like a horse pissing in a deep mudhole. When he finished, he shook it off, and went around to the back and popped the trunk. He had a big Louisville slugger in his hand.

"Get your ass out here. You candy ass."

"Take it," he said, thrusting the bat into my hands.

"What?"

"Hit it, son," he said.

"Hit what?"

"Hit it" He pointed at the black mailbox made out of old welded together pipes real fancy in a way, but backwoods at the same time. "Knock the shit out of it."

"I'm tired," I said. "I'm tired and I need something to eat."

"Hit it first!" Vaughn slapped me on the back of the head with the palm of his hand. It hurt my feelings more than anything. "Knock the shit out of her and we'll got to the Spot Cafe and surprise your mama. I'm buying. We'll have us a couple of Roadrunner specials."

I took a few lame licks at the mailbox. The cut on my thumb throbbed with the first swing. I didn't have nothing against Glenn Starkey. Hell, I didn't know him but to maybe wave at him when he was getting a haircut down to the barber shop. He had always seemed real friendly to me. He was the kind of guy apt to sit on a bench downtown and wave at people whether he knew them or not.

"Not like that, goddammit!" Vaughn ripped the bat out of my hands so hard it hurt my wrists. He pushed me in the back so I stumbled and landed in the gravel bloodying my hands and tearing a hole in the knee of my denims. "You fucking candy-ass!" Then he proceeded to bust the mailbox and the red-painted pipes into pieces. When we got back into the car he flicked on the radio and started listening to Lefty on the radio and singing some song I'd heard a thousand times but never paid attention to it. Seemed like the kind of song cows might like to listen to. Mama and me liked rock 'n' roll, not country, but Vaughn loved country music and that old tinny sounding early rock 'n' roll music. Songs with lyrics that mostly made no sense like *Be-Bop-A-Lula*.

"You got your gun with you?" Vaughn asked.

"Yep," I said. I reached behind me and pulled it out from the waist band of my jeans.

"Shoot it."

"The mailbox?"

"Shoot it," Vaughn said. "I want to know you can use it in a jam."

"Okay" I shot the mailbox twice. It looked all but dead to me anyway. A shock wave traveled from the gun to my hand, up my arm, and spread out like a spoonful of honey easing down my throat. A golden feeling of power that started in my gut and worked its way down to my balls. All fear was gone. I began to wonder what else I could shoot. What would it feel like to shoot a living thing? I felt bad about thinking it, but I had a powerful urge. The good and the bad were fighting a war inside me.

"Quit shooting up our mailbox and get the hell out of here!" Mrs. Starkey ran out on the front porch with a big kitchen knife in her hand. "I called the law! They'll be here any minute now! I lawed you all!"

"Get a load of the old lady, man," Vaughn said. "What a silly-ass bitch." Vaughn was tickled now and he motioned for me to get back in. I put the pistol under my seat. As we drove down the road Vaughn laughed and shook his head. "You think she was going to come out and cut me?" The more he thought about it, the more it made him laugh. "She must have some Indian in her. Only an Indian would show up to a gun-fight with a knife."

Glenn Starkey never showed his face, never even darkened his own door.

Strutting Game Cocks

There were only a couple of trucks parked in front of the Spot when we pulled up. Vaughn looked up in the rearview mirror, pulled a little black comb out of his back pocket and slicked his hair back: *You handsome devil* he seemed to say to his reflection. I had to wait for him on the sidewalk while he sat in the car doing God knows what. Waiting on him was irritating because my stomach was really talking to me. When he finally got out he stuffed his shirt down in his britches, yanked his belt up and down a couple of times so it landed just right over his belly. In his hand was the latest *Reader's Digest.* He didn't read the articles much, but he liked the vocabulary lists in the back. Sometimes he would have me quiz him on his vocabulary and he rarely got one wrong. He had dropped out of school in the eighth grade to "help support his family" and he said he wanted to make up for his lack of formal education.

We parked in the little lot instead of on the street where you had to pay the meter. Vaughn bought a copy of *The Fairmont Sun* out of the machine and looked through it until he came to the funny papers which he handed to me. The smell of food hit us right in the face. The bell on the door rang when we went in. It was pure-d seventh heaven: fried chicken, bread, coffee, and even apple pie with a trace of cinnamon. The wood floors were polished with a sheen from years of work boots and down toward the end of the counter the floor buckled and pitched a bit so when I stood there it was like being in a funhouse. The overhead fan was already going, but the juke box was unplugged—silent and dark against the wall.

"Let's get us a booth so we can spread out with our papers," Vaughn said.

"Vaughn," said a rotund man as he half-spun around on the barstool that practically disappeared up his ass. He had a mustache and a pair of glasses with one of the lenses darkened. He wore a wrinkled white shirt and what looked to be in the running for the biggest pair of britches I had ever seen. I had to keep myself from laughing when I remembered Vaughn had said Tugboat's clothes were made by Omar the Tentmaker.

"Tugboat" Vaughn nodded sternly.

Mama came through the swinging kitchen door with two plates, one had a tall stack of hotcakes with pats of butter arranged on the top and already sliding over, the other plate had eggs sunny side up, hashbrowns, and sausage patties. She'd quit working there and come back twice. It smelled just wonderful. My mouth began to water. She sat the plates in front of Tugboat, wiped her hands down her apron, got the pot of coffee and filled the cup. Then she looked up and saw us and the smile fell off her face into a frown.

"If it ain't the dynamic duo," Mama said, her lips turned down into a pout. I wondered who she was more mad at, me or him? She told us not to sit at the counter but Vaughn didn't want to sit at a table or a booth. She didn't like it when I spun in circles on the orange stools at the counter. Vaughn went over to a table and picked a chair up by the silver handle on top, spun it around backwards and sat in the chair with his arms resting folded on one another on the back. I started punching the buttons to turn the song selections on the miniature juke boxes at every table. The dishwasher, Lawrence, reached around the wall and plugged in the juke and gave me a wave. His mother always dropped him off and picked him up. She tried to smooth his hair for him and made him wear khaki pants—a rarity in Fairmont unless you had a business on Court Street.

"Give me a quarter to play some songs," I said.

"You think quarters grow on trees," Vaughn said and then dug in his pocket for fifty cents and slid it across the table to me.

Mama poured two little glasses of water out of a pitcher and slammed them down in front of us. She pulled out a menu and handed it to Vaughn. She knew I always had French toast with white powdered sugar, crispy bacon, and a large glass of milk. I knew that old menu by heart anyway. She sighed real loud as Vaughn just sat there and looked her up and down.

"You sure look beautiful this morning," Vaughn said. "But I bet she looks beautiful every morning, huh Honey Boy?"

"Yep." I was trying to choose between Merle Haggard and Waylon Jennings. I played them both. I flat out refused to play any disco shit.

"I guess you're teaching him to be as full of shit as you?" Mama tucked a tress back into her hairnet.

"Who me?" Vaughn said, sliding his big hand around Mama's waist and pulling her toward him. "I tell the truth, and nothing but. You are as fine a woman as ever walked the earth."

"You had your chance," Mama said. "And you blew it." She took hold of his fingers and peeled them away from her waist. "I'll be back in a minute to take your-all's orders." As she turned to walk away Vaughn swatted her on the butt, Mama turned and gave him one of her meanest looks.

"If looks could kill," Vaughn said to me and winked, "we'd both be dead."

The bell rang as two cops walked in. They were both on the young side to be cops, but they ordered coffees with cream and sugar and a couple of bear claws. The smaller one was giving Vaughn the eye, staring at him hard. Vaughn made his face impassive as a piece of stone. He had been smiling so the crows feet showed around his eyes, but now he was no longer showing anything on the outside. It was a terrifying sight to behold that change. He began to read the sports page of the *Sun*. Eventually the big cop elbowed the smaller one and gave him a worried look, and they took their coffee and bearclaws out in one of them cardboard drink holders for "to go" orders. The bell jingled again.

"Darling," Vaughn said, looking relaxed again. "I'm going to have the Roadrunner Special. And I'll need a pot of coffee. Maybe one of the little glasses of orange juice to boot. And give the young scholar here whatever he'd like, I'm paying."

"Honey Boy eats here for free. Thank you very much. He always eats French toast," Mama said. "Don't you worry about him. I'd rather you not teach him how to be a criminal like you, and you know it. Why do you got to keep bringing me heartache?" Her face didn't know to smile or spit. She scribbled our orders down. She tore the check off and put it on the wheel for Anne, the cook.

"Thank you, Babydoll" Anne poked her head out of the window so that the order wheel looked like a metallic halo over her head. "Maybe you should go take a break before the rush starts."

"My hands are shaking," Mama said. Vaughn pretended not to hear her. He was looking back at his paper. I saw Mama pull her cigarettes out and sit at the table where the cooks and waitresses always sat, back near the jukebox.

"Go ask Lorene to sit with us," Vaughn said. "Please."

"Okay," I said. I had never heard Vaughn say please before. It shocked me. There were things between them, grown-up things, that I didn't understand. But before I could get up and go over to her she came over herself smoking her ciga-rette and told me to scooch over and sat down next to me and stared down at her hands. Her hands were small and dark like she had been out in the sun lately. She had a dark brown nail polish on. Anne came over with our food and set it down in front of us. She nodded respectfully at Vaughn.

"Miss Anne," Vaughn said.

"Uh huh," Anne said, retreating back to the kitchen. She stopped and gave Tugboat a refill on his coffee.

"I ain't the same innocent country girl you knew," Mama said. "We don't need your brand of trouble."

"Trouble?" Vaughn asked. He folded his newspaper up and sat it next to him. Then he opened the Reader's Digest like he was looking for the word "trouble" in the vocabulary list. "I just want to take care of you and your boy. You know Fairmont. Not everybody wants to give you a chance. I'd see that things were made easy for you. I'd look out for you. I'd look after you both."

"We don't need looking after," Mama said. She stubbed out her cigarette in the ashtray. "What we need is to be left alone. What I need is for you to leave my boy alone. I don't want him to end up at the Church Farm, or worse yet . . . like you."

He just laughed like Mama had said the funniest thing he had ever heard in his life.

"They'll never put me in prison again."

"They call it the Church Farm," Mama added for my benefit.

Vaughn shook his head gravely in agreement.

Vaughn and me wolfed down our breakfast but Mama had to get up as the breakfast rush was starting. Everyone wanted to order at the same time. A few farmers looked over at Vaughn, but when they looked too long he looked back at them until they found themselves studying the bottom of their coffee cups. We got up and swaggered out of there like a couple of strutting game cocks. No one would dare to say anything out of the way to Vaughn. The bell jingled as we left, and I could hear the voices start up before the door even closed. I imagined that the men in their work caps probably knew more about me than I did. That's the way things are in a small town. Family keeps everything a secret from you, but everyone else knows all the juicy stuff anyway. The bell jingled as we left and I could hear the voices start up before the door even closed.

"I'd like to be a fly on the wall now," I said.

"I heard it all before," Vaughn said. "Those sons-of-bitches better look out if they know what's good for them. The Sugar Booger express is going to jump up and bite them in the ass before they know it."

Out on the sidewalk I followed behind Vaughn and looked back at my reflection. Then, I looked further into the glass, beyond my reflection, and Mama was looking back concerned. She threw an uncertain wave and I gave her the everthing's cool dippity-doo Sonny had taught me last year after we watched the second half of Giant, the best part, with James Dean. I half expected her to run out after us, but she went back into the kitchen instead.

Beck's

The next day, when the Spot started getting busy with the lunch rush I slipped out the back. Anne was huffing around in the kitchen so she didn't notice me. I swiped some leftover morning sausage links and fed them to Buddy who was waiting for me out back. The rotting smell wafting up from the Dumpster about made me want to lose my cookies. I knelt down on one knee and Buddy came slinking over on his belly licking his lips eagerly but too afraid to just walk over and take the sausages. He was like some country people I knew who were so afraid of strangers they took extra time out of their day just to stare at them.

Finally I got up and walked over to the dog and practically shoved the lukewarm meat in his face. But still he took the meat out of my hand delicately with his teeth as if he were a hightoned gentleman of breeding and some distinction. I watched him as he ate one link at a time. He wanted to follow me, but he was distracted by the sausage links. Afterward he sat down and very thoroughly licked his privates. A trucker passing by on his way to his truck told me if only he were that limber for a day he could die a happy man.

Big rigs were parked over behind the motel parking lot. Some of the refrigerated diesels were running. A whole fleet of trucks surrounded Roy's gas station down the street as I walked toward it. Some were in line to get gas. I heard Roy saying to two big men with grizzly beards down to their bulging stomachs that the mechanic had never showed up for work today so he didn't know what to tell them. Men of all shapes and sizes were scrambling around talking to each other by the garage.

Out back behind the Sinclair was Delbert's office. He was in a little trailer home where the used car lot used to be, under a sign that read in two foot all red letters, MCCUBBIN

TRUCKING. An old fashioned Peterbilt cab was mounted on top of the building. They used the old stone Gathwright and Clapp Tobacco Company building as a warehouse. Delbert and Roy fought about who could park in their lot and who couldn't. Delbert paid Roy rent for letting him park his office there so he thought all his boys, as he called them, ought to be able to park there. Roy would run off any trucker who didn't ask him if it was all right first.

Delbert wore a big white cowboy hat with a leather band and small feather sticking up on one side. He had a handlebar mustache and liked to smile at folks no matter what happened because he claimed to be an optimist. Someone could tell him his dog had died, but he would have just kept on smiling and making lemons into lemonade. This is what I gathered from his catalogues of adages—he had one for every occasion. He had a clipboard in his hand and was giving a younger blond-headed trucker named Billy Claxton instructions; meanwhile Billy had his hands stuffed defiantly in the back pockets of his jeans and would lean over and spit tobacco juice on the gravel parking lot in an angry sort of way. Delbert grinned the whole time. He knew how to talk to tough guys.

Thunder clouds were forming up in the Western sky. I began to walk quicker and the ribbing of my second-hand corduroy pants whispered every time I took a step, until the sound got to be an annoyance. I began to imitate it with my mouth just to drowned it out. I saw a truck from the potato chip factory roll by and the driver gave me a wave from behind the big glass windshield. On the side of the truck the slogan of the company was written in script, "The Golden Girl with the Golden Curl." It was such a familiar jingle on the radio that I thought I knew what it meant down in my molecules, but when I thought of the terms word for word I couldn't grasp the significance of what potato chips had to do with a blonde and her beehive hairdo. Maybe she was Old

Man Backer's main squeeze back in the olden days when things were still in black and white.

When I got to Beck's Pool Hall I could see Vaughn marching around a table with stick in one hand. He was pointing it at Punkin as he delivered some important piece of advice about life and I was outside missing it, missing everything exciting in Fairmont these days. Quickly I walked in with my head down and my hands in my pocket. It was blacker inside than 3 feet up a bull's ass and reeked of old beer sweating through the wood floors. Oral Bright was standing at a sink that was orange with rust stains, his sleeves rolled up to his elbows leaning over as he worked.

"You ask for help," Oral began. "Cleaning the chitlins and ain't nobody around wants to help, but then you say now it's time to eat the chitlins and everyone standing in line with his plate out then. You want some of these good chitlins then you got to help do the dirty work."

"That's nigger food," Vaughn said.

"But you like it though, don't you?" Oral said.

"You damn right I do," Vaughn said.

Everyone laughed like hell.

"I'm telling you—" Oral Bright turned his attention to Old Man Beck. Oral wore his orange hunting cap with his ear flaps down despite the heat. "—Glenn Starkey give the last of the Starkey millions to Kingdom County Historical Museum and Fairmont Heritage Trust."

"What else did Mr. Deep Pockets give his money away to?" Vaughn appeared to be asking Beck instead of Oral. Beck just turned his head and flailed the air with his flyswatter even though there didn't look to be any bugs in the joint.

"He give it to a bunch of charitable causes," Oral said. "Right good and proper."

Nothing was more boring to me than adults talking about money unless they were talking about their ailments like: bursitis, kidney stones, arthritis, and bland diets the doctor told them to go on.

"The Starkey millions," Vaughn snorted. "My ass."

"Hey, ugly," Rusty said to me.

"Hey, uglier than me," I said back.

"Get you a Dr. Pepper from old man Beck," Vaughn said.

Mister Beck waved, but he didn't say anything. He hadn't said much of anything to anyone since his grandson died over in Vietnam several years back. The war seemed like a hundred years ago to me, but to the grownups it had just happened yesterday. I looked up at the fancy gold-painted ceiling and the crown molding. It never ceased to amaze me how Beck's must have been quite a place, back in the old days.

"I told you I switched to red cream sodey."

"Beck's got plenty of toilet paper in stock." TC's cigarette bobbed up and down like a conductor's baton when he spoke.

"You told them what I said."

"Ah, now, don't be a pussy about it." Vaughn's cigarette bobbed up and down in his mouth. "That was some funny shit you told me. Dr. Pepper's got prune juice in it! Old Roy can be real entertaining." Vaughn called the corner pocket and sank the eight ball on a bank shot. "Rack 'em."

Punkin played at punching me in the gut but kind of gave me a slap with the palm of his hand instead a little harder than he meant and I tasted metal in my mouth but I didn't want him saying I was a sissy so I just swallowed it. He put his arm across my shoulders while I was looking at the green velvet table. The arm turned into a headlock and he rubbed my head with his knuckles; it made my hair stand on end and look crazy. I reached up and grabbed him by the nose and he quickly pushed me away. They was talking about what was better, Trans Ams or Corvettes? Blondes or brunettes?

"You going out with us tonight?" Punkin asked.

"What're you doing tonight?" I wiped at the corner of my mouth but no one seemed to notice.

"Men's stuff," Vaughn said. "If you're up for it."

Oral Bright shuffled over to put a quarter into the slot. Punched the coin in the metal arm and the balls came rumbling out of the pockets and down their shoots to the end of the table sounding like cattle running down a mountain in a flat-out stampede. Rusty pulled the triangle from underneath the pool table and started stuffing balls into it. When he had the solids and stripes arranged he pushed the triangle backward and forward a couple of times and carefully lifted it.

"Why you wear that ridiculous cap all the time?" Mister Beck spoke for the first time in about a week. Everyone stopped talking to take notice of the old man just to hear if he would say anything else.

"Keeps my brains cool." Oral pointed at his temple like he was one cagey fox. "Why you think?"

Beck shrugged and swatted another invisible fly on a table top.

"Now that ain't tight," Vaughn said. He took a sip out of his beer mug and watched as Rusty put the triangle back over the balls and rocked them back and forth again. "Put your fingers at the end like I showed you and press all the balls tight up top."

"Like this?"

"Don't boys these days know nothing?" Oral asked Vaughn. "They probably don't believe in God nor country neither just like them got-damn hippies."

"Yep," Vaughn said approvingly to Rusty. "You silly son-of-a-bitch. Just like that." Rusty started to mope so Vaughn handed him his own pool stick. It was considered a high honor by us boys because Vaughn carried his pool stick in a black leather case like a professional, like Minnesota Fats. The stick rode in the case in two separate parts that had to be screwed together. "But don't bang it up or I'll kick your skinny little ass until the shit's oozing out your ears."

"You boys ever see *The Hustler* with Paul Newman?" Vaughn wanted to know.

"I seen it on Channel 11," Punkin said. His shirt sleeves were rolled up to show off his biceps. His arms were pretty big for a teenager, but nowhere near as big as Vaughn's, but he didn't show his off. "Fucking great movie. Jackie Gleason was in it too."

"He was fat?" I asked.

"Fats," Oral corrected.

"Of course he was Fats," Vaughn winked.

"Oral is fat too," I said.

"Fats!" Rusty said. "Shit—missed again." He handed the stick back to Vaughn.

"Aw now," Oral said. "Guess who ain't getting to eat any chitlins now. I'm going to eat them up my ownself. And you know why? Because I'm fat. Really this here is all prime K.C. strip. Them ladies can't get enough of it."

"The fat ones or the ugly ones?" Punkin asked.

Oral flipped him off.

"Learned to really shoot pool," Vaughn said, banking a yellow ball into the side pocket, "Watching Paul Newman in that movie. You can learn just about everything from watching movies. But you just don't watch movies. You *watch* movies. You study them close. Then, you can learn something."

"One of these days Alice," Oral said. "ONE OF THESE DAYS . . ."

"You sound just like him," Vaughn said.

"We're working for Vaughn tonight, you know?" TC asked. "You coming?"

"Course he's coming," Vaughn said, picking out a house stick off the rack. He pulled one out and sighted down it to make sure it was straight. "You're my favorite nigger,"

Vaughn said giving me one of those ice cold looks of his. "Hey, Beck, how come all these sticks are warped?"

Beck just smiled and held up his hand in a wave behind the bar in a mysterious gesture. It could have meant anything. Vaughn, of course, hadn't expected an answer anyway. He liked hanging out in the pool hall more than Ike's Bar because the pool hall was hardly ever crowded and Beck didn't say anything and he didn't always feel like talking to folks himself. Old Man Beck just sat behind the bar doing crossword puzzles from open 'til close. In the winter he might get up and toss some logs into the wood stove where he would sit in an old recliner and spit tobacco juice into a Folger's coffee can.

The balls made a loud cracking sound and one even went down a side pocket. Rusty smiled real proud. Vaughn gave him a man-to-man kind of nod acknowledging his superior play. Rusty sunk two more balls before he missed. Then we watched while Vaughn proceeded to run the table. He had played all of us boys for soda pops and by the time he finished beating us he sat down on the bench next to the table with bottles of Mountain Dew, Coca Cola, RC, and Shasta sitting on top. He was teasing us. He handed out the bottles of soda in a way meant to show us that he was the boss but that he would make sure we were taken care of. He knew which boy was partial to which sodie. It seemed impressive to me at the time.

Punkin and me watched as Vaughn played Rusty and TC. Vaughn pretended to scratch when he was shooting the eight ball to make Rusty feel good so that he and TC could play each other. Punkin wanted us to get our own table, but I didn't have any money. We started singing all the beer commercials we could remember for Pabst Blue Ribbon, Budweiser, Busch, Miller, and Schlitz malt liquor.

"I can't go tonight," I said walking over to the soda freezer and sticking the end of the soda into the opener on the side to pop off the cap.

"You got a date or something?" Punkin asked.

"Sort of," I said. "With my old lady. She wants me to go to the drive-in with her."

"That ain't right," Vaughn said. "I don't want to hear you calling Lorene your old lady. Got it. She's your mama and you should always give her respect. I don't care who you're around. You got it? Tell me you got it."

"I got it," I said, my face felt red and hot. It was just something I'd heard Rusty and the boys say.

"All right then," Vaughn said. "You go to the picture show with her. You can meet up with us later. Spending time with your folks is always the right thing to do. They're older and they usually know better about things than you boys do. I didn't always get along with my daddy either. I know you boys don't cotton to what Danny says to y'all. And that's okay. But show him respect. My mama and daddy are a matched set. But they always meant well. You run along then Honey Boy. We'll see you later."

Vaughn never said "movie," it was always "picture show" so I decided right then to start saying it too.

"Okay," I said, backing up toward the door. "I'm going to the picture show with Mama then." When I put my hand on the handle and pushed my thumb down on the lever I could hear old man Beck way in the back calling after me.

"Hear now!" Beck said. "Hear now!"

He didn't like it for boys to leave with his bottles.

"Remember to bring your piece tonight, cowboy," Vaughn hollered. "You might be needing it." He stuffed a wadded up ball of cash into the pocket of my shirt.

The stark afternoon daylight blinded me as I stumbled out of Becks trying to get my bearings from the dark pool room. My hands were sweating still. I started to wonder why I was sweating and then I knew it was because I was so excited about what might happen. I would be able to bring my western pistol, maybe use it on some contrary sidewinding snake that might try to put up a fight. I pulled the ball of cash out of my pocket and straightened out a $50 bill and couldn't help whistling in amazement at it.

I had to see the Sky-High Drive-In sign in Columbia. I always loved looking at it. Whenever I saw the big neon sign shining like a beacon just before twilight it made me remember all the great movies I had already seen. Mama told me it was time so I pressed my body flat against the floorboard and hunkered underneath a quilt that smelled heavy of gasoline. I held my breath so I could stand it while Mama paid the attendant in the booth. She drove around the track road that made a U-shape around the gravel lot and then we started to drive over the humps.

I got up in the seat and rubbed my hands together with excitement. She pulled close to a pole, rolled the window down a few more inches, and reached out and grabbed the gray speaker and hung it on the window. When I was really little I used to go down and play on the swings with the other kids on the playground underneath the giant screen, but now the thrill of doing that was gone. It was a mystery to me, but I did not see the fun in climbing on a jungle gym, spinning on the merry-go-round, or the test of wills and teamwork of the teeter-totter. I played that I was the outlaw Josie Wales, another "great Missourian" Sonny said, but it was kind of boring now. Maybe I would feel like swinging on the playground again next time.

Mama gave me some money to get hotdogs topped with chili, cheese, onions, and relish although they didn't dance but they came in cool silver wrappers. I liked it all on my hotdog, including mustard and ketchup. I got us a couple of Cokes and a tub of popcorn. The cashier had a birthmark on her face like a brown piece of felt with hair growing on it. Other than that, she had a real pretty face. A face that seemed to me to have taken insults and turned them back again with love. She put the drinks in a cardboard carrier so I could carry it all back to the truck.

I was excited to see this double feature. Two westerns. Westerns were my favorite. The first one was an older John Wayne and the second was a new Clint Eastwood Mama said. I wolfed down my hotdog and started in on the popcorn. Just as the John Wayne movie started I made some remark about how tough he was but Mama didn't say nothing. I looked back over at her and she was already asleep. She was working a whole lot of extra hours. I hardly ever got to hang out with her even though I wanted to. I know some of my cousins loved her more than they did their own parents. When we'd go visit family all the kids would scream "Aunt Lorene!" and rush to hug her. It gave me a pang of jealousy but I understood how they felt. She was always the favorite.

The quilt was folded up between us so I unfolded it and covered her best as I could. She talked in her sleep a little and I froze until she settled back again. Then I reached over and turned down the volume on the speaker. Smoothed the tangles of hair out of her face and settled in to watch the movies. I started to get real tired in the middle of the second movie, but I kept pinching myself to stay awake. I hated to see money wasted on movies that didn't get watched at the drive-in.

"Did I fall asleep?" Mama asked later on.

"Yeah," I said.

"I'm sorry," she said. "I don't know why I'm so tired."

"It's all right," I said. "You were tired." I wanted to hug her, but we were still parked there with the speaker attached to the window. Everyone else was driving off with their lights on and radios blaring, tail lights flashing red and white. I could hear little kids whining and crying from the backseats of cars. I told Mama we would have to remember to borrow some lawn chairs next time we went.

When we got home Mama fell asleep fast. I could hear her breathing heavily almost as soon as her head was on the pillow. I snuck down the hall and got down on one knee like I was going to run a race and listened. My heart pounded in my ears. She was asleep.

The clock in the living room said it was 1:30 a.m., and I had to cut across country to get to Vaughn's. It was moonrise. The weeds whipped at my pants legs leaving them wet with dew. I stumbled into one of those nighttime spider webs and imagined a giant black and yellow garden spider coming out of its hiding place and down its web to eat me. Vaughn's Hill seemed a lifetime away.

Blooded

Later on that night after the Sky-High Drive-In: "I don't want you boys drinking tonight," Vaughn said even though he was. "What I'm asking you to do tonight requires skill and concentration. You boys got it in you. TC and Punkin I don't want you coming tonight."

"Aw man," Punkin said "why the hell not?"

"You're getting older, both of you," Vaughn said. "You get caught and it's going on your record. You boys know the ropes. I'll use you again, sure. But tonight Rusty and the Kid need to get some practice. They're both juvies, Juvy juvies, you know? The law won't catch me, but if they catch you older boys who knows what they might hit you with. It would only be a slap on the wrist for these here boys, but they ain't going to get caught. Are you?"

"They ain't catching me," Rusty said.

"That's because you're slicker than shit and faster than greased lightning."

"You know it," Rusty said.

"We're going to get Honey Boy here blooded," Vaughn said. "It'll be his first time."

"I remember the first time I went out with you," TC said. Nobody noticed what TC said since he talked so soft and rarely said anything. Around Vaughn you had to speak up, practically shout just to get his attention. Getting blooded sounded like they was going to hurt me and it made me nervous for sure.

"How did things go with you and your mama tonight at the drive-in?" Vaughn asked.

"First thing she made me do was hunker down in the front floorboard with a scratchy old yellow wool blanket so she wouldn't have to pay for me," I said.

"I taught her that." Vaughn laughed. "I taught her that. She ain't so high and mighty. Well, were the movies any good?"

"Westerns," I said. "Mama fell asleep by the time the other movie started."

"Good," Vaughn said. "She took you to see Westerns for your sake I hope you know? You don't think your mama loves Westerns, do you? Anyway, you caught forty winks so you shouldn't get too tired tonight. Did you bring it?" Patting his own handgun under his left armpit.

I patted the front pocket of my windbreaker. The weather had turned a bit cool lately. The windbreaker was red and had a big horizontal pocket that went across my chest. It felt kind of awkward having the pistol there, but until I could save up for a shoulder holster like Vaughns I guess it was the cross I had to bear.

We drove off Vaughn's place in the Ford with the Sugar Booger Express swinging
around behind us. Vaughn had a list written out in his scrawl on Big Chief notebook paper of places he wanted to hit, things he wanted us to steal, and finally he wanted us to help him load up some cattle over in Cole county where he knew there was a "downed" electric fence. Rusty and me were just happy that we were chosen to go with Vaughn. It made us feel special and chosen despite the reasons he had given Punkin and TC.

Vaughn fingered his note torn from the Big Chief notebook as we sat in the Thunderbird waiting for him to tell us what to do. We knew he wanted us to steal things from places. I couldn't help thinking there was more explanation to come, but my stomach told me he had told everything he was going to tell, said everything he planned to say. On his face was the look of determination and in his voice I saw something of the damnatory when he would break concentration long enough to acknowledge an innocent question about pulling over for a piss break in the weeds.

He drank coffee out of a tall green thermos that was solid enough to be used as a weapon. Vaughn smoked his Camels. Rusty and me smoked Marlboro Reds.

"I got you boys some sodies," Vaughn said.

"Orange Crush?" I asked.

Rusty's eyes went wide with fear. They were telling me to be quiet.

"Yeah Orange Crush," Vaughn said. "I thought that was your favorite?"

"Naw," I said. "I like Dr. Pepper."

"Your Mama said this here."

"Thats what Rafe liked all the time. I didn't have no choice but to drink it."

"That figures," Vaughn said. "A candy ass like him."

"He mixed it with Vodka," I offered.

"He might as well stuck an umbrella in it too," Vaughn said more to himself than me.

As we drove, the fog rolled into the dales filling them up with a blinding white haze. My cousins in Howard County were used to winding roads and fog on a regular basis, but we were not so adapted to watching the world play hide and seek between spaces of white blindness and abrupt dark vision in Kingdom County where it was a bit flatter. The smell of newly cut grass was mixed with the heavy humidity in my lungs and made breathing a chore.

We came out of a patch of fog and a buck stood like a sentry on the shoulder of the road. His gold eyes watching me. The Thunderbird was slowing as Vaughn tried to be careful. It was difficult for him to stop quickly with the trailer hitched on back. He rolled to a stop near the deer and I could see the animal's breath in the headlights. The buck tossed his head and his antlers were like the arms of a preacher laying hands on a sinner. Then he leaped up over the car like he was flying off into the galaxy to become a new constellation. The white of his underbelly and the hard yellow hooves floated hovering above the horizon and then I saw the stars and the Big Dipper. He grunted as he landed, one of his hooves scraping the driver's side ever so slightly. The animal threw himself headlong down the embankment and disappeared over a barbed wire fence. The silence felt like it would last for the rest of our lives.

"The spirit of the country," Vaughn said.

The Thunderbird's tires moaned a little as we drove around a tight corner overlooking the guardrail and a creek down at the bottom of the gorge. That old boy was singing about how lonesome he was. All his songs were about being lonesome and he yoddled and his quavery voice echoed across the fields and pastures. The crickets stopped chirping and the bullfrog's stopped gulping to listen to the old timey voice crooning from another time. We were heading out toward the nuclear plant. I felt superstitious about going out there because the country was rocky and wild. Lots of folks lived out thataway, but it made me nervous every time. Route O careened in feral places in a two-step with Crows Fork Creek, winding back and forth, until the road arrived at the plant.

First place on Vaughn's list was Fenton Reed's farmstead. Vaughn liked Fenton all right, but he was a farmer and he was on the list. As we approached the place, I had to admire it even at night. I knew what it looked like anyway. The house and the outbuildings all had nice red roofs. The uniformity of the red shingles just made the place look organized and tight. Fenton had two Farmall tractors and a big combine was out in the field still. A few weeks ago, Mama and me had just been driving, like Mama liked to do, and we saw Fenton's green and yellow cornfields stretching out into the blue sky where the two met. It was getting to be the time of year when folks was working hard out in the fields.

The squawk box was chattering and Vaughn turned the volume down. He listened in on the cops to see what they were up to. There was some kind of bad wreck out on Highway 54 around Kingdom City. A big rig had jackknifed on the wet pavement. A wrecker was on the way, but they said the driver was fine so they could eighty-six the ambulance. It had hardly rained all year so folks had forgotten how to drive on slick roads.

The fog covered dips in the road so you couldn't see 5 feet in front of you. Vaughn wiped at the windshield with his shirtsleeve. He had become good at mimicking Sheriff Ted Merrill's country twang and sometimes he would pick-up the mic and purposely give the dispatcher or the deputy sheriff bad directions to emergencies that didn't exist. We'd laugh our asses off when they talked back to him or said the couldn't find whatever it was Vaughn had told them about. Instead of using the word sheriff to talk about Merrill, Vaughn would call him "constable." That made Rusty and me laugh. Constable was just a funny word to us.

Vaughn parked the Thunderbird down in a gully. The car rocked and bumped so much that Rusty complained we were going to get stuck. When we parked in a copse of woods behind an abandoned shed and under an ancient pin oak, Vaughn leaned forward to tell us how he knew Fenton from the time they was boys together back before Noah and the Flood.

"I shot a ten point buck out past the river in that east pasture," he said. "Fenton's daddy took us out there when we were probably fourteen or so. Right before I seen that buck, a coyote came out. She'd been yipping off and on that night. That coyote came creeping up and I be danged if a doe didn't chase her off. I was the only one of them that got a buck that year. No I take it back. I think Fenton's mama got one too. Fenton's daddy was none too happy about it either."

"How come you're ripping Fenton off then?" Rusty asked. "If you got so much history with him?"

"Not all history is good history," Vaughn mumbled thickly. "Besides, if I wanted any shit from you I'd squeeze your head."

Vaughn looked down at his list again. His lips moved as he squinted to read in the pitch black. He snapped his fingers and Rusty turned on the flashlight and shined it on the list. There was a dog barking somewhere up around Fenton's place. We hadn't even talked about what to do in case there was dogs.

"What about them dogs?" I asked.

"Don't worry about them," he said. "Show them your gun. They know a gun and they'll respect it. Shoot them if you have to but only if you absolutely have to. If you use it you'd better run your ass back here. Make sure you get the shit first."

"What do you want us to get then?" Rusty asked.

"There's a key down in the cellar. Just go in through them double doors, down to the old coal room and the fruit cellar. There's a key on the nail to the back door. They's all at a wedding in Arkansas so we should be in the free and clear. Rusty, I want you to find his guns. They're in a fancy mahogany gun cabinet. Bust the glass. Take a hammer and crow bar in case he's got them locked."

"What do you want me to get?"

"Bring tools out the barn—he's got some nice old tools," he said, wiping his face off with a red handkerchief. "I know there's an air compressor, chemicals—everything on the list you can find. Bring it all out in the yard and we'll load her up."

He handed the wrinkled list to me.

"You know what boys?" Vaughn said. "Rusty you go to the barn instead. I want Honey Boy in the house. If you can, don't mess anything up. I respect Fenton. Take what you can see, but don't trash the place."

"Uncle Vaughn," Rusty moaned "you said for me to go in the house."

"Yeah, so what," Vaughn said. "And now I changed my mind. You might think you're slick but you can't slide on bobwire."

He made us put out our cigarettes in the ash tray instead of stepping on them outside the car. Normally stuff in his car was for show only, even the ash tray. Vaughn said he would drive up the road aways and come back so nobody would see the car just sitting there. He'd be back in thirty minutes or so and we had better be ready. If something went wrong we was supposed to cut across Fenton's property and wait on him at the bridge on the blacktop. It would take us awhile to make our way through the woodland, but it was a sight better than Sheriff Merrill catching us by the short hairs.

"Juicy Fruit?" Vaughn said, holding out a yellow pack of Wrigley's. We each took two pieces of gum.

It was the damnedest thing. I was a little scared, but I started thinking about girls more than ever right then. Rusty and me took turns punching each other in the arm until Vaughn said "Get!" First, we jumped over the cattle guard. We jogged up toward Fenton's and I was thinking about them girls. I was thinking about Regina and if she tasted like bubble gum. Next I was thinking about Tempie and laying in her yard and eating strawberries at Vaughn's. I wondered if that meant I was in love and if so—could you be in love with two girls? You weren't supposed to be according to what everyone said and the way they acted. But maybe I loved something about both of them.

We went around the first pasture on our side of Fenton's because of his big longhorn bull. It was huge. Even under the moonless sky he seemed like a gleaming white dream from a cave drawing made 10,000 years ago. He was one helluva of a beast. His balls were gigantic! A mule was out there standing next to him for the company I guess. So we took the long way around.

"You think Vaughn would want that bull?"

"Fernando? No way. Everybody knows that bull. Even Vaughn might get busted for stealing Fernando. He's probably the most famous bull in six counties. I bet he weighs 2,000 pounds. There wouldn't be any room for anything else in the trailer."

"Oh," I said. I didn't know anything about bulls.

Fernando must have known we were talking about him. He raised his head and shook his head at us and his horns were a caution. One of his hind legs went up and down like he was going to scratch an itch, but nothing came of it. The mule sidled away from him. There were some cows up aways in the same pasture looking at us all funny and chewing on their cud like patients at Fairmont State Hospital. Or like some of the employees anyway.

I had never had anybody show me stuff before. I didn't know how to change the oil on a car. Even Rusty knew how to do that. I'd never been hunting, even, and the only thing I'd ever shot was a mailbox. Mama's men were only interested in her. None of them had been daddy material, and knowing Mama's taste in men—no one she found ever would be.

I tried to pretend Sonny was my daddy for awhile to make him and Mama happy, but I just couldn't lie too good—not to myself anyway. I could lie to other people sometimes, but I could never lie to myself. Maybe only crazy people could lie to themselves. Roy called Vaughn a sociopath and said people like that could lie to anybody and not have a conscience about it. After Roy knew I was working for Vaughn, well he almost quit talking to me completely. It was weird. Then it dawned on me that Roy was afraid of Vaughn and because of that he was afraid of me. I felt bad about it, but I also felt stronger than I ever had before and that's a hard thing to give up.

When we got into the front yard we stood together under two plum trees. Vaughn was driving real slow and a pickup pulled up alongside of the Thunderbird. Rusty grinned at me. We knew he was telling whoever it was some tall tale about how he was looking for a coon dog that had gotten a little crazy. We each picked us a plum out of the tree. I made sure there wasn't any bruised spots. They felt ripe to me. I spit out my gum. Mine was sweet and good when I bit into it. Juice sprayed out of the plum as I tore some of the flesh away with my teeth. Rusty started throwing handfuls of something at me. I thought they were gravel or maybe blueberries.

"Are them blueberries?" I asked.

"No," Rusty laughed "they ain't blueberries."

"Well what then?" I demanded.

"It's goat shit, son!" He laughed and I began to chase him until I heard Vaughn honk his horn once at us.

Just as the pickup was pulling off a dog came around the side of the house close to the old pump. Some kind of ugly cur with hair as rough as bristles on a scrub brush stood there growling at us. We throwed our plumbs at him, but it didn't scare easily.

I started fumbling for the zipper on my windbreaker and Rusty was whispering cuss words at the dog. It started growling down in his throat as if to say, *I'm about to bite your ass.* Suddenly it lunged and caught at Rusty's pant's leg. I pulled out my pistol but the sight got caught and I pulled the white cotton pocket lining out with it and I was afraid the dog would attack me while I was fumbling. Mainly, I was afraid of shooting myself.

"Shoot him," Rusty said. "Shoot him!" He shook it off and ran from it backwards in circles.

"Look dog," said I. "Look, I got a gun."

"What are you doing," Rusty asked. "Shoot the mother fucker. Shoot him!"

"Vaughn said if I showed him my gun he'd know what it was," I explained as Rusty was dancing around in a circle.

"You dummy!" Rusty screamed and kept cussing. "Shoot him and show him your gun later."

The dog had a good hold on Rusty's flared pants leg again and was viciously throwing his head back and forth.

I missed the first time because the sight was still stuck to the lining I had pulled out. There was a big gaping hole in my jacket now that scared the shit out of me. I managed to get it free of my pocket and thought I shot the dog in the ass. The dog turned around and ran off hollering, but some dogs are just afraid of the guns like Vaughn said. Rusty collapsed in the yard breathing hard and looking like he might cry. Suddenly he jumped up and ran over to the end of the yard and pissed. When he came back he was laughing now. Dogs were barking, cows were bawling, and even the moon had come out to laugh at me.

"I'm showing him my gun," Rusty said, mocking me. He slapped me on the back of the head. "Wait until I tell Vaughn this one." Rusty started walking off toward the big white barn that almost looked like a church by its size.

I carried my pistol now for fear of running into another dog. I flipped the cellar doors open and went down into the dank sewer-smell under the house. Fenton's house had started out as a simple two-story, but over the years he had been successful and gradually added onto the house. The house went further back than you could see from the road. There were all kinds of shelving full of canned and jarred vegetables. There was something slightly creepy about the jars of vegetables, but maybe it was just the dark. The Reeds could have lived off the food in the cellar for six months at least.

The key was right where Vaughn said it would be. I wondered how he knew. I went back up into the fresh air and allowed the cellar doors to slam shut, found the front door, stuck the key in the lock but it didn't unlock the door at first. The fear I felt was almost paralyzing. The Reeds were in Arkansas I told myself so why should I be afraid. It was Vaughn I was afraid of. He was big too, I reminded myself. He'd once told me a story about Sheriff Merrill trying to cuff him and his wrists were so big he had to hold a gun on him until backup came—and then he had been younger and smaller than he was now.

I jiggled the key in the lock. I pulled it out. It was a little dull gold number. The key looked like it had been made back in the olden days is the best I can describe it. The lock was an old-timey one too. As I waggled it I could feel, and then see, all the hardware shifting in the door. We had lived in an old farmhouse where a skeleton key unlocked the back door, the only real entry, and I remembered shaking it all so hard the glass window cracked. Finally the catch turned and the door settled some after it swung open and banged against the little door stop. The door creaked the way doors in Halloween stories do.

The lights from the Thunderbird turned into the driveway. There was a rattling sound as Vaughn drove over the cattle guard. The drive was on a slight incline and the headlights yawed across the living room as I turned to avoid looking directly into the lights. I saw someone standing across from me totally still and kind of crouched down. Explosions started pop, pop, popping and I was scared and forgot where I was. My pistol was going click, click, click because I was firing at a mirror as a big as one of the picture frames down at Kingdom Bank.

After a couple of minutes that seemed like hours Vaughn came stumbling in with a sawed-off shotgun at his hip like Jesse James. He saw exactly where I had been standing when I shot the mirror, but instead of being mad he got kind of tickled. Then something serious flashed acrossed his face.

"I saw someone standing there looking at me," I started to explain.

"Give me that pistol," Vaughn said. "Hand it over before you kill yourself. I thought you was old enough to handle it. What if that had been me or Rusty? You would have blowed us away I expect."

I didn't want to but I gave him the best pistol ever. I figured I'd never see it again.

I followed Vaughn back to the master bedroom and he yanked the pillowcases off and handed them to me. He motioned for me to hold one open and he went over to Mrs. Reed's armoire and started tossing handfuls of jewelry into the fancy pink, yellow, blue, and green flowery pillowcase. He tied it at the opening and gave me a look like he was saying this is how you rip a place off. There was a smaller jewelry box with man's jewelry in it and Vaughn just stuffed it in his pocket. He made a sweeping motion for me to just brush all the knick-knacks off into my other pillow case including silver brushes, old family photos, a gold locket, and change collected in a jar.

"What are you all doing in here?" Rusty asked, appearing so quickly and silently in the doorway that Vaughn leveled the shotgun at him. "Shit."

"Shit," Vaughn said. "Did you get everything out of the barn already?"

"No," Rusty said. "I can't find half of it. I found a generator though. But someone's driving down the road."

"Damn it," Vaughn said. "Talk about a cluster fuck. Grab the hunting rifle off the living room rack and let's make like horse shit and hit the trail."

We had all tumbled out on the side porch. Someone was coming and it looked like a cop car.

"Fucking Sheriff Merrill," Vaughn said.

I jumped in the backseat with the pillowcases, Vaughn and Rusty in the front. Vaughn looked over his shoulder and pushed my head down in the seat out of the way so he could see out back. I could feel his energy now. He was like a cornered junkyard dog. Dangerous. What did the sheriff think he was doing messing with Vaughn? Maybe he didn't know it was Vaughn. Maybe someone had tipped him off. It was hard to say. Even though we made fun of the sheriff's hillbilly way of talking, I was afraid of him. Folks told stories about how he had had to kill a man once. They said that's why he walked with a limp now, because he'd got himself shot by a mental case, an escapee down in Potosi, name of Scofield.

The Thunderbird groaned as Vaughn used the entire front yard to get turned around
with the Sugar Booger Express behind us and the lights was shining in Merrill's eyes, but he had the spotlight on us when my head popped up to see over the seat. Rusty was grinning from ear to ear and Vaughn handed him my pistol and the crazy sumbuck was ready to shoot at the law if Vaughn said do it to it. The tires started spinning and the gravel was raining down on the truck and trailer for a second and we was barreling at the cop car like a bat out of hell. Merrill turned to point his cruiser right at us and at the last minute Vaughn veered to the right and we traded paint. Everything slowed down and it was like we was in a movie and we were about to die, or the three of us had been staring at the sheriff like this for a hundred years. I could see the green lights from the sheriff's dash shining up in his face like he was a ghost wearing a cowboy hat. A look on his face that was worried and irate at the same moment. And I swear he looked right at me and his eyes said, *You're an outlaw, and I aim to catch your skinny ass.*

Click, click, click said my pistol in Rusty's hand who was at no angle to be shooting anyway.

The next thing I knew we weren't even on a gravel road no more. We were on blacktop and the yellow line down the middle of the road was flying by like dots blending into a continuous blur of yellow. What had happened to time? How did we get on this road? I sensed the familiarity of the road, but I wasn't sure which road it was. On a straight stretch I could see the red lights whirling and the siren was screaming at us to come back and face the music. I wonder who would come to my funeral and if Mama would finally realize how much she loved me. Merrill's top lights were flashing but we had left him in the dust for the moment.

"I'm sick of this shit," Vaughn said. "Here's where we lose Constable Merrill for good."

The Thunderbird whipped off onto another gravel road going past King's Row and the trailer wheels were up on one side for a second. We were flat out getting it. When we came up on an old rusted out bridge Vaughn stopped the car and got out.

"What the fuck is he doing?" Rusty asked.

He climbed back in the car and began to drive up and back and it just didn't make no sense to me what Vaughn was doing. He was about to get the trailer and the car stuck on that bridge is what it looked like to me. Finally he had the trailer positioned in front of the bridge and he used a mallet to pop the tongue off the ball and he started laughing. That's when Rusty and me realized what he had done. He had parked the trailer across the bridge and there wasn't no getting around it. I guessed the days of the Sugar Booger Express had come and gone before they even got started.

"I'll just call the trailer in stolen tomorrow morning," Vaughn said. "Let's see them try to pin it on me. I'll call old Ike Scoffed on their ass if they do. Ike's the best damn lawyer there is. For the right amount of money he's a goddamn artist when it comes to parading up and down in front of that judge."

The flashing lights of the police cruiser receded behind us back at the bridge. Vaughn made a strategic turn or two and finally got back on the blacktop. We passed a roadhouse that made me wish I had a sodie about then, but it was all motor-cycles out front and besides that Vaughn said Sheriff Merrill was dumb, but not that dumb. It made me think how Aunt Oleta always like to say, "I may be stupid, but I ain't dumb." It didn't make sense to me either.

Vaughn lit a cigarette and inhaled deeply. I was too stunned to do much of anything. When he thought we were safe he turned off the CB and we listened to an old hillbilly station quiet and low. Nobody said nothing for a good half hour. Rusty looked to be moping.

"What's wrong with you, boy?" Vaughn asked.

"I just wanted to get one good shot off at old Sheriff Merrill," Rusty said. I could tell it wasn't just talk, he meant it to.

Those Poor Little Heathens

Aunt Oleta was wiping vomit off Clarence's chin and undershirt. Mama was out to make me into a good person because she felt guilty about not being around and working at a tavern. Aunt Oleta was actually my great aunt and Sonny used to say she was ten years older than dirt. Aunt Oleta was good at making Mama feel guilty about falling lax in the mothering department. She said I needed a Christian upbringing or my soul was in mortal danger of the fires of hell. Aunt Oleta and Grandma Kimbrough would gang up on Mama and when she felt particularly weak she'd send me off to Aunt Oleta's to go to Redeemer Pentecostal Church where they raised holy hell every Wednesday, Sunday, and at the Thursday night Bible study. Then Mama would go off on a wild tear her ownself.

"You boys ready to go to the tent revival tonight?"

"What are you asking him for?" I asked.

"What do you mean? Clarence loves going to church. He's a part of the family of God."

"Shoot," I said. I was trying to tone down the cussing for her sake. Mama always warned me not to be a cusser around Aunt Oleta. I guess that ruled out smoking and drinking too, but I didn't have the nerve to do that around Mama, even, and definitely not around Aunt Oleta. She had a fierceness few could match.

"What did you say, young man?"

"Shoot," I said again.

"We both know what you mean when you say shoot," Aunt Oleta said at me. "It's just another way of cussing. A boy your age ought not to be so broad spoken. You ought to just go ahead and say what you mean as to say shoot."

I was surprised she said that since it made so much sense. I was making the S sound when her eyes shot me a reproachful look.

"Don't you dare," Aunt Oleta said. "Not in this house. Don't make me take the spoon to you. I used to take the spoon to your mama's hindend and I'll do the same to you if that's what it takes. Don't think I'm too old. I've dealt with tougher customers than you. I had three boys and a girl all living at home at the same time. And believe you me, you aint nothing compared to that."

"Yes ma'am," I said.

She had a whole drawer full of wooden spoons that looked like they had been around since before the Stone Age. She stirred soup and iced tea and anything else that could be cooked in a pot. Spoons were also used as hindend whackers. She'd whacked me hundreds of times, but she'd threatened to do it thousands of times. When she threatened me with a wooden spoon she always smelled like lilac perfume mingled with the onion smell of her hands. There was a collection of ceramic pickaninnies painted all kinds of gaudy colors lined up on a shelf on the wall, because Aunt Oleta bought most of them at yard sales. She said they would be worth a heap of money. I wondered what Mama Horne would think if she saw all of them making their ridiculous round-eyed faces with dewrags on their heads.

I watched the green cat clock on the kitchen wall. The clock was in the shape of a cat and the tale hung down and moved back and forth along with the cat's eyes. It had a crazy smile on its face too. She'd bought the clock down at Gasper's truck stop of all places. She'd had it for as long as I could remember, since before we had started moving all over the place. All I knew was that I wouldn't want to look at that nutty cat clock every time my stomach growled. Just looking at the cat clock threw my head off balance, but then that was how it was in general at Aunt Oleta's house.

Aunt Oleta's face was lined with wrinkles that made unlikely designs on her face. There were lines that seemed to
make circles around the outer edges of her face like rings
marking the age of a tree. I watched her put on makeup at her
vanity and she looked allowable at first—that is until she actually made a facial expression. Then her caked on makeup
would crack as her wrinkles bumped up craggy fractures like
an earthquake. Pink powder verily puffed out from her face
like an Indian's smoke signals. She was old, that was all. I
never could tell who she was trying to impress. She still had
her own choppers—it seemed impressive enough. How did
anyone get so old? It seemed like something a body had to
work at, being so ancient and all.

Her hair was blindingly white. A large puffball on her head
like blue cotton candy. She liked to wear jewelry mainly to
impress the other old ladies at Redeemer Church. She wore
dangly earrings and sometimes reading glasses across the
bridge of her nose to give people dirty looks when she didn't
agree with what they had to say about Jesus or one of the Bible stories. At her throat she usually wore a cameo or a cross.
She had a gaudy collection of stick pins to wear on her dresses that said things like "God Loves You" in fake silver and
diamonds. She had an unbelievably high singing voice that
could potentially shatter glass I thought when she sang one of
her "specials." She dressed up to go out in public, but she
was getting slightly bowlegged just like her own mama. Every
night she took a bottle of rubbing alcohol and rubbed her
legs from the knees down and the room would fill with the
smell of alcohol.

Clarence's head was lolling back and forth fighting off
Aunt Oleta's attack at his face with her dishrag. He was making noises like he was annoyed with the rough treatment.
Clarence was real big too. I guess I wasn't the first person
who wondered what would happen if Clarence ever got mad
at Aunt Oleta. Clarence had jet black hair Aunt Oleta cut in a

bowl style haircut twice a month on a red and white step stool with a bathroom towel to catch the hair. She usually cut my hair, too, but I never liked it because she parted my hair on the right and since I have some freckles on my face she always made me look like Howdy Dowdy.

"Stop it," Clarence whined. "Don't. Clarence does not like that, please." Clarence talked like someone who had stuffed cottonballs in his mouth.

Mama said Clarence was a surprise to Aunt Oleta when she was around thirty-five years old. She and Uncle Odie didn't think she could have anymore children, but Clarence ended up being born mentally retarded. Some said Aunt Oleta should have put Clarence in Fairmont State Hospital and forgot about him, but she stood up for her boy. She was one tough biddy, even back then.

Aunt Oleta had always been the type that if you throwed her in the river she'd float upstream. So if someone had told her she ought to raise up her retarded boy she probably would have stuck him in the asylum but instead they said the other, and so she'd raised him. Now Clarence was thirty-something but he seemed older and Aunt Oleta was up in years and she still made three meals a day and took care of Clarence who had a hard time feeding himself, although he did manage the toilet. I didn't even want to think about that. Uncle Odie had died of a heart attack before I was born, but I always wanted to hear his side of the story. Aunt Oleta said it wasn't no surprise he died of a heart attack, because it ran on the Selby side. Uncle Odie had been a blue baby she said as if that meant something to me. I could tell it should have, but the words "blue baby" just made me think of a picture of a blue man I once saw in a book about the Hindu gods of India in Fairmont Public Library.

Aunt Oleta put a nice white dress shirt on Clarence, but I didn't know why she bothered. He'd be drooling on it soon enough. Sometimes he stared at me and said he liked me.

Clarence would get to telling me that Jesus loved me and then he'd kind of get stuck and tell me it over and over again. He got the giggles pretty easy. When I got bored in church, I'd sometimes make faces at him. He'd start off smiling at me and then put his hand over his mouth. Finally I would stick out my tongue or push up my nose and he would laugh so hard Aunt Oleta would have to take him out of the tabernacle and out to the parking lot where everyone could hear him laughing at least through the first part of Pappy's sermon.

"Pappy" was what everyone called the preacher at Redeemer Pentecostal Church. Some folks called him "Brother Pappy." The name out on the sign said Reverend Cordell Redmond, but I never heard anyone call him by them two front names except for some of the old people like Aunt Oleta but like as not she called him Pappy too. He put funny sayings up on the sign out front like, "HONK IF YOU LOVE JESUS!" There were quite a few Jesus lovers in Fairmont—if all that honking meant anything. He used fifty cent words like "edify." He said the Church was meant to edify one another. I was all for it if someone would just tell me what it meant.

From what I had gathered from Aunt Oleta and listening to the grown-ups talk. Brother Pappy had fought in the Pacific Theater, wherever that was, during World War II in the Army and got shot up. They said he had a Purple Heart and had a bullet lodged near his spine, still. While he was overseas he got a number of tattoos and almost all of them were on his arms so when he preached in the summer in short sleeves now it looked kind of funny to hear about God's righteous anger at the Egyptians while I watched a green hula girl shake on one forearm and a snake wrapping itself around a dagger on the other. The old church didn't have an air conditioner so some people got crabby and complained about his tattoos behind his back. He said them tattoos was a sign of his shame and kept him humble. God didn't want folks getting tattoos according to Pappy.

When he came home from the war Pappy opened up a liquor store in Fairmont and started sampling his products with a vengeance he said more than once from the pulpit. Men always laughed real hard when he got to that part. Then Pappy got the call to preach from God. He'd had the call his whole life, but had fought hard against it. He had given up drinking. It took him longer to give up the demons of cigarette smoking. There were demons whose sole purpose was to make people pickup the smoking habit according to Pappy. Pappy had given up smoking five years ago, he said, although he had been a preacher longer than that. He talked about how he used to love smoking even more than drinking. It seemed to make everyone respect him more because he knew what sin was all about first hand and he had overcome it by God's grace.

Once Mama Horne told me and another little boy not to chew our Juicy Fruit in the temple of God. Brother Pappy heard her and said, "Those boys *are* the temple of God because the Holy Ghost lives in them." Mama Horne sure was embarrassed and I always liked Brother Pappy after that but being around him was like being next to a burning bush—you just wanted to move away from him because the sparks might fly off him and land on you.

"Brother Pappy says it's high time you got baptized, Honey Boy," Aunt Oleta said. "Baptized?" I repeated. "I don't want get baptized." I knew getting baptized meant Brother Pappy dunked you under water in Blackmore Lake, but that's about all I knew about it. I remembered the Bible story when John the Baptist baptized Jesus, even though John the Baptist thought it should be the other way around. John the Baptist said, "I must decrease and he must increase." At least, I thought that's what he said in the Jesus movie I saw. I guess I would probably have to go around decreasing and doing the Lord's work after getting baptized.

"Now listen here," Aunt Oleta said. "You don't have sense enough to know what you want. You think you can run me around here picking up after your mess and that don't mean nothing to you, but that you could do me this one little favor. The one little thing I ask you to do and you say you don't want to do it. Well, you're getting baptized and that's it. How else are you going to do the good Lord's work without getting baptized?"

"I'm getting baptized today?"

"Did I say anything about today?"

"No ma'am," I said.

"No," she said curtly. "But by the end of the week, on the last day of the revival meeting you will be baptized along with the others down to Blackmore Lake. Then you can start serving the Lord instead of running around with Elston Vaughn all the time."

I didn't much know what to say and before I could think of anything Clarence spoke up.

"Clarence doesn't want to get baptized either, please," Clarence said.

"Clarence, you've already been baptized," Aunt Oleta said.

I wasn't exactly sure what serving the Lord added up to, but I guessed it meant I was going to be a preacher. If God had called me like he'd called Brother Pappy I sure didn't remember picking up the phone. But Aunt Oleta had it on her mind that I should become a preacher. There was a boy about my age down in the Ozarks what preached. He was on the local news once, but there was something frightening in the way the boy hollered at folks. He held his little Bible like a full grown preacherman in one hand and shook it wildly at people and screamed at them and said they was all sinners and needed to repent. The woman on the news called him

"The Boy of God." But I wasn't studying on being no boy of God.

Vaughn would laugh his ass off if he could see what a mess I was in now.

"Go get Clarence's tie off his bureau, Honey," Aunt Oleta said.

"Go get my tie, Honey!" Clarence said, bobbing his head as he spoke. "Get my tie," he said again and the last word drew out like a cross between a sigh and a giggle.

"Hush it up," Aunt Oleta said to Clarence.

"I'll hush it up," Clarence said. "If you hush it up, thank you."

"Don't talk to your mama like that," Aunt Oleta said.

There was hardly anything in Clarence's room. There was a dresser, a chifforobe filled with his clothes and a Norman Rockwell Calendar on the wall above it, an iron twin-sized, bed that looked impossibly small for him to sleep in. Just the thought of him laying in that bed with the covers pulled up to his chin with his big head and mop of hair poking out was comical to me. There was a strategic picture of Aunt Oleta in a gold frame bedside. It's a wonder he didn't have nightmares. Aunt Oleta had a fancy bed with wooden pineapples carved in the bedposts. She told me the pineapples meant hospitality and that one screwed on and off. When folks visited, Aunt Oleta said, and you got your fill of them you just screwed on the pineapple and that meant it was time to go. I wanted to wear one like a hat--that's how ready to go I was.

"That Honey Boy's a bad influence on you, Clarence," Aunt Oleta said. I could hear from the sitting room, as Aunt Oleta called it, so I stopped to listen. I learned most of the good stuff I knew by keeping my ears open because I was nosy like Vaughn said. I always wanted to know it all. "After we get him saved and baptized I guess he can go back to his mama and then she and God will have to lookout for him."

"Honey Boy's a bad influence on me, thank you," Clarence said solemnly. "He makes me laugh too much. He makes me laugh too much, huh? He makes me laugh too much, huh?"

"Yes," Aunt Oleta said. "I'm not deaf. I heard you the first time."

"Clarence is not deaf either, thank you," Clarence said. "Why didn't you say anything if you heard me the first time?"

"Because Honey Boy makes you laugh too much?" Aunt Oleta said to throw off his line of questioning.

"That's right," Clarence cackled with pure delight. "He makes me laugh in church and everyone turns around and looks at me."

"I know it," Aunt Oleta said. "I wonder what would happen if he knew about Vaughn? If he knew who Vaughn really was?"

"If I laugh too hard," Clarence said. "It makes me have to go potty—thank you—thank you very much."

I backed up to the other side of the sitting room and started whistling. When I came into the kitchen Aunt Oleta looked at me over her glasses as if I had taken too long. She jerked the clip-on tie out of my hand. Her lower lip quivered like she was about to say something to me but decided against it. She buttoned Clarence's top button while his head pivoted back and forth leaning so far back in the kitchen table it looked like he might flip it over any second. It hit me that I was freezing cold—it was middle of summer at that. Aunt Oleta was the only person in our family who had air conditioning and she kept it so cold it put gooseflesh on your arms. It might be cold, but she had the place so clean you could eat off the hardwood floors in the dining room. There wasn't no house moss or slut's wool on her floors.

"Clarence does not like wearing ties, please," he said.

"Don't you want to look nice for church?" Aunt Oleta asked.

"Clarence is not deaf either," he said.

"You're just acting ugly now," Aunt Oleta said. "What do you think Jesus is thinking to see you acting this way?"

"I am not ugly," Clarence said.

"Here," Aunt Oleta said. "Let me get a treat for Clarence. Clarence likes Coke. He wants a Co-Cola, doesn't he?"

"Clarence like Co-Cola, thank you," he said.

"I like Co-Cola too," I said.

"Hush," Aunt Oleta said in a don't wake the baby tone of voice.

We heard a car pull into the driveway and honk its horn.

One of Mama Horne's kids came to pick us up in an old black Cadillac to take us to the tent revival because Aunt Oleta never had a driver's license, or owned a car. Mama Horne owned the taxi service in town and drove folks around herself sometimes, but not too church. She didn't charge folks for taking them to church. Usually she worked as the dispatcher. Everyone called Mama Horne, "Mama Horne," so when white people called her Mama I knew they was just saying it because that was her name. But when black people I knew called her Mama Horne that was a whole nother thing, because I didn't know which of them was really her kids and which of them were just calling her Mama Horne. Everyone was saying she came from a big family. Now, if their last name was Horne who were calling her that, then I knew but otherwise it was anybody's guess. I called her Mama Horne too.

The big man behind the wheel waved and he looked familiar. If I recollected correctly his name was Luther, but for some reason unbeknownst to me he was generally known as Simmie to everyone except the old folks. Luther hopped out and helped Aunt Oleta get Clarence situated in the big backseat. Clarence's arms and legs went out at odd angles like his bones were made of rubber. Clarence had difficulty doing the simplest things, but at the same time he could accomplish the greatest feats of flexibility like bending his fingers backwards, almost completely touching the backs of his hands without any visible sign of discomfort. His legs were messed up since birth. Aunt Oleta said it was congenital.

The big man huffed and puffed and beads of sweat popped out on his forehead as he hefted and shifted Clarence like he was a doll. Clarence was big too, like I said, but Simmie was so gigantic he made Clarence look like his little brother. He had a pretty good-sized afro but it looked good on him because he was a big man I guess. Another interesting thing about Luther was the spots of white skin on his hands that looked just like a white person's. I figured he must have a white great granddaddy, but I wasn't for sure.

As soon as it looked like he had Clarence sitting just right in the back, Clarence would start to slide on the seat of his pants into the floorboard. Normally Clarence sat in chairs just fine but he got more attention by acting even more helpless than he was.

Clarence grabbed Luther's big hand and kissed it.

"I'm sorry," Clarence said, "that was not appropriate, please."

Clarence laughed and patted the top of Clarence's hand to let him know it was all right.

"Thank you, Luther," Aunt Oleta said. "I don't know how I'd manage Clarence."

"Think nothing of it, Miss Oleta," Luther said. He pulled out a red handkerchief out of his back pocket and dabbed at his face and squirreled it away again before getting back in behind the wheel. "Who this fine young boy with you?"

"That's Lorene's boy," Aunt Oleta said with a wave of her Bible. "Honey Boy."

"Honey Boy?" Luther said. "I haven't seen you since you was a real little thing. You turning into a fine young man. You probably don't remember me, do you?"

"I think I do," I said. I didn't remember him, but if I had known him how could I have forgotten such a large man? His name had popped in my head, but I wasn't sure how I knew it. He held out his hand for me to shake, and my own hand disappeared in it.

"Honey Boy's getting baptized this week," Aunt Oleta said in a prim matter of fact tone of voice.

"You kidding?" Luther said. I was afraid he might make fun of me, but instead he surprised me. "Me too! Man, we aint never going to forget it. Our sins will be washed away. Thank you, Lord. You and me will be washed in the blood of the lamb and our sins will be thrown in the sea of nonremembrance. Praise his name."

"Praise God," Aunt Oleta said.

I wondered how Aunt Oleta could say "Praise God" one minute and then be calling me on the carpet about one of her pet peeves the next. My own notion about God was that he probably wasn't too particular judging by the caliber of folks I saw at church. She told me God works in mysterious ways, and I guess I couldn't argue with her there. I felt a little bit better about getting baptized now if big Luther was going to do it at the same time. The biggest fear I had about it was that Brother Pappy would get all excited with the Holy Ghost, like he did sometimes, at the exact moment he had my head dunked underwater. I was kind of afraid of the water a little and didn't like getting dunked, not even in the swimming pool. I hadn't even learned how to swim yet because I was so scared of the water. First time I got a chance I'd ask Luther to make sure Brother Pappy didn't hold me under the water too long.

The closer we got to the land Redeemer Pentecostal owned the more the sun kept trying to hide behind the clouds. Church was in town next to Ike's Bar, but the tent revival was out off Highway 54 right smack in the middle of an area called "Four Corners" because it was where land from four different farmers had met—until Redeemer Church bought a few acres off of them. I could see the white tents like the off-white canvas of the circus, but it was a more sobering experience to know that this outfit meant to save souls for the glory of God. Souls, Brother Pappy told us, bound for the Lake of Fire talked about in the book of Revelation. The sky above was gunmetal gray and looked to be ready to be ready to tear loose on us any minute.

On KLIK radio there was a story about the Fairmont police burning a crop of somebody's weed. Luther started laughing real hard about it. He was trying to get Aunt Oleta to imagine the cops standing down wind as they burned the magical mystery weed and getting the munchies, but Aunt Oleta gave her regular expression of non-amusement. She told him that Christian people were not amused at the antics and results of those under Satan's power. Luther only said, "Yes Ma'am."

We saw a line of six boys from the military academy walking so they stretched across a lane of traffic. Kids in town called them "Krauts" even though few, if any, were German. Actually, most of them were rich kids from Mexico and further south. Sometimes they rode in Mama Horne's taxis wedged in together like sardines. Rusty like to call the taxis "clown cars" if we were at the theater and we would count how many climbed out of the backseat. It was little short of amazing.

When I got out of the backseat of the Caddy I was surveying the huge tent when I felt something strange at my feet. When I looked down there was sawdust on the ground under my tennie-runners. There was a gap on one side of the tent and I could see people sitting on rows of metal folding chairs. Some ol' boys in overalls was looking at the big fan that wasn't working right--it was meant to blow the tent up or keep everyone cool but I wasn't for sure which.

Beyond all the chairs was a little stage with an old-fashioned wooden podium where the preaching would be done. A fat lady everyone referred to as Miss Nanna was being helped by a boy about my age wearing a white shirt and tie. Miss Nanna wobbled back and forth between the boy and her four-pronged aluminum cane singing about the old rugged cross.

"Miss Nanna," Luther whispered "she too big for a man but not big enough for a horse."

On the one side of the land, where there wasn't some pitiful corn or soybean trying to grow, was a little pond. A whole herd of cows was standing in the pond up to their necks watching us because of the heat and there we were wearing uncomfortable Sunday clothes for the most part about to die. I knew everyone would pray that those thunder clouds above us would turn lose some rain, especially the farmers. Clyde Ogilvy was a farmer who said we were going through the worst drought since the 1930s. Clyde remembered how bad things was back then as a boy because his daddy and granddaddy had been scratch farmers and he had lived in a shack where he could see through the boards.

There were two little boys and girl on the far end of the pond away from the cows dangling their feet in the water from a little wooden pier. They was drinking root beer out of them bottles that kind of looked like dark brown bottled beer. One of the little boys waved at me and I suddenly wished I could rip off that old tie I had to wear and join them, cows and all. There was a little shack up north of the pond with clothes drying hard on the pulleyed clothesline.

"Those poor little heathens," Aunt Oleta said. She handed me a Dum Dum sucker. She wanted to shut me up when she said "hidy" to Brother Pappy. I was not above accepting all kinds of bribes.

She took me by the arm and led me into the tent where mainly heavy ladies were waving fans at their faces oily from the humidity and the tent hadn't even filled up yet. Oft as not skinny little old men sat beside the big ladies just like Miss Nanna's husband Doc who was a nice old dude who broke horses down in Texas when he was a young man or so he once told me. I couldn't help wondering how the horses knew anyone was riding them he was so skinny. He also had a hole in his throat he said he got from smoking too many cigarettes. He wore a little bib around his neck so people couldn't see it so easily and so dust didn't blow into it. He would press his finger to his neck and say, "How are you today, young man?" in what sounded like a robot's voice.

"THIS IS THE DAY THE LORD HATH MADE!" Brother Pappy said extending his hand to Aunt Oleta and me. Luther was trying to push Clarence in a wheelchair but it was rough going over the sawdust. Clarence wasn't crippled, but he did have a tough time getting around what with his elastic bones and all. "I hope you're ready for a miracle today. We should be expecting a miracle every day of our lives. Isn't God good?" I noticed Brother Pappy's garage sale suit, and a blue tie with loud browns and yellows working in the design, and his oxblood shoes and that he always looked to be pitching forward on his toes like he was going to run the 50-yard dash.

"Amen," Aunt Oleta said. "Brother Pappy, I've been talking to Honey Boy and he is ready to make Jesus Christ his Lord and Savior. So when you call for folks to come forward who would like to accept Jesus into their heart then you be sure to be on the lookout for Honey Boy."

"Now that's entirely up to him," Pappy said. "What about it, Honey? Are you ready to profess your love for the Lord and ask Jesus into your heart?"

"I guess so," I said. "I guess that's what I'm here for."

"There caint be no guessing to it," Brother Pappy said, shaking my hand in his big paw. "Jesus said if you deny him before men, he'll deny you before the angels."

"I don't know much about it I guess. I know I don't want to go to Hell." I knew I was bad, but I hoped Brother Pappy couldn't see it. I shot a mailbox and spent time running with the wrong crowd, cussed and drank beer. I'd kissed loose women. I knew I was so bad even God could not care about me anymore. Jesus must hide his eyes ever ytime Aunt Oleta drug me to church.

"We'll take care of him," Brother Pappy said with a scheming nod to Aunt Oleta. Pappy clapped big Luther and Clarence on their backs and stalked off toward the fan the men in overalls were having trouble with. I fully expected Pappy to lay hands on the fan and it would supernaturally start working. Prayer was his answer to everything no matter if it was a person or a machine. I'd seen him do a few miracles before.

After a lot of standing around under the tent the big fan kicked on and the seats filled up. Lord, did it ever get hot then. Folks were sitting elbow to elbow with the mingling smells of Old Spice, lilac perfume, and sweat. I was trapped right on the front row on account of Clarence and Aunt Oleta. I had to sit between her and Luther. Luther was clapping his hands as Brother Pappy started singing a song:

> *This is the day! This is the day!*
> *That the Lord hath made! That the Lord hath made!*
> *I will rejoice! I will rejoice! And be glad in it!*
> *And be glad in it!*

There were so many people singing and praising God it seemed unlikely that the Devil could be right here in our midst, but Brother Pappy assured us he could be. So Pappy cast out the deaf and dumb spirit of the Devil that would cause any poor unsaved souls not to be able to hear the good news. I honestly didn't think any demons would be dumb enough to mess around with me, not with big Luther sitting right next to me.

Brother Pappy was walking up and down on the stage in front of us. Sometimes he got real quiet and then he'd holler JESUS or GLORY real loud and I tried not to laugh when Clarence was over there in his wheelchair making poot noises. The sun went down and it never did rain even though Pappy and some of the Deacons were trying to call it down out of heaven! We all felt expectant. Jesus was about to show up any minute. The world was in such a sorry state Jesus was about to show up and cash in our chips for the Father.

Brother Pappy said he could feel the Holy Ghost settling down on us. He pointed to a woman and said he saw angels hovering about her and did she know why them angels was all around her head like a golden halo glowing in the night? The old lady in the black and white polka-dotted dress stood up and ran in place bawling: "Hallelujah! Hallelujah! Hallelujah!" Pappy said them angels was there because of her prayers and her good works. Then the old lady fell down in the sawdust with her hands in the air and I knew she had been slain in the spirit and was now speaking on tongues. It was her heavenly language. Since she was talking directly to God the Father it didn't need no human interpretation is what Brother Pappy said.

Folks did stuff like that at Redeemer Pentecostal and then the music started playing and Mama Horne came running down the aisle like a screaming banshee. Normally she said stuff like "Amen Brother" and "Preach it, Preach the word" but tonight she was filled with the Holy Ghost and going plumb nuts dancing in the presence of God. It was better than having color-cable television. But it did shed new light on when grown-ups told me to straighten up and act right.

"We are not like the uptown church," Brother Pappy said. He did not have much respect for the "uptown church" but I understood it to mean all the churches besides ours especially the big denominational ones. "We believe signs and wonders will follow the elect. One day a man came up to me in Cooper's grocery store and he said, Pappy, I hear people fall down in the floor and start flopping around in your church. And I said to him, Brother, there's always room for one more on our floor. Come on down! That fella didn't know what to say to that. I'm hear to tell you all! You are the elect of God and you're entitled to the promises in the Word, because they apply to you. You, the one sitting in the seat where you are sitting. Can I get an amen?"

"Amen," said the church.

"Just to show you all God's power," Brother Pappy said. "I'm going to ask Sister Hayes to come up here. Maybe someone can give her a hand if necessary."

Sister Hayes was a lady who looked to be crippled by something. I wasn't sure if it was a car wreck or some disease. She was dressed in her Sunday best dress and even wore high heels, but she had crutches under her arms and had to practically drag her feet all the way to the stage. A couple of deacons and Luther got up and helped her onto the stage with Brother Pappy. Pappy put his hands on either side of the woman's face. She had curly black hair dropped down in greasy ringlets framing her face. She wore large round glasses that made her look like a female hoot owl. Pappy murmured something just for her, something private, and we all held our breaths waiting to see what would happen.

"Lord," Pappy said. "You said where two or more are gathered in Your name as agreeing on anything touching earth or heaven that You would be there, Sir. We come to You in humility and in faith. We know faith is the substance of things hoped for, the evidence of things not yet seen. Father, we ask that you heal our dear Sister. We ask that you heal her from the top of her head to the soles of her feet. We know you love Sister Hayes and that you will do this because your word says you will because you are a mighty and loving

God. We ask you to heal Sister Hayes in the name of your son, Jesus. And we thank you for the healing in Jesus' name we pray, amen."

Sister Hayes's face was bright red. Tears streamed down her cheeks. If nothing else the force and power of Brother Pappy's personality seemed to change her for that second and I believed in God and the power of Jesus like I'd never believed in nothing in my whole life. I knew who Sister Hayes was but I didn't know much about her except that she was usually very pale and sad. Whatever had happened to her legs had crushed her on the inside too. She was not one to say two words, especially to kids like me. But she looked different now, Brother Pappy would have used a fifty cent word like "transformed." She tossed her crutches to either side of the stage, turned and lurched toward the podium and she bellowed, "Thank you, Jesus!" It was the grandest noise I ever heard come from her lips.

"Everybody praise God!" Brother Pappy said.

A body would have thought Jesus played for the Cardinals and had just scored the winning homerun in the World Series against the Yankees. Them old people shot right out of their seats like they had springs attached to their butts even the ones with leg and back trouble. Everyone was hooting and hollering. Sister Hayes started in dancing around behind the pulpit like a drunken Indian dancing an Irish jig. She was using them legs even though they was skinny as match sticks. All the musicians started playing their horns and the piano player started pounding out an upbeat gospel song and Mama Horne grabbed Brother Pappy's microphone and started swaying and singing a song she was making up the words to right on the spot, she was singing something like, "Oh Jesus! Get down with the Lord!" I never knew church could be this much fun. Luther jumped up and started dancing and twirling around there on the front row. I would have been going every night had I known how much fun it was.

I snuck a peek over at Aunt Oleta and even she was kind of prancing in one spot on her tiptoes, but that was about as excited as she would allow herself to get. I remembered she told me she had been raised Presbyterian so even though she considered herself a holy roller and Jesus freak it was hard for new traditions to grab hold of her I guess.

"Praise God," Brother Pappy said in a way that said he meant to be heard. "Praise God. Thank you, Jesus." He began praising God in tongues for awhile then and everyone started calming themselves down or the Holy Ghost left them alone for a minute or two. "Now, we're here to do the Lord's business." Slow repentant-type music began to play.

"And what's the Lord's business you ask?" Pappy said. "He's in the business of saving souls. You all have to ask yourself: If I were to die today would I be ready? If the Lord were to call you home, would you go to heaven? Do you know beyond a shadow of a doubt that you are a child of the King and bound for Glory? If you want to know this for certain, then I want you to come up here with me. In fact, I want to ask everyone to close their eyes. That's right, everyone bow your heads and close your eyes. The Holy Ghost will speak to you in groanings, he'll speak to your heart. If he's speaking to you right now, then I want you to come forward and ask Jesus to come and live in your heart. You will never have to be uncertain again. Surrender to Him. It will be the greatest thing you have ever done with your life, I'm here to tell you. So come on down . . . oh, yes, thank you, Lord. I thank you for that one . . . oh yes, thank you Brother Luther."

Luther got up and knelt down on his massive knees in front of Brother Pappy. I knew Luther was once a star football player in Fairmont High School, but he had to drop out because he didn't pass some of his classes. He also had to get a job to help his mama support his six brothers and sisters. But one thing I knew about Luther was that he was tough. It crossed my mind that if Luther was tough enough to go up front and kneel down in front of everyone that I could probably do it too. So I knelt down next to big Luther and he put his heavy arm across my shoulder. Then with much fanfare and whoop-de-doo Brother Pappy came over and led us in what he called "the sinner's prayer" and we both made Jesus our Lord and Savior and became born again that very moment.

Even God must have known things couldn't have stayed at such a high pitch.

Otherwise everyone would come to the tent revival and get saved and then the world would have to come to an end. I guess it wasn't in God's plan for everything to come to an end yet. A light drizzle began to piddle down outside the tent. A bat came flying into the tent and flew around one of the wooden posts holding the tent up. Some of the old people were calling it a dove, and saying it was a sign. It might have been.

"It's a bat," I said quietly, but no one heard me, it flew out of the tent just as quickly as it appeared.

Brother Pappy must have been feeling the Holy Ghost running through his veins because he said the Lord was not through yet. He believed God had one more miracle to show us that night. The miracle God was going to show us would take everyone's faith to make it happen. He wanted everyone to get in a circle and hold hands, but there were too many people for that so Brother Pappy told people to make smaller circles within the larger circle and hold hands and so the folding chairs had to get moved around a bit. People were praying and singing and dancing and speaking in tongues but I kept my eyes open because it seemed like Jesus would come back right quick. Pappy had said on many occasions that Jesus would return like a thief in the night, here it was a Sunday night, anything could happen.

Pappy whispered in the ear of Deacon Ralph, who in turn whispered something to Luther and before I knew it I was helping Luther lug Clarence and his wheelchair in the absolute center of all circles. Aunt Oleta stood in the circle with us too holding onto Clarence's hand. Brother Pappy told Clarence that God called him to do a great work for the Lord.

Clarence said, "Jesus loves me this I know."

Brother Pappy held his hands straight up in the air as if God was sending the Holy Ghost into Pappy's body. I expected thunder to crack and lightning to come through the tent and zap us all. It was beginning to rain a little harder outside and the tent seemed to be sagging in the middle.

"Do you believe the Lord wants to heal you, Clarence?" Brother Pappy asked. "Do you believe it from the bottom of your heart?"

"Yes," Clarence asked a little wild-eyed. His head lolled back on his neck like it did when he felt overwhelmed by something like greenbeans mixing with macaroni and cheese. "Actually I am not sick, Brother Pappy."

"Deaf and dumb spirit," Brother Pappy began. "COME OUT of this young man's body! I command it in the name of Jesus Christ, the Lord of Lords and the King of Kings, the Alpha and Omega! Come out and leave this boy whole!"

Next thing Brother Pappy said nearly scared me plumb to death. Pappy said to me, "Pray for Brother Clarence. Pray for him. Ask Jesus to heal him."

My eyes were closed, but they popped open all by themselves when Brother Pappy said that. Pappy's dark face was intent on communicating with the Holy Ghost or something, because he didn't look at me. Everyone started getting real quiet. I knew I had to say something. I don't think I had ever prayed for someone before, besides a God help me kind of prayer of the hail Mary variety that just about anyone will pray if they're in a jam and only a miracle will do. I swallowed and said, "Dear Lord, heal Clarence. We all know he is retarded. Make him normal, like all of us. Aunt Oleta won't have to have Luther come over to lift him up so she can clean up after him no more. She's plumb too old to keep doing that forever. And, Lord, while you're at it, help Mama meet a nice man who can be a good daddy for me. Thank you, Lord, amen!"

"Amen," everybody said. I felt something new I had never felt. I belonged. I was part of a large group who at that moment loved each other and me. It felt strange. Overwhelming.

But then Clarence did not change. He was still a retard. He still could not walk too good and said kind of funny things. I thought at first God was going to do things with Clarence a little at a time instead of all at once. Maybe he would straighten out Clarence's bones first, and he would stand up and walk around. Then he would start speaking in a very educated tone like one of the teachers at school. Instead he laughed and showed us his some of the silver molars in the back of his mouth. Where was God; what was He doing? Why did God do some miracles and not others? So many questions but nobody seemed to know the answers, not even Brother Pappy. If Pappy didn't know, then I wasn't sure anyone ever would since he was so much closer to God than everyone.

Blackmore Baptism

By the end of the week we were all standing knee deep in Blackmore Lake with our pant's legs rolled up high on our calves. Everyone from Redeemer was there standing around looking happier than they normally looked. After some of the men and boys had thrown stones into the water to make sure there werent any snakes around, particularly cotton mouths, we gathered closer around the lake. The blue sky reflected off the water. I had to squint it was so bright. There was more redneck polyester suits than you could shake a stick amongst the men that day. The old ladies wore brightly colored dresses, the pinks and purples of the fabric the likes of which I only saw on Easter stretched across the incredible girths of those good ladies.

Brother Pappy said the angels in heaven were rejoicing that Brother Luther and them (including me) was saved and getting baptized. When Brother Luther came out the water dripped off of him and he rubbed his fists at his eyes like a giant's baby that just woke up. Brother Pappy was saying words at me, but I couldn't concentrate on them much because I was worrying about getting dunked. He already told us what he was going to say earlier at our practice so when he dunked me it was like dying a little bit. The people standing around were watching me like my soul went to heaven and they did not seem to matter. I don't know if God was inside me, but I knew the sky was blue and that there were puffy white clouds in it. Everything was quiet. One of Brother Pappy's large hands covered mine which were holding my nose so water wouldn't go up it. I was laying flat out just under the water's surface and I knew Brother Pappy was right close to God. I could feel the heat coming out of his body and heating the lake, and something was happening to me. I came out

of my body and floated above Blackmore Lake and I could
see everybody and I finally understood.

Then the sun was glaring in my eyes. A brightness too bril-
liant to explain made me close them. When Brother Pappy
pulled my head out of the water I kind of sputtered, whatever
I had understood before did not make sense again. People
touched my back as I walked out of Blackmore as if they
were blessing me or trying to get something from me. I felt
like crying, but I didn't know if that meant I was happy or
sad. I felt different for the rest of the night, even while getting
ice cream cones at the Blue Star.

The Law Dog

I hadn't been home for a week when Vaughn pulled up in a green Dodge pickup and parked in the yard outside our trailer. There was a gunrack in the window behind him with two rifles on it and a Confederate flag sticker in the window. I was not paying attention to how straight my rows were as I pushed the Briggs and Stratton across the yard but now I was worried it wouldn't suit Vaughn even if it wasn't his yard. Buddy was in the bed of the pickup smiling at me. I didn't know how to tell Vaughn how I got Jesus now and couldn't run with him anymore, but I had a feeling he already knew.

"Howdy there, Kid," Vaughn said to me like I was a complete stranger.

"Hey Vaughn," I turned off the mower.

A little orange Pinto drove by in a bucking fit. Vaughn turned at the same time to see the Pinto back up. A pretty black woman got out of the car wearing a nice dress, heels so high she had to take funny small steps. I'd seen this before. Sometimes when folks saw your lawnmower they stopped and asked for gas. It was my chance to be like the good Samaritan although that always sounded like a type of fish to me.

Vaughn put on his mean face.

"Can I buy some gas off you all?" she asked. "I just ran out of gas. I only need enough to get me down to Roy's 66."

"I got some gas," I went to the porch to get the gas can. "I don't know if it's enough to get you to Roy's or not."

"Thank you," the lady said. "You are a lifesaver, hon. If you give me your can I'll fill it up for you and bring it right back."

"Now listen here, sister." Vaughn tugged at his belt, hiking up his pants. "You just get back in your car and peddle your ass to someone who gives a good goddamn."

"But Vaughn," I said. "She said she ran out of gas."

"Shut the hell up," he said over his shoulder. "You barely got enough gas to finish mowing. Let this bitch go get her own gas. Your mama works for her money. This one's probably eating the government cheese and has her a sugar daddy paying her bills. Ain't that right, baby? If she takes off those white women shoes, I expect she could walk a heap easier since she's probably used to going barefoot everywhere."

"Okay," she said. "I'm leaving now. I know who you are. Oh, yes I do. I don't care if the whole town afraid of you! You shouldn't treat people like they trash."

"What did you say to me?" Vaughn moved quicker than I expected he could as he closed the space between himself and the woman. She jumped in the car and locked the doors. Her mouth was moving and her teeth were flashing and I couldn't hear exactly what she was saying, but I could guess. I knew she called him a cracker a couple of times. He went around to his truck, pulled out a tire iron. He smiled the whole time as he beat that ugly-assed Pinto up. People was coming out of their trailers now to see what all the fuss was about.

"Crazy motherfucker!"

"How you like that? You spear-chucking slut!"

"Oh you better be praying," the lady hollered, "because I'm praying for your dumb ignorant soul."

The woman kept trying to get her Pinto to turn over. It started spitting and choking. Blue smoke came out of the exhaust like it was being strangled, but then the car began to lurch forward a few feet at a time. Vaughn gave it a kick and knocked a red taillight out with his boot. A black man in a little red and white trailer at the end of our row came out with his shoulders hunched down like he wished he was invisible. The Pinto lurched forward and pulled over in front of his place. He waved at us scared shitless of Vaughn with an appeasing smile on his face. The woman, I never noticed her before, looked as if she was the old man's daughter. She was telling him to go down there and kick that white man's ass. He murmured something to her and patted her back trying to comfort her as he pressed her toward the door of his trailer. Vaughn turned back to me laughing his ass off. He didn't think there was nothing wrong with what he done because he was white, and he told me everytime we saw anyone black that the white man was naturally superior to the black man. He loved Mama Horne in his own way. He said he respected some of them. It was scientifically proved, he told me, that niggers were not as highly evolved as whites. He sat down on the porch step like nothing at all had happened except sweat was pouring down his face. It was then that I knew this Jesus stuff was not going to be too easy.

"Don't ever go around trusting anything *those* people tell you," Vaughn said.

"Why don't you like them?"

"Because they're common" Vaughn raised up his hand like he didn't want to talk about it no more. He lit up a cigarette. "They want you to feel sorry for them because they's niggers. They want us to feel bad about being white. Well, I got news for you, the white man was created in HIS image. Says so in the Bible."

"When I stayed with Mama Horne she said she used to watch you when you was little," I said.

"Watch your mouth, boy." Vaughn turned his face away from me. "Don't be too smart for your own good." He gestured with the burning cigarette in his hand. It had a green smell to it like Missouri ditchweed. "You don't know anything about it."

"Yes sir."

"I hear Lorene shipped you off to your Aunt Oleta's." Vaughn said. "You look different. Hell now. Well, ain't that the shits? I guess Pappy redeemed you? Saved your soul? And I suppose you're a dyed-in-the-wool Jesus freak now? Going to heaven and all."

"I guess I am," I said. "I don't know. I guess I just don't want to be bad no more. Luther got born again, I thought he seemed tough so it must be a good thing to do."

"Tough?" said Vaughn. "Who you talking about? Luther? Simmie, you mean. Simmie's the biggest candy-ass I ever seen. I could whip his ass with one hand tied behind my back. Since when you been a nigger lover anyway? Is that what Oleta's been feeding you? Oleta can kiss my lily-white ass."

"I don't know about any of that," I said. My legs felt weak. Getting yelled at set me off. It made me want to run or punch something but I couldn't hit Vaughn.

"You think anyone's tougher than me?"

"No," I said. "It ain't go to do with tough."

"You think Pappy's tough, huh?" Vaughn said. "Just cause he fought in the war and has tats. It don't take much to impress you, does it? I was in Vietnam, *boy-san*. I was in the shit. Them boys in World War II did all right, but Vietnam was a head trip. You probably think that was a long time ago, huh? Well, it ain't so goddamn long ago. I can't even sleep at night for thinking about the slant-eyed sons-of-bitches I killed. And you think Simmie and Pappy's all tough and good to go with Jesus? I guess you really believe all that happy horseshit. I can see it on your face. They converted you. You know what you are? You're a damn proselyte! Know what that means?"

"Nope."

"Means you been brainwashed." Vaughn pulled out a Reader's Digest with his latest vocabulary list in it and the word proselyte circled in red. He turned the magazine around and showed it to me.

"Brainwashed by who?"

"Brainwashed by Pappy," Vaughn said. "He just wants people in there to put money in the collection plate. Besides, he used to be the worst drunk around. I even drank with him a few times. Why he used to have his own liquor store and drank as much as he sold."

"Everyone knows that," I said.

"And Luther . . . you think he's such a tough mother? He ain't nothing but a nigger. Now ain't that right?"

"I don't know," I said.

"Well now, I do know." Vaughn was goading me. He poured two fingers of Black Label Jack into a glass and took a sip. "But I want to hear you say it."

"What?" I said, but I knew what. It wasn't that I thought or never said it, but he was so worked up about it. I ain't saying I'm perfect or pretend that I wouldn't say it when I had but he wanted me to say it to control me. He wanted me to feel bad about being friends with Luther and getting saved by the blood of Jesus. He didn't want me to walk around being forgiven. No, he wanted me serving him in the clutches of sin.

"I want you to tell me what he is! What did God make that boy in his infinite and perfect wisdom?"

"What?" I asked again. "He made him a good person for one."

Vaughn made a sound like a buzzer with his mouth. "Wrong answer. You know what."

"What do you want me to say, I'll say it."

"Quit yanking my crank." Vaughn took a gulp of Jack. "Say what he is."

"What he is," I smiled.

"Don't be cute," Vaughn reached over and cuffed me across the face. "What is he? You say it you little son-of-a-bitch or you'll wish you had!"

"A NIGGER!" I shouted. "HE'S A NO GOOD GODDAMN NIGGER!"

Vaughn had pure hate on his face, but suddenly it dissolved into a slow smile.

"There you go, boy." Vaughn sat back in his seat.

"Vaughn," I said. "I don't want to be bad. I give up on running the roads."

"Bad?" Vaughn said, all crazy like. "I brought your dog over here. 'Cause I don't want him on my place. He's a big pussy just like you. I put my hand out and you know what he does?"

"No."

Vaughn pushed his weight forward and opened the door and hopped out of the truck. He looked at me hard and then hitched his jeans up higher on the roll at his belly so I could see a hairy belly button for a second. Then he looked at Buddy, the dog's head came down and his ears flattened down around his head. Vaughn tried to pat Buddy on the head but the dog stuck his tail between his legs and cowered on the far side of the truck bed.

"See that!" Vaughn said, like he had won a bet off of me. "Get out! Get out of the truck." Vaughn's face expanded and his lips flattened as his upper teeth came over his bottom lip. He let out a harsh whistle at Buddy. The dog jumped out of the truck, came over and slammed his body into the back of my legs as if I could protect him.

"What do you want him to do?" I said. "Start barking and growling at you and clamp down on your arm? That's how them rednecks and Kluckers train their wormy dogs."

"Don't get smart with me, Kid," Vaughn said.

I clamped my mouth shut then. He stood there staring at me like I was a crossword puzzle he couldn't figure out. Vaughn leaned with his arms across his chest against his new truck. I never seen the truck before. It wasn't exactly a new truck, just new to him I guess. It crossed my mind that maybe he had requisitioned it. That's what he said when he stole something. My mind was working a mile a minute now. I wasn't sure how, but I had to get away from Vaughn. I knew how he could do people like Glenn Starkey, Fenton Reed, and how he had killed Rafe and gotten off scot-free. If I said the wrong thing to him he might do something to Mama or me. There wasn't nobody to ask for help either. Everyone was too *ascared* of Vaughn to help.

"Where'd you get this Dodge?" I asked, putting my hands on my hips like I was a tough old cobb, some salty dog who hung out at Mike and Laura's bar in Fairmont drinking shots of Southern Comfort with beer chasers.

Vaughn gave me a mean-ass look like he wasn't going to answer and leaned down with his face in my face. "You plumb tickle my ass, Kid." He shook his big shaggy head like a big black bear. "Look here, I ain't saying I'm sorry but I just don't like when folks fill up kid's heads with fairy tales. You know I wouldn't never hurt you or steer you wrong, you know that don't you?"

"Sure," I said. I said it like I believed it too. "I know you're on the lookout for me."

"I got your back, Honey," Vaughn scratched his big sideburns. "Some day I'm gonna sit you down and set things straight with you and your mama." He reached into his wallet and pulled out a $20 bill. I shook my head like I wasn't about to take it. My hands were in the back pockets of my jeans and he stuffed the bill into my shirt pocket. "I owe you for that. If you don't want it, give it to Lorene. Buy some groceries or something down at Cooper's. You look starved, you're such a skinny-assed kid."

"I get enough to eat," I said.

"Is your Mama home?"

"Nope," I lied. He knew I was pissing on his leg. We both knew she was peeking through the curtains at us. I didn't want him going in there and pitching a fit. "She's working over there at the 3 Sister's Cafe."

"What's she doing?" Vaughn asked.

"Waiting tables."

"She quit the Spot?" Vaughn asked.

"No sir," I said. "The Spot don't like it when you come by so they cut her hours."

"I want you to take a ride with me," Vaughn said. "Go around to the other side and get in." He waved at Mama and the curtain closed. He pulled out a cigarette and lit it with a silver Zippo. "Ride on down to Dixie and I'll buy some pickled pigs feet. You know they have a little grill in the back now?"

I decided it couldn't hurt nothing. I did like the barbecue ribs at Little Dixie store. He smoked as he drove listening to some shit-kicker radio station that I didn't much appreciate.

"That's ol' Lefty." Vaughn shook out some cigs from the pack and I took one. Back to my wicked, wicked ways I guess, but you couldn't fake it with Vaughn. We flew past the barbed wire fences and blackberry briar and hedgerows of sumac growing along the sides of the road and the ditches were full of Queen Anne's lace thriving under the mean sun.

Vaughn was country smart for someone who was proud to tell you he never went past the eighth grade. He took me down to Dixie store and we sat on the little red vinyl stools at the counter. The counter was next to the glass case where you could pick out your meat, but Mama never shopped here because she said it was too expensive. Just as we come in there, there was a galvanize tub full of ice and clear bottles of beer. The place had wooden floors and smelled powerfully of rotten fruit.

He ordered deep fried catfish with some cottage fries they give you on the side there. I ordered a Coney dog and a root beer.

"Where does root beer come from?" I asked.

"Where do you think?" Vaughn asked me annoyed. "Comes from the root of the beer tree."

"Beer tree?" I asked. "I never heard of a beer tree before."

"Why do you think they call it *root beer*?"

He went over to the freezer and pulled out a six pack of PBR, pulled the tab off one and stuck it in the ashtray, and sucked down half of it in one slurp. He picked up the salt shaker and shook out some salt around the lip of the can. It seemed like a funny thing to do but his face said he liked it like that every so often. When the big-boned woman finished cooking our food she brought it over to us with a look that said she disapproved of him drinking his beer there. Like he wasn't supposed to drink it in the store, but she decided to let it slide. Everyone knew you didn't tell Vaughn what to do.

When we were finished eating, Vaughn spun around on the stool like maybe he was ready to go and maybe not. "I'm still kind of hungry. How about you, hoss?"

"I could go for some sweet," I said.

"Damn straight," Vaughn said. He went over to the cookie aisle and came back with some Oreos. He sang a little ditty: "Little girls have pretty curls, but I like Oreos. Ore-os." He shoved a double-decker in his mouth. He held the bag out to me while making mmm-mmm sounds. He washed down the Oreos with a swig of beer.

"I usually take mine with milk," I said.

"Hell Kid," he said. "That ain't nothing but easy to fix. Go grab you a carton. They've got them little chocolate cartons."

I went over and came back with a half-gallon of milk and there was a picture of a missing little girl on the back of it. She was a pretty little thing too. Could have been my little sister if I had one.

"Ain't afraid of breaking the bank are you? I meant them little bitty cartons," said Vaughn.

"Maybe I'll go steal a cow for you later on tonight." I grinned at him. Just being around Vaughn was letting the Devil back into my life. I knew that. I was already doing the things Brother Pappy said not to do. Not more than a week had gone by and I was a backslider. It ain't easy to keep Jesus in your heart all the time. Now I guess I had to worry about grieving the Holy Ghost next. What was I going to do? Cast the demons out of Vaughn? That was big league stuff. I didn't think Brother Pappy and every fiery-eyed Jesus freak at Redeemer all praying together at the same time could have done that.

"Maybe you will," his head tipped back like he was thinking about who might have a milk cow for me to steal.

Vaughn was using his fancy words to impress the big-boned blonde behind the counter. He was making eyes at her and she was starting to get all moon-eyed over him too. He started telling me all about himself, but the problem was everytime he started reciting his autobiography it seemed like the details changed. He said he hailed from the Crackerneck region of western Missouri and was kin to Jesse James. "I'm butthole cousins with George McCreedy. You probably don't know him, but he was the last man hung in Kingdom County for killing a piece-of-shit highway patrolman name of Saunders."

"Is that all for you, hon?" The blonde put our check down and bent over the counter to show Vaughn her big titties.

"I'll let you know," he winked. "Ain't this better than the apothecary?"

"The what?" I asked.

"Dunavant's," he said.

"Oh," I said. "The drugstore."

"Well," Vaughn began, more to the woman than to me "I guess we better make like horse shit and hit the trail."

"Come back and see me," she said. "Hon."

"Will do, baby." He winked again, grinning broadly.

When we got into the pickup Sheriff Merrill eased up beside us in the Dixie parking lot. Vaughn didn't even bother to start the engine. His hands tightened on the wheel, but other than that, Vaughn was cool. He liked talking to the sheriff, because he said he had Merrill's number. He had measured the man up and down years ago and knew just how hard to push. Merrill had been sheriff in Fairmont ten years before time began. He was a tall man with thinning white hair like the cotton in an aspirin bottle that made him look trusty on a election campaign poster. Everybody in town liked Merrill, except Vaughn. Vaughn said he "respected" him but that meant he was afraid of him.

"Sure is hot, ain't it? How you been, Elston?" Sheriff Merrill asked, sticking his head into Vaughn's window.

"Better than you," Vaughn said. "I ain't knocking on death's door like you, old timer."

"Listen," said the sheriff. "A word to the wise: Everyone knows Raffert Clearwater didn't die of old age . . . it wasn't no accident either. If I was you, I'd lay low for awhile. Stop visiting folks at midnight and taking inventory and stop harassing people. My God, boy, when do you ever sleep? Your daddy and me cut teeth together and you ain't nothing like him."

"My daddy is dead," Vaughn said, the mocking tone gone. Now he sounded serious and threatening. The muscle in his jaw was working and even though I could tell Sheriff Merrill probably had his hand on his gun I began to worry a little. "Not only is he dead, but you don't know shit about him and me so I'd appreciate it if you kept your ignorant redneck comments to yourself."

"You're right," Sheriff Merrill said, backing up out of the window. "I ain't got the right. You ain't nothing like the Vaughns I knew, most all them is dead now. But I'll make you a promise right here and now—don't mess with folks and you won't never have to see me darken your door. You read me?"

"I got you," Vaughn started the Dodge now. "I got you a long time ago, Constable. You might be seeing me sooner than you think. You going to be telling Jesus how sorry you are for mean-mouthing me one day, old man."

"You might be slick," Merrill said "but you can't slide on bob wire."

The rushing sound of a flock of starlings flew overhead like bullets. They flew as a group across the sky, first one way and then the other, as if they were being fanned by the thumb of a god.

The Sheriff was trying to talk to Vaughn still, but every time he started to say something Vaughn revved the engine up real loud so he couldn't hear him. I'm ashamed to say it, but it made me laugh to see Sheriff Merrill's face everytime Vaughn revved the engine. Vaughn wasn't laughing though. He had his lip curled like he was some kind of mad dog that had lunged to the end of its rope. Merrill's eyes were like a horse's that had been beat by the farrier, wild-eyed and helpless at the end of his tether.

We pulled out of the Dixie parking lot in a hail of white dust and gravel. I turned around to see Merrill still standing there shaking his head in disgust. Vaughn snapped the radio on and there was Johnny Cash singing about prison. Vaughn was pounding the steering wheel with his hands like he was playing the drums. I knew it was bad then, because Vaughn started talking to himself. Sheriff Merrill was only doing his job, but he had done pissed Vaughn off. Vaughn was showing his devil face now.

I'm going to drive the Jesus right out of you, Honey Boy.

I thought Vaughn was going to drop me off at the trailer, but instead he got out before me and told me to wait outside. My heart shot up to my throat. He yanked the trailer door open and it smacked the side of the trailer, and then ricocheted shut. Vaughn was going to do something to Mama.

I tried to think of something else other than what was going on between him and her in that bedroom. There was the sound of a woodpecker beating on a tree out in the pasture. The deep sonorous booms of train cars hooking up off in the distance. Up above I saw a jet trail running across the sky like a white scar just under a half moon in the afternoon sky. I tried to push all my bad thoughts out of my head but I knew it couldn't last for long. Then I heard him yelling, her hollering back. I popped open the glovebox and my pistol was there. I took it out and there was two bullets in it. I held the pistol up and then I saw my scared-shitless face in the side mirror and put it back in the glovebox. The cicadas were thundering in my head all of a sudden. Through the noise I heard Mama's voice.

"Help!" she said. "Help!"

Suddenly I was in the trailer with the pistol in my hand. One of the lamps was smashed on the floor. The legs of the coffee table were broken on one side. I could hear Vaughn and Mama in her bedroom, but the door was closed. I could hear the springs on the bed squeaking, not like they was doing it, but like he was probably trying to hold her down. I cocked the pistol, the sound of it like a hammer on an anvil in my ears, and held it up in front of me with both hands. I stopped at the door and listened and Mama said "Oh" and so then I slammed the door open. It sounded like Vaughn came off Mama in a hurry, his pants down around his ankles, he tripped and fell on the floor. Mama's eyes was big and her top was off and she was laying there in her bra and her jeans was unbuttoned. I was hypnotized by the fear on her face for a second.

"Honey, don't do it," Mama said. "Honey, it's all right. I'm okay. Mama's okay. All right?"

"You all right?" I asked. Tears were coming down my face, but not why you think. I was mad. The anger came over me and it was like I was drunk with it. If his head popped up right then I was going to shoot it off. The whole trailer shook. The room swam through the tears of my blurry vision. The adrenaline of hate ran red through my veins.

"Mama's just fine, Honey," Mama said. "It's okay. Look at me. Vaughn and me are just going to talk. Go put that gun up now. Everything's just fine."

"Okay," I said. "I love you Mama."

"I know you do," Mama said. "Now go outside for awhile."

"Okay."

Just as I lowered the pistol Vaughn's head came up real slow. "You all right there, Kid?"

"Yep," I said.

"You was going to shoot me just now, wasn't you?" Vaughn asked.

"Yep," I said. "I just about did."

"That's all right," he said. "I don't blame you one damn bit. It takes balls, son, and you got them."

"I don't care about that," I said. "Don't hurt Mama no more."

"No sir," Vaughn said. "I sure won't."

I shut the door. Tossed the pistol on the kitchen table. I never wanted to see it again.

I went outside, Buddy came out from under the trailer and I patted his head and dried my eyes in his fur. I hugged his warm black body to mine. When I let go he turned and licked my cheek. I felt and smelled his foul dog breath in my face. I called the dog. We ran out past the pond. I wandered around in the woods with Buddy to get away from people. You thought you could be reborn like the good book said, but the evil in people made it impossible. The hell of it was, the more you thought about trying to be good the more opportunity there was to be bad.

It didn't make sense to me why folks was the way they was. I wondered why I was the way I was. I got mad sometimes in school, because I always had to move. Everytime you go to a new school someone's always got to mess with you. Boys want to try you out to see if they can get away with picking on you or see if you will stand up for yourself. And if you ain't rich, girls like to make fun of your clothes and holey tennis shoes. But getting mad the way I did was way beyond all that school stuff. I wanted to kill Vaughn, just because Mama said it was all right, hadn't made the feeling go away . . . not yet anyway.

I guess I walked for a long time, because the next thing I knew the sun was hanging low in the evening sky. I saw bats circling around in the dusk hunting insects under the street lights. When I come up out of a copse of woods, nearby was White Cloud Cemetery. All my people had been buried there they said, but I didn't feel very close to them. Where was they when I needed them? I knew Mama's people was buried there, but what about my daddy's? Was Vaughn really my daddy? Most of the time I just tried not to think about it. I knew folks said I was a bush colt. My daddy should be taking care of Mama and me. I wasn't big enough. I didn't know how to take care of her, or me for that matter. Who would give a kid a real job? It was against the law for a kid to have a grown up job.

I didn't know what to do with myself now that all my anger was used up. Pulling a gun on Vaughn hadn't been a smart thing to do, so I was afraid to go home yet. Instead I walked around on the old windy wagon road that wrapped around the cemetery inside the black iron gates until I found some Kimbroughs. The oldest one, *Charles beloved husband and father*, with the biggest headstone, died in 1888. Kimbroughs sure were thick in that part of the cemetery under a couple of big pin oaks, but they couldn't help me now. Oh, I listened for them old time voices on the outside chance they had something useful to tell me. They didn't say nothing. There were even some kids, younger than me, with tiny markers set in the ground so far down and so long ago I couldn't even hardly read them. I knew they were all waiting for me, but I wasn't planning on leaving for the great hereafter any too soon. I used to be real careful about walking around the outline of their coffins. You could tell where some of them were by the way the grass grew, others had little stone fences around them, and there were some that looked like little gardens. Only the kind of garden you didn't ever want to be in.

Then, looking down I could see the rotting bodies in their best suits and dresses grinning their skeleton heads off made me mad. I don't why. I started walking all over the bodies underneath me daring the devil to come up and do something about it. I didn't want to wait until I was a hundred years old to have to deal with him. None of the bodies moaned or warned me off, but at least I didn't see them in my mind any longer. Their voices and grasping bony fingers stopped begging me for their old lives back. I wished they could help me, but they were all dead. They couldn't keep from dying so I didn't know how I thought they could do anything for me.

"That there's the yellow fever wing, Captain," The voice belonged to an old black man with the whitest head of hair I had ever seen was leaning on a rake. He was standing underneath a large pin oak. I could just see him out of the corner of my eye. He was wearing wool work clothes and a battered navy colored cap sat on his head at a cocky angle.

"Oh," I said.

"Uh huh," he said. "You better watch yourself or something going to sneak up on you too. Folks like to believe they will see death coming up on them and they'll know what to do then. Well, that ain't so. Old Death like to sneak up on you like a Tom cat after a field mouse in the marsh grass. You mind what I say."

I turned toward him thinking I'd be a smartaleck, but he was over by the Williams mausoleum scratching at the bald ground surrounding it. No grass was growing around the Williams monument, while the rest of the cemetery was a shining green—even though there was a drought going on. It looked like someone was using the crypt like a miniature house. The old man had his back to me, his dirt raking like he was making drawings on the ground and using the rake as a brush. The closer I walked to him the more quickly he worked on his drawing until he disappeared around back of the tomb. Just before I got around the side to hear him whisper to two blackbirds sprung out of the brushwood and into the heavy air as silent as the souls under the earth. The old man was nowhere to be seen. I looked for the pictures the man drew in the dirt. It was a one-winged angel standing over a snake crawling up to a tree where a pair of women with bird bodies were playing a harp and a flute like they was calling the serpent. I can tell you I didn't know what it meant exactly, but I thought it to be about temptation and that the man must be my soul-guardian angel.

Just outside the cemetery was the marker for the Confederate dead of Kingdom County. The marker was erected by the United Daughters of the Confederacy, to which both Grandma Kimbrough and Aunt Oleta belonged. It was kind of a funny shape, tall and gray and like pictures I had seen of the Washington Monument. There weren't any names of men who'd fought in what Old Roy called the *War of Northern Aggression*, except for Colonel Fisher whose kin had gone on to become the richest people in town and build the first mansion down on Hillcrest where all the big houses were. A couple of years ago I'd had a paper route delivering in that neighborhood and dreamed I might live in one of the big houses some day.

A black and white cow was lowing, its head stuck over a barbed-wire fence. Buddy was sitting there looking up at me, "She's talking to you" I told him.

Buddy got up followed his tail in a circle and sat down again.

The cemetery was giving me the heebie-jeebies so I headed out toward a dump. One of them fat nuclear bees flew near my head until I waved it off. We had lived nearby out in that part of the country one summer when I was little. It was out west of town, and there wasn't nothing around but old-timey wash machines—the kind you had to put clothes through the wringer; old refrigerators; and people's trash. But the real treasure was a junked '61 Lincoln Continental that I used to sit in and pretend I was driving to some real swank place like Las Vegas or Hollywood.

When the sun set I went down to a creek and drank a handful of water. My stomach was beginning to growl so I rummaged around until I found these wild blackberry bushes down near Dry Fork Road. It wasn't too long before my face felt sticky, and my fingers were a dark purple. I could smell my own sweat too. Sleeping out at night didn't scare me, but I didn't have a sleeping bag or blankets. I didn't want to wake up covered in dew either. The knees of my pants were muddy too. It wasn't long before I started feeling sorry for myself and wishing I could go back home.

The Goat

Vaughn's swirling horns poked out of his head. He had the body of a mountain goat. He hopped from stone to rock, leaping up the face of one of the Ozark cliffs. I knew it was somewhere around the Lake of the Ozarks. I tried to keep up with him, but I was beginning to lose sight of his hairy body as he skipped from rock to hillock, the sound of his hooves clicking softly, as he disappeared into the sunshine peeking over the next ridge. A sound came out of his mouth, but it didn't sound human. It was like a coyote singing the blues to the scrub pines.

The Aluminum Curtain

T he next morning it felt like God was watching me as I caught a few winks in a cottonwood thicket. I was laying there feeling pathetic. I was thinking about how my whole life I'd got rooked over one thing or another. But that kind of thinking don't get you nowhere. No one wants to hear that crybaby shit so I told myself I had to get up and do something. Besides, I couldn't sleep because the goddamn gnats was trying to share the shade with me.

I decided to go to Lover's Leap and have a look at the town from the bluff. Kids didn't go there much, because of the story about Icepick Annie. Icepick Annie killed her husband and then took a nosedive off Lover's Leap. I didn't believe the story about her anymore. At least, not the part about jumping down the rock face. It wasn't really high enough except to hurt you if you jumped except to give you a bad case of road rash. Unless you broke your neck by diving headfirst maybe.

On the way I saw the strangest sight. On the trestle out past White Cloud Church I saw a horse hanging upside down with one of his hooves kind of caught between the tracks. I stepped behind an old railroad depot that wasn't used no more and watched. He was a roan saddlebred and by my guess he was a little over 15 hands high. He wasn't the prettiest horse you ever saw, but the farmers who owned him were keen to get him down. The fire department was there in hardhats and thick gloves with ropes up on the trestle. The fire chief almost hung the horse dead with the rope he was using to pull it toward the bank. I couldn't see how, but they got the horse's leg free, but they did and he fell into the shallow creek upside down. I thought that horse was a goner for sure, but he jumped up on all fours and his whole body shook. Everyone cheered then and I figured that sorry looking horse was going to be all right. I have no idea how a horse could have gotten himself in such a fix.

From Lover's Leap I saw Tempie downtown outside of Monkey Wards so I made my way down the ravine around the poison ivy and the bloodroot. I featured her buying barrettes or pins, thimbles, and dress patterns like Mawmaw or Aunt Oleta. The clock tower from the college began to chime when old man Churchill, who looked like a bulldog, gave his speech about an aluminum curtain everyone thought was hot stuff. Sonny referred to it in his making fun way by saying aluminum instead of what everyone knew it as "The Iron Curtain speech." I saw a picture of the geezer in a top hat flashing the peace sign so I thought he must be kind of hip, but Grandma Kimbrough said it meant V for Victory back then. Someone back in olden times got the idea to bring a bombed out church over from England brick by brick and put it up at the college and created a museum down in the basement. It was supposed to be a tourist attraction but why anyone would want to come here unless they had to I just couldn't imagine. Churchill looked just like W. C. Fields. I could picture him saying, "Go away kid, you bother me" as well as anything.

Lover's Leap wasn't as bad as it sounds. Years ago someone had put a stone stairway down the rough face of the ravine. I guess maybe some company or other was going to build something up there, but now there was just a park where neighborhood children could swing or teeter-totter. A flock of swallows flew out of their nests on the sandy rocks embedded in the little cliff.

"Hey Tempie," I said when I got there.

Her hand shot up to block the sun from her eyes, "Hey, Honey Boy, what're you up to?"

"Nothing much," I said. She looked prettier than the last time I saw her. The whites of her eyes were amazingly white like boiled eggs. No lines of red at all streaked them. Her eyes were a very light blue with streaks of black in them. Her skin was tanned. Her skin was golden and glowing.

"Where you been?" Tempie asked. "Everyone's looking for you."

"They ain't looking too hard," I said. "I been watching."

"You sure are dirty," Tempie said. "Your clothes are just about black. Are you hungry?"

"I'm starving," I said. "Can you get me something to eat?"

"At home," she said. "Come on. You know, you stink too."

"Honey Boy," Roy hollered, but he was pumping gas for a woman wearing a purple church hat in a Mercury. "You'd better go on out to Vaughns! You hear me? Your Mama's out there."

"All right." I waved to him but I didn't have no plans of doing any such thing yet.

I could feel the heat from the macadam on the thin soles of my tennie shoes as we walked the couple of miles out to Tempie's on HH. She must have been bored, because it was getting awfully warm to be walking out in this heat. Even the air from the cars whooshing by us was warm.

"You ought to be ashamed," Tempie said. "Your Mama was crying and crying when Vaughn and them boys was helping her move your all's stuff out to Vaughn's."

"Boys?"

"You know," Tempie said. "Punkin and them."

"Oh."

"You want this?" Tempie asked, holding out half of her Hershey bar to me. She had seen me staring at it. Just seeing that chocolate had made my mouth water. I shoved it in my mouth and was probably quite a sight to behold with my checks all puffed out full of Hershey's chocolate like I was some new breed of squirrel. Tempie was laughing at me and her brown eyes were wet and beautiful.

A crazy nut was honking their horn behind us and driving so as to make the tires moan and squeal. Tempie and me jumped off the shoulder and a beat to shit car skidded onto the gravel shoulder causing a cloud of dust to form, choking us. For a second I thought we were going to have to jump into the irrigation ditch for cover. I knew it was Tempie's older sister Becky by the no-muffler rumble of the car Tempie called the green weenie. Becky was a skinny-assed blonde who was always hollering about something. She was seventeen and already had two snot-nosed kids.

"What are you two doing?" Becky demanded. Her frizzy hair was losing some of its feathered style and was floating in puffy strands. "If Daddy catches you with him he's going to beat your ass. You know his mama is living with that crazy son-of-a-bitch, Vaughn? I can't believe Arlene puts up with his shit."

"Mommy! Mommy!" Her son Jerry was braying like a sick calf.

"Jerry and Sherry!" Becky yelled over her shoulder. "Shut the fuck up before I have to jerk you out of this car and leave you behind."

"She took my car," Jerry said.

"Tough titty said the kitty." Becky's green eye shadow had me hypnotized, it was so hideous. She was all googly-eyed, her lip was up in a snarl. Her words slurred. She made me sick everytime I had to look at her. I couldn't believe she and Tempie were blood relatives. The car was sputtering like it needed some work.

"Honey's going to eat with us," Tempie said.

"Who said?" Becky shouted. "Did Mom or Dad say?"

"Neither of them," Tempie answered. "Cause they don't know yet."

"Mmm hmm," Becky said. "When they find out they'll throw you both out. Look at his clothes. They're almost black! Goddamn boy, you stink, what are you? Part pig?"

"No," I said.

"What?" Becky said. I didn't say nothing. She liked nothing better than to argue. "That's what I thought. You all want a ride?"

"Yeah," Tempie said. "That'd be great."

"That'd be great," Becky mocked.

"MOM--ME! MOM--ME!"

"Goddamn it, Sherry!" Becky hollered over her shoulder again. "You two have hit my last nerve!"

"Why don't you scream at them a little more while we melt out here," Tempie said, in her own smart-aleck tone. Believe me, you had have to have a smart mouth just to survive in the Ridgewell house.

"All righty," Becky said. "Hurry up and get in before the car dies. But you're going to get me in more trouble with Dad."

"That's okay," Tempie said. "You're always in trouble with dad, so what's new?"

"I know it," Becky grinned. She gave Tempie a big smooch on the cheek suddenly laughing. I could smell the booze on her breath. "You're my favorite sister, even if you are a shit."

The car died. Becky banged on the steering wheel with the palm of her hand. Her face turned red and puckered up like she was sucking on a lemon.

"How could you do this to me?" Becky asked the car. "Tempie, you and the pig get out and push. We got to pop the clutch now. I'll push from this side and jump in when it's time."

The heat beneath my shoes threatened to melt the rubber I had left. The trunk was hot when we put on our hands on it to push. Tempie made the crazy motion, twirling her finger by her head and rolled her eyes because of Becky.

"One, two, three . . .PUSSSH!" Becky hollered.

The car didn't budge at first. We needed one more big guy to do it right. Becky had a big mouth but she was a tiny thing. I thought we might have to get the kids out of the back to push too but slowly the car began to move, faster and faster as we picked up momentum; then we hit the downside of the hill. We let go and fell down to our knees onto the boiling macadam. Becky jumped in and popped the clutch, the car roared to life, and she was revving it the entire time. We ran around to the passenger side and got in breathing hot and heavy. On the radio was the voice of Freddy-fucking-Fender singing "Wasted Days and Wasted Nights." That song irritated my ass every time I heard it.

"I hate this song," I said.

"Well, I like it," Becky said, "and it's my car so if you don't like it you can walk."

I hated it when kids who had their own car to drive ended every argument with "it's my car and you can walk!"

"That gave me a stitch in my side," Tempie said.

"Don't be a baby." Becky flicked Tempie's ear. The kids laughed about that in the back.

Becky drove us toward their house in a new subdivision. We swerved all over the road because as far as I could tell she never once looked in front of her. She was watching Tempie talk, or me, or screaming at her kids. It was like everything she said was her way of winning the argument, even if no one was arguing with her, or getting the last word. It wore me out just listening to her, but lots of people in Fairmont talked that way. It was probably something in the water.

"Your Aunt Oleta sure is a religious nut," Becky said. "She's worse than Tempie here. Daddy's little angel."

"Yep," I said noncommittal.

Tempie elbowed me in the arm.

"I heard you are too," Becky said. "You probably think you're better than everyone because you've been saved, huh? I know how you all Jesus freaks think. You think you're better than me? Huh? Honey Boy? That's a stupid name."

I knew when to keep my mouth shut.

"He doesn't think he's better than nobody." Tempie came to my rescue. "He's a helluva of a lot better company to talk to than you are!"

"I ought to pull over and smack your smart mouth," Becky said. "You been born again?" Her face turned purple, flecks of spit appeared in the air in front of her. Brother Pappy told us that the Devil could use anybody to do his work. Jump right in their bodies and make them do his bidding. Well, right now I could sure believe it. I was tempted to put my hand on the back of her head and cast out the demon of hard-headedness with my fist. It would have served her right too.

"Whatever," Tempie said. "Some people are so dumb, so immature, even if they are old enough to know better. Isn't that right, Honey Boy?"

I shrugged.

Freddy Fender was really wailing now *Don't you remember the day that you went away and left me?* I couldn't take it anymore! Becky was annoying as hell. The kids were screaming in the backseat. Freddy Fender was getting on my nerves the most so I started howling out the song. I just cut loose. Everybody got really quiet then, even Becky.

"Why should I keep loving you-ooh-ooh? When you know you're not true-ooh-ooh? Why should I call your name? When you're the blame for making me blue! OW OW OOOOOHH!"

Becky made us get out and walk from there. I didn't mind. Walking was better than listening to someone talk crazy to you all the time. I don't know what got her so worked up. I was about to stick my foot up her ass anyway. I knew folks that seemed like they was mad at God for something. I can't say I knew anything about whatever arrangement they must have had with God that didn't work out. Maybe Becky asked to be a movie star or a rock singer and God said no to that prayer?

"I'll be praying for you!" Tempie bust out laughing.

"I won't be!"

"Did you see her face?" Tempie said. "When you started howling just out of the blue like that? Why should I keep loving you-ooh-oh?"

"I hate that dumb song," I said. "Aunt Oleta likes it. She thinks it's far out."

When they said His ways were mysterious, I sure could believe it. Sometimes I prayed for really big things like Mama would find a great job and get married to someone she could stand for more than a few months, but God never saw fit to answer that one. One time I lost my house key on the playground from the chain around my neck. I prayed that God would help me to find it and he did! God sometimes helped me with little stuff, but not the big things. I don't know why He's like that. That's probably his way of teaching a moral to your story.

Tempie's daddy had been working at National Brick since he had been a teenager. It was one of the better jobs in Fairmont, even if they did have a habit of laying people off now and then. The unused claypits were full of water now used mainly for fishing and swimming, but they were also chock-full of souls of all the men who worked there according to Mama Horne. Everyone knew Mama Horne was telepathic, but Vaughn said she was just "intuitive."

The Ridgewells had a nice split level brick house on Woodrow Avenue. They lived almost like millionaires it seemed to me. The Ridgewell house had upstairs and downstairs, two living rooms, and two bathrooms. They had color television sets in the living room and the bedrooms. They

even had cable television which meant they got eleven channels. I sometimes got hypnotized by the time and temperature
channel that showed a row of clocks and gauges, and a chalkboard they called a "community bulletin board." The camera
panned back and forth down a line between the chalkboards
and the clocks in a slow comforting way.

Mr. Ridgewell even had a downstairs den with a bar, and
deer's heads and bass trophies on the walls. He was a big man
who normally spoke in an even tone of voice. He worked
hard at a regular job and seemed to love Tempie's mama. Mr.
Ridgewell did manly things like hunting, fishing, and fixing
clogged drains under the sink. I guess I admired him in a way,
but he had a way of looking at me like I was lower than dogshit. He didn't think I acted tough enough. Nobody did. I'd
learned to be tough on the inside.

Becky went to her room down the hall and immediately
slammed her bedroom door shut. Jerry and Sherry stood outside her door begging to be let in. Tempie gave them
popsicles she brought from the kitchen freezer. She told them
to go outside and watchout for Daddy. If he showed up, she
said to come running in and tell her right away. Those kids
were in seventh heaven, licking them red, white, and turquoise rocket popsicles.

Tempie hustled me into the kitchen. It was a big kitchen
with new linoleum on the floors and the newest appliances.
The places I'd lived in all had Frigidaires from the 1940's and
old white gas stoves in them. I don't know why but I hated it
when Mama would decide to defrost the fridge. It unsettled
me for some weird reason. The Ridgewells, on the other
hand, had a lime green self-defrosting fridge with two doors
and an ice machine on the outside door. All their leftovers
were nicely stored in brand new Tupperware containers instead of old butter bowls or wads of aluminum foil. Tempie's
mama even sold the stuff at Tupperware parties.

Tempie got last nights roast beef and ketchup, heated up leftover mashed taters and macaroni and cheese with a little milk mixed in over the stove for me. Rusty would have called it "roast beast" if he had been there. She said her dad was going to buy a microwave for her mama for her birthday, but everyone knew microwaves cost around five hundred dollars. They really were rich. Her mama didn't even work neither. She was in her bedroom with a headache, but people said Mrs. Ridgewell was an alcoholic.

"You sure are nice to me," I said.

"You'd do the same for me," Tempie said, stirring the taters. She pushed a strand of hair over her ear. Her head was down, but she looked up at me with her eyes and smiled. My heart did a flip-flop. She was good at that. She put a blue plate in front of me at the kitchen table with a big glass of milk. I was in heaven. I stuffed a bite of roast beast in my mouth. She gave me a look that meant I had to say grace first. I bowed my head with my eyes closed even though my hands were shaking because they wanted to tear into the feast. After I thought I'd bowed my head long enough I said, AMEN. It was funny how religious Tempie was when nobody else in her family was. Her mama said it was a phase, but I didn't think so. She wasn't nothing like any other girl I knew. She watched me eat with real glee. She put her hand over her mouth as if to say she was sorry for laughing at me.

"I can't help it," I said with my mouth full already. "I'm hungry."

"I know," she said. "Honey Boy, why don't you just go out to Vaughn's?"

"You don't know why?"

"No," she said.

"Because I pulled a gun on him," I said. I slurped my milk. She pointed at my milk mustache and handed me a napkin. "He don't forget nothing. I don't know what he'll do. Probably kill me."

"He wouldn't do nothing to you, Honey Boy," she said. "Not you."

"Yep," I said. "I think I'd probably disappear forever. No one would ever hear from Nathan Kimbrough after Vaughn catches up with him."

"I guess no one knows what Vaughn might do," Tempie said. "Word is he shot Glenn Starkey in the neck for no reason."

"Did they arrest him for it?" A piece of macaroni flew out of my mouth onto the table.

"Gross," Tempie said. "No. Sheriff Merrill picked him up with a couple of deputies. They questioned him, but Vaughn denied it. Said it wasn't him that shot Starkey. There weren't any witnesses. Some people say Starkey must have done something to make Vaughn mad. Nobody just shoots someone for no reason."

"Vaughn just hates farmers," I mumbled through the food bulging my cheeks out.

"Then he must hate half the people in Kingdom County," she said.

"I wouldn't doubt it none." I dipped the roast beast into the ketchup and stuffed my face with it until my cheeks were bulging.

"Daddy says Sheriff Merrill is scared shitless of Vaughn."

"Who ain't?" I asked, not expecting an answer. "Good food."

Tempie left while I finished eating and came back with one of Mr. Ridgewell's T-shirts and some fresh socks. There wasn't nothing much she could do about my dirty pants, because her dad was going to come home pretty soon. She took a washrag with soap and washed my face and neck and dried me with a dishtowel. Tempie even kissed me on the forehead. It made me blush hard. She saw me blushing and got bashful all of a sudden.

"Daddy's coming," Jerry said, running in. He had red Kool-Aid all over his lips like he had been kissing a monkey's butt. "Better hurry, Honey Boy. Better hurry."

I felt my heart hit rock bottom. I didn't want to leave. Tempie took me by the hand to the basement. I wished I could live here, but I knew I wasn't meant for nice places like this. I went into the bathroom they had down there and saw they had Dial hand soap. I washed my hands with it. It looked nice on the soap holder like it was sitting on a little throne with its name on it. It smelled good. It sure beat the hell out of Irish Spring. "Manly yes, "my ass! Mama bought it because Irish Spring was about the cheapest soap you could get. Their Dial soap was too good for me. I smelled my hands for a minute after I dried them off on their fluffy and nice Tide-smelling towel. They had squeezably soft Charmin toilet paper too. I started rifling through the medicine cabinet and found Arrid and Secret deodorants. I can't tell you how I longed to be able to have these nice things. It made me feel sad just thinking about all the name brand things I'd never have unless I stole them. Mabye that's why Vaughn did what he did. I thought about taking some little stuff just because I could but Tempie had been so nice to me I decided against it. I knew I'd have to harden my heart against all the stuff I couldn't have so much that even the name CHARMIN made me mad at it. *Get mad at that toilet paper! If I can't have it, it can't have me!*

When I came out of the bathroom Tempie was standing there with her arms crossed.

"What took you so long?"

"I'm sorry. I cannot abide Charmin toilet paper. It irritates my ass."

"I heard something else," Tempie pulled me by the arm to the door to their backyward. "I'm kind of scared to tell you this."

"What is it?" I asked, draining my glass of milk.

"Sonny's back in town."

I had a great idea. I would build a raft and float down the Missouri river. I got the idea as you probably know from the book about Huck Finn, but the Mississippi was too far away although the Osage and Missouri were more doable. The other problem was I wasn't any good at building nothing. I had a hard time hanging a picture without banging my thumb with the hammer. I caught a ride all the way to Jeff City with these old folks, looked at the river and it scared me. It was so wide. I had been fishing in that river before, but never alone. I still couldn't swim either so it ended that dream right there. I just hitched another ride with a trucker going back to Fairmont on Highway 54. That Huck must have been a brave kid. Me, I was too much of a chicken to do more than dream about floating down a river. At least Huck had Jim. Who did I have?

I imagined trying to jump from the bridge into the river over and over again. It got stuck like a film strip in my mind. I didn't want to kill myself I just thought about trying it. Off behind the bridge was the State Capitol where all the laws got made. It looked like something straight out of Spartacus or Ben-Hur. It made me think of a church or Mount Olympus, where the gods lived, where they were apt to throw a lightning bolt at poor people. Aunt Oleta always liked to tell how her daddy, that is my great granddad, helped rebuild the capital after the fire a long time ago. It made me feel proud and even patriotic, although I knew it wasn't cool to be patriotic according to Sonny.

The Prodigal

I decided to go out to Vaughn's when I heard Sonny was back in town. I knew Vaughn probably wouldn't care so much about me now that he had some competition for Mama. Vaughn was standing straddle-legged over his outdoor barbecue pit off to the side and out back of the house which was mostly just bricks and mortar clay. I suppose he was going to fix it up so he could barbecue pork steaks. The blue vein in his forehead stood out as soon as he saw me walking up the gravel road. Mama's car was in the drive so I breathed a sigh of relief.

"Look at what the cat dragged in." Vaughn held up a can that made a pop when he squeezed out the lighter fluid onto the charcoal. His other hand gripped a spatula like it was a crown and he was the king of the cookout. "You better go in and tell Lorene you're back, because she's been worried sick about you. She's been laying up in bed and won't even go to work. Hope you're proud of yourself."

"All right" I gave him the bird when he turned his back.

"Then come back out here," he said. "Maybe you can give me a hand with this pit. You and me's got some unfinished business to talk over."

Before I could go inside Buddy came out stiff with his tail in the air kind of growly in the back of his throat. I squatted down on my haunches and whistled to him and he came right up and nuzzled deep in my hands. He whined and took me by surprise, licking my nose before I could pull my face back. Dogs always got to get right in your face like that, if they like you.

When I went inside, the house looked a mess. Arlene normally kept the place spic and span, but not only was it dirty and cluttered furniture was overturned and broken. Arlene was in the kitchen standing at the sink smoking. Her hair was greasy, she wore no makeup, but I couldn't tell that until I got up close to her because the heavy bottle green drapes was pulled shut all over the house. Her lips was pulled tight across her face. She did not smile at me. There were dirty dishes for days stacked in the sink, on the counter, and on the Formica table.

"If you're looking for your mama," Arlene said. "She's in my bed. Sleeping in my bed."

"Okay," I said.

"You two don't belong here. You can go out and tell him I said that too, because I don't care. Take your mama and get out. Don't let him stop you." I felt bad for how everything was. I could understand why she'd be upset and try to take it out on us, but that didn't mean I liked it.

"I'll try to get her to leave with me," I said. "But I don't know if she will, or if Vaughn will let us."

"Oh," Arlene said, going at her nails now with an emery board, "I just bet she won't want to leave. Why would she? She's got my man all to herself. She's got me and Sugarbaby waiting on her majesty hand and foot. This is my house I hate to tell you."

"Okay," I said. Looking at her out of the corner of my eye because I was afraid to look at her head on. I wasn't afraid of her. She had always been nice to me. This was the kind of situation that just wasn't right, but I doubted there was anything to be done about it.

Mama was lying on a full-sized bed on a stained mattress. There was a little jag of sunlight peeking in between the curtains and falling across her legs. Her hair was messed up like she hadn't combed it in days. She had auburn baby-fine hair that got tangled easily unless she took good care of it every day. On Sunday afternoons she sometimes used to have me brush her hair.

She looked real skinny laying there. The stained chenille bedspread was bunched up underneath her. I sat down on the bed next to her and let my fingers play with the fringe. There was stale cigarette smoke with a sickening mixture of woman and man sex. I had smelled it before. I couldn't breathe so well because the smoke sucked all the good air out of the house. My asthma was kicking in on me.

At first I thought she might be dead she lay there so still. But she must have sensed something was different because she kind of turned over and then sat up like a jack-in-the-box. Just as quickly though, she threw herself down on the mattress and the springs squeaked. I could tell she'd been crying. She burrowed her face into the pillow.

"Don't look at me," Mama said.

"Why not?"

"I just don't want you looking at me," she said.

"Ain't you glad I'm back?"

"Yes," she said.

I moved to the very edge of the mattress. The silver horn-rimmed glasses of hers was sitting there on the bedside table, not that she ever wore them anyway. They was way out of style too. Viceroy cigarette butts were overflowing in a red glass ashtray. Slims was Arlene's brand. The ashtray was imprinted with words in white: *Stolen from the Magnolia Inn.*

"Go away." her words were muffled in the pillow.

"Mama," I said. I felt a big lump come up in my throat like my Adam's apple would burst. I didn't say nothing I just waited for her to turn over or say something else. I don't know how long I sat there waiting, but finally I took her by her narrow shoulders and turned her over. Her face was bruised. It hurt me so to see her that way, but what could I do? Mama looked at me with a forlorn expression and I learned what every kid learns sometime in their lives, that their mama ain't the strongest person in the world. I didn't want to know it, but there it was looking me in the face.

"I told you not to look at me," she said. "Go get me a beer."

When I went back in the kitchen Arlene was gone. Sugarbaby was standing there in front of the fridge with the door open drinking some red sweetwater straight out of the pitcher. She clutched it in her two little hands as if she thought I might take it from her. As I walked toward her, she let the pitcher slip out of her hands and the glass shattered, the glass shards and Kool-Aid went everywhere.

"Uh oh," she said and started bawling. Quiet at first like little kids do, and then she was wailing like her dog had died. I tried to calm her down but she just wailed and hollered as I got a dirty dish towel out of the sink and soaked up the mess. I tried to be real careful about not getting any little pieces of glasses in my hand. Of course, I managed to cut my finger and I looked at the little cut. I squeezed my fingertip and watched the blood pop out. I sucked it for a second. Washed my hands. Found a Band-Aid for my finger. Sugarbaby's eyes looked like she had the pink eye or the flu. To make her happy I put a Band-Aid on her elbow and pretended she had a hurt and kissed it for her.

"Where'd Arlene go?"

"Mama went fishing," she hiccupped.

I grabbed a PBR out of the fridge and took it into Mama. I found some leftover macaroni and cheese and beanie weenies and put it in a bowl for her even though it was cold.

She was laying with her back against the pillows. She had her glasses on and was smoking. There was a black velvet picture of Elvis on the wall. She turned on the radio, there was a fella singing out of his nose about a town called Oxford.

"Come here," she said, patting the mattress. I sat down next to her. "Oh, Honey, I'm so happy you're back. I was real worried about you out there somewhere all alone. I thought you had run away from me forever."

"I wasn't running from you," I told her.

"I know," she said. "I didn't want you to see me this way. I don't know what to do. Just don't make him angry. He isn't mad about the gun thing. He was proud of you. The way you stood up to him is something he respected. He's just tetchy. He don't mean nothing by it. Vaughn's luck has about run out I think, but he won't let me leave. He almost killed Glenn Starkey. People are out for blood now, but they're so scared of him they don't know which way is up. I was there, Honey, when he shot Glenn. I saw the blood."

"Mama," I said.

"He won't let me alone either, Honey," she said again in a little girl's voice. It scared me to hear that voice coming out of her. I thought she would make me feel better, but I could see she needed me to be the strong one now.

"Mama," I said. "I'm going to get some help. Guess who's back in town? Guess? Sonny."

"Aw baby," Mama said. "One's just as bad as the other. I don't want to fight no more. I can't take another beating. I'll kill myself before I let him beat me again. A person can only get beat so much before they begin to hate themselves. How can this be happening?"

"You didn't do what they said you did, did you? Did you really hold a gun on those folks?"

"Oh, honey," she said. "Don't make me talk about it. Please, don't make me."

"Okay," I said. "But you did it, didn't you?"

She nodded.

"Well," I said. "Try not to worry about it. He made you do it. You didn't want to, he made you. Just remember that."

"There's something else," Mama said. "Something I don't want to say. It scares me to tell you, because it's true. But when I had that gun on Marshal Clevenger I could see in his eye that he was scared—and I liked it. Lord help me, but I wanted to shoot him. Not because Vaughn said, but more for the reason that it would have pleased me to do it. Do you understand?"

"I think so" I grabbed on to her hand.

"No," Mama said. "You don't. I don't know how to say it so I'm just going to come out with it. Years ago I worked for Vaughn. Stealing things. I was just a girl. He took me with him when he knocked off some gas stations and liquor stores. Nothing too big. Then, I started helping. I was a natural. It was the first thing I was good at besides drinking. But Vaughn thought he owned me. Nobody owns me. I'll kill myself first. I think that's what he's waiting for."

I was struck dumb. My heart raced. This woman could not be my mama. The woman who carried me and had me and raised me for the better part of my life.

"I'm no good as a mother," she said. "I guess you noticed already. But I tried Honey Boy, my Honey Boy. I tried for you. For both of us. You need to make sure you get away from him--away from Vaughn. He's the devil, no, worse than. If I leave he'll kill me this time. He already said it. But you're my hope. You get away. You go directly to Aunt Oleta. She'll raise you up right. You hear me? Tell me you hear me."

"I hear you," I said.

"Shut up that blubbering!" Vaughn beat the wall to the bedroom from outside. "I ought to take you across town and have you committed at the state funny farm. You're plumb nuts, woman."

Mama made motions with her hands that I should go into the living room and let her rest. She put a finger to her lips. It broke my heart to see her in that state. Her mascara was all over her face and she was shaking.

I did what she said. I went out and sat in front of the television waiting for Vaughn to come in for the longest time, but he never did. I had to move all the shotguns and rifles leaned up against the sofa just so I could sit down. Sugarbaby was asleep on the floor sucking her thumb with Mrs. Beasley even though she was too old for either one. Vaughn just stayed outside with his cooler of beer, smoking and looking at that big crater that he intended to be a catfish pond rubbing a rifle thoughtfully with an Outers kit.

There was a bulldozer parked right in the middle of the hole in the orange mud of clay. All of mid Missouri seem to be full of clay that stuck poor people in the ground where they stood so there was no way they could get ahead in life. It was like quicksand. It started at your feet just because you were born there; then it sucked you down to your knees when you were a teenager; and finally you had a wife and kids and it was way past your waist, your face was just barely sticking out so you could draw your last breath. Vaughn was born under the clay like a prehistoric creature that ain't supposed to exist anymore, just waiting to pull Mama and me down under the surface with him. I tried to imagine Mama holding a gun on someone, but the image just wouldn't stick in my mind.

I found my clothes folded up in a cardboard banana box. I grabbed a fresh set of clothes, went to the bathroom to take a long bath. The tub was an old-fashioned claw foot. The claws even had what looked like porcelain toenails. I tried to figure what kind of animal the claws reminded me of but I finally gave up and slid into the water after I had it nearly full. The water felt good and warm, even the soap, but it was hard to relax because I kept thinking Vaughn would barge in or start banging on the door any minute. It felt good to put on clearn clothes even if they was somewhat wrinkled.

There was the sound of a bird's wings behind me in Mama's bedroom. I looked up and saw a queer looking bird flapping around the room. I picked up one of Vaughn's flannel shirts and crept towards it, but as I crept closer I realized with a sick horror that it was a bat. I'd always heard if you saw a bat in the middle of the day it was an evil omen. It usually meant the bat was sick with rabies too. Fluttering around, it looked big, but after I caught it on about the fifth or sixth try, and Mama screaming, I saw it was a tiny little thing really. Even the fangs hanging out of its mouth were pitiful. Up in the corner of the bathroom, near the bedroom, was a big hole in the ceiling. There was also a stain up there from the rain. Anything could get in here if it wanted to, I couldn't believe Vaughn was so far gone that he'd let the place fall to such a sorry state of affairs. I took the bat outside and threw in the air and off it went.

I sat there with Mama for awhile until she fell asleep. I took off her sunglasses still pushed back on her head and put my hand on her cheek. When we'd left California, I'd thought she was safe from bad treatment, but she had come back to another Sonny. Another woman beater.

Right then, I knew I'd have to do something to try and save her myself. Sheriff Merrill was useless. Even the highway patrol, Stafford, wouldn't do nothing. So I decided to find Sonny, and I'd get him after Vaughn somehow. Even though they was brothers, they both liked Mama, and I knew that would get him mad. Why would he come back, except for Mama anyway? They was bound to lock horns sooner or later.

The screen door smacked shut behind me as I lit out for town through the fields. I could hear Vaughn hollering, but I think he was calling for Buddy not to follow me. There was a hot-wired barbed-wire fence in front of me that I almost ran through, but I skipped down the length of the fence and cut over toward Danny Vaughn's pasture.

Sorry Daddy

I tore through the honeysuckle. A trail led across the dirt road and up to another barbed-wire fence. I pushed the third wire down with my hands and squeezed through. There were fresh piles of cow dung everywhere I looked. The Vaughns called them piles "landmines." A cowpath, straight as a plumbline, led up and then down over some hills, past some conifers and ironweed. I hustled down the dogtrot, because an old Stallion called Stargazer lived in this pasture and he was known to get after any kid's ass. The Vaughn boys said they used to double dare each other to cross the field alone "You ain't got hair one on your cods if you don't . . ." one or the other of them would say.

In the shaded woods was a creek with cool water gurgling 4 feet deep. Most creeks that summer didn't have nothing but dry bones and memories of fish, but Stinson Creek was fed by Blackmore Lake so it always had some water in it. While I was sitting there on a rock scraping cockleburs off my socks and shoelaces, a water moccasin swam across the widest part of the creek. I skipped a couple of pebbles in the general direction of the snake, but without really aiming at it.

Up in the pasture was an old wagon, the kind horses used to pull before trucks or when vehicles were considered a mere convenience, and I stopped to look at it for a second. I had to bend at the waist to walk up from the creek. There was an abused Corvair sitting there rusting not too far away. I looked back behind me and I could see Stargazer and some of the other horses cropping the grass short on the other side of Hungry Mother. The stallion stamped one of his hooves at me and I could just makeout his high-pitched neigh to show that he was mad at me, but that was about it.

There was a black spot in the field where Rusty had been playing with matches and burned down the barn. It was one of them big red variety of barns that had sat on the hill since eighteen-something or other. I bet he caught hell for that. Them boys would tell you stuff like Rusty burnt down the barn playing with cigarettes and matches, but then not tell you the good stuff. Like did his daddy, Danny Vaughn, beat his ass with a belt or a shoe or did he just take his fists to him?

Rusty said he didn't like having the reputation of being a barn burner, but since it was his own barn then folks would know it was accidental. But I for one thought Rusty burnt it down to be contrary. He seemed like the kind of kid to take an ass-whipping just to get everyone to pay attention to him for a minute. When his brothers would get on his case, whether he was in the wrong or not, Rusty would say, "I don't give a damn," and his voice would get real high-pitched like a girl's. He'd get a snarl on his face too and look around defiantly like he was going to take every one one of us on. I had a bad feeling he would end up in jail someday.

I began to think Punkin might drive me into town if he was at the house, but I had to cross the woods, where no one would ever go, because the Vaughns was always warning kids that them woods is where coal mining used to go on and there were abandoned shafts under the land like anthills. It seemed like a lie to me. I don't know why. I got the feeling there might be other reasons they didn't want us mucking around back there. Like maybe they had killed someone and buried him back there, but I didn't know for sure. Sometimes we went back in them woods anyway, but no one ever fell through. The old folks said we might could fall through the earth and we'd be down there in an old shaft and no one would ever find us again.

"You boys are just into trouble all the time," Danny Vaughn said. He was taking a pocket knife to a tree branch that was about an inch or more in diameter. "Hellatious trouble is what you're going to face up to when I hear about something you did. You understand? Where's Punkin?"

"I don't know," Rusty whined.

"He's working on that piece of shit of his," TC said.

"Tell him to get his ass up to the house," Danny Vaughn said.

"He won't come because I tell him," TC said. "He's out there bush-hogging."

"Tell him, I said," Danny Vaughn said. "Daddy said come! That's all he needs know. Tell him not to make me come down there to beat his ass. If I have to go catch him, I'm really going to be pissed off then."

"I'll tell him," Rusty said, trying not to laugh. Then he walked down to an old barn they used as a garage. Rusty was singing a tune that went, "Punkins getting his ass beat, Punkins getting his ass beat." Then he started whistling the theme to *The Andy Griffith Show*.

Danny Vaughn muttered to himself the whole while Rusty was gone. Most of it didn't make much sense. TC stood there with his hands in his front pockets with his head down. TC was wearing a straw cowboy hat and he was trying to keep a straight face while his daddy was on his tirade. Danny was talking something about being stationed overseas when he was a young man, and be damned if he was going to start taking lip from his own whelps. He talked about Nixon and Lyndon Johnson and followed all that with a steady stream of cursing. Rusty was gone for about twenty minutes and I thought maybe they run off together to avoid their daddy's madness. Then directly I saw them walking side-by-side up to the gate. Rusty climbed over the paintless gate near the latch and Punkin followed, but it was clear he didn't want to come in. He looked like he'd rather bush-hog the whole county than face his daddy.

"Did you want something, Daddy?" Punkin asked.

"What?" Danny said from the porch. He spit brown juice so it landed expertly near Punkins shoe.

"Did you want something from me?" Punkin asked. "Rusty was talking about you wanted something. He said you was going to beat my ass over something."

"That's right," Danny said. "Did I tell you not to go into town yesterday?"

"Yeah," Punkin said. "But I had to go into town to get a ball for the truck to haul that old Corvair out of the east pasture like you said."

"I don't give a good goddamn what I said," Danny said. "When I tell you not to do something, you don't do it. When I say jump, you ask how high. You got me, chief?"

"Daddy," Punkin said, his hands on his hips. One of his legs was commencing to shake. His hands slid off his hips and he was beginning to look at the switch in Danny's hands and his right leg was shaking just below the knee. "You told me to move that goddamn Corvair and that's what I was trying to do. You can't fault me for that."

"You're going to get your ass whipped," Rusty said.

"Fuck you, motherfucker," Punkin said, he turned and shoved against Rusty's chest hard so that he fell on the gravel. "You hear me, fuck you!"

"Daddy," Rusty moaned. Making out to be hurt worse than he was.

"Don't take it out on him," Danny said. "A man's got to pay for his own mistakes."

"This is bullshit," Punkin muttered. "TC tell him. Tell him."

"The old man ain't going to listen to me," TC said. "He's got a mind of his own."

"Such as it is," Punkin said.

"What the hell did you say?" Danny hollered. "You're disrespecting me to my face now."

"I'm saying," Punkin began. "I'm getting too old for you to whip. All you do is lay around here drinking and farting and expecting us to do all the work."

"I was going to beat your ass before," Danny said. "But now I am going to tear you a new asshole."

"You got to be shitting me," Punkin said.

"I shit you not," Danny said.

"I'd have to come over and there and bend over," Punkin said. "Or you'd fall over with a heart attack trying to catch me."

"Beat his ass, Daddy," Rusty said.

Danny came off the dilapidated porch unsteadily because of all the Pabst beer he'd drunk with most of the bark off the willow switch he had in hand. The switch was about four or five feet in length and Danny swooshed it back and forth a couple of times, an ornery whipping sound like an angry humming bird flying by your ear, to give Punkin something to think about. The problem was Punkin didn't have anywhere to run to so he just stayed there, but his feet were trying to tell him to run. He looked like he was doing an Irish jig from the waist down. To make matters worse all he was wearing was cutoff blue jean shorts. The old man caught up to him and began to chop at his hairy white legs with his switch. Punkin would kind of leap in the air like he was doing the high jump but the switch was catching the backs of his legs. Big bloody welts were bubbling to the surface of Punkins legs and all the while Rusty was hollering for the old man to beat him good.

Punkin was shouting like he was at Redeemer Church, but instead of saying *Hallelujah* he was saying *Son-of-a-bitch*! The whole time the old man was giving him a lecture on the history of the United States since World War II so it didn't make much sense why Punkin was getting the switch. But I guess it only had to make sense to one person, and that was the man with the switch. So I knew right then Punkin wouldn't give me a ride even if he could. He was likely to beat the shit out of me just for asking. Besides, how much time does someone need to recover from an all-out, knock-down, drag-out, ass-whipping like that?

Punkins face went beet-red with anger and he drew back and punched his daddy in the chin and dropped him. Knocked him plumb out. We all just stood there stunned, but no one more than Punkin and we did the only thing we could which was to pick the old man up and walk him up to the porch to sit on the porch swing. The swing moved and we dropped his narrow ass on the floorboards and the swing came back and clocked him in the back of the skull. We managed to wrestle him on to the swing. It was the first time I noticed how thin and frail he actually was. Danny was a tall man, but TC. said anymore he probably only weighed a hundred and thirty-five pounds. His unkempt salt and pepper beard gave him the appearance of someone much larger. The smell of beer was strong coming off the old man.

"Sorry Daddy," Punkin said when Danny came around.

"That's fine boy," Danny put his hand on the back of Punkins neck and pulled him down so their heads were touching. "You a good fine boy. You laid your old Daddy out now and that's the way things get to be eventually. You lucky I'm drunk or it would have been another story so don't go thinking you can do that all the time."

"I won't Daddy." Punkin had tears coursing down the dirty channels of his face.

The old man looked like he might start crying and carrying on too. He was real mellow now. Not a normal thing for him. He prided himself on being a man. All of the whoppers he told us about his coming up days were always about the fights he'd been in. He never went looking for it like his younger brother Elston but when trouble came to him he relished the idea of a man who fought with his hands. So much so that he often had the boys fight each other too. They liked it sometimes but it was predictable in that the older boy always got the best of the younger. Danny called that hard knocks.

"Hard knocks time." the old man wiped his wet eyes on the tail of the Dickey's shirt he was wearing.

"Not now, Daddy," Punkin said.

"Not yours," Danny said. "You already took care of business. I don't' want you boys acting like pussies. I call out Rusty and . . . Honey Boy!"

"What?" I thought the fighting was what they all liked to do. I never thought I'd be called into it.

"Unless you're a candy ass," Danny said.

"Ah Daddy," Rusty said.

"You all don't want the word getting out how you're a couple of candy ass-Mama's boys now do you?" Danny laughed. He was embarrassed about Punkin knocking him down and now we had to pay for it.

"I'm too much bigger than Honey Boy," Rusty said. "I might hurt him."

"Look how s-s-s-skinny he is," T.C. said.

"That's all the more reason he has to prove himself," Danny said. There was a finality to it.

"Honey Boy was raised by his Mama and his Aunt Oleta," Rusty said. "He ain't used to fighting. I might make him cry."

I didn't say nothing, but now Rusty was starting to make me mad.

"I might scar his face, Daddy," Rusty said. "He's about as pretty as any girl I ever seen at the Junior high." He gave me a big teasing smile and, when Danny wasn't looking, flipped me off.

"Let's go," I stood up.

"You heard the man," Danny said. "Let's get after it!"

We both took off our shirts. We was both about as skinny as could be. Much to his surprise I went at Rusty and threw a wild roundhouse left that missed and I was off balance. Rusty shoved me down hard on my ass. I tried to stand back up but the grass smeared away from my shoes and I fell down again. He looked at his Daddy and started dancing around like he was Sugar Ray Leonard with his fists up in the air. He was skinny as one of them black boys in Africa who ate nothing but rice with flies crawling on his faces but he had big bones he'd grow into one day. His fists alone were twice the size of mine.

I got up off the ground slowly, determined to connect my fist with his big shit eating grin. Rusty danced in and shoved his face in front of mine and darted away just as quickly. He didn't think I could do anything to hurt him so he wasn't too worried about me. I threw a couple of soft jabs in his direction and he batted my fists away easily. I could see he fought with his older brothers all the time and I wasn't nothing. The more I missed the madder I got. He finally danced in and slapped me across the face with an open hand. The biggest insult yet.

"Oh ho!" Rusty said. "I bitched slapped you. Now how you like that!"

"Sounded worse than it was," I said. "It didn't even hurt." My nose was bleeding. He came back at me with jabs and a couple of wild hooks that raked across my cheeks. I went down on one knee. I thought I was going to black out. I shook my head a little.

"You want to stop?" Rusty held out his hand to shake.

"Naw," I spat blood out of my mouth. Even my teeth were bleeding. "I'm going to stomp a mudhole in your ass and walk it dry."

"Listen to that," Danny said.

"Big talk," Rusty said.

"A bad ass," Punkin said.

"If he wants an ass whipping. . ." Rusty motioned to me to come at him like a boxer.

I remembered some stuff Sonny showed me. It was mostly about suckering people into thinking you were weaker than you were and then really giving it to them. I stopped crying then. I let my arms down closer to my sides. I started stumbling around a little to make him think I was completely out of it since I pretty much was. Rusty didn't really want to hit me no more. He stepped in and threw a half-hearted jab and just as he did I caught his arm at the shoulder with my left hand and pulled him toward me and gave him a forearm in the throat with my right. I crossed my right leg behind him and pushed him down. He went down hard and the back of his head bounced on the ground. It was my chance now so I leaped down to straddle his chest, pinning his arms, and bludgeoned him in the face with wild right and left crosses, him begging me to stop. Everything was blurry and a white hot anger had taken over like I was possessed by some demon spirit. I even reached over and grabbed a big rock I fully intended to cave his head in with but Punkin stepped in and took it away from me and gave me a shove so I went flying off his brother.

Everyone was silent for a minute. They were all looking at me like I was crazy. Until Danny started laughing his ass off. The other boys joined in too except for Rusty. Rusty finally got over it and he came over and held out a hand and pulled me to my feet like they did in their fights. I could see I'd earned his grudging respect.

"I guess Honey Boy is a true blood Vaughn after all," Danny said. "I think he was about to put the hurt on you."

"I'd've been okay," Rusty said.

"He ain't but a little thing," Punkin said. "And look what he about did to you. I think you'd be better off fighting a pole cat."

"He's tough enough," Rusty said. "I'll give him that."

"I'm sorry, Rusty," I said. I felt real bad about it. The anger had just taken over for a minute.

"Don't be sorry," Danny said. "That's what I want you boys to learn. You take care of business and you find a way to win. This is what me and your uncles used to do for fun when we were coming up. Course Daddy made us do it too, but we're better men for it now. Gave us character. Besides that, it was good training for the Army. We didn't take no shit from no one we didn't have to."

"I feel bad about it," I said.

"Who taught you that move?" Rusty asked. "Can you show it to me?"

"It just came to me is all."

"Well, it works," Danny said. "Yeah, you got a temper on you, don't you? Just like Sonny and Elston. When you fight it's for real, ain't it?"

"I guess so."

"I thought you was a pussy," Rusty said. "Sorry. We still friends? You ain't going to go beserk on me again?"

"Naw," I said. "You're safe for now."

Wish I Was in Heaven Sitting Down

I waited for Rusty to get by himself which took awhile because he was chopping wood. His daddy kept calling him a twerp. Rusty took off his shirt and it was amazing to see how fast his body was changing between chopping woods, lifting weights, and starting to grow hair on his chest. Rusty told me he was born without two ribs on that side, but I didn't believe him until I seen that. When the boys got to playing rough with him he would tell them to be careful of his ribs. He could still chop his fair share of wood and it wasn't long before he was putting them together into cords.

Danny drank himself to sleep on a brown recliner on the porch while Dot was working in the kitchen. Rusty snuck off behind the outhouse to have a smoke. I didn't want to spook him so I made a big deal about scuffling my feet and whistling as I walked through the weeds.

"Hey Rusty," I said.

"Where the hell did you go anyway?" Rusty said. He walked up and punched me in the shoulder. On his wrists he wore studded leather wrist bands. "We thought maybe you drowned in Blackmore or got lost down in Wildwoods."

"Neither one."

"Where you been?"

"I guess you heard about me," I said. I stood there with my hands on my hips and my legs kind of cocked out. "I pulled a gun on Vaughn, and so I had to hide out."

"I heard," Rusty said. "I couldn't believe it. I told Punkin and them that I didn't know the little shit had it in him. Well, I guess you do."

"Yeah, I sure am dumb."

"Everyone will think you're a badass now," Rusty said. "Check this out." He pulled out a leather case and inside were metal throwing stars. "You ever see anything like this? These are throwing stars like the ninjas use." He took one out and threw it at the outhouse, but it bounced off and into the grass. "Shit."

"You couldn't hit the broad side of an outhouse," I said.

"Aw, man," Rusty looked terror-stricken. "I hope I didn't lose it. Help me look for it."

After we found the throwing star he pulled out a package of rolling papers and a little sandwich bag and started making a joint. He rolled it up like he'd been born to it, licked it, and twizzled the ends. "Hit that one time."

"I don't know," I said. "I heard Sonny's in town and I got to find him."

"Is he?" Rusty said, like he already knew. I noticed he was wearing brand new painter's pants, a striped shirt, and a leather belt with little Indian beads in a cool Southwestern design on them. I'd never seen him wear new clothes before and thought maybe Sonny had brought them for him from California. It sure made me jealous. "Him and Uncle Elston will run into each other soon enough. Why you looking for Uncle Sonny?"

"Well," I said. "You know my mama's there, right? Arlene don't like it much. Vaughn won't let her leave. I figured Sonny could talk to Vaughn about it."

"When them two meet," Rusty began, "it's going to be all she wrote for somebody. I'd put my money on Uncle Elston. Ain't nobody as tough as him. He ain't scared of nothing neither."

"You think Sonny's a chicken or something?"

"No," Rusty said. He lit the tip of the joint and inhaled deeply and handed it over to me. "There ain't no cowards in the Vaughn family. You got to go into town to find the chickens working at the savings and loan or the chamber of commerce. No. The Vaughn men will come after you with both barrels. You ought to know."

"I know it," I said.

Rusty's eyes were already puffy and red from weed. His hair was strawberry blond and the breeze combed it so the ends stood up like he just saw something scary. I took a big drag and coughed and he tried to shush me but I couldn't seem to stop. He passed the joint to me again and I took another hit even though I was still coughing.

"Hell, we oughn't to be worrying over all this shit," Rusty said. "I know where Punkin and TC stash their beer on the weekends. What say we go find it and get falling down drunk."

"All right," I said. "It'll be good to hang out with someone I know for a change. I must have been out in the woods for near two weeks. Wished you'd been out there for company."

"Bullshit," Rusty said.

Rusty checked to see if his daddy was still asleep on the porch and then he took me out to the barn the Vaughns used to dry their tobacco crop years ago. Now there was just a rusting Nash Rambler and an ancient steam-powered thresher in there. In a meat freezer was some warm Stag beer. We popped open a couple of cans and Rusty smashed his into mine.

"See," Rusty began. "We done right getting high first. If you get drunk first and then get high the two effects kind of cancel each other out. So it's best to get high first and then start drinking." Rusty was a regular philosopher when it came to drinking and getting high, but I think he learned most of it from TC. But I guess I was ready to do something crazy because I was so upset about Mama.

We was getting real drunk. Everything Rusty said seemed like the funniest thing I ever heard. He showed me his mare, Rosa Lee, and her newborn paint horse which he hadn't named yet. The foal had disturbing eyes as blue as the sky and it looked like he had mascara on too. I guess I got stuck staring at the foal so Rosa Lee came over and whinnied at me and bucked in front of me. Her hooves flew just a few feet away from my head.

"I don't want to eat your baby," I said.

"She's a good mother is all."

"No doubt," I said, but I couldn't help feeling a little offended.

We smoked some more of Rusty's wacky-tobacky. Rusty and me started running through the fields until we got a stitch in our sides, falling down, trying to climb trees. Mostly we laughed. I told him I saw his daddy whip Punkin's ass with the green switch and his face got very serious for a second, and then we both busted up laughing again. We drank a twelve pack pretty quick and then I was cussing that he didn't have no more beer. Then Rusty got pissed off at me and the next thing I knew we was rolling around in the dirt rabbit punching each other. He monkey-flipped me. I dropped kicked him but not too hard. Just playing around. I went into what I called my "slow motion Bruce Lee High Karate" until he put me in a headlock. I accidentally punched him in the eye. It got swolled up. He made two big roundhouse swings that I stepped back away from as he lost his balance sitting down hard on the seat of his pants. I watched him while he fought off genuine tears. It was as much hurt pride as anything. I told him I was sorry. Rusty said he was afraid he might accidentally hurt me, because he had wires in his hands. He started in on some crazy story about how the doctors put wires in his hands to make him stronger. He held them in front of his face and flexed his fingers into claws like even he was amazed by the latent power there. We raged at each other like that until we got arm-weary and started laughing again.

"You ever see that space movie?" Rusty asked. "The one where the computer takes over?"

"Yeah," I said. "It was pretty good. It was kind of long."

"In the year 2001, I'll be about 35 years old," Rusty said. "When I get that old you won't find me in no Kingdom

County. I'll be living in Hollywood I bet or down at the beach in Florida. I don't know if I'll be an actor or a race car driver or what by then. I might become a singer and have my own rock band."

"I just hope I'm still alive by then. I mean, the way things have been going. Just this summer Jesus could have called me home several times over. Vaughn might have killed me for one."

"He might yet."

"A bear could have got me for another," I said.

"There ain't any bears around here no more," Rusty said. "Daddy said he saw one in the woods around here when he was a boy, but there ain't supposed to have been no bears around in a long time." We walked out past the old summer kitchen where there was a pickup camper shell and some PVC pipe stacked against it. We kept an eye out for random piles of cow flop. I could see a dog through one of the windows of the camper snoozing away like it was his bedroom. Looked like it might be part lab and part shepherd—the best kind of dogs.

"There's still coyotes though."

"Yep," Rusty said. "There's still coyotes. They know how to live around people. They're smart. Sometimes Daddy and the boys and me get our rifles and we go shoot all the coyotes we can find. Daddy says they ain't as thick as they once was.

"There's pictures of him and some of the old folks with over a hundred rabbits tied up on lines near the outback kitchen."

"You like your daddy?" I asked.

"What?" Rusty said. "I guess so. I never thought about it like that. He's all right. He ain't perfect."

"What do you think it be like if you never knew him?"

"I don't know," Rusty said. He knew what I was thinking about but we were starting to straighten out a little so he was too polite or tired to ask me anything. Rusty showed me a couple of his prized arrowheads. I couldn't help thinking about that first time he punched me in the gut. We were best friends now. He suggested we should become blood brothers and he took out his pocket knife and sliced at his thumb and squeezed it so a little bead of cherry bubbled up. I wasn't sure I wanted to deliberately cut myself, but I did it so he wouldn't think I was a coward. The first couple of times I tried to cut my thumb nothing much happened. Finally, I cut it real deep and blood was running down my arm. We pressed our thumbs together.

"We're blood brothers now." Rusty looked about as serious as he was ever capable of looking other than when he was pissed off at one of his brothers.

"All right," I said. "Blood brothers. The bloodiest."

Rusty looked at all the blood running down my arm and whistled. He handed me a red handkerchief from his back pocket like Roy would do. "You could fuck up a wet dream," he said. I wrapped the handkerchief around my thumb and squeezed it tight like Rusty said to do.

"Check this shit out!" Rusty rolled up his shirt and showed me his homemade tattoo that looked like Vaughns. "It said the name VAUGHN and had a lightning bolt."

"Cool," I said. "It looks a bit rough, but it's cool."

"It ain't supposed to be professional. It's supposed to be tough."

"Oh," I said. "You are good at it."

"You want one? I could give you one?"

"Naw," I said. "That's all right."

"You probably ain't tough enough anyway."

"You think?" I said. "Well, you got the stuff do it?"

"Up at the house."

"Bet," I said.

He ran back up to the house. I threw stones into the pond while he was gone. After awhile I started to think I needed to go to Aunt Oleta or the cops he was gone so long. I couldn't live like this much longer. I'd just about decided to go back home when Rusty showed up with his backpack. He brought us a block of cheese and saltines to eat. When we finished eating he pulled out a couple of beers. Those beers tasted real good too although they were a little warm but like they came straight from pure mountain water like the commercials said just the same. Next, he pulled out a pen with green ink and his pocket knife. He looked at me like he wanted to know if I could handle it.

"What do you want on your shoulder?" he asked. "You want your name or something?"

"How about a cross?" I said.

"That could be cool," he said. He narrowed his eyes and rocked back and forth like he was imagining the kind of cross he wanted to do.

He made me take my shirt off and then went to work cutting on my shoulder. It bled some but he took back the bandana I'd wrapped my thumb in and dabbed at the blood on my shoulder so he could see what he was doing. When he had it carved out like he wanted he went to work on the green ink pen. He took off the top and started sucking out the ink and blowed it on my arm. He smeared it all over where he'd carved in the cross and the words JESUS WEPT. He rubbed the ink down into my skin.

"I might become a real tattoo artist when I get older," he said. "How you like that? JESUS WEPT?"

"Tough man," I said. "You do have a talent for it. I would have rather had SINNER."

"Thanks bro," he said. "Well, this here is funny. It's serious and funny."

"You know," I said as we looked out over the catfish pond. "I don't even know how to swim."

"You know how Daddy taught me how to swim?"

"Nope."

"Took me out in a fishing boat on the Missouri river and threw me in." He smacked his hands together at an angle. His eyes laughing as he lip-farted.

"That's what everybody says."

"What do you mean?" he asked.

"Everyone says they're daddy just up and throwed them in," I said.

"Well," Rusty said, wiping off his knife in the Johnson grass. "It's the best way to learn. Sink or swim."

"Sounds like BS to me," I said. I knew I shouldn't be cussing, but it came natural to me when I was around my cousins. I could remember Aunt Oleta saying that cussing was the same as spitting in the face of Jesus considering everything he done for mankind.

"You know what you need?" Rusty asked. "You need to get some poontang."

He was always talking real frank like that. He had to make everything sound dirty, but I think it was because he was really afraid of everything. He was forever talking about sperm, hard-ons, big titties, and that type of thing. I had this feeling that one day they would put him in the funny farm even though I loved him like a brother. Then, I knew he considered me a real friend because he took off one of the leather wrist bands and gave it to me.

"This is cool" I snapped on the wristband.

My head was sure beginning to hurt now. My stomach felt like it was going to come up so I went over by the cattails near the pond and puked. I felt better. We crawled under a weeping willow tree where it was nice and shady. Despite all the mosquitoes and gnats humming around I must have passed out in just a few minutes.

Later, I halfway woke up and felt myself being carried by strong arms across the field. I pretended to be asleep because I didn't want to have to walk. I pretended it was Jesus for a minute taking me up to heaven. Then, I made up that it was my daddy. It turned out to be the last time I was ever carried when someone thought I was asleep.

The Parliament Hotel

When I awoke I found myself in a strange room. I pushed myself up on my hands. My head hurt and my stomach was doing flip-flops so I lay back down on the bed. I had all my clothes on and I was lying on a crazy floral bedspread. The bedspread's pattern was so busy it made my head spin. I had the feeling someone was in the room with me which was giving me the creeps so I got up and went to the window and pulled open the blinds. I was looking down on Fairmont courthouse so I knew I was in the Parliament Hotel. It used to be a fancy place once, but now only winos, bums, and people on welfare lived there.

"Hey Kid," Sonny said, as he kicked the door open. He was carrying a brown paper bag from Cooper's grocery store. He pulled out a plastic container with a dozen doughnuts, a quart of milk, and a bottle of Co-Cola. "The Co-Cola's for you. It'll help straighten your stomach out."

"Thanks," I said. I had to open the bottle on one of the tiny kitchen drawer handles since he didn't offer up no bottle opener. "I'm sick as a dog." I sneezed.

"You and Rusty really tied one on yesterday," Sonny laughed. "You two are a couple of lightweights. It was only about 5:30 when we found you boys out back of the barn. TC said you was a couple of crazy little fuckers."

"We was bored was all," I said. "Their TV don't work." I felt plumb rundown. Not just from the drinking either. All that time sleeping out of doors gave me a stuffy head.

Sonny went, "Well, ain't that the shits." He wore a white T-shirt and a pair of bell-bottom jeans. His hair fell straight down to his shoulders and it looked kind of greasy. He looked like the Jesus in Jesus Christ Superstar. "Couple of hellions is what you all are."

"Did Rusty tell you I was looking for you?"

"And I found you instead," said Sonny. "We must have some kind of psychic connection, I expect. Don't worry. I know why your mama runoff. I ain't mad about it. I shouldn't have been hitting on you two. I wanted to tell her I was sorry and all, but I hear she's staying out to Elston's?"

Sonny went over to the tiny black and white TV and flipped the dial around the horn, but it only got channel 8 and 13—channel 17 came in a little if he held the rabbit ears just right.

"Yeah," I said. "That's why I was looking for you. Mama don't want to be there. Arlene don't want her there either."

Sonny kind of laughed as he leaned against the wall and looked out the window and watched the traffic drive by "I bet she don't."

"Vaughn's gone crazy," I said.

"He's always been nuts."

"No," I said. "More than usual. He shot and killed Rafe Clearwater and probably Glenn Starkey. I never heard if Mr. Starkey lived or died. That ain't too normal, is it?"

"No," Sonny said. "But that's Vaughn for you." He stuffed half a doughnut in his mouth and chewed it up. He grabbed the quart of milk and opened the carton and polished it off from the carton. "Would you look at that. Ed Southard's driving a brand new Lincoln Town Car. How do you think he's affording that?"

"I don't know him."

Sonny went over to the grocery bag and pulled out a newspaper "Oh, yeah. Glenn Starkey lives." He tossed the Fairmont Sun so it landed with a smack on the little table. "It looks like they're going to charge Elston with attempted murder."

"I guess that's a good thing," I said.

"Sort of," Sonny said. "Everyone might be better off if Elston was to spend some time in the joint. Although he'd be running it within a week if I know him. It says here, "Mr. Vaughn pleaded guilty to the terror of the people. I ain't exactly sure what that means, but he's got that ringer lawyer. Pays him with blood money."

There were a thousand things I wanted to say and ask Sonny. Like for one, I wanted to know if he had it in him to go up against him since Vaughn was his older brother and all I didn't think he'd do it. The Vaughn family had this honor code the boys told me about. No matter how much they fought amongst themselves, they'd always go to the wall for each other when it really mattered. Sonny turned the TV off and looked out the window for a spell. He was thinking about something. He pulled out a gold lighter and as he flipped it open a flame 6 inches long leapt out and lit the Marlboro dangling from the side of his face. He looked at me and smiled slowly and the lid to the lighter clicked shut.

"What your mama say about me?"

"That you're meaner than a black snake," I said. "She said you and Vaughn piss through the same quill."

Sonny went, "My, my, but ain't that the truth. We were buddies once upon a time."

"But you're the only one can save her," I gulped.

"Save her?" Sonny said, pretending to look surprised or flattered. "She don't need saving. Her and him has got quite the history together, more than me and her. Anyway, if she wants to live with Vaughn and Arlene under one roof, birdshit shingles and all, it ain't my business. The place used to have spitholes in the floor for chewing tobacco juice."

"We re-roofed the place earlier this summer," I said.

"Well," he said. "It used to be birdshit shingles. Anyhow, if you were re-roofing his place why don't you want to live there?"

"This all happened before he kidnapped Mama," I said.

"What all?"

"Before I pulled a gun on Vaughn," I said. "I didn't want to tell you I done it, but there it is. I pulled a gun on him and had to go into hiding." I was afraid to tell him it was his gun I used. I got up and went to the bathroom and took a whizz and then blew my nose. I felt like I could lay down and die. I puked in the toilet. It was so *acidy* it burnt my throat.

"What?" Sonny laughed.

"I'm puking."

I came out and he gave me a little bottle of Coke to drink. He sat there while I explained everything. I told him how I'd slept out by the dump and met the sign painter and got to smelling worse than a billygoat. Sonny didn't seem too excited about taking Vaughn on man to man, "mano a mano," he called it. I could tell he was still sweet on Mama and he said he'd think about everything I'd told him and decide what to do. I knew better than to trust him with all my heart, but I just hoped he'd do the right thing by Mama as I seen it— even if it was for his own reasons.

"You know," Sonny said. "Your Mama's funny. She likes to eat hamburgers with peanut butter on them. She also used to eat peaches and cottage cheese all the time."

I said, "I know it."

He walked over to the john and took a piss with the door left open. The cigarette butt hissed in the toilet bowl as it hit the water. He flushed the toilet and had to jiggle the handle a couple of times. Sonny even washed his hands after he was done.

When he came out he grabbed my wrist quick as a snake and slapped something into my hand. "This belongs to you."

When I looked down I saw it was Rafe's knife. I had wondered where it got off to.

"Oh thanks," I said.

"It ain't nothing but a thing, man," Sonny said. "I'll show you something I got for your mama." He pulled out a little black velvety box and tossed it to me. I opened it and there was a nice little ring inside. "Think she'll like it?"

"Oh, she'll like it good enough," I said. "Is it real?"

"Doesn't it look real?"

I shrugged "Hell if I know."

"You think I shouldn't ask her?"

"I think you should save her first," I said. "She's been waiting her whole entire life for someone to save her."

"You're one cool customer," Sonny said. "You know that? Do me a favor, would you? The next time you talk to Lorene, tell her I'm sorry. Tell her I'll never lay a hand on her again."

"I feel kind of puny," I said.

"You don't got to whine about it. It's just a cold from sleeping out in the fields or a hangover or a little of both maybe."

He showed me a pair of the toughest looking boots I'd ever seen. He said he bought them for me on the way back from California. I couldn't wait to wear them. Now, I could kick the shit out of anybody dumb enough to mess with me.

"You'll be cool like James Dean," Sonny said. "They're engineer boots. I used to have me a pair when I was a little older than you are now." He rolled up my jeans a couple of turns for me.

"Thanks Sonny," I said in a real nasal tone of voice. The boots made me think of the tough guys Mama and me saw at Rafe's races. Maybe it meant I'd be tough now too. Like just putting them boots on would give me muscles. I smiled to myself thinking about the day I would be a man and kick some major butt when it came to men who beat up on their wives and kids.

"Well now." Sonny clapped me on the shoulder.

I rested up there for a good three days in misery before I got back on my feet. Sonny bought me Spiderman comics and all the 7UP and orange juice I could drink. I got to wondering if didn't Mama or Aunt Oleta or anyone wonder what happened to me. Didn't they care? Didn't nobody love me?

Sonny went out and got himself a job at the state hospital tending "the criminally insane" in the Bigg's building. I couldn't hardly feature Sonny up there with all them nuts but I saw him around a time or two wearing his white cotton uniform smoking. He said about half the people worked there was crazier than the patients. Then he smiled crazy at me to show me what he meant. I could tell he liked them all just the same.

Revelations

We took the elevator down to the lobby of the Parliament. In the office, a balding man with hair growing out of his ears in the office mumbled something at us. Sonny stuck his tongue out at him and gave him the bird, but he was looking down at his newspaper. It was getting close to noon. When we stepped onto the sidewalk I could tell it was going to be a scorcher. Several blocks away the new tar on Bluff Street going out past the Sinclair station shimmered in the heat.

"Time to rambunculate," Sonny said. It reminded me of how Vaughn was always coming up with some crazy word.

I recognized Sonny's El Camino right off the bat, because he always had to do things for show. Then, I remembered that day when Mama told me about her own mama and sang about the glow worm, someone banged on the door and sat outside in the drive with the radio on.

"Want to drive it?"

"Can I?"

"Hell no," Sonny said. "Get in. We're going to go see Mawmaw."

There were orange cones down the middle of the road. The smell of hot tar in my nose and the ground shimmered with heat. Sonny cursed softly to himself as the sound of flecked black gravel flew up from his wheels and threatened to ruin his paint job. A man in an orange hat and vest held a sign in his hands that said SLOW. All the bugs in the world were making noise all at once. The little creatures were saying: "Rejoice!" Grasshoppers were everywhere and nobody could seem to stop them from eating everything up. A man was pulled over on the side of the road in a Buick with his hood up and steam coming out of the engine.

Mawmaw Vaughn was a tough old bird. She was a member of
the United Daughters of the Confederacy and when I was a
little kid I used to wonder if she had been alive even back
then.

She had outlived three husbands, but the first one, the important one, had been Craigie Vaugh. She was the eldest of all
the Vaughns and the only one that salty group would kowtow
to because she had earned her place at the head of the family.
All the men had died at relatively young ages of heart attacks
or from fast living.

She lived in a three-story house at the end of the gravel
road on Vaughn Road. At one time the Vaughns had been a
family to be reckoned with. They made most of their money
as big time farmers. Later, the family fortunes changed and
they started running stills during prohibition days, and probably some cattle rustling on the side too. At least, that's how
Punkin told it to me. Lately the Vaughn line had lost its salt
according to Elston, and Mawmaw.

The house Mawmaw lived in had once been quite a sight
to see. It had four columns on the front porch bigger around
than most oak trees, although a wringer-washer sat listing under the library window. I heard tell there had once been a
chandelier above the second floor gallery until it fell down
during a thunderstorm. On the inside were two living rooms
that they called parlors in the olden days, a library, and dining
room. There were wall sconces that used to be powered by
gas before electricity came along.

Bulky dark furniture that looked like it was made for giants
squatted on the hardwood floors. Mildewed red and green
velvet curtains framed the windows. The kitchen was gigantic
too. Behind the kitchen was a place where they used to grow
plants where the walls and ceilings were made of glass. Mawmaw had still managed to hold onto most of the land even

though she allowed what she called "sharecroppers" to rent the land from her for farming.

The inside had beautiful dark wood throughout, but the place was going to pot without a family to live in it and a man to fix things up. Mawmaw lived on the first floor, because she couldn't get up and down the steps too good. Her bedroom was the front parlor. The front parlor had once been the men's parlor. She used to charge people two dollars a head to come in and look around. An old black man, Woody, usually led the tour, but no one could understand him too well. He called every white man "Captain" in a respectful tone but also in a way that made them realize he could probably kill them if he decided to do it.

There were statues from France in the house and family paintings from the 1800s. There was a picture of a Vaughn talking to President Truman in the dining room. There were swords and even a suit of armor brought in just for the tourists.

When we pulled into the driveway Sonny pointed at the barn that had been converted by him and some of the other men into a house. The second story had a nice newer addition to it but it looked like a barn on the lower half and an apartment from halfway-up. Sonny used to live in the apartment before he took Mama and me to California. It seemed grand by comparison to the studio apartment we were jammed into just outside of Los Angeles.

Sonny parked the in the circular drive. We both got out. He took his time looking around. We both looked out the front archway we had just driven under. The rusting iron gates had been thrown open for so long wisteria vines were growing in a kind of pleasant decay. The ruts in the driveway were near impossible to drive a car through they were getting so deep, but still none of the Vaughns would come to fix the road or anything else. Mawmaw didn't want anyone to put themselves out. So in the winter time they parked outside the

gate and walked her groceries through the snowdrifts to the
back door, if Woody wasn't around to do it.

At the door, Sonny banged the knocker real loud before
walking in. When we lived in the barn we just came in and
out of Mawmaw's house as we pleased but it was more con-
venient to use the path that went under the trellis, grew as
much poison oak as it did ivy, to the back door. A big walnut
tree was out there dropping big green bombs on the ground.
I'd seen more than one sassy dog that had been surprised by
the walnut tree and yelp like someone threw a rock at him.

We lived there when it was hot. I'd go into the kitchen to
get a drink of water. She might be setting at the kitchen table
reading the old family Bible. She wouldn't let me dirty up
glasses so I used the aluminum dipper that hung on a nail
over the sink. Truth to be told, I preferred using the dipper.
The water out of that dipper tasted sweetest, even though
everyone drank out of it. She always kept some sugar cookies
in a clear glass jar with the words COOKIES stenciled in
white lettering on the side.

Soon as we stepped inside everything was the same as I
remembered. It was dark and cool and smelled of old wood
and the musty smell of moldering flowers. The sound of Wal-
ter Cronkite's voice echoed in the foyer. I hoped to get my
hands on one of them swords before we left, but I sensed
that we were here for something important.

"Who is that?" Mawmaw's voice croaked from her makeshift bedroom. "Who's there?"

"It's me Mawmaw," Sonny said. "And Honey Boy."

"You all get in here," Mawmaw said. "I can't get up to answer the door. My bursitis is acting up."

I followed Sonny into Mawmaw's room. They had double-
doors about 12
feet high. Inside Mawmaw was sitting on a high-backed wood
chair with fading royal purple velvet was what she sat on. She
sat on the edge and I could see her stockings was the kind

that only rolled up to mid-calf and they weren't suntan color like Mama wore neither. She was leaning forward with her weight on a walker.

"That's quite a chair Mawmaw," Sonny said. He went up and threw his arms around her.

"Ain't it though," Mawmaw said. "Woody got it down out of the attic for me. It's pretty comfortable too. But you know what it really is?" She smiled an impy smile. "A potty for grown people."

Sonny croaked, "Good Lord."

"It's all cleaned out," she said. "It just makes me laugh, but if I didn't tell no one they'd never know the difference. Not that anyone comes to see me unless I'm sick, and they think I might die. Vaughns from all over just can't wait to take this old house apart for the hardware."

"Hardware?" I asked.

"The doorknobs and stuff like that," Sonny explained to me.

"Oh," Mawmaw said. "Why haven't you come to visit me since you've been back? Don't you love me anymore?"

All I could think to say was, "Mawmaw."

"Lorene hasn't come to see me either," she said, settling with her back up against the plush chair. "And she's just down the road a piece at Elston's. Is she there now? Maybe we should call her and ask her to come over? It would be nice to have some company for a change."

"We had to come the back way," Sonny said.

"My Sonny," Mawmaw said. "You kids should learn how to get along before it's too late. Life's too short for all this carrying on."

"I know, Mawmaw," Sonny said.

"You know I got a roast in the pressure cooker with your name on it," Mawmaw said, including both of us somehow with the sweep of her arms.

"Roast beast," I said, imitating Rusty.

"Oh yes," she smiled. "That's what it surely is."

"We come to ask you what to do about Vaughn." I said. I walked over to the ashtray stand because one of the rusting swords was there. I pulled it out but I didn't swing it around like Zorro, because I knew it would upset Mawmaw.

"What can you do about him?" said Mawmaw, like she was philosophizing. "He's always been mean as gar broth and ashes. And you Sonny, you should know how he is because you're just like him. That's the reason you boys don't get along because you're just alike. When you was little things you used to follow Elston around. Why—you were his shadow. When Craigie died seems like that affected Elston funny. Your Grandpa and Elston always had a special bond. He started going around getting in trouble. It's in your genes anyway—causing trouble."

"Mawmaw," Sonny said. "It's different. Vaughn's more than just bullying people. He's harassing people. He shot a man."

"I heard about it," Mawmaw said. "The Starkeys better watch out."

Sonny hissed, "Mawmaw."

"I'm not approving of how he done people," Mawmaw said. "But he's blood. You got to stick together with blood no matter what. You hear me? Sonny, you should know how it is. So you take it to heart, Honey."

"Mawmaw," Sonny said, "I've got just as much love for family as anyone, but Elston's about as nuts as they come. I love him. Tried to get along with him—he's my brother—but I can't stand to be around him."

"I know it, baby," Mawmaw said. She pursed her lips. A fire lit up her eyes. "But you heard what I said. You listen at what I say."

Funny thing I learned was how families like to keep secrets from the kids. The younger you are the more likely it is you're going to get sent out of the room when the grown-ups talk.

Only now nobody was sending me out of the room. The trouble with family trying to keep things secret is that everyone else in town already knows the truth anyway. Sometimes you find out the most amazing things from neighbors or from someone blurting it all out.

"Does the boy know?" Mawmaw asked Sonny, looking at me from the corner of her eye.

"I don't think he knows," Sonny said. "But I bet he's got an idea about it."

"Why don't someone tell him? Why don't his mama tell him?"

"I guess she thinks he's too young," Sonny said.

I always hate it when grown-ups start talking about you when you're standing there. It's almost like you're invisible. It's not so bad if they say good things, but things like this is when it gets weird. One of them was going to tell me something so I sat down on a travel trunk that was handy and laid the sword down next to me. Sonny was looking at me funny and for a second I thought one of them was going to say Sonny was my daddy. It wouldn't exactly be a shock, but to know for sure would be something else again.

"Anybody ever tell you who your daddy is?" Mawmaw asked.

I shook my head side to side. "Nobody ever said for sure. They dropped hints."

"Well, well," Mawmaw shook her head as if she was disgusted. "It's a fine thing when a young man don't know who his own daddy is. How's a boy supposed to grow up right? I mean, even if it ain't the perfect situation a body ought to know one way or the other."

"Don't tell him Mawmaw," Sonny said. "Let Lorene do it."

Tell me, I wanted to say. *Tell me.* I snuck a look at Sonny. He looked real fidgety, so I could tell it probably was him. His face was all red like he might explode any second, but he couldn't stand up to Mawmaw when she decided something for sure. No one could.

"Baby," Mawmaw said. "The boy ought to know."

"Who?" I croaked. "Who's my daddy?" I figured I knew it was Vaughn, but I didn't want it to be. I didn't want to be him because he was bad and that meant I was bad too. Not just bad but maybe even crazy or evil.

"It's Elston," Mawmaw said. "Elston is your daddy. I don't know why they all wanted to keep it from you. Elston and your mama was married. They didn't stay married too long. I don't know how they managed to keep it a secret from you this long, or why they even tried. Everyone knows. Maybe they was just too backward to tell you, Honey. Don't hold it against them no more than you can help. They were just country kids that didn't have as much sense as you could slap in a gnat's ass with a butter paddle."

"He's my daddy," I whispered. I wanted to deny it, but now I couldn't fool myself like I had been. "*He's* my daddy."

"Craigie tried to tell them not to get married," Mawmaw said. "But when your hormones are pumping at that age, you ain't about to listen to nobody."

"He's, my daddy," I said. "Sonny, I thought Mawmaw was going to say you was."

"I know you did, Kid," Sonny said, pushing his forefinger and thumb into his eyes to pinch at the tears there. He kind of sniffed, inhaled deeply and then exhaled. "I'm sorry. It's all a big mess. Nobody knew what to say to you. We figured you're just a kid and eventually you'd probably find out for yourself."

"It's all right boys," Mawmaw said. Her face looked ancient and destroyed until she sighed as if she were putting up her memories like nice china after Easter supper. "We're all family here. I got to go check on that roast."

The roast smelled good. The pressure cooker was hissing in the kitchen.

"Mawmaw, Mawmaw!" Sonny hollered, following her into the kitchen. She would put her walker out a foot and then walk slowly until her feet would catch up. It was almost as if the thing was part of her. "I love Lorene. I love her more than Elston does. And now you tell the boy that Elston's his daddy!"

"I can't believe it," I whispered to myself. Vaughn is crazy. I figured if Vaughn was crazy, I was crazy too, or I'd end up nuts too. I'd already heard they had to send Craigie to Fairmont State Hospital to die. Everyone said he was a bad to drink. So the Vaughn's were crazy alcoholics, and that was all she wrote for me.

I heard Mawmaw and Sonny off in the kitchen. Sonny's voice came to me high-pitched, but Mawmaw kept talking quieter and quieter until I couldn't hear her no more. Then the kitchen door slammed and before too long I heard the El Camino turnover and roar off the back way. I felt bad because I didn't try to follow after Sonny, but we were two different people and now I find out he was my uncle instead of my daddy like I guessed.

There were pictures all over Mawmaw's room of everyone when they were kids. Even the pictures of Vaughn and Sonny when they were boys made them look tough. When they were littler than me they had crew cuts. Then as they got into their teens they had ducktail haircuts greased back with Brylcreem or whatever. There were even some of my grade school pictures on the wall. Some of my school pictures I could barely remember what state we were living in when they were taken.

There was one picture that dominated the room. It was of my great great grandfather and grandmother. The picture had made a big impression on me when I had seen it before all those years earlier. It was oval shaped with an olive and black background behind a thick glass from another time. In it, they were quite old with white hair as fluffy as cotton candy. Mawmaw said they was just poor dirt farmers and that

Grandpa Vaughn loved his mules Kate and Betts as much as he loved Grandma Vaughn and maybe more. But the thing that confused it all in my mind were all the religious pictures hung on the same wall.

The Last Supper hung to the right of Grandpa and Grandma Vaughn. Off to the left of the bubble-like oval frame was Jesus in the Garden of Gethsemane, so my great grandparents were vaguely like religious figures in my mind. Probably because I never met them. Mawmaw had Grandpa Vaughn's obituary from the newspaper. He had died out behind his haystack off the highway out past White Cloud Church. Suddenly , I felt a link I had never known before. Even though all the Vaughns drove me nuts I now had more people to belong to and I didn't know what to do with them all.

Mawmaw brought out a picture in a gold leaf frame of Mama and Vaughn standing next to each other behind a cake as tall as the Empire State Building. They both looked like movie stars. Vaughn was handsome. Mama looked worried, but still pretty at the same time. Mawmaw took out a tissue, dabbed at her watery eyes.

"I'm going to keep this picture for you," she said, sounding quavery. "Some day, when you're old enough, I'll give it to you." She wrapped it in tissue paper and put it back in the cedar chest she kept it in with shoe boxes full of black and white photographs.

I vowed right then I'd never call him "Daddy." I was so mad at him the anger boiled up in my face but they Mawmaw ask me what I was thinking. Bad shadows were in my head. I tried to remember Mama and Vaughn when they were still together for such a short time. The memories must be there stored in my daydreams like a double exposed picture I'd found of Mama, me, and a man whose faith was blurred. Just thinking about these things made me think I was going to faint. The light ran out of the world and tilted forward at the same time when I imagined sneaking up on Vaughn while he napped on his couch and hitting him in the head with a hammer. I felt bad after that. It made me a bad person I know, but I got so mad the world seemed to tilt at an angle like riding on the scrambler at the carnival.

The sound of a vehicle revving its engine outside. I looked out the window expecting to see that Sonny had come back for me but it was Vaughn's green Dodge. His truck just sat there framed under the archway. I couldn't see him, but the truck was unmistakable. My throat felt tight, almost like I had a sore throat. Vaughn did a U-turn in the gravel and headed out the back way to Fairmont. I didn't know if he was following Sonny or if he was just on a beer run.

"The good Lord's got his hand on you, Honey," Mawmaw Vaughn said. "You might not believe it right now. Things are going to turn out how they turn out, but someday, if you don't turn sour, God's going to see to it that things work out for you. So you stay sweet. Can you do that for me?"

"Okay Mawmaw," I said. "I'll try." I wanted to ask her if she was a Holy Roller or just a regular Christian, but then I decided it probably didn't matter to God. Either way you probably had your bases covered. Some people were white and some were black and some were Chinese—I just happened to be a Holy Roller Jesus Freak without even meaning to be. I mean, that's just the kind of people I got associated with as Aunt Oleta would say.

"I think it's time," Mawmaw sighed into her tissue. She blew her nose like a trumpet.

"Time?"

"C'mon," she said. "Get your Mawmaw's walking stick and the little Bible off the writing desk.

The stick was a gnarly staff that made me think of them three wise men what that came to see the baby Jesus. The Bible was red ("dusty rose" Mawmaw said) with her name written in cursive in gold leaf *Comfort Vaughn*. "Comfort" had always sounded like a funny name to me, but it suited her. Just sitting with her at the table made me feel better. She smelled like lilacs. Before I knew it she was up and out the side door heading toward the gold fields of wild hay and weeds. Up ahead over the field a mockingbird was chasing a crow.

"Mawmaw! Where we going?"

She stopped walking and even though she was limping I probably wouldn't have caught up with her.

"Where we going?"

"Found a mouse in my well" Mawmaw turned back toward the field and opened the first gate. "It's bad luck."

"Yeah," I tried to be agreeable.

"It's bad luck," she called over her shoulder. A couple of neon blue dragonflies darted by on the wind with the pollen white in the air almost like it was snowing.

I followed Mawmaw through two more gates she unlatched at the post. Even with her walking stick and dusty rose Bible she handled the hitching and unhitching of the gates with an ease that made it easy to see the young girl she might have been a jillion years ago. We come up to a place I'd heard the Vaughn's call the "old homestead" that amounted to a swaybacked shack with a painted orange tarpaper roof. There was a rusty pump in the ground next to the house. Half a picket fence stood, but there was not a drop of paint on it anymore. The privy was still standing, a home for wasps, and the half-moon carved in the door made me wish I had lived in this house, but I'm not sure why. I guess because the few old folks still creeping around talked about how happy they were back then even if it was the Depression.

She walked right passed the old homestead to a tiny cemetery with a kind of funny wrought iron fence around it except it was a family plot so there wasn't nothing to laugh about. The weeds were almost as tall in there too. Mawmaw left the gate to the plot open for me. She looked down at something on the ground between her feet. My heart hammered in my chest and I got the chills at the same time. I did not want to look at what she wanted me to see. I walked up next to her, did something I wouldn't normally do anymore, and slipped my hand into hers. At first, I thought it was just an ordinary marker from a long time ago except this one was new. I stared at it trying to understand what it meant. It didn't dawn on me for a minute. The name was the same as mine, except the Nathaniel Kimbrough buried there had bee born almost a full year before me. He only lived one day.

It got me started crying. It was like I had died once before and then came back again. There was always an empty hole in my heart and now I knew what it was. The other Nathan wanted his name back. I heard a sound like a baby, but it was just that mockingbird. Mawmaw's face turned to mine. I didn't want to see her for a minute, but she reached over with her hand on my chin to turn my head to hers.

"Now you know," Mawmaw said. "I know your Mama gets distant. This thing ruined her. She became a totally different girl when the baby died. Poor thing. It never lived long. Elston wouldn't have nothing to do with her after the baby died for a while. He would have murdered himself with grief if he could have. I don't know why. I tried to talk sense into him, but he wouldn't hear it. He went back with her long enough. He give her another baby, but then it was too late. I tried to take care of your Mama. After you was born I let you all stay out to the barnhouse. Now the baby is up in heaven in the arms of the Lord Jesus."

"No he ain't," I said.

"What you mean . . . no he ain't?"

"I mean somebody's been talking to me," I said.

"Who? A baby? Make sense child."

"No," I said. "A man's been talking to me in my head. I bet it's him. Only kind of growed up." I scuffed my shoes at the ground. Squatting down I traced the copper-colored name with my finger. The name that was mine and his. We shared something. Maybe we were the same person is what came to me but I couldn't make sense of it to myself—least of all Mawmaw. So I clamped my mouth shut about it and Mawmaw looked at me like I had two heads.

"Well," she said. "Maybe you do hear voices. Could be, you'll be a preacher or a healer."

Roy's 66

The beans were blossoming everywhere out in the county. I heard farmers talking out in front of the hardware store about how the crops were in the last phase of their growth. The old men, some in cowboy hats or caps, would stare out across the plain to the northwest searching the horizon for signs of rain. The crops needed more rain before the harvest another six weeks away. A decent harvest and the farmers could keep their heads above water and buy a new clutch for the combine or maybe new tires.

A dozen or so Kenworths and Nationals were parked behind Roy's gas station in the gravel lot behind the station. There was a white and powder blue National parked in front of the diesel tanks fueling up. The trucker had his door open and he and Roy were jawing about something with big grins on their faces. The trucker was a big guy everyone called T-Bare. He had a reputation as a *Super Trucker* so the cops were always on the lookout for his rig. I remembered him because he was one of the few you could tell liked kids. Roy turned around and waved at me. I had to wait in front of the glass window while he did business, but I could tell he had something to say.

"Got to get some Pusholine," T-Bare said.

"Where you heading?"

"Chocolate Town," T-Bare said.

After Roy was done bullshitting he turned to me, "If it ain't the Dr. Pepper Kid! How's the world treating you?"

"Not too bad," I lied through my teeth.

"The terror of Kingdom County!" Roy hollered over the hissing and grinding noises of T-Bare's diesel pulling away from the pumps. "Here he is folks! Right here in my station! Someone call the cops!"

T-Bare tooted his air horn and we waved him onto Highway 54.

When we went back inside the station Roy's CB radio crackled. We heard T-Bare's voice talking to us, "66 Roy and Honey Boy, you got your ears on? I say Roy 66, c'mon back."

"This is 66 Roy. What do you want, T-Bare?"

"Give me to senor Honey Boy," T-Bare said.

It was real exciting that a trucker wanted to talk to me on the CB. Everybody around seemed to have them these days. Roy held out the CB and I took it from him. He pointed to remind me to push the thingy down so it would work properly. I tried to think how they talked.

"That's a big 10-4, T-Bare," I said. "This is the Honey Boy. What's your 10-20?"

"Ha ha," T-Bare said. "If you hang your head out the window you can probably still see the backside of my 10-20 now. Y'all take care. Try to stay out of trouble if you can. Don't be running with no outlaws."

"4-10, good buddy," I said.

The sound of static the, "You're a natural at this. When you get old enough we'll have you hauling loads in your own truck. Tootle-loosky. We gone."

"Roger Dodger," I said, since I'd used up what little CB jargon I knew.

"Oh, tell him to watch out for Bear traps," Roy said.

"He's calling Vaughn an outlaw?"

"Well, Vaughn used to be good people, but he's been different ever since the war. Usually,
Roy was big on making pronouncements about people, good old boys, politicians, and sons-of-bitches alike. He told it like it was but in such a way nobody took offense even if they weren't one of the good ones. Roy had a knack for making them feel like they were somehow.

"Different how?"

"Like there wasn't nothing he wouldn't do different is all," Roy said.

"Why do you think that is?"

"What?" Roy cocked his ear toward me.

I was going ask again but I could see he was pretending not to hear me on purpose. Probably afraid I'd tell Vaughn and then the shit would hit the fan.

"Y'all is outlaws like Jesse James," he said.

"No we ain't."

"No?" Roy said. "That ain't how Starkey tells its. Everyone tells old Roy everything soon or later."

"Ain't seen you around lately, Honey Boy!" Wiener hollered from under a Pinto.

"Well," I said. "I been around. Here, there, and yonder."

We walked to the office and Roy hung back so I could go on in first. There really wasn't much in the office besides a wooden counter with the register on it, a cooler for beer and another for sodie, a rack with some candy bars, gum, and Slim Jims, a couple of gumball machines, and a calendar with the picture of a curvy girl in a swimsuit tacked up on the wall.

"If you need anything," Roy said. "Let me know. You need a place to stay you could have the back room behind the office most any night. I've got an old cot in there too if you need it, but let's keep this between you and me. I don't need Vaughn or anyone getting after my ass."

"I appreciate it," I said and then spit like one of the old men. I tipped back a Dr. Pepper with him. It sure was good going down. The heat was already climbing and it wasn't even 10:00 yet. The sodie was frosty-cold with little pieces of ice sliding off it and running down my arm. The floor of the gas station had a green and white checkered design filthy with grime and oil, and decorated with several heel-crushed cigarettes. I could hear the sound of mowers not too far down the road. "Things ain't that bad yet."

"You a tough old cob," Wiener stood in the doorway between the garage and the office like there was a boundary there he dare not cross. "For a kid."

"Check this out" I showed him a leather wrist band with metal studs on it. "My best friend give it to me."

"That's tough," Wiener said. "What happened to that nice young man you and me used to know, Roy?"

"I don't know," Roy said. "This one's going to end up in juvie like some of them Vaughn boys he runs with if he ain't careful."

"Shit," I laughed.

"That's what I'm talking about," Wiener said. "Such language. I get your Aunt Oleta wouldn't like to hear that."

"Vaughn pulled a gun on Marhsal Ron Clevenger the other night," Roy said. "Clevenger gassed up here before he left town and he told me the whole story. Vaughn and Arlene pulled guns on Clevenger. When he radioed the county sheriff for backup they told him just to make sure Vaughn didn't kill nobody. And that was it. They're all scared shitless of the man. I don't blame them either, because he's dangerous. He ought to be locked up away from decent people."

"I know it," I said.

"I guess you know your mama's out there?" He squinted at me.

"Yes sir," I said. "She don't want to be there, but she can't get away."

"That ain't how I heard it."

"What do you mean?" I said.

"Well," Roy said. "Way Clevenger told it, Lorene was there too. She and Arlene both had the drop on him. They was standing there outside their trucks all holding rifles and shotguns and shit. Clevenger didn't have a chance. Hell, they didn't even pay the man $300 a month to be marshal. He resigned, up and left town. Even the truckers are getting nervous about stopping here in Fairmont."

"Why are you telling me all this?"

"Because I like you, Kid," Roy said. "Life has handed you a raw deal. And one day, Elston Vaughn ain't going to get off scot-free no more. He's been accused of murder, but I guess it ain't the first time. We'll just have to see how things play out."

There was a ding-ding sound; I turned and a family in a station wagon were parking in front of the pumps.

"Got to get back to work, Quick Draw," Roy said.

"I'll get them, Roy," Wiener said.

"Nope," Roy said. "I better take this one my ownself."

"Okey doke," Wiener seemed disappointed. He had a reputation for being great with engines, but bad with making change. He crawled back under the Pinto.

The man got out of the station wagon wore Khaki pants and a blue shirt. The woman had blond hair and wore a lot of makeup. There were two kids in the backseat playing with a golden retriever. I watched as Roy pumped their gas, checked their oil, and cleaned their windshield. I watched the way the man leaned toward the smiling woman and the way the kids yipped happily in the backseat. I figured they were going to Silver Dollar City together. Finally the man paid and they drove off. I walked out of the office and watched them drive out of sight, my mouth hanging open because they look so perfect, like a TV family.

I asked, "What was that?"

"That was the Atwill family," Roy said, walking over to the next car. "Thomas Atwill's Vaughn's new lawyer. He's a slick one. Figures he's got the world by the balls because he's from St. Louis and everyone around here ought to bow down to him. The Sun says he asked for a change of venue for the trial because Vaughn gave Starkey the red ass."

"What's a venue?"

"Place," Roy said. "They know everyone around here wants to see Vaughn in jail so they want to have the trial in another town where people don't know what a hardass he is. It's the State of Missouri versus Elston Vaughn."

I didn't tell Roy that Vaughn was my daddy because I didn't want him to hate me. I figured he might know already anyway, everyone probably knew a long time before I did. Now, it sounded like Mama had gone off the deep-end too but Roy was one for stretching the truth. I just couldn't believe she was pointing shotguns at sheriffs. First chance I got, I'd definitely ask her about it. A trucker pulled up to the diesel pumps and the dinger went off loud out in the garage. "Looks like Little Ed's got him a load." Roy hopped off his tall stool at the register and went out the front with a wave.

I started reading the *Fairmont Sun* to get all the news. I was getting real sick and tired of not knowing what was going on in this town. I found a piece on the Neighbors page about Aunt Oleta that talked about her being "of the home" and Roy said that just means she stays at home all day instead of working. Her hobbies included needlework, planting flowers, playing bridge, and she has made thirteen quilts—presently at work on number fourteen. She probably felt all high and mighty being in the paper.

On Roy's little black and white television of Roy's they were showing footage of Vaughn, Arlene, and Mama moving in lapsed time in the Little Dixie convenience store with guns pointing at the clerk. It was bound to be in the paper tomorrow. They showed the same footage about three times. I didn't put anything past Vaughn. I knew what he was capable of, but seeing Arlene and Mama was just pitiful. Mama looked dangerous and beautiful. I didn't know she even knew how to hold a gun, but there she was with a rifle. Her lips seemed to move in one of the frames, and I wondered if she was threatening to blow someone's head off. It was like something I'd seen about Patty Hearst only she was carrying a sawed-off carbine.

I was from a regular family of outlaws. It was like the family business or something. Maybe it was the only thing I'd ever be good at since it was in the blood.

When Roy wasn't looking I swiped a pack of Marlboros. I didn't figure he would miss them.

Father and Son

There wasn't nothing to do now, but go back to Mama. There wasn't anyone to run to anyway. I could have stayed with Aunt Oleta, but in her way she could be as bad as Vaughn only going the other way. With her everything was Jesus and what everyone ought to do was done, but real life ain't like that. My life wasn't like that. No one cared if I did right or wrong. Vaughn wasn't no good for Mama, but I didn't know if I should get her to run off with me or if I should steal a gun from somewhere and end it all myself. Not that Vaughn had her holding up places with him she was bound for jail and on the highway to hell. It terrified me to think about killing someone, especially Vaughn, but these were desperate times. Maybe I couldn't kill him but it didn't stop me from thinking about it, but I had to do something.

I thought maybe I would get a ride from someone but didn't nobody stop as I walked out to Vaughn's. Roy had given me one of his gas station hats to help protect my face because it was peeling from sunburn. I was real prone to sunburn. A southerly breeze kicked up but it didn't help cool things off because it was a hot wind. A swaybacked horse neighed to me from a pasture behind a row of pine trees. I whistled and he came trotting up to a stop like a private getting an order to halt and rotated his ears to the booming sounds coming from the brickyard. I jumped over the ditch and petted the horse's nose. He was lonely like me. There was a part of me that wanted to leap over the fence and become a horse and not have any dealings with people. I wondered if I'd be an appaloosa maybe or an Arabian mix would be nice. Most likely, I end up a jackass.

As I walked up the steep grade to Vaughn hill I could see the Dodge in the driveway. I didn't know if I should feel relieved or scared. Vaughn was likely to beat the dogshit out of me. I heard some dogs barking now and one of them was Buddy. He saw it was me and came flying down the hill and almost knocked me over. I patted him down real good and he licked my face. Some of the other dogs wanted to get petted to but Buddy wouldn't let any of them near me.

"Honey Boy's here, Honey Boy's here," Sugarbaby started singing and ran inside the house like she was scared of me.

Arlene looked out the kitchen window at me, but gave me a dirty look and closed the curtain.

I heard a chainsaw running in the back so I walked around and saw Punkin and Vaughn working without their shirts on. The pair of them gave me a casual glance like I had never gone anywhere. They were cutting up trees from a brush pile that had been building up all year. Punkin and the boys would deliver pickup truck loads to folks in the county as a way of making a little money. Vaughn didn't normally trouble himself with their wood project, but it was just him and Punkin which made me think they was planning something. Punkin was still walking funny since Danny had beat him with that switch. Punkin wouldn't talk to me, wouldn't even look at me, and he had some chewing tobacco tucked into his bottom lip.

"What do you want?" Vaughn asked.

"I just come to get Mama," I whispered. I meant to sound tough, but the air came up and through my mouth so all I could do was whisper. It was like the air had suddenly gotten thicker. Buddy plastered himself against my leg.

"You're a day late," Vaughn said, revving up his Poulan chainsaw and taking a couple of steps toward me. "And a dollar short. Your Mama done cutout of here, or didn't she tell you? You probably think she loves you so much and all. She didn't tell you she left, did she? She don't love you or anyone else except herself."

"You're a damn liar," I said. "I know she's here. Everyone knows she's here and I want her to come with me." Buddy bared his teeth and started growling at Vaughn.

"What did you say to me, boy?" Vaughn said. He pulled his pocket knife out of the sheath attached to his belt. "I though I heard a mosquito, didn't you Punkin?"

"I don't hear nothing," Punkin said.

Vaughn strode over and tried to pick me up by my shirt but a couple of buttons popped off. I tried to ward him off and pushed against his big forearm and bicep but that just made him smile in a cold way. Buddy clamped his teeth on Vaughn's leg and he howled. He kicked Buddy in the head and I heard him yip. Vaughn threw me on the ground and straddled my chest and held the knife close to my face. I heard the back door slam open and Sugarbaby was slapping her daddy on the back and screaming nonsense, "Play with me, Daddy!" He turned a little and smacked her across the mouth and she went flying ass over elbows. With her bawling now, I could tell he felt bad about doing it so he got off me and let me get up.

"Shit," Vaughn said. "See what you made me do." I didn't know if he was talking to me or Sugarbaby, or maybe Buddy. Punkin took his axe and sunk it into the cutting stump with a solid *ku-chunk*. He didn't say nothing just turned on his heel and made for his daddy's house.

"Arlene!" Vaughn hollered. "Get my 12-gauge, the East-field!"

We all waited until Arlene came out onto the porch with the 12-gauge.

"Don't do it, Daddy," Arlene said, trying to talk to him all girlie and everything which wasn't really her specialty. She handed him the shotgun like it was a snake with her fingers. "Don't do it, Daddy please."

Vaughn wasn't listening to her though. He was looking at me. Sweat was pouring off his face by the bucket and his lips were mumbling like he was cursing me out but nobody could hear what he was saying. He checked to make sure the shotgun was loaded and not on safety. His eyes bored holes into mine. My legs went weak as he stomped over to me and I fell down to my knees.

Instead of pointing the sawed-off shotgun at me he went over to Buddy who had his ears plastered down on his head, rolled over on his back, with his tail curled up between his legs. He was trying to tell Vaughn, *I don't hate you. I was just trying to protect that boy.* There were two loud booming sounds and Buddy's body jumped and didn't move anymore. There was the sensation of warmness across my belly and thighs and I looked down to see that I was in the act of pissing myself. It was like it was happening to someone else. Buddy was dead and I hadn't done anything to stop Vaughn. I had been relieved he was going for Buddy instead of me and the relief had kept me from doing anything about it.

"I know who you are," I said, standing up and brushing off the woodchips and dirt off my clothes. "Mawmaw told me. She told me all about you and Mama."

"What?" Vaughn asked. "What did she tell you?" He threw the shotgun down in the yard.

"That you're my Daddy," my legs were shaking and I felt so weak I thought I might fall on the ground. "And what a sorry son-of-a-bitch you are too! If there was anyone in all of Fairmont, all of Kingdom county, I wouldn't want to be my daddy it would be you! All you do is treat people like shit. You tear things apart. You don't care about nothing, least of all me or Mama. You just want to show everyone what a big man you are."

I saw his head drop for the first time ever. It was like someone bigger than him had socked him in the stomach. Then he looked over my shoulder and I turned to look too and it was Arlene giving him a shaming look as she walked back inside like a zombie. She had left Sugarbaby out there to watch it all. When I turned back around his face had already set back into the meanness it had come from. He picked Sugarbaby up and swatted her on the butt to send her inside and that's exactly where she went--bawling all the way. There was another stump he sat down on with his back to me. The cicadas were chirping loudly and suddenly I felt weak. Like life was hopeless for me. I was just a kid. Why was I even trying? It was the grownups who were supposed to sort all of this shit out, not a kid, not me.

"I ain't your daddy," Vaughn said.

"What?"

He turned and glared at me, "I said, I ain't your daddy. Mawmaw gets some romantic notions in her head sometimes. She's old is all."

"Even Sonny said so."

Vaughn said, "Shit." He kind of drawled it out. "And you believe that lying sack of green shit? He's probably the one you ought to be talking to now."

"It don't matter," I said. "I already seen the wedding picture. I know. Where's my Mama at Vaughn?"

"I told you I don't know," Vaughn said. "Man, you're just like her. She hopped into Arlene's truck and booked it out of here early this morning."

"Where'd she go?"

"How the hell am I supposed to know that?"

"I've got to find her," I said. "I heard you made her and Arlene pull a gun on that Marhsal Clevenger."

"What would you know about it?" His elbows were resting on his knees with his hands holding each other. "I told Clevenger if he didn't mind his own business I have to blow his damn brains out. The chickenshit resigned less than an hour later. I heard it on the scanner. We just drove out of town big as you please. There was a bear in the grass out on the highway but he never batted an eyelid."

I wanted to bawl like a baby about then. How could this man have so much hate in him? Didn't he ever want to do right? Seems like he just wanted to tell people what to do or beat them to a bloody pulp if they didn't. It was depressing to think this man was my daddy. Now, I didn't know if he was or not but it seemed pretty likely. I looked more like Mama. I was small like her. Right back to square one, but either way I was a bastard or Vaughn was my daddy. I don't know that one state of affairs was better than the other.

"Go get me a beer," Vaughn said.

"Why don't you get up off your fat ass and get it yourself," I said.

He moved fast for a big man. He threw me down and started punching me in the head and chest. After the first punch I was pretty much out of it. His face was inches from mine, and even some of his sweat dripped on my face. I tried to get up a couple of times. He seemed to have problems holding me by the wrist because we was both sweating. He kept saying like I thought I was a big man now because I had growed a couple of inches over the summer. And if I was such a tough guy, could I take a punch?

When he finally let me up I ran across the backyard from him and started hollering, "Sonny's going to kill you! You hear me? Sonny's going to kill you and if he don't, I will!" Because at that moment I did want to kill him. I wanted to see him suffer too. I wanted him to suffer for the way Mama and me had suffered. About all the men Mama had been with had treated her bad. I wondered what hope I had to grow up and become a good man. That was about the time that coming up with a way to kill Vaughn was the only thing I could think about. I didn't care if I was caught or not, only that Vaughn was dead. Before I turned away I saw Buddy lying there in his own blood. I wanted to pray to God and Jesus, but it didn't seem like any of that would do any good. Maybe the Devil would be more willing to jump in with this type of situation so I decided to pray in my mind:

Dear Jesus or Devil, either one of you is welcome to my soul if you would help me this one time. Help me do something about Vaughn. I don't know what. Kill him or put him in the clink for life. Just do something for a change. Help me this one time and I won't ask about nothing else again.

That was a lie.

Kingdom Dazed

A bluish-green ford pickup pulled over to the shoulder. The sun reflecting off the chrome bumper blinded me worse than a lightning strike. When I reached for the handle the truck lurched forward and then came to a stop. There was a big dent on the passenger side in the front fender. I stretched for the handle and the truck revved forward again. A smartass! Finally the driver let me catch hold and I swung the door open and peeked in.

The old man had a crewcut and large ears that would have stuck out no matter what kind of hairstyle he had. He had a smashed-in nose, and his face had craters. His head was too big for his spindly body and shaped like a pineapple. Rusty would have said something like how he'd make a good poster child for abortion.

"You should have seen your face," the old man said and by the way he talked it was plain he didn't have a tooth in his head. He smiled at me real big too as if to give me a good look at his gum line. "Speaking of which, it looks like someone beat you like a dog."

"Yeah," I said.

"Want a ride or not?" He was hard to understand because he kind of slapped his lips together when he talked, but it wasn't nothing I hadn't seen before.

"I'll take it if you'll let me get my cotton-pickin foot in the door," I said.

"Get your ass in here then, you little son-of-a-bitch," the old man said. "First, get us some refreshments out the cooler back there." I was used to playing down my natural reflexes to assholes so I shrugged to myself and did like he said.

There was one of them Styrofoam picnic coolers in the bed of the pickup, freshly packed with ice and cans of beer.

There were fishing poles, lures, and what looked to be tackle boxes of the sort that had all kinds of colorful bait and hooks. I pulled out a couple of beers, but they hadn't had a chance to get none too cold yet. He had Olympia and Hamms beer in there together.

"Now we're cooking with gas," the old man said. "You going to town?"

"Yep." I said.

"Are you a boy or a girl?" he asked me.

"I'm a boy," I said, jutting my jaw at him. "What do you think?"

"Well, you could have fooled me. You too pretty for a boy. Anyway, who you belong to?"

"I'm a Kimbrough on my mama's side and a Vaughn on my daddy's," I said.

"Oh shit," he sucked up some beer. "You all ate up then, ain't you? My name is Vernon. What's your handle?"

"Puddintame," I said. "Ask me again and I'll tell you the same."

The old man drove 35 miles an hour all the way into town. Even on Highway 54 where the speed limit was 55 mph he still just drove slow as hell. His head kind of bobbed side to side like his spinal cord wouldn't hold his big pineapple head on straight. He sang a rendition of "Amos Moses" like an idiot. He did the laughing part real good but that was probably because he wasn't right in the head. He was smoking a fat stogey and wearing a stained, dirty green jumpsuit. He looked like an escaped convict from the Church Farm in Jeff.

We passed a stand where a little Amish boy selling his family's baked goods stood up out of his chair and waved at us.

"Them Amish couldn't sell natural gas in hell," the man said. He broke into something that passed for laughter, but it sounded like he was choking to death. Then he said it again, to make sure I heard him.

Every minute or so the old guy would look at me and smile and laugh hunched over the steering wheel. I figured him for an old *prevert* for the way he was looking at me. Or he was loopy as a loon anyhow. He reminded me of something Mama would say when I would ask her where she was going. She'd say, "I'm going crazy, want to come?" The geezer got real happy when I told him I was going to the Parliament. He asked me if I had a room there, but when I said no he started cussing me and kicked me out on Bluff Street. I flipped him the Bird.

I walked a couple of blocks and then up to Court Street where the richest people in town lived. At the head of the cross street to Court was a big house with a wide driveway that curved in an arc, a stone driveway that only well-to-do people could have afforded to have build. As I made my way down the street I couldn't help wondering about the people inside. What fabulous lives they must lead. I figured they must all be doctors, lawyers, dentists, politicians to live in such big houses . . . millionaires. For the most part, the houses belonged to the people who owned all the businesses in town. There were lawn jockeys and boxwoods planted by design on the home turfs of folks determined to show they were better than everyone who they thought wasn't good enough to darken their doorsteps. I would never have enough money to be as hoity-toity as those people.

"There are always the haves and the have nots," I said to myself, remembering something Aunt Oleta used to say.

On Court Street, where the richest people in town lived, was also the funeral home where everyone around here ended up eventually when their time came. I'd already been to a couple of funerals there myself, and I guess it scared me to think someday I would die in Fairmont, like I was too good for that to happen, but at the same time I was scared I wouldn't be there with the rest of my people too. Sonny had told me when a person died they siphoned out his blood and filled him with formaldehyde to preserve the body so people could have an open casket. It really scared me to think about it, because if you had your own blood a miracle could still happen and you might come back to life! Another thing I thought was maybe when your blood was gone from your body so was your soul. Your body and soul are separated forever then. Maybe you couldn't get to heaven then. Blood was a big deal to God in the Bible.

The brick streets of downtown was closed off with sawhorses for the Kingdom Days Festival. There was arts and crafts booths and families was walking around holding hands and pushing strollers. I saw some kids eating cotton candy. The Optimist Club was giving horse and pony rides next to the fire department where the firemen was making their rig gleam like a ruby.

The old man everyone called the Prophet was on the square handing out his damnation pamphlets dressed in black. He looked out of place all dark and dour among the brightly colored banners, booths, games, and families walking on the brick streets around downtown. It was like looking at a villain in a Western who carried a Bible in one hand and maybe a pistol was tucked away on his person somewhere in case someone were to challenge him. Even when he smiled at little kids eating hotdogs, it looked like his face might crack. The streets were crowded but people walked to the edge of the wide sidewalks where he stood in front of the courthouse as if they were afraid he might snatch their souls against their will and throw them down to hell. But good and evil don't work that way. I took one of his pamphlets. He wore sunglasses and looked down at me with a sneer on his face. He didn't care about anybody. There wasn't any love in his heart.

"Jesus loves you, young man."

"Think so?" I asked. "Well, you don't know shit."

Tempie was dressed up like a southern belle with her hair hanging in loopy curls and wearing a hoop skirt, because her folks were into that kind of thing. Some people next to them had a life-sized tee-pee set up on the empty lot next to a law office. A makeshift jail was set up in front of the courthouse where they were pretending to throw all the rich people and then other rich people would post their bail for charity. An ice cream booth had my attention but I didn't have any money on me. My head started swimming just looking at all the people walking back and forth. It made me feel dizzy being around so many people.

"Daddy doesn't allow me to have gentlemen callers." Tempie hugged my arm up against her. She was imitating what she and her mama figured a Southern girl would talk like. "How're you all, Honey?"

"What are you doing today?" I asked. She smelled like Grandma Kimbrough's lilac water. She wasn't nothing but a bean pole, but she looked like a real girl in her dress with her face painted up.

"I haven't got the foggiest. Mama and Pappy made me get gussied up," she said. "How do I look, sir?"

I looked her up and down and blushed. I was too embarrassed to say much of anything, "You look all right."

"You don't look so great yourself." She pushed me away from her suddenly and disappeared in the crowd. I didn't know what she was so mad about but women are touchy about how they look. If I didn't tell Mama how beautiful she looked with just the right amount of enthusiasm she'd get all upset just like that. I guess that's how women do and you got to used to it.

The Prophet moved to the corner in front of the Savings and Loan with his Bible open in one hand and the other one was going like a piston. He was deep in the Spirit and giving everybody what-for where it concerned their salvation. His face looked wild like he just came out of the wilderness from eating locusts and honey like that story about John the Baptist: "GOD'S JUDGMENT IS UPON THE WICKED!" he cried out. People moved away from him. No one wanted to believe it was them that was wicked. When I thought of Vaughn I knew God's judgment did not come soon enough for some. They had the right to do all the evil they wanted until they died or someone killed them. Badness came out of some folks like a terrible infection and couldn't rest until everyone else had it down in their systems too.

The Prophet seemed to point directly at me: "ENTER INTO GOD'S REST, O SINNER!" He stood there with his eyes closed and his face squenched up. I expected that light from heaven to come down on him, the Jacob's Ladder, and take him up in a "twinkling of an eye." But the time of Tribulation, he was fond of preaching on it, was near "but not yet at hand." He said other stuff too, but I was too busy to listen. I was a kid. I had plenty of time to rest. Time to rest when you're dead is what Sonny used to say.

A girl what looked like she was fifteen with a cute little redheaded baby girl propped on her low-slung hip, spat back at the Prophet, "I ain't no sinner. I go to church, motherfucker!"

"Here now," an old man's voice in the crowd said in response.

Standing there with the families of Fairmont all crowded in one place, I started to think about those fires of hell. The men and women in their fancy town clothes burst into flame around me. A little girl with a balloon was suddenly grabbing and smacking at her yellow dress because it was on fire doing a little dance in her patent leather shoes. An old man in his ancient western suit fell on the ground, rolling around, trying to put out the hellfire that enveloped him. Fire was everywhere. Human nature being what it was people would kill each other to make sure the fire didn't land on them. They'd offer up the person standing next to them first. I saw God standing on a cloud, he looked exactly like pictures I'd seen of Zeus, pitching balls of fire down on everyone on earth.

Wrath. God's judgment, I could see it, would be visited on folks who already thought they was good enough to go to heaven.

Then just like that all the fire was gone again. Everything was pretty much normal except I was panting a little bit. A pregnant lady with long hair down to her waist asked me if I was okay. I could only nod. No wonder everyone thought them Bible prophets was nuts seeing visions and stuff.

"What's wrong with that big boy, Mommy?" the pregnant woman's little boy asked clutching at her hand and making me think of a monkey wearing his little sailor's suit.

"THE DEAD IN CHRIST SHALL RISE FIRST . . ."

The Prophet's voice trailed after me like God's finger poking my conscience. I just wanted to get away from that talk. It seemed like to me that God made some people act crazy and I certainly didn't want to do that. Living in the same town where the state funny farm was always had kids wondering who was insane and who was normal. It appeared to be a dead heat to me.

The smell of food was making me hungry so I sat there on a bench probably looking pathetic, because a woman dressed in an old gown that poofed out around her twirling a little umbrella that she called a "parasol" gave me her big pretzel to eat. I wolfed it down and went over to the Parliament. I didn't see Sonny's truck parked out front, but I thought he might at least give me some spare change for rides and a slushy.

I rode the rickety elevator up to Sonny's room and knocked and waited and knocked. I could tell by the way the door sounded that nobody was there. When I went to the elevator and punched the button nothing much happened. I kept waiting for the elevator to come back up to me but it never did no matter how many times I punched the button.

The back steps were as good as it got so I walked down them and noticed the shiny part of the floor, where millions of footsteps had worn the boards smooth near the rail. The rest of each of the steps still held its varnish all right. On the ceiling in the lobby was a fancy bright tin decor like they'd had since the olden days I was willing to bet. When I walked in front of the office, the man who worked there asked me if he could help me in a way that asked *what the hell are you doing here* and *get out*. When I told him I was looking for Sonny, he suddenly became disinterested and started watching the Cardinals game on his little black and white.

"Sonny and a woman checked out about an hour ago. She was a goodlooking woman too. Why she would want to run with such trash is beyond me?"

"What did she look like?"

"I don't know," he said. "She had wavy dark hair and a nice figure."

"What's the score?" I asked.

"2-1 in the bottom of the fifth," he said, taking his cigar out of his mouth as a matter of civility. If someone asked you the score to the Cardinals game, it was a big deal, even if the someone asking was just a punk kid. "Brock's up," he said it sounded like the crowd was booing, but really they were saying "LOU!" I'd never been to a baseball game, but I'd always wanted to go. A boy's daddy should take him to at least one game in his life.

When I went out onto the sidewalk the heat reflected in my face, suffocating me. The police station was right down the street and I thought about telling them my mama was missing. I knew how that would end up, though: me living with Aunt Oleta. No thanks. A part of me felt abandoned, but another part of me was kind of interested in the way things was happening like an invisible giant was controlling all the foolish things people did.

Across from the Spot Cafe there was a crowd for a race between three different groups of people pushing beds on wheels across the parking lot. It was a funny thing to see, but then seeing all those people together having fun made me think just how alone I was.

Everyone was having fun despite the fact that just about everybody was scared to death of what Vaughn might do next. I didn't know anybody who would stand up against him now. I thought Sonny might, but since him and Mama left town I figured it was up to me now. Mama had run away from things her whole life and that didn't seem to work too well. Sometimes you got to take care of things yourself. Vaughn would probably kill me eventually but I had to do something instead of just waking one morning finding myself "poleaxed" like Old Roy would put it.

There was one thing I was meant to do. Nothing else mattered.

The King's Daughters

I went to see Grandma Kimbrough at the nursing home. Angie, an attendant who had just graduated from high school, told me Grandma had practically quit eating and talking. While we were talking, an old guy was hollering from his room down the hall that his catheter had slipped out again. I didn't know what a catheter was but the old man sounded like he was dying. To be honest he sounded like he was drunk. So I started down the halls that smelled like they had been washed the bug spray. I followed Angie into the room where all the caterwauling was coming from. The old guy had a big toothless grin on his face and nodded his head eagerly. Angie rolled her eyes at me. I gave her an embarrassed wave and backed out of the room.

The sound of clarinets pulled me into Grandma's room where she was sitting in a rocking chair near the window. I sat on the foot of her bed and watched her looking out the window. She acted like she didn't know I was there. She looked up into the sky with her hand planted against the window. One of her biggest fears since I could remember had been getting sent to King's Daughters some day. King's Daughters was a place where they took care of old ladies who had completely lost their marbles and the ability to feed themselves and use the toilet. Here she was.

Her left hand was shaking in her lap. She was holding her mouth at a funny angle too like she was getting ready to make a smartass remark. Seemed like something worse than a little rheumatism or alzheimers, but when I went out into the hall I couldn't find Angie anywhere. Just old people standing in the halls. There were quite a few people seatbelted into highchairs. One old guy with cataracts over his blue eyes looked right at me, and with his legs crosses kicked his leg like a flirty girl, and bawled: *YAHOO! YAHOO!*

"Howdy Pardner!" Ruby Korsmeyer said to a little old man who had a now permanent look of surprise on his face. The old dude's head came up like a turtle's coming out of his shell. He grabbed her by the hand and started laughing his old man's laugh. Even sang the chorus with her the best he could without teeth. I hoped somebody shot me before I got so old I didn't do nothing but sit in a wheel chair all day long.

Ruby was one of Grandma Kimbrough's roommates. She was wearing her trademark red cowboy hat that balanced on top of her Jiffy Pop hairdo and at least once a day she made her rounds through the nursing home singing to everyone like she was working a Vegas strip joint according to Mama. Ruby used to be a backup singer for all the big names at the Ozark Opry in the early days and she wasn't no spring chicken then either.

"Howdy!" Ruby said to me.

"Hi Ruby," I said.

"I know you're not no cowboy," Ruby said. "But I was once in love with a cowboy and I'm going to sing a song about it and goes something like this . . ." And then she tore into some cowboy love song that even had yodeling in it.

Grandma Kimbrough was moving her mouth like she was talking to someone, but no words were coming out. Maybe she thought she was singing. I hoped to God I didn't end up in such a state. I loved her but I hated seeing her that way. Ruby went on down the hall like the born entertainer she was. I heard her shout another howdy at someone. Grandma once told Mama that Ruby loved the menfolk and then I heard her loudly whisper, "She's a slut!"

She seemed to give up on talking then and looked at her hands folded up in her lap. Being nosy like I am I started snooping. On her dresser was all the old black and white pictures in frames I had seen a million times. There was a picture of my Mama squatted down next to a bird dog when she was a real little kid. There was a blurred picture of a man with his hand on my shoulder when I was about half the age I am now. The man looked familiar. It reminded me of Sonny, but the face was blurred as if someone had jerked just as they snapped the picture.

Grandma had been beautiful when she was young, but it was a long time ago. To me time seemed to barely move but it looked like it must pick up steam at some point. It was hard to believe Grandma hadn't been born looking the way she looked, older than the hills, rubbery skin and squishy veins that gave way when I squeezed her hands.

"Take me with you," Grandma said. "Take me with you. Don't leave me in this place. They are trying to kill me here. They've been poisoning my food."

I knew it had been a mistake to come see Grandma. She wasn't right in the head and I needed to find someone that had it together in their heads instead of full of rusty memories and cobwebs.

"Look out for Mama," Grandma said in a little girl voice. I didn't know if she was talking about her Mama from the olden days or mine now.

The No-Account Boy

A pair of jays was harrying a crow, crying out at the larger bird as they took turns poking at it with their beaks in mid-flight. The blue jays were protecting their nest. Even though the jays were smaller, together they could drive the crow away. I saw some jays dive bombing the neighbor's cat after one of the baby birds fell out of the nest. Eventually the baby died, but they terrified that cat. It had to run under the neighbor's Cutlass Supreme until the birds forgot about him.

I had to get my hands on a gun. I dearly regretted leaving my pistol on the kitchen table at the trailer. It crossed my mind to break into Vaughn's Dodge and get whatever piece he had stuffed in his glove box, but the dogs would raise up a racket and I'd never get close enough. Buddy wouldn't be there and that tore me up inside, but I kept it together.

Roy was letting me crash out in the backroom on his cot. He brought me sandwiches from home, bratwurst and Saltine crackers some days. Other days he made peanut butter and jelly on Wonder bread– he'd even bring the prizes they stuffed in Wonder bread like iron-on decals. Roy covered for me when Sheriff Merrill came around asking questions. Aunt Oleta knew about Roy and the Dr. Peppers so she came by with Luther and Clarence looking for me. I was surprised she'd trouble herself over a no-account boy like me, but there she was chicken squawking out front. I could smell her lavender perfume lingering in the air even though she was gone. Roy played dumb with everyone. Called me a nuisance and a no good child. I told him he didn't have to be so convincing.

"Oleta's still got some knockers on her," Roy said as he ate a little bag of red carmelized peanuts he had pluck off the sale rack. "You think she wears one of them Cross Your Heart bras?"

"Gross," I said. "Who cares? Besides, she's so religious she wouldn't have nothing to do with anybody. She's too holier than thou."

"I'll tell you what . . ." Roy chewed on his peanuts with his front teeth. "If she gets to heaven she'll ask to see the upstairs."

Drinking all that soda pop was teaching me to cut loud and dangerous belches. Roy liked to tell truckers to pull his finger when they came in to pay on account. On account they ain't got no money, Roy liked to say. It was obvious to me that he thought he was some kind of laugh-riot. There was a lot to learn from Roy. He had special soap to take the grease off. He showed me how, even without the soap, he could use gasoline to wash oil off just as good. Off and on trucks pulled up delivering things for the office or the garage. Roy signed his name on papers instead of giving paper money. Boxes of stuff were piling up. Roy had me stack the boxes in the back. Vaughn would have called it swag. Then, later, Roy had me put things out on the racks in the office or stack up quarts of oil and brake fluid in the garage.

"You don't have to give them money when they deliver your stuff?"

"I sign my life away." He smiled. "They all have different due dates for bills I got to pay by check later on."

Roy was a good business man and people liked him. On the other hand, Vaughn might know a lot about being an outlaw but he never did show me anything useful like how to change the oil in a lawn mower or change a flat on a bike. I wondered if I could run a business someday. Maybe I could be like one of the nickel millionaires in town and buy a house on Court street.

"What do you think you're going to do, Kid?" Roy looked out the big window watching the traffic go by. "I'm glad for the free labor and all, but you can't stay here forever. You can't stay much longer either. Everybody around comes into this station. I been saying I ain't seen you, but other folks have seen you in here. You're going to have to get before we both get caught."

"Can't I stay one more day?" I asked.

He tipped his hat back like cowboys do in the movies with the tip of their pointy finger pushing up on the brim and sighed heavily.

"I reckon Elston Vaughn really is your daddy."

"Yep," I said.

"I been trying to think what you can do," Roy said. "I don't know what to tell you. You're going to have to figure out for yourself. Maybe you're going to have to go back to your mama or stay with Oleta. I know, I know. She's a religious fanatic. Got it bad for Jesus, but she might be the only can protect you from Vaughn, legally."

"Legal ain't protected no one so far." I said. Besides, Mama run off again with Sonny."

"True," Roy said. "You sure are a smart kid. Well, you could always go back to Vaughn and just do what he tells you. We could call you Little Vaughn and you could grow up to be just like him. How about that? You might even come in here and hold me up one day. Haul off all my Dr. Pepper!"

"Oh Roy." I laughed. "I'd never do nothing like that."

"You would be doing me a favor if you did."

"What?"

"You're the only one who drinks Dr. Prune Juice."

"That's why I'm the only one around here ain't full of crap," I said.

"Look who it is!" Roy said. "Get in the back room now."

Just then we seen Vaughn's Dodge barreling down Highway 54. No doubt he'd heard about me hiding out here. He was going to come in and beat up Wiener and Roy, or shoot them. I could just feature it all in my mind now. I ran back to the office and slammed the door shut, but then I opened it just a little. I could see Roy walking out to the pumps like Vaughn was his favorite customer through the crack. Roy started pumping gas for Vaughn. I could see Vaughn smiling holding a bottle of Jack by the neck. He'd say something and then take a nip. He offered some to Roy, but he just smiled back all *I'm on duty or I'd kill the rest of that whiskey for you* but then suddenly Vaughn looked offended and was pounding Roy's chest with his finger. Someone probably told on me by now. Vaughn paid Roy. He looked three sheets to the wind. Whiskey crazy. I'd seen that look before. He hopped in his truck and roared off nearly colliding with a Blazer.

"The jig is up," Roy's face had gone white.

"What happened?"

"He knows you're here," Roy said. "He said to send you home. I'm sorry, Honey Boy, I truly am. You're going to have to go on home now."

"I don't think I can," I said. "He might kill me."

"Whatever you do," Roy said. "Don't tell me where you're going so when I say I don't know where you are I can do it with a clear conscience. Stay out of trouble if you can."

I shook Roy's hand and he nodded gravely. He looked down at his work shoes as if he might want to say something. His lips moved a little, but then he just looked back up at me.

"Take care of yourself, Kid."

Some with a Kiss, Some with a Gun

My heart almost exploded in my chest. I was walking down the gravel road trying to take a shortcut back to town when Vaughn pulled up next to me. He nodded for me to hop in. I was afraid to do it at first. Then I was mad for him shooting Buddy. I cut a sidewards glare at him. He moved his head back in a gesture that said not to get high and mighty, so I had to cover up my honest feelings. He was wearing a blue chambray shirt, there was the odor of new mowed grass, and weeds from the side of the road the county tractors were working on and the smell of honeysuckle and that whisper tickling my ear kept saying, *Get long gone.* When I opened the door to climb in there was a little puppy dog thumping his tail on the seat and looking like he was grinning at me.

"Oh man," I jumped in the truck, put the pup on my lap and began stroking his head and rubbing behind his ears.

"Look at the size of those feet," Vaughn said. "He's going to be a big one."

I couldn't help thinking about Buddy then. A pup couldn't take his place. I knew he hadn't been my dog, but he was one of the best friends I had had for awhile. Animals were friendlier and kinder than most folks I ever met.

I went ahead and shut the door. A person who could give a pup to a boy couldn't be all bad I tried to tell myself but what if he just shot it too? I couldn't bear to see it happen again. The midday glare made it hard to see anything except in a haze of white light like those people who said they had gone to heaven in a tunnel after they died and then later came back into their bodies. Seeing Vaughn made me feel like I had come back into my body.

He put his hand on my shoulder and turned to look into my eyes "You know I think a whole helluva of a lot of you," Vaughn said.

"I guess," I said.

"No," he said. He wouldn't leave it alone. "Look at me. I really do. Tell me you believe I'm telling you the truth."

"I believe you," I said. "But . . . what you done . . . wasn't good . . ."

"I know it," Vaughn said. "I ain't proud of myself. But don't ask me to apologize. I don't never apologize. I want to make things up to you though. I want us to be pals again. Don't you want that? Hell, I'll take you to the carnival when it comes and let you ride the roller coaster . . . buy you whatever you want . . ."

"Why would you do all that?" I asked. "I'm just a kid."

"No you ain't," he said. "You're THE KID. And don't nobody mess with the Kid. You're like a son to me. That's something that counts with the Vaughns. You get adopted by us and you belong forever."

Vaughn was bending over backwards for me although I didn't know why. Probably just trying to trip me up. I could tell he felt bad about killing Buddy, but I was afraid he was crying crocodile tears so to speak.

I could have hopped out. Slammed the door. Climbed over the barbed wire fence and ran through the hayfield and probably he wouldn't have chased after me. But just as I was considering what to do, I felt the puppy's tongue on my hand. I smiled sourly. Vaughn turned on the radio and gunned the engine.

"Want to go fishing?" he asked.

"Sure," I said. "Why not?"

I was biting my tongue not to cuss him out.

"Reach under the seat and see if you don't feel that bottle of Jack."

I bent forward but couldn't find it at first. It had rolled back a ways but finally I pulled it out and held it out to him.

"Unscrew the cap for me since I'm driving."

"Here you go." The smell of it burnt my nose.

"Thanks," he tipped it back like it was lemonade. "Oh, that's what I needed."

No matter how wrong Vaughn did me, I couldn't seem to walk away. At least, he wanted to have me around, more than I can say for most grown-ups who don't even like kids. He already had his poles and tackle box in the bed of the truck like he'd known I was going to go along with whatever he said.

Or maybe he would have went anyway.

"We're going to do us a little ichthyology," Vaughn said. I had nary an idea what in the name of Judas Priest he was talking about.

He pulled off the road shoulder under a sycamore. We was near a branch that connected off the Vaughn's Hill creek. I don't know that it had a name. Probably, it did, but I just never heard it other than "the creek." Vaughn gave me a length of rope to tie around the pup's leather collar. The puppy was black with some brown on his forelocks. He looked like pups I had seen that were shepherd-lab mixes. His little red tongue lolled out as if he were happy to follow us.

"We'll teach him to ride in the bed of the truck and bark at people and show his teeth," Vaughn growled, putting his hands like claws on either side of his head, as if to show me what it might look like. Vaughn had me carry the tackle box. He carried the poles and a cooler with beer I figured and hopefully some Cokes or root beers.

The creek flowing past sounded like the voices of children laughing. There was a mini waterfall where the water was white like soap or cake frosting and bubbling. A crane was standing stock still on the opposite side of the bank plucking at a frog. I had never seen one of them before that I could remember. It gave us the eye for awhile. It looked like it could have been as tall as Vaughn. Finally it heaved itself heavily into the air and flew off from us, and the trees made it hard to see where it went.

We sat our equipment down and started tossing stones sidearmed into the falls. Vaughn pointed and the head of a water moccasins made its way to the far bank. He tied the pup to a tree with a little rope he'd pulled out of his pocket. The pup tugged at the rope and whined at us. There was a fallen tree that stretched across the width of the creek, and another tree lay down on its side, too, perfect for us to use as a benchseat while we fished—after we chased off a snapping turtle that was trying to get sundrenched.

Vaughn had me working on untangling the lines while he drank PBR. After thirty minutes of messing with the equipment, he finally pulled out his pocket knife and cut the lines and started all over again with new gaffs, lure; he even had a gig over to the side just in case. He was talking about how good some fried catfish would taste, but we'd have to take it back to the house so Arlene could fix it up. That meant we would have to stay out there for awhile to catch enough for everybody.

"That water sure looks good," Vaughn said after awhile. "Let's jump in."

He took off his shirt and his chest was muscular and so hairy he could have been part ape. He had a pretty good-sized beer belly on him, too.

He was all set to jump in. He had taken off his boots and his hand was on his belt buckle when he noticed I was just sitting there. His eyes were on me funny now.

"Tell me you know how to swim," he belly-laughed.

I shook my head and wished I could go hide under a rock.

"Well, I be damned," he said. "Don't your mama ever think to teach you nothing?"

"I don't know." I cut my eyes over to the pup I had decided to name Star because he had a white spot on his forehead. He was chewing grass as happy as he could be. I wished I could change places with him, or even go wild and disappear into the woods and live down in the Ozark mountains, where no one would think to look. "Mama barely knows how to swim either. She's afraid of the water."

"She's afraid of a lot of things. Now, let's skin off those clothes," he clapped his hands. "We ain't going nowhere until we taught you to swim like a dolphin."

"That's okay," I said. I wished he would just forget about it. It entered my mind he might drown me for sure.

"My ass!" Vaughn said.

The terror rose up in me and I started to breath hard and heavy.

"Stop that, now," Vaughn said. "You're going to start hyperventilating and then what're we going to do. You ain't getting out of this one. You'll never be a man if you don't learn how to swim."

"How old were you when you learned to swim?" I asked, hoping to get his mind off teaching me.

He thought for a moment. His big head hung back on his neck like he was looking up to heaven to find the answer: "I don't remember ever not being able to swim. We were all country kids. We were always down at the creek playing and fishing and swimming. I must have been real young. Now, off with them blue jeans. C'mon, down to your comfortables. We're going to do this!"

The rock bluff on the far bank rose up. I could see the layers of strata, and I prayed the whole thing would rise up and kill me like a bug so I wouldn't have to learn to swim. I wished I knew how already. It was just those dreams of swimming, legs thrashing, and something grabbing your legs and pulling you down to a rocky lair.

Vaughn tied the pup to a little tree in the shade where he could get to the water if he wanted a drink. I took off my clothes and stepped in the water. Vaughn dove in and disappeared under the seagreen water surface and for a moment he was gone and the world was silent and calm. When his head came back up and he was sputtering,

I knew what I had to do. The Bible said to "gird up your loins" whatever that meant. I thought it just meant get ready—so I did. I kind of ran out into the water up to my waist and waited to die.

"You're so pitiful looking," Vaughn laughed. "Look how skinny you are! Now, for this to work, you've got to trust me."

I nodded.

"Do you trust me?"

"I guess," I said. "As much as I trust anybody."

"Damn," Vaughn said. "You sure are awful cynical for a kid. It ain't good to start out that way. You haven't even had any women problems yet."

I shrugged.

"What you got to do is lay down on your back and let your legs float up to the surface." He demonstrated for me.

It took me a few tries to get the hang of it. He came up to me and put one hand at the small of my back, and the other he put under my head. The smell of the whiskey enveloped me in a fog.

"Don't go rigid," he said. "Relax. Close your eyes. Don't think about anything. Take a long, deep, breath." He began to breathe deeply through his nose and out through his mouth. "Good."

"It's hard to relax when you know you might die any minute," I said.

"Don't I know it," he said. "That's why you got to live every minute the best you can, because you never said a more true statement in your whole life. Now, breath deep again."

His voice sounded like it was coming to me from across the country. I made up my mind to die if I was going to or if Vaughn decided to kill me I might as well just let him. The sky was yellow-white when I closed my eyes. I felt my legs float up again to the top as if they had a will of their own. I forgot about the Voice. The notion that Vaughn was a bubble left of plum was something I just refused to think about.

It was tough to make my mind think about nothing. I told myself to "just. . .be." Lights exploded behind my closed lids, lights of a new heaven and a new earth. The feeling was beyond description. My body was lifted out of the water, and I opened my eyes.

"I think you fell asleep," Vaughn said. "Turn over, because now you're going to do the dog paddle."

His hand slid around to my belly. He told me to kick my feet like I was riding a bike underwater and then make my hands into cups and get them going. At first, it didn't work. I couldn't get everything going all at once because I was afraid of going under which is exactly what happened. After doing that a couple of times I started swimming for real. I was swimming somehow. It was the biggest thing I had done since I'd learned to ride a bike. I dogpaddled all around the creek and after awhile I even did a few actual strokes over my head. The puppy was barking and carrying on like he was excited because I was doing his kind of swimming. My fear had vanished. I was a swimmer now. I still wasn't in love with the idea of sticking my head under the surface though. Something about it was too much like dying to me.

We tried to fish more a little farther upstream, but when we hadn't caught anything but the same snapping turtle twice and tiny crappies. Vaughn said it was a good thing we were sport fishermen anyhow. We packed up our stuff and drove to a roadside joint called Butch's that also doubled as a mom-and-pop grocery store and they fixed us up some greasy burgers dripping with cheese and home fries. I tossed my burger scraps to the dog. He was likely to be a good dog, but I wasn't about to let Vaughn off. Let him give that dog to some other sucker.

Back in the truck, the dog had its paws on my lap. We were flying down one of the narrow back roads. The wind was whipping my hair around. Vaughn actually looked happy; It didn't look right on him. I didn't want to ruin the day or make him mad but the questions were swirling in my head. He had a way of controlling me, but I felt helpless to do anything about it. He could be so cruel that any little kindness, like giving me a Heinz 57 dog seemed twice as important as it would have if he acted like other kids' dads did. I couldn't help the feeling of relief washing over me like a damp washcloth when you're head's on fire with fever.

"Why ain't the cops come after you yet?"

"What's that you say?"

I looked out the window and began my old game of making Fingerman run through the fields and then leap over the telephone poles as we drove along.

"Spit it out," Vaughn said.

"Why ain't the cops come to get you yet?" I looked at him when I said it.

"You might say I have friends in high places." Vaughn smirked. "Really you just have to know how to work the systems like the richies do. Money makes the world revolve around the sun. You can do most anything if you line things up proper."

"Not everybody wants money, do they?"

"What a naïve kid you are." Vaughn said every big word, like naïve, with a jokey tone. "You are right. Some people can't hardly face their conscience, but there are other forms of persuasions, *boy-san*."

He grunted and he whipped down a gravel road I'd never been on before. There wasn't a green county sign marking this particular road so I took it for a long driveway. It needed a little gravel here and there but it was understandable since it was a lot of road for an individual to buy gravel for. It was a twisty curvy; we drove by trees that had had their tops sheared off by last year's ice storm. It had been particularly bad out here, and nobody had come out and cleaned it up like in town. There were single wide trailers with cars on blocks in the front yards, and they'd be followed by a truly nice, respectable old farmhouse. It was a real hodge podge down this road.

After six or seven miles of this, we passed an old silo by the road and I could see another blacktop road ahead. Before we got to the road, Vaughn shoved an 8-track of Jerry Lee Lewis into the deck. The Killer was belting out "Hold on I'm Comin'."

"Man, he's good" Vaughn turned up the volume. His hair was still wet from swimming and it made him look not as scary as normal.

"Yep," I said.

"Beats that disco shit to hell."

There was another farmhouse just over the rise. I knew it was important because we started slowing down. Vaughn turned the dial on his CB, every so often a dispatcher told the cops to go here or there. The police codes were easy to figure out especially after Vaughn had already explained that the pig's car and badge number were the same. It was simple for Vaughn to figure out how long it would take for anyone to get where he was when he wanted to push it.

"Whose place is this?" I asked. "It's pretty nice."

It was a two story white house with a recently painted red barn and the star symbol painted in white around loft level. It was easy to see it was a horse place rather than cattle. It was kept up too neat for cattle and didn't stink to high heaven like hogs. I could just make out a nice machine shop behind the house and someone with a sense of nostalgia had even kept the old outhouse, but no doubt they didn't use it no more.

There was a fairly new catfish pond down a little further. The grass around the banks was patchy.

"Whose place you think?"

Vaughn pulled the Dodge into the drive and I saw MERRILL on the mailbox. My heart was thrashing around in my chest. This wasn't like skipping school or turning over an outhouse at Halloween. What were we doing there?

A sound of a train crying off in the distance. I was trying to see just how drunk Vaughn was. His mood could change on a dime. Just me asking about the cops was all he'd needed. It was like everything was a threat or a challenge to him.

"Oh my God," I said.

Vaughn laughed but not like he thought it was funny.

"Give me that .38 that's underneath my seat," Vaughn said. "I got this motherfucker here."

I jumped quick to obey, "Okay."

"Good."

"Check to see is it loaded."

"It's loaded," I said.

"Put it on the seat."

I did it.

A big black shepherd came loping up to the truck and Vaughn took a shot at it with the .38 but missed. It turned and ran back to the house. Vaughn laughed loud then. It pissed me off, just looking at his cruel fat face. I couldn't get the picture of what he done to Buddy out of my head. He grabbed the neck of the bottle between his legs and took a big swig of Jack and sloshed it back and forth in his cheeks like mouthwash. A pretty woman in a dress came out on to the porch but only for a second. Her hand had gone to her mouth.

"Big Vaughn is here for you, baby." Vaughn revved the engine with a sneer on his face.

"What are you going to do?"

"Get that rifle down," Vaughn said. "Don't hit me in the head with it."

My hands were shaking, I was so nervous. I was afraid I might drop the rifle on Vaughn's head.

"Just hold on to it in case I need it."

A tall, rail thin man in a straw cowboy hate now came out in the woman's place. His hand didn't run to his mouth; instead it went to the big iron that *wasn't* on his hip. It was Sheriff Merrill and he was walking toward us, but he seemed smaller wearing his civilian clothes.

"What are you doing, Vaughn?" I asked.

"Come and get it, son," Vaughn . "Ain't we having fun now?"

He now started revving the engine like a madman. The engine popped a couple of times in the process. Merrill stopped where he was as if to guard the house with his body. That was fine by Vaughn. He put the truck into drive and started barreling toward Merrill. When it looked like we weren't going to stop, Merrill started backing up to the oak tree the circle drive went around.

"Hey Ted! You ready to die? Teddy boy!" Vaughn took the Dodge around the circle drive. He was holding the .38 out the window and pointing it at Merrill now. Merrill looked confused.

Vaughn was going to kill the sheriff. I could see the papers now. I was too terrified to move, although I should have gotten down in the floorboard. "You want some of me? Here I am? You want some of me?"

"Get out of here, Vaughn! This is my house!" Merrill was red-faced and shouted back.

"I kill people who get in my way!" Vaughn said. "I kill their wives and their itty bitty daughters! Hey, you got an itty bitty daughter, don't you?"

"Get out of here Vaughn! This is it! You ain't getting away with this!"

Merrill said some other strangled words too, about being the law, but I couldn't make them out. Vaughn cussed back at him. He straightened the truck out after about three loops, and down the drive we went. The scanner was alive now. Merrill's wife had called in the incident to the dispatcher. They would send a car to come out here, but they wouldn't get here for fifteen minutes. We'd be long gone down another back road by then.

Suddenly Merrill's face was in the window with his hands on Vaughn. The truck was still making circles around the drive. The sheriff hollered at us everytime we circled back around. Vaughn batted the sheriff in the face with the butt of the .38 when he tried to hang on to the door, and then he disappeared out of the window and was lying on the ground holding his hands over a bloody gash under his eye.

"Check your mailbox, Teddy" Sweat was pouring down Vaughn's face. "There's a special package for you."

"Son-of-a-bitch!"

"Ooh wee!" Vaughn laughed. "That will teach him to watch his ass, I do believe. I'm going to be that man's shadow."

"Are you crazy?" I said.

He looked at me very soberly now. "Don't never say nothing like that to me again."

We barreled out of there but when we came back to the mailbox Vaughn got out and fished his hand underneath his seat. There was a fat envelope with the word LAW DOG scrawled on it. I had to keep the puppy from lunging out the door when Vaughn got out. He stuck the envelope in the mailbox and hefted himself back into the truck and slammed the door.

"What was in that?"

"What do you think?" Vaughn laughed like I was the world's biggest goober.

"I don't know, man," I said. "Money?"

"The rent," Vaughn said. "A thousand smackers. Sometimes you have to grease the wheels of justice. Let that be a lesson to you. Next time it'll be a rattlesnake we're putting in there if he don't act right."

He turned on the gravel road as smooth as you please. He put the pedal to the metal as the pastures, fences, ditches, and old bridges flew by like they were the ones moving and we were sitting still. We must of hit every pothole on that road. Vaughn threw the .38 down in the seat between us where it bounced toward me like it was looking for help. Here was my chance. I glanced at Vaughn but he was looking down the road. I could just grab it, point it and shoot! All this hell would be over.

I grabbed it.

"Don't point that in my direction."

I put the gun back in the glove box and slammed the little door shut harder than I needed to. I saw my pale reflection in the side mirror. I could feel his eyes drawing a bead on me even though I wasn't looking at him. If he'd told me he could read minds I'd have believed him because what I felt was always on the surface. Sometimes he seemed all right like when we went swimming, but being nice could be one of his mind control tricks. I looked at him, stared him in the eyes, and what was looking back was a flood of blackness from a dark river. It would be easy as sin to fall into the blackness and never make it back out.

The Mouse Trap

Rusty brought a thirty-aught-six to the Stillman mausoleum. He was carrying a gunny sack at his side. Tempie had a candle for us to put in the tomb and talk until late if we wanted. She also brought us some leftover biscuits and bacon strips. Her mama, Irene, made some good country-style biscuits. After Tempie prayed over the food we devoured it all in no time flat. I was half-hoping Rusty had some Cokes in his sack, but he said he didn't so we washed them down using one of them olden-time pumps out behind the shed on the cemetery grounds: you had to pump the handle like crazy to get a trickle of water.

The sun was now setting pinkish-orange in the west. A full moon was dripping red with blood and looked like you could reach out and touch it with a fork. Day was making its slow exchange with night. Instead of sitting inside the mausoleum we crawled on top beneath that awesome moon. We'd look up at it every so often like it was a god about to speak, but it looked down on us with its bloody eye and stayed silent the way gods tend to do these days. The stars and the midnight blue sky looked like you could float up there and bump your head on the ceiling of the earth.

If I needed more proof that there ain't gods or heroes, remembering Sheriff Merrill laying on the ground holding his bloody nose was plenty. I was going to need help. My mind went through all the big men I knew who were tough, but compared to Vaughn they were pussy cats. I couldn't see Luther calling him out. Why would he? Even Uncle Sonny wasn't going to try to whip him. He'd even left Missouri to get away from Vaugh. It wouldn't do nogood to call the cops either because they would have come and got him by now if they could.

When you lose all hope you stop thinking about being saved. If I knew anything it was that I was too young to give up trying just yet. I didn't have nothing to lose so it made it easier because I didn't have much to gamble with in the first place.

It was getting warm outside, and I could smell someone burning brush not too far away. All three of us had our noses in the air testing the evening breeze and listening to what there was on the wind.

"So you think you can stand up to Uncle Vaughn?" Rusty handed over the thirty-aught-six. "You're going to need this."

"No," I put my hand in the air. "You keep it. I won't need that."

"What are you going to do, Honey Boy?" Tempie asked.

"The hell you ain't going to need it!" Rusty said. "You better take it. It belongs to Punkin and he'll probably beat my ass for it. He won't know I stole it for you, but they figure I pinch anything not nailed down."

"You do!" I said.

"I know." He looked proud the way he said it.

"I think you should just stay away from Vaughn." Tempie shook her head so her hair rippled back behind her and fell into place like Jessica Lange in King Kong. "Stay out of trouble. Go live with your Aunt Oleta for awhile. I know she drives you nuts but she'll see that you're safe until you're your mama comes back."

"I've got a plan and it ain't going to Aunt Oleta's," I said.

"Your Aunt Oleta is crazy as a loon," Rusty agreed. "So what is the master plan?"

"I don't really want to say. I'm afraid you'll try to talk me out of it partially, but I'm going to need your help too. No adults will help me, but I can't sit back and watch Vaughn do what he does to people. There's a part of him that wants to be good . . ."

"I can't believe that," Tempie said. "He's plain and simple of the Devil. The only way things would be good between you and him is if you're serving him. Serving him is the same as doing the Devil's will."

"Kinda dramatic, ain't ya Temp?" Rusty laughed. "He ain't OF no devil. He's a bad man and that's all you need to know. Us Vaughns in general is bad. Not evil like from the pit of hell, but we're outlaws. I don't think it's right for you to go against another outlaw either. It's like it's against the code. How would it have looked if Billy the Kid had gone against the Outlaw Jose Wales? Besides that, if you turn him into the cops then you're turning your back on your people. That would be wrong. Without your people you ain't got nothing. It don't take a brain surgeon to know that. It's what Daddy says too."

"Like you do what your daddy says?" Tempie stood up with her hands on her hips. "Who are you to tell Honey Boy how he should live his life? He's been born again in the blood of the Lamb and baptized! He's a new creature! You're no example he should follow."

"Well say a prayer for me then," Rusty said. "Besides, just what kind of creature are you now? One of them Born Again Jesus robots? Are you going to fall down on the ground and start having seizures the way they do?"

"Listen," I said. "Don't you two start in. I wanted to talk to you because you're my best friends. What I aim to do is make it so everyone around here goes after Vaughn at the same time."

I could get along with either of them alone, but together they were too different. I wanted to be as good as Tempie, but it was in me to be as bad as Rusty. He wasn't all that bad anyway. I could see myself being more like him in the long run. I'd never seen a perfect person before. I mean, they talked about Jesus but he lived back in the Roman times or he might not have existed at all. It was confusing. I asked Brother Pappy why Jesus didn't appear in front of people and say, *Here I am* and then everyone would know he was real. Brother Pappy had said, *No, it don't work that way. You have to have faith.* He said he did appear to his disciples after his resurrection and some of them wouldn't believe either. It still seemed to me that I'd for sure believe if he did a miracle in front of my eyes like that. Brother Pappy said we lived in a different *dissipation.* I wasn't tracking what he was saying for watching the tattoo of the hula girl on his forearm.

"They're already fed up with him," Tempie said.

"Yeah," I said. "But not enough to stop him."

"What's this plan then?" Rusty said.

"I'm thinking I'll start doing things and see that they're blamed on Vaughn. I ain't proud of these things but I'm desperate. I'm thinking I'll do the same things or worse that he's been doing."

"How's that make you any better?" Tempie said.

"It don't."

"I mean," she said. "What's the difference?"

"It's the best plan I've got," I said.

"It's like mice trying to trap the biggest tomcat around with a rubberband and a paper clip," Tempie said.

"Maybe it's God telling you to do it?" Rusty smiled at Tempie. I could tell he was trying to make her mad so she would leave.

"That's a bunch of bologna!" Tempie objected.

"I know what you could do," Rusty was fiddling with the gun. "You could start burning down churches! You burn one down and give an anonymous tip to the police department that you seen Vaughn do it. You know, as a concerned citizen!"

"Ah, you would think about burning things down." I clapped him on the shoulder. "You'd probably help me with that?"

"Damn straight," he said.

"That is the most horrible thing I've ever heard," Tempie buried her face in the palm of her hands. "Just terrible. Burning down the house of God. That might be grieving the Spirit, and for that there is no forgiveness."

"See," Rusty said. "Goody Two-Shoes here is going to rat you out like a coward."

"No I am not."

"Like . . . a girl," Rusty added.

"I wouldn't do that."

"That's why they don't send girls to war," Rusty sniffed. "They can't be trusted. They'll get you killed if you ain't careful."

"How dare you, Rusty James Vaughn!" Tempie huffed. "You're just saying that because you want to set things on fire you old firebug. Everyone knows how you burned down your own daddy's barn. In olden times they would have hung you up by your neck for that!"

"And if words were bullets . . . you would have won the war."

"What are you talking about?" Tempie sat back down. "What war are you talking about?"

"The war of Tempie won't shut the hellup!" Rusty laughed.

"Let's quit all this jawing!" I said. "What do you think I should do, Temp?"

"I already told you."

"I mean," I said, "about my plan?"

"I can't help you with that." Tempie's voice went all husky. "If you go through with a plan to burn down the Temple of God I will never speak to you again."

"Aw c'mon, Temp." I held out my hand palm up and she slapped it hard. "How else can I stop Vaughn?"

"It's not your job to stop anyone. Vaughn is already a lost cause. He'll get his due at the White Throne Jugement."

"Judgment Day?" Rusty leaned over the edge and spit on the ground. "You're waiting on your Holy Roller Rapture? Christ on a stick!"

"THAT'S where you're headed Mr. Rusty Vaughn!" Tempie fumed.

"I DON'T GIVE A DAMN!" Rusty came right back. That was one of his favorite sayings. Anytime someone told him about the consequences of doing something he ought not to do he said it. "I'll take pussy any day over walking on streets of gold or flying around with angels playing harps. You can worry about heaven when you die. You got to live now!"

"Actually," I said, "I don't like that church burning plan much either. Maybe I could do other crimes like bust the window out at the hardware store and call it in like you said. I don't know."

In case there was a God I sure didn't want him to be mad at me. One minute I believed in God and then the next it seemed crazy. It was a good story. The people who made it up and put it down on paper knew how to make it real interesting, but I had more questions than anything. It really bugged me that I could pray as hard as I was capable and God wouldn't answer the prayer on something important. I even tried to make deals with God like *If you do thus and so for me, I will serve you the way you want.* It just didn't cut any ice with Him. I'd even prayed about this whole mess with Vaughn. It was spinning out of control. God wasn't paying attention, though the Devil was all ears. I decided I'd pray in tongues for awhile from now on, if I ever prayed again. Then I could say it all in the Spirit and then God would know if I was talking his spiritual language the way Brother Pappy said. Brother Pappy got me going on tongues after I got filled with the Spirit. He prophesied I'd be a preacher some day. All that didn't stop me from acting and thinking bad though.

"Burning churches sure would get everyone's attention," Rusty said. "It would make them high and mighty people in town sit up and take notice. Think about all the snotty church people. We could burn down the Presbyterian, the Catholic, and Lutheran churches first. All the richie-riches goes to them churches. Why, before long all that would be left in town would be bars and then maybe they'd be the new churches! Naturally they'd want to lower the drinking age some then. Gary Putnam is from Texas and he told me that down there you can drive when you're fifteen and drink when you're eighteen."

"That's a whole nother country," I said. I could see Rusty was probably going to start burning churches himself now that he'd gotten all jazzed up about it.

"Don't do it, Honey Boy" Tempie grabbed my hands in hers and looked at me with tears coursing down her cheeks like she was saving me from the Devil himself if she could talk me out of it. She was my good angel. "You're both going to end up in juvie or Boy's Town."

"Some of my best friends are in Boy's Town," Rusty said. "Gary Putnam got send up there last year for selling pot at the junior high. Jason Coates got sent to the military academy, but that shows you the difference between a poor kid and a rich kid."

"I'm glad I'm not rich then," I said. "I sure wouldn't want to get yelled at and wear them godawful uniforms the Krauts got to wear."

"No doubt," Rusty said.

"Oh, Honey Boy," Tempie cried. It made me think she was an actress on one of Mama's soaps.

"It's something I got to do" I took my hands away from hers. Her hands were white and flopped around on mine like doves having a seizure. I felt bad about it, but I just couldn't keep running like Mama always done. It was in me to do that too, but I wanted to fight against it.

"All right, then get out of here, split tail!" Rusty roared. "We don't need your kind of help! Why don't just go tell on us now! Be a rat fink! See how many friends you got then!"

Tempie started crying hard. She seemed as tough as the Rock of Gibraltar, but now her pale face was red with heat, and tears welled up in her eyes. I hated to see her that way but Rusty was laughing at her. He could be cruel sometimes. It was in him to be a shitbag to people. I couldn't help laughing at him the way he took so much pleasure in hurting people. He could be a real Looney Tune sometimes. I knew one day he'd do something so crazy it would make the papers. It made me worry about him since I knew it to be the truth way down in my guts. But the crazy look he had on his face plumb tickled me at the same time, and I laughed out loud.

Tempie quit crying suddenly and looked at me in disbelief. I knew she thought I was laughing at her, at her pain, but I wasn't. It was one of those misunderstandings in life that were constantly happening as far as I could tell. She let herself down the side of the mausoleum, took off running, and never looked back. She ran down the cemetery lane lined with cedars under the orange glow of street lamps.

"Get on out of here!" Rusty yelled after her. "Tell Jesus I said hi!"

"Tempie!" I yelled. "Come on back!"

I elbowed him in the arm and shook my head.

"That was a shitty thing to do."

"What?" Rusty said. "I was just kidding her. Besides, you ain't never going to get that stuff! She's too uppity for you. You think her daddy is going to let you marry her and have babies? You going to end up marrying fat Grace Ann Washburn or one of them fugly Lynch girls!"

"Fuck you," I said.

"Ha-ha," he said. "Anyway, I'm glad your girlfriend's gone. C'mon."

He jumped down with his gunny sack in hand, and gestured for me to lower down the gun which I did. We could have went anywhere on Vaughn's Hill to be alone but here we were in the center of town. If we got caught screwing around here, who knew what they'd do to us. Probably send us to juvie.

I leaped over the side and landed hard on my feet. Rusty had the thirty-aught-six up to his shoulder and was sighting like he might squeeze one off. I put my hand hard on his shoulder like I seen men in a war movie do. "Don't make me slap you," I said, joking.

"What?"

"Nothing."

"That's what I thought."

Rusty pointed the gun at someone's house, across the street, on the other side of the cemetery.

"Bitch," I said.

He very purposely leaned the gun up against the trunk of a skinny pine with a grin tugging at his cheek. I knew what he was up to. He walked up to me and put me in a headlock. We fell to the ground and flipped and flopped there. I finally worked an arm through his headlock, put a hand on his face like a zombie coming up out of the earth, put the Iron Claw on his face, and pushed him off me. I rolled him over on his back and when he couldn't get up, I patted his head. I let him up then. I didn't want to make him so mad he'd try to kick me in the balls later. Even though he was bigger than me, he just couldn't take me in a fair fight. I knew he respected that, but I was careful not to brag about it. Why make someone feel bad about the obvious? I'd seen boys do it all the time in the schools I'd gone to. A big kid would beat up a smaller kid and then crow like he was the world's heavyweight champ. I hated guys like that. Punch a guy like that in the face while he's talking tough, and he's ready to be your best friend two

minutes later. Bullies don't want nothing to do with someone
who will fight back.

Rusty got up, laughing and shaking his head. He was
amazed every time that he couldn't take me. He was bigger
and stronger: I couldn't beat him when we arm wrestled. It
just didn't add up.

"That's what I thought, boy," Rusty said. "And I did say
boy."

"Boy," I said. "I'll smack your lips together. Don't make
me slap you, boy!"

"That's what your mama said to me last night, boy," Rusty
said.

"What?"

"Nothing."

"That's what I thought," I said.

It was our standard "Who's on first?" type routine. We'd
say variations of this to each other over and over. I couldn't
remember why or how it got started, but we said it all the
time just to be funny. It kind of lightened the mood a little. It
was a relief to know you could just relax, say stupid shit, and
laugh. A guy had to goof off sometimes to keep from going
nuts. If you were too serious all the time, you'd either go mad
or you blow someone's brains out. You might even blow your
own brains out if it got to be too much pressure.

"Seriously," Rusty said, dusting off his jeans. "How the
fuck do you do that?"

"One day it will become clear when you can finally take
the pebble from my hand, Grasshopper," I said in my best
fake Chinese voice.

We went into the mausoleum. I lit the rusty green Cole-
man lantern that Tempie had brung us, and we laughed at the
shadows it made on the walls after I adjusted the flame. I'd
have to think about how to make things right between me
and Tempie again, but I decided not to worry about it so
much.

Rusty pulled out a box of cherry Swisher Sweets cigarillos. He handed me one and I lit his first and then mine. These were our favorites. Smoking was wrong but then even people who went to Redeemer stood outside after the church service smoking and flicking their butts into the gravel parking lot.

We sat back and smoked them like old codgers at the tavern. Rusty got on his evil grin and pulled out a half-pint of green label Jack, took a sip, and yipped. I never drank stuff like whiskey, but I took a nip to be sociable anyway. Jesus *had* turned water into wine at a wedding once. The whiskey burnt like acid crawling down my throat. If there had been a haystack nearby I could have lit it on fire with my breath.

"Indians," Rusty did his best Jack Nicholson imitation. "That makes me think, man. If you could live anyway you wanted, how would you live?"

"I don't know," I said. "I guess I'd be rich."

"Naw," Rusty said. "Who wouldn't pick to be rich? I just mean, what do you think you'll do when you get older?"

"I don't know at all," I said. "I feel like I got a full plate now. You tell me. How you want to live?"

"I'm going to get me a Harley one day" Rusty smoked thoughtfully. The cherry end of his cigarillo glowed like Rudolph's nose. "I want to just drive around the country and see things. Be free from living the way the world wants you to."

"How will you make money?"

"I don't know," he said. "Maybe I'll go into the Army. But that's just what I'm talking about. At school they say study hard and go to college, but I ain't no good in school. Ain't nobody in our family ever been to college. I don't want to live like all the nickel millionaires in Fairmont. I want to be fucking free, man."

"Sounds like a TV show," I said. "Rusty Vaughn IS Harley Man. He travels from town to town solving crimes and shooting the shit out of the bad guys with the gun he stole from his lazy-ass brother."

"I like that," Rusty said. "That sounds good. Become an actor like Clint Eastwood."

"That shit about killed my stomach." I held my gut.

"That's because you're a pussy."

I went outside and puked up the food Tempie brung us.

When I came back in Rusty looked a little green around the gils. He had a cigarillo clenched between his teeth and was making hand shadows of an eagle on the wall.

"Better?"

"Yeah," I said. "So are you going to back me up on this thing with Vaughn?"

He took the cigarillo out of his mouth, put the cherry out on the floor, and shoved it back in the box for later.

"Sure," he said. "I think you're a little crazy. Who would go after Vaughn?"

"I know," I said. "It's almost like we're related."

"I guess I'm crazy too."

"I'm Crazy number one and you're Crazy number two."

The night around us went quiet. The frogs down at the creek stopped gulping. I know Rusty was thinking the same thing I was. Maybe someone saw our light and was coming to check it out. A Night watchman or something.

The sound of someone walking in the cemetery besides the ghosts in their gauzy white rags was coming toward us. We were frozen looking at each other with our mouths open. Rusty blew out the candle. He'd left the gun outside against the pine tree. Maybe Tempie had gone straight to Vaughn and told him everything.

The laser beam of the flashlight appeared in the opening and shone in our eyes. We were screwed now, and we knew it.

"What are y'all doing now?" Tempie said. "I hope I didn't scare you boys?"

"Hell, naw!"

"Hey Tempie!" I was glad she had come back and wasn't too bad.

"Get in here!" Rusty said. "Hurry up before someone sees that flashlight."

"You were really mad at us earlier, huh?" I asked.

She didn't say anything, but she smiled, and her head tilted down to the concrete floor like she had the world's most precious secret

Don't Throw Your Love on Me
So Strong

One night I was walking by McNally's. Truthfully, I was looking in on Vaughn. I couldn't believe it, but Luther was in there with his hands all over a girl Mama used to work with name of Misty. Luther had done been saved, but now here he was getting drunk in a bar. Aunt Oleta would be appalled, to say nothing of Brother Pappy. I'd've asked Pappy for help, but he had a way of making all your troubles seem like they were your own fault. *Admit it and quit it.* Next thing you knew, you'd be bawling about something that wasn't even your own doing. He knew how to play the guilt card, Mama once said. I cashed in my chips on that old game.

"Honey," Luther hollered, drunk from inside. He came out and stood in the doorway. The door was hanging open, though they was running their air conditioner. "Honey, wait there, I'm coming." The blonde was clutching at his shirt a little unsteadily like he was a life preserver, but he gently pried her hands off the folds of his silk shirt with a butterfly collar.

"What are you doing in there?" I asked. "Ain't you saved?"

"Now don't get on your high horse with me, man." Luther said. I think he meant to talk to me seriously, but he was too tipsy to keep a straight-face. His eyes were bloodshot and glassy.

"You're drunk," I said, thinking I could keep him from asking questions about me if he was busy defending himself. "How many fingers am I holding up?"

"Which one of you?" he joked.

"Just as I suspected," I said. "You're three sheets to the wind."told y

"When you was little," he began "you looked like the smallest little man in the world. The way your Aunt Oleta used to dress you up made you look like a midget. I'd say to her, Lookee here you got the world's tiniest man. You could put him in a carnival. Little Nat Kimbrough . . . the World's Smallest Midget! Folks would pay fifty cents a head to see him. Right about now you look like Piglet."

"Oh, stop it," Misty Westhues started tittering, and so I thought the glass she held might shatter, it was so high and screechy. The alcohol smell was almost as strong as her drug store perfume. Luther and other men I knew had talked about her before. Everyone said she was a good time girl. What that meant was that she was easy to get in the sack.

"You welshed on your promise to God." I pointed at him. "Kids like me never doing nothing right much less get saved proper. You expect a grownup to get it right even if he ain't white."

"Now you listen here," Luther said, "You better watch that kind of talk! I'll knock you down; don't think I won't. Where you been, Honey? Everyone been looking for you. Your Aunt Oleta is worried sick. She's a good Christian woman and you shouldn't ought to worry her like that. I got a good mind to throw you down and tie you up and take you over to her house."

"Now you're just talking bull-goaded drunk," I said. "Aunt Oleta will be fine. Have you seen my mama or Sonny around?"

"I heard they left town, man," Luther said. "Sonny scared of Vaughn. Everyone is. I ain't scared of him, but you won't catch me hanging around his haunts. Sometimes he comes here and I go out the back door."

"And you ain't ascared of him?"

Luther whistled. "Hell no. But I am a judicious judge of character, and that's why I hit it when that dude comes around. He starts messing with me, and I'd have to kill him. Then I'd get sent to the pen. Dig?"

"You might not have to worry about Vaughn much longer," I said.

"I know," Luther said, looking around. "They had a big meeting at the VFW, and the men decided to protect the families of the girls who saw Vaughn shoot Starkey. He likes to torment peoples so they don't testify against him. Well, after Clevenger hightailed it out of here, Mayor Foley said it was the last straw. And, so they going to form a watch of deputized men who follow Vaughn around and *observe* him."

"Vaughn would kill them the first time around," I said.

"Don't I know it," Luther said. "He's always bragging about how nobody can catch him. He'll never serve a day in jail. Vaughn said he paid that lawyer, Atwill, such good money that he better get him off for anything bad he does in this lifetime or the next."

"We ain't air conditioning the whole world," the bartender bawled. "Close that door!"

"All right," Luther said, backing up into the bar.

"I guess I got to go, too," I said.

"Where you been staying?"

"Just tell Aunt Oleta I'm okay," I said.

"Close the got-damn door!"

"I better go in now, Honey," Luther said. "Give me a call if you need anything."

"I am looking for something," I said. "Do you know where I can get a gun?"

"Shitfire boy!" Luther howled. "Don't be coming around here talking about getting no gun. Crazy motherfucker! Get on out of here."

"Hi there, Honey Boy," Misty said. Misty made Luther look stone cold sober. She was wearing a tube top and was showing off quite a bit of titty. She wore a corsage made up of pink carnations around her wrist. When she was sober, she was pert and cute, although a little bit wide across the backside. Now her hair was all mussed, and her lipstick was smeared from kissing on Luther and who knew who else. Some men said Misty was a friendly girl; others called her a nympho, but she seemed like a decent enough person. only bound to hurt herself. She could be hard to resist.

"I always wondered why they called you 'Honey,'" Misty said. "Is it because you taste so sweet?" She grinned and leaned around Luther's big arm. "I could just eat you up, Honey Boy, but that wouldn't be right."

"Leave that boy alone," Luther said. "He ain't got sense as it is. If he busted a nut on you, his head would blast off to outerspace."

"Come on in here, Honey," Misty said. "You want a Smith and Wesson?"

"GET THE HELL OUT!" the bartender said, and pushed Luther and Misty outside and locked the door. People inside, mostly men, let up a roar of laughter at what the bartender done.

"Don't worry he'll let us back in." Misty laughed and did a high kick and one of her high-heeled shoes went flying out into the street like a red shooting star.

"He's just a child." Luther wagged his big finger in front of her face. He was set on lecturing her. She appeared to sober up for a second and flashed him a big cheesy smile. Misty was cute, not beautiful, but she had a great smile. Not only did she have a great smile and big titties, but she knew how to flirt. She was major league in the flirt department. In her face, there was still traces of the little girl she had been. She had a cute little beauty mark on her cheek. I knew right then that Luther was a long gone daddy when she flashed him those ivories.

"But a child need to become a man someday," Luther went on, "Here he is asking do I know where he can get a gun and he ain't even ever had him none yet. Kids today got their priorities mixed up, if you go asking Luther."

"You need a gun, Honey?" Misty said. "Hell, that ain't a problem, but you got to give your Aunt Misty something in return. Guns ain't cheap, you know?"

"Guns don't grow on trees, either," Luther giggled. "Show him that nickel-plaited automatic you got."

"You ain't my aunt," I said.

"But I want to be," Misty said, bending her knees and talking to me like I was little baby. I resented the way she was talking to me, but at the same time it affected me in a powerful way that made it hard to breathe.

"Come and go with us," Luther winked at me real big over his shoulder.

Misty leaned heavily against Luther causing her skirt to ride up her back so I could see her panties. She was giggling and started hiccupping. I could see Luther's Cadillac parked in front of Dunavant's. He opened the back door and shoved her in like she was a sack of dogfood.

"Get back there with her," Luther said. "Take care of her for me."

"Yeah," Misty said. "Take care of me, honeylove."

Luther was driving slow, too slow.

"Grandma was slow," Misty snorted. "But she was old!"

Luther drove down by the college in the black part of town. "We in niggertown now. That's what everyone call it, don't they?" I nodded that he was right. "Mmm hmm. At least you don't try to lie about it. You call it that too sometimes, I bet. That's all right because you're my man. Just don't go around talking like that around me. I'll have to kick your ass then, but you my man! We got saved together. That makes you my little brother in the eyes of the good Lord, don't it?"

"Luther." I said. "I got something to tell you. It might be a shock."

"You can't shock your brother Simmie," Luther said. "We're down here now so call me Simmie."

"Simmie," I said, but it didn't sound right to me. "How about Brother Luther?"

"All right now," Luther said. "You call me Brother Luther and I'll call you Brother Nathan."

"Okay," I said.

"Now what you want to tell me?" Luther asked. "Did Misty pass out on us?"

"Vaughn is my daddy," I said.

Luther just looked at me in the rearview with no expression on his face, but it was hard to see him in the dark as he looked up at me in the mirror. His right arm was across the top of the seat as he drove. The top of his afro just touching the car ceiling made him seem more like a giant than ever, but what I said bothered him. Maybe he thought I was going to snitch him out to Vaughn. Everyone was scared of Vaughn but I thought maybe Luther wouldn't be for some reason. Not really scared of him, the way most were.

"I got something to tell you, brother," Luther said. "That ain't no news flash."

"What?" I asked. "You knew? You knew all along?"

"Pssst . . ." he laughed. "Everyone knows Vaughn's your daddy. Anyway, we all knew you was a Vaughn for sure. That ain't nothing. Didn't you know? Didn't Miss Lorene tell you? All that time you all lived out to you grandmother's?"

"Hell no," I said, "he killed Buddy too."

The King started wailing on the radio about being all shook up.

"You like Presley?" Luther asked.

"Yeah," I said. "He's a good singer. Someday I'd like to sing like him and stuff."

"Well," Luther said. "Why don't you? You know he started off singing in church in Mississippi? You could do the same thing. He started off imitating black folks. That's all you gotta to do. Be white but sound black. He just ripped off Big Dad Arthur. You ever hear of him?"

"Nome."

"Buddy?" Misty slurred "who the hell is Buddy?"

I felt like crying again just thinking about it.

"Buddy's a brother," Luther said. "He was blacker than the ace of spades too." Luther grinned at me in the mirror. "He was kind of a crazy one though."

"What do you mean?" Misty asked, sitting up and trying to push her hair up behind her ears.

"He liked to run around town naked, sometimes on all fours," Luther said. "Pissing in people's yards and shit."

"No shit?" Misty asked.

"He shits you not," I added.

"And, man, did he like the bitches!" Luther whooped. "He was one bad mother! Baddest blackest nigger I ever seen."

"He was my best friend," I said. Luther putting Misty on was making me feel a little better.

"And Vaughn killed him?" Misty asked. "Is that what I heard you say?" I nodded in the affirmative.

"Vaughn gets away with everything," I said. "The system don't care. Mama's apt to wind up in the jailhouse now. Vaughn's a badass; most of the Vaughns are, but people get to a certain point where fear turns to hate. Even the meekest little animal will turn around and fight if you corner it. I seen it on Wild Kingdom with Marlin Perkins where a rabbit turned and fought off a fox. Chased it even. That's what you got to be like. A rabbit that will run right down the throat of a fox just to stop it from coming at you."

"That shit's true right there," Luther said. "True shit."

"I heard about your mama" Misty rubbed my forearm back and forth. Her hand was soft and smelled like coconut lotion. "Just so terrible. Why don't she just leave him?"

"Can't," I said. He won't let her. It's like he thinks she's his property.

"What a jerk," she said.

"It's worse than that," I said. "It truly is. Don't let it out that you say anything bad about him or next thing you know he'll be following you everywhere."

"What are you going to do, Honey?"

"Stop him," I said. "I don't know how yet but I will."

Luther looked straight ahead like he was afraid I'd ask him to help. I didn't blame him. Nobody could stop Vaughn. He was a throwback to the Wild West days. A person willing to do anything he had to do, even kill somebody, he had to do to get his way. I wondered if I could be that way because that was the only way to beat him.

I'm Going with You Baby

Luther drove us out east of Fairmont. We parked out under a pin oak by one of the clay pits where killdeer and squirrels had taken over. I remember Grandma Kimbrough talking about how she was born in Wildwoods. It wasn't a town or anything. It was a place where people said there was ghosts because of the abandoned church and cemetery. The Wildwoods was past most people's notice except for maybe the strip mining that had gouged their pits into the countryside. Grandma said Wildwoods was a magical place. She talked about the voices of the dead lodged into the limestone cliffs and muttering downstream in the brook. There were some pretty thickets. Strange little copses here and there. Queen Anne flowers growing wild everywhere. Right now everything visible in the dark was all ink blot shapes like scenery for a slasher flick. Grandma talked about the voices of the dead lodged into the limestone cliffs and muttering downstream in the brook.

The wind was shaking the trees and a cool breeze began to blow through the windows of the Caddy. There was thunder rolling off in the distance and echoing off the hills. The first sign of rain in weeks. Some drops began piddling on the windshield, but nothing too heavy.

"Give us a few minutes," Misty said to Luther.

"Give her hell for me, HB!" Luther laughed. He reached under the front seat and pulled out a half-empty bottle of cherry wine. "Misty will teach you all you need to know about coursing."

She looked about half sober now. Her eyes looked at me like I had never been looked at before. She held the palms of her hands up to my face. The look on her face was almost religious.

"Look what I've got for us?" Misty said. "Luther ain't the only one with a secret stash of wine. Well, it's his really but he won't mind. Have some."

The wine tasted so sweet it was like drinking cherry-flavored cough syrup. She wouldn't let me hold the bottle. She made me tip my head back into her lap and she poured it in my mouth until I choked and had to sit up. The rain was sprinkling on the roof of the Caddy again and making a soothing rhythmic sound. We laughed about Luther out there in the rain.

"He's afraid of the thunder," Misty whispered. "Hey, flip the key to batt and put on some music."

"Okay," I said. A girl was singing on the radio in a style that made me think she could be from Fairmont somehow. She was singing about calling her name and I'd have a friend. It was a song that gave some comfort.

"Do you think I'm pretty?" Misty asked.

"Yes." I turned to put my hand on her cheek.

"You're very sweet" she combed her fingers through my hair. She let me kiss her, and not no little boy kiss either. She was looking at me all horny. My hands were shaking with wanting to do whatever she wanted and fear of what I wasn't sure. We kissed each other and used our tongues. I put my hand on her breast, and she pulled down her tube top so I could touch her skin where it was warm, and if I was quiet I could hear her heart beat. I felt her smile at me even if I couldn't see it as if she enjoyed my excitement. Her hands were at the small of my back and she pulled me against her. She put her head back against the car door and moaned and I kissed her neck. I could feel her hand on the back of my neck pushing me down to her breasts. I traced her smallpox vac-cination scar on her shoulder. She laughed prettily and put her other hand to her breastbone, pretending to be scared of the size of me in her hand. Her face dipped down like a moon at night and swallowed me up. Her mouth moved up and down on me. It was like camera flashes and the peace that passes all understanding. Time quit moving and we were floating in the darkness. If this was the road to hell it was the right turn for me. The green dashlights glowed brighter than the moment before.

"Just hold me, Honey Boy," Misty said, and I did, listening to her heartbeat and the thumping in my own chest. They were not beating in time, her heart drummed first and then mine. It made me feel alive for real. Tears ran down her face in tracks. People thought just because she was boy crazy that she didn't have feelings, but I knew different. Everyone needs somebody to love them.

"I love you," I said.

"You don't know what love is," Misty said. "Not until your heart has been broken for real you don't, but you have changed now. Haven't you? There's something different about you. I'm not sure what it is."

"I thought I was saved," I said. "But now it's like I was saved in a different way."

"Am I a bad person?" Misty asked. "What I did with you . . . does that make me bad?"

"You're a good person," I said. "Don't let nobody run you down."

She smiled and put her arms on my shoulders and her head down on my chest. It seemed strange she would want to know what I thought, but I could sense it the way she pushed against me. I felt she had this burning desire to know how other people saw her. I guess it didn't matter how old you were a person needed folks to approve of them. To trust them and care with all their heart. I knew she didn't love me and that her being with me was all about a wanting of something that would eat her up someday if she wasn't too careful.

Snake Dreams

I woke up in the middle of the night from a dream that I was drowning. I had tried to face down a glowing snake in Blackmore Lake. It talked to me. It told me I would remember everything it said, but I'd do what I had to do.

I grabbed hold of it there in the water by the neck and it grew three times its former size. His big neck was pulsating and glowing a slimy green color and he took me down deep in the brackish water. My lungs were about to burst. Finally, I couldn't take it anymore and I started breathing the water in my lungs like a fish. He took me so deep down there I saw a city that was on fire. It was the city of the dead and even if I didn't go there now the snake told me I would soon enough. I knew I could let go of him and that's where we stood when I woke up thrashing around on Danny Vaughn's couch. There was white fuzz on the television.

Low music was coming from Rusty's room. He liked to sleep with the radio on. Once he had told me he liked to listen to women singing at night so he could pretend she was singing only to him. It wasn't going to be easy waking him up either. If he had been born a superhero his super power would have been the ability to fall asleep instantly and anywhere. Still I went in there trying to be quiet like you do even if you really want to wake people up. I put my hand on his shoulder and shook him, but he didn't even move. His mouth was hanging open like he was trying to catch flies and I laughed to myself.

"Rusty," I hissed. "Wake up. Rusty? Wake up!"

"Did you make that sandwich for me?"

"What?"

"That my sandwich?" He was talking in his sleep.

"Naw," I said. "I made it for me and you can't have none."

"Aw man," Rusty said.

"Wake up," I said.

"Why you messing with me when I'm trying to sleep?"

"Get up," I said. "I need your help."

"What time is it?"

"I don't know but I need your help."

"Doing what?" He turned his head and now he was facing the wall.

"I'm fixing to do something bad."

"Okay," Rusty threw back his blankets. "I sure hate for school to start this fall. I'm having too much fun this summer."

"You got any red spray paint?"

There is a Way

It was still dark outside. The only light was bluish-white in the backyard by the barn coming from high up on a pole. The air was still at this hour and sound was amplified like the earth was encased by a curved glass lid like the one they put pie over at the Spot. No matter how quiet we tried to be every little sound echoed off the hills behind us and down to the valley below. A dense fog lay in every divot and cleft. I had the gunny sack with the spray paint in it. Rusty walked ahead of me to the machine shop. He wanted to bring the thirty-aught-six but I told him it would be too much to hold on the ride into town. Rusty had started lifting weights all the time earlier in the summer with a weight set that went up to 125 pounds he'd found in the barn. He was starting to look a little bigger now.

I waited for Rusty by the machine shop. He went all the way down to the barn. After awhile I heard him cussing, the sound drifted to where I was, so I shushed him. I could barely make out the indistinct shape of the barn and suddenly he emerged out of the gloam pushing his Suzuki dirt bike. He'd been riding the trails with it and practicing jumps out at the clay pits. He would turn fifteen before long and then he was determined to start racing in the 125 class. We had to get down the gravel road a little ways before starting it up so his mama didn't come running around and raise cane with us. Rusty pushed it down the long drive and out onto the gravel road. When we were about a half-mile down the road, probably still not far enough, he got on and I slipped behind him. I held my legs back out of the way while he jump-started it. The first time nothing happened, but the second time it started right up.

"That's the first time it started in over a week," Rusty said.

"Cool," I said.

"It's Copacetic," he answered.

The gunny sack was hard to hold and hang on to Rusty's belt loops at the same time. When he was by himself he would fly down the hillside pasture across from his house but it was too dangerous to go down double. The land also belonged to someone else but that had never stopped the kids from playing over there or swimming in the creek. We had to hurry now before the sun came up.

We were flat out getting it down the gravel road. It was hard to breath until I tucked my head down behind him. His hair was streaming out behind him like a flag. It was about that time when you could tell the sun would be up before too long. The wind stung my eyes so that they watered like hell. The world looked bubbly and wet through my tears. It was cool on my arms and I wished I'd grabbed a jacket but it was too late for that now. I was always getting cold.

When we got into town and passed the Fairmont Funny Farm and the Dairy Queen we knew we were almost there. We turned on the main loop and found ourselves on the square. The buildings looked lonely and bored almost like they were waiting for us to get there and liven things up. It was that hour of morning in a town when even a whisper echoed off the courthouse and sounded like a shout. Rusty parked on the sidewalk in front of the Savings and Loan. I gave him one of the cans of red spray paint. I shook my can real good and sprayed HELL TOWN and VAUGHN on the alley wall of Pearlman's Jewelry store. Rusty smirked and wrote FAIRMONT SUCKS! We made our way down the North side of the square spray painting things like DIE, VAUGHN WAS HERE, SATAN (of course), YOU HAVE NOW ENTERED HELL, skulls, bones, and just crazy lines all over J.C. Penneys, Westlake's Hardware Store, Dunavant's Drugstore, and Cole's Office Supply. I hoped that would be enough to get folks all upset at Vaughn enough to put him away, but somehow I knew it wouldn't be.

"Let's do the courthouse next!" Rusty said.

"No!" I said. "That wouldn't be right."

"Why not," Rusty said.

"Just because," I said.

"That ain't no good reason," he smiled and I could tell he was going to do it anyway.

"I'll kick your ass if you do," I said. I meant it too.

"What?"

I didn't trust myself to explain it. They had the war memorials on the front lawn of the courthouse. Every day they put out the red, white, and blue on the pole unless it was a day when they flew it at half-mast. I'd heard all the old men talking about the wars they'd been in to some degree or another. It was the ones who had been in Vietnam who intrigued me the most. They wouldn't say Jack about what happened. It made me wonder if they'd been tortured or something. I didn't care about the courthouse itself. Hell, I'd heard the original one burnt down when Grandma Kimbrough was a little girl back in nineteen aught-something. Everyone I knew went to court there got thrown in the clink. And, it wasn't that I am so partiotic but the people who fought in them wars deserved more somehow. I couldn't hardly get out of my mouth to explain to Rusty.

We stepped back off the sidewalk to admire our handiwork.

"I don't know, man," I said.

"What?"

"I just don't know."

"Don't know what?"

"I just don't think anyone's going to buy that Vaughn did this." I looked at him with a I-think-we-done-screwed-up smile.

"Who do you think they'll blame it on?"

"Us," I said.

Rusty looked down at the red paint on his hands. He showed me the dot of red on his index finger. Mine matched his to a tee.

"Naw," he said.

"I guess we can't take it back now."

"Don't look so glum, chum," Rusty said. "We're juvenile delinquents. This is what we're supposed to do."

The sun was about to come up. An orange-red haze was splotched on the horizon like orange sherbet ice cream.

An old man appeared from around the corner. He was shuffling down the street to take up his position in front of the courthouse. He looked about ninety. It was the Prophet. Nobody took him seriously except when the Spirit moved him to preach, but then they just crossed the street to avoid him. I hadn't thought about him since the Kingdom Days festival.

The Prophet's general message was your standard one: everyone bound for Hell and fiery brimstone. He slobbered and spat like a mangy mad dog. A person would of thought he was personally going to drag you down to hell himself. I got the feeling he liked talking to everyone like this and that rubbed me the wrong way. Why would anybody be happy about people going to hell? It made me see red just looking at him. Each of his messages did end on an uplifting, if not terribly specific, positive note: *There is a way.* He had a funny Yankee accent that made him seem even more strange like a film strip they showed us at school on President Kennedy before Lee Harvey Oswald blew his brains out down in Texas. *My fellow Americans, you are going to hell unless you repent!* The prophet would look up into the sky with an expression of peace, but it seemed fakey to me. Some people bought into it. They'd stuff a few bills into his dry hands for his trouble. What did he spend the money on? Mad Dog? I think he stayed down at the Tanglewood nursing home, but he still had his walking priveleges.

His clothes were all black like Johnny Cash. He had a cane and he was blind so we weren't too worried. He liked to come down to the square everyday and hand out his come-to-Jesus tracts. He had a big stack of them with a rubberband holding them together. His face looked like a battered suitcase, but made to last like old stuff was. One of his eyes was completely misted over but he could see out of the one a little. He preached on the square when the Spirit moved him. He had some definite ideas about Jesus coming back in a chariot with the prophet Elijah. He preached how the crows fed Elijah when he was out in the woods. I could see crows feeding him too pretty easy the way he dressed. If he just had wings he could fly around town sqawking with them about the end times. I could picture him in my mind sitting with his feet hanging on to the phone line like bird's claws and his hands tucked into his armpits like wings.

Everytime I asked the old geezer what his name was he told me something different. The first time I asked him he said he was Isaiah or the Voice-of-One-Crying-in-the-Wilderness. The second name sounded like an Indian name to me, but it was Bible. Besides, why would they call him the Prophet when he never prophesied anything no one had ever heard or even given someone on the street a word of knowledge. He was just another dead head trying to tell people what they ought to do.

One afternoon I was drinking a Mountain Dew on the square and I said, *Hi Isaiah*. I thought Mama might be impressed that I knew him but he pointed at me trying to scare me, his good eye bulging, and he said he was *John the Revelator*. I am not completely dumb so I knew for sure he was just saying names from the good book. Aunt Oleta had forced me under the cruel rule of her wooden spoon to learn the order of the books in the Bible so I guess he was going to say he was Jeremiah, Ezekiel, Daniel, and Hosea next time around. He thought he could give me crap because I'm a kid.

"Anyway," Rusty nodded in the direction of the old man, "we could spray paint the old man. Then, he'd have something to bellyache about."

"Naw," I said. "That's a good idea though. He'd be known as the red prophet."

"We'd better get out of here before all hell breaks loose."

"Wait!"I said. I dragged the gunny sack with the paint cans in it.

"What?" Rusty said. "We got to get out of here before we get caught."

"Hey there, Methuselah!" I shouted at the old man.

His head shot up. It was like a baby's head in comparison to the rest of his body. A hooked nose like a vicious beak took up the middle part of his face. The battered hillbilly hat he wore reminded me of the kind the Puritans wore on Thanksgiving except without the buckle. He had probably been one hell of an ass kicker in his younger years. I wondered if he had been in World War I or II maybe. Maybe he had never done nothing. It was hard to say.

"Who is it?" the old man hollered at me. "Who accosts me at such an unholy hour?"

"It is me . . . I!"

Rusty was walking behind me like he was afraid the guy was Moses. "The Son of Man!"

"You two talk funny," Rusty said.

"The son of a what?" The old man motioned like he was all bad. "Come closer."

"The Son of Man," I said. "I've come back! Aren't you happy? Have you been handing those tracts out like I told you to that one time in that dream like a good boy? C'mere, give me a hug."

I started walking toward him with my hands open wide.

"Here now!" The old man backed away like he was afraid, which was funny because he shouted at people all the live-long day like he was a *pure-d* badass in the Army of the Lord. "That's blasphemy. Don't blaspheme, young man!"

"How can I be blaspheming," I said in the most godlike voice I could muster. Rusty wasn't laughing. He was jerking on my arm like he was drilling for oil. "When it's me . . . the I AM . . . you've been waiting for me to come back. Here I am! I came back on the wings of a dove. Don't you want to worship me?"

"Worship you?" The Prophet held out his cane now like a sword to keep me at arm's length. I was plumb tickled now and it was all I could do not to start laughing my ass off. "You are not Him. You are the spirit of Antichrist in the world! I'd recognize you anywhere."

"No," I said. "Tsk. Tsk. That's you! You ARE the Antichrist but you don't realize it because you are old and crazy now. Remember when I called you in the beginning? You were young. You still had your mind and your good looks. Now, look at you. I think it might be time to call you home, ole son."

"Let's get of here, man," Rusty hissed. "This sucker is crazy. Crazy people make me nervous."

"He thinks he's so holy he needs to tell other people not to go to hell because he knows he's going to heaven," I hissed back.

"So?" Rusty said.

"You ain't never had no religious training," I said. "That's why it don't bother you."

"Come over here so I can get a better look at you," the old man said. "I don't get around too good these days."

"You mean so you can WORSHIP me?" I was trying not to laugh at the expression of horror on Rusty's face. He was afraid of the Prophet, not because he believed so much in God, but out of supersitious fear that if he messed with the old man then God might see it and send him to hell and *do not pass go*. Any other old man, he would have kicked his cane out from under him and stole his good eye if he could have but he was looking around for thunderbolts at the moment.

"What good do you think this does?"I grabbed his stack of tracts. "What good does this do? Aren't most people in Fairmont pretty good people? They work hard, pay their bills, and raise their families. Why isn't God happy with that?"

"I wouldn't know, young Antichrist," the Prophet said. "I just try to do the good Lord's work. He'll sort it out in the end. I am the voice of the latter day crying in the wilderness!"

"Well," I said, "that's where you're WRONG. I AM HERE TO SET IT RIGHT NOW! THIS IS THE END TIME! FOR YOU!" I sighted down my arm like a rifle and pointed my finger at him.

"Dear Jesus." the Prophet grabbed his chest and fell down against the bank. "Help me. Help me." The old man wheezed so quietly nobody could have heard them if they had been standing at the end of the block. He was a good actor though so you couldn't take him too seriously. There was a chance he was faking. His legs were underneath him the way no old man's could comfortably rest thought so there was that. His Mayflower hat fell off his head and rolled away from him.

"Dear dear," I repeated. "Your snow man hat fell off. You've about near melted. We'll have to fix that." I shook my can of paint and sprayed a big P on it. "Look here, man, I've beautified your Mad Hatter hat for you. P for Prophet. Maybe when you wear it you should think about how you might be the one going to hell. Huh?" I stuck it down over his head so that it covered his giant cauliflower ears.

"You" he wheezed. Then he topped it off with a dramatic, "AWWWG!" His chest heaved up with one claw on it, then his body went back down on to the sidewalk, and, man, I'd kiss your ass if he didn't look deader than fuck.

"Oh shit," Rusty said. "Is he dead?"

"Christ," I said. "To think I was ascared of you."

"You killed the prophet." Rusty looked at me with horror in his eyes like I'd walked under a hundred ladders.

I felt bad about it too. He looked most surely dead, but it made me mad when people like to make out how much better they are than you. Especially if those people think they are better than you and won't respect you as another human being. I guess it still don't get me off the hook for treating him like that, he's old and all, or putting that giant P on his hat. I bumped Rusty with my elbow and jerked my head so he'd follow me. We walked away from the old man backwards down the street, still talking, but about Tiger basketball.

"You see Sunvold and Stepanovich the other night?" I tried to sound all casual but loud enough for the Prophet to hear.

"Nope."

"They really lit it up," I said.

"I'd like to go to a game sometime," Rusty said.

Then, I saw it. The old man's head came up off the sidewalk a little and he slid off his sunglasses to regard us with his one good eye.

"The old man was playing possum," Rusty whispered.

He heard him and let his head rest back on the pavement.

"I know who you are!" The quavery voice of the Prophet followed us. "The god I serve will bring you low one day. There will be a day of reckoning. The White Throne Judgment applies to the Vaughns! After judgment those who are not righteous will be cast into the lake of fire."

"You ain't righteous!" I hollered back at him.

"He was playing possum and you knew it." Rusty bumped my arm with his elbow.

"You ain't no true prophet," I said. "I know you can hear me too. You ain't no prophet at all. I'd say you're the golden idol of prophets. You're worse than any of the Vaughns I know because you want people to worship you."

Rusty had his hands on me and was pushing me away now. He was grinning like a new idea had just hit him. The more I yelled and hollered nonsense at the old man the more he shook his head and kind of snorted like he was trying not to laugh. I was getting worked up now. I took a swipe at Rusty for laughing at me. My fist grazed off his chin and then he reached over and smacked my face with an open hand to get me out of it.

"Christ, Honey Boy," Rusty said. "Give the geezer a break."

Rusty got on his Suzuki and I waited for him to start it before I got on behind him. I told him to drive into the alley and we threw the sack with the empty DOT spray cans into the Dumpster behind the tavern. He started flying down the alley a little too fast but that was how he always rode. Rusty left a black mark and skidded out onto the street, and lo, and behold we came face to face with a cop at the stop sign just gripping his steering wheel under the early shade of a pin oak. Why he didn't just take off, I wasn't sure. He just sat there with one foot on the ground to hold us up, revving the engine and staring holes into the cop.

"Let's go, Rusty," I said.

"Cop," he spat over his shoulder.

"He ain't going to do Jack," I said.

"Not until he sees the number we did on the square, anyways." Rusty chuckled.

When I thought of what had happened with the Prophet, I began to wonder if I wasn't even worse than Vaughn. I knew plenty of judgmental people and didn't do nothing to them. Even thinking someone else is judgmental sort of made the person thinking it judgmental, too, when you got right down to it. It made me feel awful just to think about it. It seemed like the religious people I knew got off on telling who was going to hell and who wasn't, but I didn't see them saving any more souls than anyone sitting on a bar stool. I liked most of the folks down at the tavern better than the most of the church people. I wondered why the Prophet thought he should be some kind of living reminder to everyone that he thought they probably weren't going to heaven. I had my doubts God was excited about people like him either. Why didn't He let people go to hell in peace?

The cop finally turned off and went back toward the police station. We were both thinking he might circle around and follow us. As soon as we made it past the state hospital Rusty gunned it so suddenly I thought I was going to fall off. We plummeted down the steep hill and my stomach came up into my throat. We were expecting the law to be on our ass any second. Rusty stood up as we went up the hill to look back over me and as he did a buck stood in the road as if to keep us from passing. Rusty lost control, and we went flying into the deep ditch off to the right. Just before we hit I thought: *So this is how I die.*

Nightwomb of the Grave

Next day I went over to Aunt Oleta's and she gave me the biggest dressing down you ever heard even though I hand-picked a bunch of wildflowers for her. She was wound tighter than Dick's hatband that day, but she was glad to see me and made me eat a leftover salmon patty with a side of macaroni and cheese after she fixed my face up with a big Ace bandage. A tree branch or something had scratched my face worse than a wildcat. I thought it made me look tough, but she insisted on making me look like a dork with a big bandage on my face. She said I looked plumb wild, and she made me strip down naked right there in the kitchen, which I didn't want to do because of the tattoo Rusty had given me. I tried to turn away from her so she wouldn't see and she near about had a conniption fit! She licked her fingers and tried to rub it off but it wouldn't come off. She gave me a mean look and let go of my arm and just pointed to the bathroom in silence. I took a bath with Clarence peeking in and pestering me not to use all his Mr. Bubble the whole time. Aunt Oleta threatened to burn my clothes, but instead, before she hauled them off to the laundry room.

Rusty had broken his arm in the wreck and was going to be laid up for a while. The Suzuki was toast. As it turned out, that cop we saw must have been asleep because he never chased us or came nosing around to ask about the job we did on the shops downtown, but it did make the papers.

Aunt Oleta told me Grandma Kimbrough had died in the King's Daughters nursing home. It was real sad to hear. I remembered how one particular night, I'd stayed over with her. I laid on the white clean sheets in bed next to her after smoking weed with Rusty, and I asked her if she could see the blue-green moonbeams coming in her window like I could.

She said she could and told me to go on to sleep but in a kindly way. While Aunt Oleta was telling me about it she was looking at what looked like a restaurant menu. When I looked over her shoulder I could tell it was from the funeral home. All about their rates. She told me she was the executor of Grandma Kimbrough's estate. It sounded official, especially when she threw an extra syllable or two in there, but all Grandma had now were pictures in shoeboxes, second-hand furniture, thirteen children (eleven of which were still alive), twenty-three grandchildren, and twenty-four great grandchildren. I was one of the great grandchildren and none of us ever got one of her special-made quilts as far as I knew.

Mama didn't make it to the visitation or the funeral. I knew that would tear her up when she heard about it. I sure was worried about her and I could tell Aunt Oleta was too but she just said, "Your Mama's plumb wild" as if that it explained it. Clarence was griping about his clothes as usual, and he kept grabbing at his crotch. Aunt Oleta would ask him then if he had to pee. Clarence just giggled and kept grabbing at his tallywhacker like a prevert. Aunt Oleta pretended not to notice for a change. It just egged Clarence on if she frowned at him for it, so she just let the dumb bunny go at it for a while.

Later the whole hee-haw gang was gathered at the Dubois Funeral Home to see Grandma Kimbrough off. It didn't even look like her to me. They put too much makeup on her face and I swear she could have been younger than Aunt Oleta if not for the fact that she was dead. Everyone made a fuss about how wonderful she looked. It bugged me that they didn't make her look the way she was supposed to. There was a rosy glow to her cheeks I had never seen before in my entire life. They had put too much makeup on her face.

I stared down on her laying on white lace in the casket and tried to remember something nice about her. "Pro-found" as Vaughn probably would have said, quoting from one of his

Reader's Digest word lists. I remembered her sugar cookies and punkin pies and how good they were. I remembered her collection of salt and pepper shakers that were packed away in boxes filling up the entire closet before she got put into King's Daughters. I asked her one time why she collected them and she surprised me by saying she didn't. She laughed at the look on my face. She said people gave them to her on her birthday one year and after that everybody assumed she was collecting them.

"Why didn't you just tell them you weren't collecting them?" I asked.

"I didn't want to hurt their dang feelings," she said.

For some reason I thought Grandma Kimbrough might suddenly get up out of her rose-colored casket and fix us all some fried chicken to eat. She was always right spry so it wouldn't have surprised me either. I prayed quietly that God would raise her up from the dead like Jesus did Lazarus. I looked around from the corner of my eyes in case someone might guess at what I was doing and maybe get on my case. I could see Aunt Oleta stroking out about it now. *Honey Boy! You don't go raising people up from the dead unless God tells you to do it! And if He didn't tell me, he sure enough didn't tell you! Now look, everyone is a mess and carrying on with Grandma come back to life!* But Grandma didn't move. They embalmed her I tried to tell myself to quiet my nerves. There was a minute when I promise her eyelids fluttered, a finger tremored, and I swear her chest rose and fell with living breath, but she was stone-hammer dead all right.

I ain't dead so quit looking at me, young-un.

You look dead.

Well, I ain't, but seems like now I can see you been up to some things.

I guess that's how it goes, Grandma.

Ah hush, boy. I'm tired. Go get me an extra quilt off the divan. It's cold in here.

On the radio they talked about how somebody defaced public property on the square. A few minutes later, the worse part, they said they found the Prophet dead on a bench in front of the nursing home. They suspected foul play and the authorities were looking into the incident. I had killed someone now. Not directly but I was the cause. The responsible party. I was just as bad or worse than Vaughn. The way he acted it was like it was his instinct taking over, but I let my own pride get in the way. I'd shouted that old man down to the land of the shades like he was always trying to do the whole of Fairmont. He'd be under the streets of National Brick now, yelling up about the error of their ways.

I knew nobody was going to blame Vaughn for spray-painting downtown either. They'd know kids did that. There was still a little red spray paint on my trigger finger that I couldn't wash off, just like blood. What had we been thinking? We would catch hell for that one. If they accused us of killing the old man, we'd get taken down to juvie hall. I could see it now. They'd put Rusty up on the witness stand to testify against me. I'd go to prison for the rest of my life. Aunt Oleta would come visit me and shake her head and tsk tsk because I hadn't gone to church enough. I figured Mama would visit me a couple of times before she got too busy with a new boyfriend and left the state of Misery again. Rusty would be in there with me for something else eventually at least. Vaughn might even come visit us too. Now, wouldn't that be funny? Not funny ha-ha either.

I'd have to pull out all the stops now if I was going to do any good. The more I thought about loving God and being good it seemed like the worse I got and the worse things went on around me. That must have been what Job thought too back in the Bible days. I liked them stories, but I sure couldn't figure what guys walking around in dresses and sandals had to do with me. I figured I was on the dog trot to hell, anyway, so why get all excited about it now.

Later on they buried Grandma on the poor side of the cemetery where all the Kimbroughs were laid to rest. There was some talk of what Grandma was like. She loved all her kids. She'd never learned to drive in her eighty-nine years but she wanted to toward the end because she didn't want to be a burden on anyone. There was talk of the Day of the Lord and the twinkling of an eye. After that everyone went back to their cars and trucks. No one watched as they lowered her down into the ground. I wondered if people weren't like annuals or perennials and if maybe they'd spring up out of the ground down the road sometime. I hoped maybe I would get rich somehow one day and have my own family mausoleum. I'd be separated from Grandma and all the old people anyway since I was a kid. There wasn't any comfort in thinking about being buried next to my cousins. It would be safer to be buried with the old people. I don't know why I thought that, exactly, but I guess it's like when you're itty-bitty and the flashing lightning and thunder bellowing like a dragon makes you sit up in bed of a night and scream for your mama. She's the only one who's going to hold and comfort you.

Burn, Baby, Burn

If I could have found out what church the dead Prophet had gone too I would have burned it down. Now I had to pick one out for sure. The first real problem I had was getting out of Aunt Oleta's line of sight. It hadn't taken her long to realize I'd been on my own for a while and now I couldn't move without her commenting on it for over a week. She was of the kind that thought someone was going to kidnap kids and steal them away. I tried asking her who had ever been kidnapped in the history of Fairmont, and she waved her arm vigorously in the air, her back arm meat flapping, and choked back her rage to spit out, "You hear about it everyday!" I'd never heard about it at all, much less everyday, but you couldn't talk sense to her anymore than you could to a rock. Maybe it had to do with Clarence being a retard but she was a mother hen and felt perfectly justified.

When I'd been little I'd ask if I could go outside in the summer and she'd say, "It's too hot outside so wait until later" and then in the evening she'd say, "You can't go outside, the mosquitoes will get you!" Eventually I learned not to ask, I just went outside and took my chances with sunstroke and the swarms of malaria-ridden mosquitoes rising up from out of the cattails in the pond.

She took Clarence shopping down at Cooper's grocery store. Every time she went somewhere without me she said, "Don't you go nowhere." She knew I was apt to walk off without so much as a "See you later or kiss my ass."

I saw Luther pull up in front and off they went. I took off the new garage sale nerd clothes I'd been wearing that Aunt Oleta had given me. I couldn't believe my own reflection wearing a purple button up shirt with a pair of red, white, and purple checkered slacks. Believe me "slacks" was exactly the right word for them. My clothes, a T-shirt and jeans, were practically black before but now they'd been washed and folded so I put them on to feel more like myself again. I kicked off the dorky Hush Puppies, knockoffs she'd had me sashaying around town in and traded them back in for my engineer boots. I went down to the garage and found an old rusted gas can. There was a little gas sloshing around but not enough to do what I wanted, and also the cap wouldn't come off. Some pencil dick had put it on crooked and now it was stuck. I used a pair of pliers and loosened it, finally, so I could dump the dregs out in Aunt Oleta's rose bushes just to vex her. I'd probably catch hell for that, too.

I found a battered Radio Flyer wagon and put the gas can on it and headed out to Roy's gas station. First I needed money so I raided the change jar up on the fridge that Aunt Oleta saved for the collection plate and for the Ding Ding Lady or the Ooga Ooga Man drove through the neighborhood. The Ding Ding Lady sold snowcones out of the back of her little red hatchback and rang a bell; the Ooga Ooga man honked the horn of his yellow jeep that made the sound you'd expect to sell ice cream. My hands were shaking. I thought I was going to puke. Everytime I thought about what I was going to do, my hands would start sweating worse than when I talked to Tempie.

I was pulling that dopey wagon when Sonny pulled up in the El Camino. He'd been working on it because now it had yellow and orange flames going down the sides. I didn't want to see Sonny just then but I perked up at the thought that Mama might be with him.

"Honey Boy . . . are you having a good time?" Sonny hollered through the passenger window. He had his arm across the top of the seat. Sonny was cool without trying hard at it. I always wanted to be like him but deep down I felt like I wasn't tough enough. One time he said I thought too hard about things and used too many fifty-cent words for a kid. And said I was a little bit queer acting, too, which nearly killed me—I just wanted to be cool and tough like him. I was getting hard to insults and tough talk these days, but the people you feel the closest to are the ones who can hurt you the most.

"Not hardly."

"Nice wagon you got there."

"Hey Sonny," I dropped the handle on the wagon and stuck my head into the passenger window hoping he had the air conditioner on but he didn't. He claimed not to like AC and preferred the air blowing in the window, no matter how hot, just like Mama. "Where's Mama at?"

"She's at my room in the Parliament for now" Sonny tapped his hands on the steering wheel to Eric Clapton coming out of his 8-track. "We can't stay there long. We just parked around back and we're getting a few things before we get the hell out of Dodge. We had us this sweet little place down at the Lake. Your mama wanted to see Lee Mace's Ozark Opry."

"Well, ain't that fun?" My lip started quivering on its own which pissed me off. Tears were welling up in my eyes but I was trying to fight them off too. I was trying to talk without crying and not doing a very good job of it. "I hope yall had a *grand* . . . old time."

"What?"

"I hate country music," I said, just to get a rise out of him. "I hate everything country! That old fake hillbilly act they do on that show makes me want to spit." The tears were falling down my cheeks, and when the waterworks got going, they'd won't stop until they run their course.

"Well don't watch it then."

"I won't!" I said. "Lee Mace looks like a fuckin' hillbilly Frankenstein!"

"Good." Sonny stuck his tongue out at me. "I know he does. What a mouth you got today! Don't cry like a little girl. Lorene wants to see you as quick as we get back."

"When will that be?" I wiped the tears off my face with the back of my arm.

"In a few weeks or so, but we got a little business to take care of. Elston was running her ragged. We kind of been hiding out. The law has been after your mama for holding up places at gunpoint with him and Arlene. I mean, you understand we got to lay low. Who would ever thought your mama would go on a crime spree?"

"Sonny," I said. "Can I come with yall?"

"Sorry," he said. "No can do, Kemosabe! It's too dangerous. We're trying to keep her out of jail until they catch Vaughn. Otherwise they'll probably try some bullshit and pin everything on her. You understand?"

"Yeah," I said. "I guess that sounds right. I heard about one of the gas station robberies one night on Channel 13. Dick Preston told it before *Star Trek* came on."

"You don't say?"

"Well," I tried to make my voice sound hard. "I guess you can tell Lorene I'll catch her when gets back."

"Aw, don't be like that kid," Sonny said. "Your mama loves you. Believe me. Nobody loves you like that woman does."

"Let her tell it to me, then."

"Don't tell me you've turned into a little sissy-girl living with your Aunt Oleta and going to church?"

"Yeah!" I said. "What do you know about where I been living? Yeah, I'm going to start wearing a dress tomorrow."

"Everyone like's a little ass, but no one likes a smart ass." Sonny laughed. "Hey, where did you get that tattoo on your arm? Cool cross. 'Jesus Wept,' huh? I'll say he did."

"He most certainly did," I said. "Rusty gave me this here tattoo."

"Rusty's got a talent," Sonny said, "but he lies like a moth-erfucker."

"What are you going to do with that gas can?"

"Aunt Oleta needs it for the lawn mower."

"Here." Sonny reached across the seat and gave me a $50 dollar bill. "Put that in your piggy bank."

"What's this for?"

"For you, holmes," A smile crept across his face.

"Is this money from one of the robberies?" I whispered, although no one was around.

"Could be," Sonny said in a way that made it clear that was exactly where it had come from.

Sonny looked up the street and his face went dead. It was like someone was holding a gun on him. I looked over my shoulder and a fire truck went by. You would have thought it was the cops, the way, he kind of sank down in his seat. All it would take was someone to turn him in and that would be it.

"I've gotta go, Honey Boy," Sonny said. "I'll tell your mama you miss her. She wanted you to stay with Oleta. I know she can be a little over the top, but just hang loose."

"All right," I said. "I'll do my best."

"Don't tell Vaughn you seen me either." Sonny tightened his grip on the steering wheel and revved the engine up. "You hear? Him and me is about to have a difference of opinion over Lorene among other things."

Sonny did a U-turn and disappeared over the hill. I studied the $50 bill for a minute and stuffed it down in my pocket. It looked like a work of art to me. Just looking at it, I wasn't sure if I should frame it, spend it, or eat it. I might have to get a wallet sometime, and then I could put my bank robbery money in it and a few pictures. School would be starting before much longer and I could trade pictures with the kids in school. There was a tall kid named Rick I'd been friends with years ago when I went to school in Fairmont. He might be around still. I'd get a picture from Tempie and Regina, too.

I grabbed on to the handle of the wagon and took off down the sidewalk. I hoped it didn't fall apart before I made it to Roy's. I got to thinking I probably could have just carried the can it by the handle, but there were a couple of other things I might need as well. It made me think I might have to get back out to Vaughn's and get my pistol back off him. I tried to think of a way to get it without pissing him off. Maybe if I said I needed to practice with it. He might want me to rob a credit union if I said that, though. I'd never heard of a kid robbing a bank before. A kid would probably have to shoot the guard in the leg right off the bat to get the bank tellers and farmers in there to take him seriously.

I was in a hurry to get to the gas station, but the sidewalks were so cracked with crabgrass that the wheels of the Radio Flyer kept getting hung up, and I about yanked my arm off by the root. I'd pull it along a little ways and get stuck in a rut. On and on it went all the way there. It sure was vexing a lot like everything else going on. I was working up a sweat by the time I got there.

"The Dr. Pepper kid rides again!" Roy hollered as I pulled up. He was always dressed exactly the same, every day, in that blue gas station suit with his work hat on and his white hair sticking out from under it. It was nice to know there were a few good ones around, and they always stayed thataway.

He was talking to an old lady in a Lincoln Town Car. She waved with her fingers as she pulled away like she was flirting with him even though they was both old and lined up like a Rand McNally road map.

"Hey Roy!"

"Where's the fire?" Roy said.

"What?" I was thunderstruck. Maybe Roy was psychic.

"I say," Roy adjusted the brim of his cap. "What's the hurry?"

"Oh," I said. "Aunt Oleta wants me to get this gas and cut the grass."

"I'm glad to see you helping her out," Roy said. "That's what family ought to do for one another."

"Yep," I said. "I just need to get some gas."

"All right, then," Roy filled up the gas can and I handed the change over to him.

"You got to piss?"

"No sir," I said.

"Then why are you fixing to break into an Irish jig?"

"Hey Roy," I said trying to sound casual, "Can you break a fifty?"

"Say can I what?"

I was holding the bill out to him, as proud as could be, until he snatched it out of my hand.

"Where in the hell did you get this, Nathan Kimbrough?" Roy was more serious than I'd ever seen him before. "Don't lie to me, either. I ain't in the mood for it! Your mama or Vaughn give you this?"

"I promised I wouldn't say," I said.

"Whoever give it to you is a dumbshit," Roy said. "I know exactly where it came from. You go flashing big bills, any bills, and people will know what's what. People ain't that stupid although the Vaughns would like to have it so." He turned his back to face the office and changed the fifty into smaller bills. "Here. Now, spend this very carefully and slowly. Don't make a big deal out of it. Anyone asks you it was money for your birthday or paper route. Got it? This is serious, boy!"

"Okay," I said. "Geez, I got it."

The dinger went off and Sheriff Merrill's cruiser materialized out of thin air. I thought I was going to piss my britches right there. Had Rusty or Tempie called the cops on me to stop me from finishing my mission? Or did the cops just want to talk to me because of who my mama and daddy were?

"Good afternoon gentlemen." Sheriff Merrill hung his arm out of his window.

"Morning Sheriff." Roy suddenly put on his business smile and turned away from me. "What's the good word?"

"Same old shit," the Sheriff said. "Different day."

"You got that about right." Roy gripped the black rubber hose, opened the little door with one hand, unscrewed the cap, thrust the nozzle inside and jabbed the flipper down on the pump in one continuous graceful motion. The man could be poetry around the station. "Did you see Junior down at the Spot this morning? He said he had a dog he wanted to sell you for."

"I bet he does, but no, I didn't see that fat ball of grease. I went to school with him in a one room schoolhouse out there off of County Road 113. We used to scrap like two pups fighting over the same tit. We even shipped off to Korea at the same time."

"I believe he might have mentioned that," Roy said.

"Seems like I recognize this one here."

"Yeah," Roy said. "He's one of the regulars."

"My eyesight ain't as good as it used to be. Is that Clyde Barrow, or Pretty Boy Floyd?" He stared at me from under his goofy looking cowboy hat like he was a Texas Ranger. It was like he was going to stare a hole through me. He looked a lot tougher without Vaughn around to scare the shit out of him.

"Just me," I said.

"Well, just me, I got a question for you. Have you seen your mama and Sonny Vaughn around? Now, don't answer too fast. I want you to think about it long and hard. If you know where they are then you need to tell me. I think between Elston and Sonny your mama don't know which way is up and I want to help her. In fact, hop in the car here for a minute. Sit next to me. I've been wanting to talk to you for some time."

"Okay." I looked to Roy. He raised his bushy white eyebrows a gave a negatory shake to his head.

I walked around the car, slid into the nice leather seat and thunked the door shut. He hit a button and his window went up. I hadn't been in too many cars with electric seats or cop cars period before. The air conditioning was cranking, which told me all I needed to know about the Sheriff right there. The car was clean, but it smelled of cigar smoke. The CB crackled and fizzed, and I nearly jumped out of my seat the first time it barked and a woman with a nasal voice started squawking. There was a pump action shotgun of some variety in a kind of holster so if he had to jump out shooting, he could. I wondered how many times he'd done that and how many people he had shot. There was a cage that separated the front and back seats. I was glad he hadn't put me back there.

"You like running the AC?"

"That's a funny question." Sheriff Merrill took a half-smoked cigar and lit it. "Real funny. I do, in weather like this. I'm getting kind of old, and I do like to stay cool when the mercury rises."

"My Mama doesn't like AC," I said. "She said it doesn't feel natural to her. You get too cold and then you can't adjust to how hot it really is outside. That's how some people get sun-stroked so easy."

"Is that a fact?"

"Yes sir," I said.

"It is best not to want what you can't have either," the Sheriff said. "Makes it easier that way. It was you who was with Vaughn the day he came out to my place to stir things up, wasn't it?"

"Sir?"

"Listen, young man," Sheriff Merrill's voice was right curt and loud now. "Let's cut through the bullshit. I need to find the rock where your mama and that shitass Sonny is hiding under, and I mean to know just that quick! Don't worry we're going to get Vaughn too, but first I want your mama. Hear me, boy? If you don't start spitting out the right answers I'm going to take you to jail and whip your little ass and then lock you up for obstruction of justice!"

He put a death grip on the back of my neck and shook my entire body. He was a big man and now I had no doubt what he might do to me or anyone else. Vaughn had made a fool out of him too many times and he didn't want a kid to do the same.

"Where are they?"

I wasn't sure what to say.

"Don't tell me you don't know! Where are they?"

"You're hurting me." Tears sprang in my eyes.

The pressure he was putting on me made it feel he was going to fold me up like clothes in a suitcase. I was shocked the law could do this in broad daylight with witnesses. I couldn't think. I didn't want to tell where mama and Sonny was but I was afraid of Sheriff Merrill and what he might do to me if I didn't. I tried to elbow his arm off me but it was like I was a gnat flying against the tooth of a lion.

Just then a freckled fist was beating against Merrill's window. I could hear shouting too but it seemed to come from far away down a tunnel. The sheriff let go of me and when he did, I opened the door and fell into the searing white gravel. Gravel as white as angels blinding me with their glory I was so relieved to get away from that iron grip. I crawled on the ground until I bumped into Roy's leg.

When I could see again Roy was picking me up off the ground and wiping the dust off my shirt and pants.

"I told that son-of-a-bitch I was witness to what he done and I'd press charges too if he didn't leave you alone. You okay, boy?"

"I'm all right, I think," I said. "There's a reason the Vaughns don't trust the law. They ain't no better."

"I ain't never seen Sheriff Merrill like this before," Roy said. "Something is going to blow up between him and Vaughn before long. Best take your gas home and go cut the lawn. Lay low for a while. Don't be throwing all that money around. Find something worthwhile to spend it on."

So it was hard to lay there until Aunt Oleta and Clarence fell asleep. Aunt Oleta was a big believer in the early bird-worm idea. She went to bed at 8:30 every night come hell or high-water so she could beat the sun up in the morning like it was a personal bet she had going with the sun. I couldn't help laughing to myself as I stepped out the window and featured her opening my door to holler "RISE AND SHINE! UP AND AT 'EM!" The joke would be on her then. There wouldn't be no rising nor shining. Clarence would ask where I was about 150 times, which gave me an idea. I drug my leg back into the window. I found a pencil and notebook paper. Aunt Oleta was always talking about the Rapture and the end of the world. She claimed to know she was saved and knew she was going to heaven. I wrote her a little note to give her something to think about:

Dearest Aunt Oleta,

I feel real terrible about this, but you were right about everything after all! Jesus appeared in the sky and gave me a quick minute to jot down this note. I have been taken up to heaven in the rapture. I guess they took me since I'm still a kid and all. We are precious in his sight. Jesus loves the little children of the world. I figure if you and Clarence keep making it to church and praying and being good then you won't have too many problems with the antichrist. Don't let them tattoo you with 666 either, but you know that already. I'll be watching you from heaven and praying that you can resist the false prophet, the antichrist, the four horsemen and deal with all them other problems that John wrote about in the Bible. I'll be cheering for you!

In the Twinkling of an Eye,
Honey Boy

P.S. Please read this to Clarence or he will ask you 150 times where I am.

It might have been mean, but I thought it was a pretty good joke. I could see her getting madder than a hornet about it and wanting to take the wooden spoon after me even if I was too big for it now. I went out the window and went behind the carriage house where I'd stuck the gas can. I wanted to tell Tempie what I was up to but I was afraid she might tell on me for my own good. On the other hand, Rusty was always up for something like this. He was probably already lurking around somewhere nearby. I'd called his house after dinner and told him the plan.

The gas can was heavy. I couldn't take the wagon because it was louder than hell. We might have to take turns carrying it to whichever church we was going to burn down. I'd been thinking about it ever since we'd come up with the idea. I'd imagined myself doing it too and I knew no matter what my reasons were, I'd be in big trouble if I got caught. They'd probably put me on an island like they did to Steve McQueen in Papillion it was so bad. I'd seen that on the late show awhile back.

The street lights cast shadows that looked like Sheriff Merrill and Vaughn sneaking up on me. There was the sound of cats fighting a couple of streets over. I wished there was a way to hide the gas can. Anyone who drove by and saw me would know who to point the finger at so I tried to keep to back streets and alleys. There was a little alcove by the back door of the library that I thought would make it hard to see me so I waited there. I had a good view of Court and St. Louis Avenue.

Then one of the black hands reached out of the night to grab my shoulder, but this one belonged to Rusty.

He had a cast on his arm, but he wasn't using the sling anymore. A bunch of people had signed their autographs on it.

"Hey man." Rusty took a cigarette and tossed it up into his own mouth and lit it with a Bic like a magician's trick. "You ready?"

"Damn straight," I said.

"We got three churches to pick from right here on Court," I set down the gas can. "What do you think?"

"I purely do not give a damn," Rusty sneered, exhaling a fog of blue smoke. "How about all of them?"

The Presbyterian church across from the theater was smoking deep purple and the air was like breathing velvet into our lungs where we hunkered down by the Dumpster in the alleyway. We had to use the entire can of gas on a corner of the church. The fire just didn't want to catch, but it was finally licking up the back section and shooting up like a new species of animal. Rusty thought it was the type of paint at first protecting it. I said it might be God, but he smacked his leg and laughed like an old codger.

"The fire sure is loud," I said.

"Yeah, it is!"

"I didn't expect that."

Rusty was trying to shake out any gasoline that remained in the can. I could hear it sloshing every time he shook the can at the fire. He got a considerable amount on his own clothes until I wondered if he wouldn't go up like a torch himself. The flame reached out and purred at the new gas Rusty pitched at the church.

It was time to get on down the road. I noticed someone coming around the corner in a familiar looking pickup, parked, and started watching the church smoke and burn.

"Oh damn," the driver said. It was Vaughn. I heard him talking to someone on his CB. I snuck around to the side of the church. I could see the movie theater directly across the street where I'd sat in the balcony and watched a matinee in the balcony of the terrible new Flash Gordon.

I watched Vaughn leaning back against the truck with his arms crossed in front of his chest. I shouldn't have been surprised to see him there. He had terrible insomnia, and he'd drive all over town and up and down the back roads when he couldn't sleep. He could be the most generous person in the world one minute and then the next he might try to kill you. He'd probably insist on helping the fire fighters put out the church fire. Even if they told him no (which they wouldn't) he'd still do something to help them. It didn't make any sense but that's how Vaughn was. I couldn't let him get the credit for dousing a Church fire.

The morning light hadn't made its way over the lip of the world yet as we slunk like coyotes down behind the business-es. Vaughn claimed he believed in God and read the Bible daily but somehow I doubted that shit. Rusty gave me a dime and I made an anonymous call at the pay phone in front of the Dairy Freeze that we'd seen a man who looked like El-ston Vaughn leaving in a Dodge truck from burning down the Presbyterian church. Maybe that would do it. If the cops saw him now, after our call, they'd haul him in. No matter what he said, everyone would think he was lying.

Darker Blues

I heard something was happening downtown on the police scanner, but then it went quiet. There was the smell of hot tar and weirdness in the air. The tar smell gets up in your nostrils, and you can't get it out for a while. I needed to get into town from the trailer court. The neighbor lady would have given me a lift, but she had a flat, and her car was sitting under her carport like a lame-duck. I looked at it for a minute in disgust, but I had never changed a tire before in my life. A smartass old man walking by asked, "Flat tire?"

I nodded.

"Well," he drawled, "she's only flat on one side."

Old people were always saying crazy stuff that didn't make no sense. I walked back into town. It didn't take more than twenty-five minutes.

Cars and trucks were lined up on the square and for three blocks in each direction. The Heritage Festival was still going on, so that it wasn't exactly a surprise, but instead of families walking around hand-in-hand, I noticed it was men alone for the most part. The Heritage Festival was a week long, and the Fourth of July celebration was hot on its heels. A woman's voice came over a loudspeaker singing "The Star Span-Spangled Banner." The lines across the streets down on the square were decorated with red, white, and blue paper looking things in the shape of flags and Liberty Bells.

There was an old ancient threshing machine on display that was in such good shape it looked spitfire new. A one-armed man talked about how along with the steam engine a grain separator, and the water hauling wagon were necessary long ago. There was a water-monkey who hauled about fifty barrels a day depending on the load. The water came from a nearby pond or creek. He told us about how he'd backed off a truck into the pond and the engineer was frantically blowing his whistle because he was running so low on water. There might be as many as forty people to help out with driving the teams. The farmer told how today a combine could be run by one man now, but it could cost as much as $70,000 to buy. The man telling the story was wearing bib overalls. He had a real interesting way of talking until he started telling what the women had to do in them days so they wouldn't feel left out.

Men were gathered in little clumps around pickups with gunracks and talking in low tones. Nobody was smiling either. I recognized some of the men as longtime residents of Fairmont, but others must have come in from farms around the county. It gave me the chills when men's cold eyes would look into mine with no expression. They all knew what I never had; they knew Honey Boy Kimbrough was from Vaughn blood. I was pretty sure none of them knew that I had been involved in some of Vaughn's thievery, but I still felt guilty. I was guilty. They could have opened fire on me and I'd've deserved it. I felt like a Judas.

Vaughn's truck was parked out in front of Ike's bar. Since it was afternoon I just walked right on in. The place was packed with men, unusual for so early in the afternoon. It was downright eerie. Vaughn was sitting at the bar and I could just make out his face, reflecting back at me from the mirror behind the bar. He looked completely relaxed. Arlene was sitting next to him with her shoulders slumped and a hangdog expression. Normally, out in public, she put on this tough woman act but anyone could tell something was about to happen.

"Let me tell you about quitting smoking, son," Oral Bright was yapping in Vaughn's ear like he didn't have a care in the world. "This was a couple of years back you understand. My mama mentioned how much she wanted one of them little lapdogs. Uh, what do you call them? Chihuahuas. Yeah, that's it. And she told me she wanted to quit smoking. So I up and told her, 'If you quit smoking, I'll buy you one of them little dogs for you my ownself.' Well sir, she called me up one day about two, three months later."

"Say she didn't," Tugboat said.

"Now you're not listening to me," Oral said. "So I buy her the dog and everything's hunky-dory, right? Well, a couple of weeks later, I go over there and guess what I saw?"

"She wanted you to buy her a drink!" a rude voice in the crowd said, with a bunch of laughter following it.

"I went busting through the door to see her" Oral's voice went highpitched. "And I be goddamned if she wasn't smoking a cigarette and petting that dog at the same time!"

The men in the smoky bar laughed like thunder, but like they was nervous more than anything. I heard stagey whispers about Vaughn being a firebug and a murderer!

A couple of men walked over to stand directly behind Vaughn. One was dressed with a cowboy hat and had a handlebar mustache. The other man was wearing a John Deere cap, dirty and abused. While they were talking the cowboy purposely bumped against Vaughn as if to intimidate him. When Vaughn spun around on his stool I thought he might take out his pocket knife and cut the cowboy's heart out. Instead he smiled real wide and bought the man a Budweiser— the King of Beers. I'd never seen him act intimidated before.

Vaughn saw me standing at the door and he motioned for me to come over. I expected he'd be madder than hell, but he just smiled as if we were at a family reunion.

"Get this boy an Orange sodie," Vaughn hollered at the bartender.

"That's okay," I said. I didn't especially like them because they had so much fizz.

The bartender said he didn't have no orange sodie, but he slopped some orange juice in a glass in front of me.

"What's going on here?" I asked.

"I guess everyone's having a powwow about ol' Vaughn," he said. "I thought you might know something about it."

"It's news to me," I said.

"Maybe you could do me a favor," Vaughn said low. "Out in the truck's your pistol. Maybe you could go out and get it for me."

"What?" I asked. "How? If you think it's crowded in here, you should see it outside. Everyone will see me."

"Come on, son," Vaughn said in a way that I could tell meant he was really calling me his son. "You're a smart kid. You'll think of a way."

"We just need to go on home, Daddy," Arlene said. "Let's go on home."

"That might not be a bad idea," Vaughn said to her as if he was discussing her grocery list. "These son-of-a-bitches has always been out to get me, but they won't. They won't get me today, tomorrow, or ever."

When I went back out on the sidewalk a half-dozen pairs of eyes from across the street and down the sidewalk cut in my direction. Sunlight was glinting off the old Fairmont water tower. I stood stock still for a minute, but then I had to pretend I didn't see them and got over to the Dodge. The doors were unlocked and the windows were down. Vaughn's rifles were still on the gunrack. I slid on in and sat there for a minute. Muscles in my face were twitching and there wasn't nothing I could do about it. I felt like I couldn't gulp down one more swallow of air. For a second, I thought I might faint but I didn't.

Uncle Sam was standing across the street pointing his finger at me from way up on high on his stilted legs mouthing the words: I WANT YOU.

I opened the glovebox carefully. I was sure everyone knew what I was doing. Everyone in Fairmont knew I was his flesh and blood. I hefted my pistol and started to stick it in my waistband at the small of my back, but then I remembered to see if it was loaded. The chambers were empty. I threw a bunch of napkins and receipts out of the glovebox and found four bullets.

Many things were going through my head at once. My head felt like when you eat ice cream too quick. I could give Vaughn the pistol with no bullets in it, but if he noticed I was giving him an unloaded gun there would be hell to pay. I decided then not to go back into Ike's. Vaughn would come out eventually looking for me and I would stay put. I'd finish this thing myself. Maybe I could end it all and no one else would have to be hurt by this man, Elston Vaughn. Mama could come back if she cared enough about me and we could live a normal life here for a change.

Bob and Grealy Guthrie was standing by a pickup behind me. And Fenton Reed and some of his clan. Some Clearwater boys, mainly teenagers, was down wind of Ike's with deer rifles out already. I turned my head and sat with the pistol in my hand watching the door to Ike's place.

Arlene stepped out first with her hand up over her eyes, shielding her eyes from the sun. Vaughn had probably sent her out so she wouldn't get hurt if anything happened. She stopped and gave me a look I didn't understand and then kind of dog-trotted across the street to the Spot Cafe where she went inside. She joined the ladies who had their faces pressed up against the window.

I couldn't help wondering where the cops were. In a case like this, although there had never been a case like this that I knew of, there would normally be a couple of cop cars with at least the county sheriff or maybe the highway patrol. Since Vaughn had scared off Ron Clevenger as marshal, no one had stepped forward to claim his old position, but I couldn't blame them.

The temperature was beginning to climb along with the humidity. I rolled down the window all the way. The time and temperature was flashing on the bank sign and it made a clicking sound when it showed the time and flipped to the temperature. It said 96 degrees, and that seemed cool compared to last week, when it had run over 100 degrees. I checked up in the visors for cigarettes, but couldn't find any. My hands were shaking.

Then the big green door to Ike's came flying open and Vaughn was standing there like it was any other day. He had a six pack of beer in a brown paper bag under one arm. All eyes were on Vaughn. The men on the sidewalks started backing way as he stepped out onto the street. Bottle flies were buzzing around and one landed on my hand. The green of the fly was an amazing color. How could something so disgusting still be so beautiful?

Vaughn eased into the pickup and set the brown bag of beer between us. He pulled out a pack of cigarettes and tore the cellophane off deliberately and lit one up and laughed to himself as he inhaled. He pulled out a can of beer and took a slurping drink out of it. He put the key in the ignition and started up the Dodge.

"I got the gun," I said. He just nodded. "They're going to kill you, you know?"

Vaughn looked down one length of the sidewalk toward the cafe and grunted. He looked down the other way, but there weren't too many friendly faces. When he was looking the other way, I held the pistol up to his head, aiming just behind his ear. I saw his eyes, eyes full of pain, glance up into the rearview mirror, and I know he saw me pointing the gun at him. His lips moved, and I thought he was telling me, *Do it*. He kept his head turned for a long time like he was giving me permission to go ahead and do it, but finally I lowered the gun.

"They've all got guns," I said.

"I know it." He made a motion with his head like he had a tight shirt and tie on in church.

A farmer named Charlie Ward and a tough kid called Red Clearwater were easing up on both sides of the truck. Vaughn took another drag off his cigarette but just sat there for a second.

"Get out of the truck, kid," Ward said.

"Get out, Honey," Vaughn said. "It's going to be all right by and by. You want to know what I believe? I believe this has all happened to me before and I'm going to see you and your Mama again one fine day. You can count on that, son."

My throat locked up on me and I grabbed the door handle, but before I could get the door open I saw Red put his rifle up to his shoulder. Just as he was pulling the trigger Vaughn looked up and jerked his head so hard to the left it cracked the window. Blood splattered on my face and arms. I wrenched the door handle, and Ward grabbed me away from the truck. Red was moving in for a closer shot to put Vaughn down for good.

But instead the Dodge burnt rubber for a second and the side mirror clipped Red in the ear and knocked him off his feet and out of sight. The Dodge backed almost straight back and rear-ended a Nova parked in front of the courthouse. Suddenly rifles were firing from every direction. Men were coming out from behind their vehicles with deer rifles—a few even had pistols they were using to pellet the Dodge in an effort to stop him.

The Dodge zig-zagged its way down Main Street.

"Don't let him get out of town!"

"Goddamn it!"

"He's going to remember every last one of us," Fenton Reed said aloud so everyone could hear, but not to anybody in particular.

"He won't be too ready to give us any shit now," Ward said. "At least, I don't think he would."

People came flooding out of the buildings around the square like they was on fire. Arlene came running out of the Spot screaming at everyone, "Murderers! Murderer! You want to kill him!" Men looked down at their boots, but some of the younger ones laughed and said things like, "That was the idea anyway." The man from the First National came and led Arlene into his bank so she couldn't go out to her truck and get a gun. She kept staring around at people afraid she'd be next.

Nobody noticed that I had the pistol in my hand so I began to tuck it in my pants but it was too hot. I had fired all four rounds into the Dodge when he peeled out of town. Red came over and slapped me on the back as if to say good job.

I wondered if the men would get together and chase him down or what. But the main families who'd wanted to see Vaughn dead were saying it wasn't worth jail time and for everyone to shut up about it. No one was to say nothing about what happened. Charlie Ward, the Guthries, and Fenton Reed said they was going home. Red Clearwater was the only one who wanted to hunt Vaughn down. It was kind of weird but while I was looking at Red a zag of lightning flashed behind his head out of a cloudbank in the west. I took it for a bad sign like Mama Horne would have told it.

"I say we go nail that motherfucker." Red was clicking the safety on and off on his rifle. "He killed my cousin, and the law let him run free. It's now or never if you ask me. Anyone would kill a dog with rabies—well, ain't this the same damn thing?"

The men didn't seem to agree, not even most of the known hotheads. When the women came out of the shops and started talking sense to their men the whole posse seemed to lose steam.

Off down the street, the pavement was shimmering in the heat. The smell of new tar burnt inside my nose. I felt like it was up to me again. I was going to have to find my own way out to Vaughn's Hill and take care of things the way my people did once and for all.

Feel Like Doing Something Wrong

As people started thinning out on the square I sat at one of the benches on the courthouse lawn. It was one of the oldest original courthouses in Missouri. It still had the nice mansard roof. There was even a cannon ball lodged in one of the pillars from during the Civil War. Folks passing through on vacation always said they expected the cannon ball to be bigger when they read about it in the guide books. "Well, that's it," was about all anyone local would say back to them.

There were war memorials in the courthouse and on the square. The stone marker on the lawn was for those Kingdom County residents who'd sent their sons to fight in Vietnam. Vaughns had died over there. Vaughns had been fighting in wars going back to the beginning of the country and their names were on the plaques. It made me feel proud, but I wasn't so sure I wanted to go anywhere to fight anyone, not for love nor money. I had my own war right there in Kingdom County.

"Where you going, kid?" Red Clearwater's neck veins standing out.

I looked over my shoulder and went, "I need to see a man about a horse." Then I walked to the corner of Court Street and Liberty and jumped into his Chevy sedan and despite him screaming cranked her up and drove out of town. That Chevy could flatout get it too. I had to avoid an outhouse some high school boys probably flipped over— they did that old joke on Halloween too. A high pitch whine sounded like it was coming from far away. At first, I thought the noise was coming from the engine. I looked over my shoulder to see if the cops was chasing me, but nobody was behind me. I nearly put her in the ditch when I looked out front again.

The sound grew louder and higher pitched and it was in my ears like a voice talking to me. The voice was telling me what to do. *Kill Vaughn*, said the droning voice. *Kill Vaughn*. I didn't want to but then again I did. It seemed like someone was telling me to do it. I didn't know if it was the Devil or not. *Kill Vaughn*. It was me. Definitely me. Coming way down from inside of myself I told myself to do it. I didn't want to, but I was going to. The way deep down me had the axe over the run of the mill me.

Blood in the Mirror

There weren't any clouds but the sun seemed to disappear. As I was driving Red's Chevy out of town, I passed Royce Stafford coming in. The Chevy was whining up high as I passed under the yellow caution light on Main. I figured he would pull a U-turn and come after me with his lights flashing and siren blaring, but he didn't. Someone had finally called the cops, but I noticed it wasn't Sheriff Merrill coming into town because Merrill was a chickenshit. I could just barely see over the steering wheel with my leg stretched out so I could push down the gas pedal. The highway out of town looked long and narrow, stretching toward a steep hill up ahead, and the ditches rose up steeply on either side. I wasn't used to driving and I tried to feature keeping that Chevy down the middle of the road.

In the side mirror I saw the blood on one side of my face, and I told myself that it wasn't my blood. Red's bullet had ripped through Vaughn's cheek if I could believe my own eyes, but Vaughn was tough so who knows how bad off he might or might not be. First thing I did was get off Highway 54 right away and head out on Route O, where I passed Stinson Creek and got onto a dirt road that ran out into a stand of pine trees in the woods, in a little holler to wait things out. On the inside I felt like this old boy in a jungle movie who got sucked down by quicksand until nothing was left but his panama hat.

I knew I was taking a chance on waiting. Red and some of the others might run out to Vaughn's to finish the job, but I figured it would be better to wait. I found a Glock in Red's glove box. While I waited, I listened to the radio, but Red's car only had an AM, so I had to listen to about the only station you could get in Fairmont and that meant country and western music, but Merle Haggard was better than listening to myself think. Looking out past the barbed wire, I could see the field hay was mowed and cubed. A wren was making noise from the branches of a sycamore. In the distance I could hear the sound of boards being cut with a bandsaw.

There was a little mudhole the rain from the morning had made so I used one of Red's oily T-shirts in the backseat, tore it, and dipped it into the water and tried to wipe Vaughn's blood off my face but all it did was smear. It made me want to get sick if I let myself think about it. From here, I told myself I could let the men take care of it. But they couldn't be relied on and neither could the law in this part of the country. Red had half a carton of Camels under his seat and I felt like a pirate finding treasure. I gratefully smoked most of the afternoon, until my throat was raw and sipped on some hot beers and tried not to get too drunk like Vaughn had taught me. It wasn't easy. I passed out as the corn waved ever so slightly in the field.

The Darkest Hour

When I awoke the sun was beating down fiercely on the roof of the Chevy. The edges of the world were blurry to my eyes. I thought a Pepsi-Cola sure would go down easy about now. I patted my shirt pocket and realized I still had the better part of Red's carton, but my throat hurt. Despite the bright sun rays in my eyes, and the fluffy clouds passing across the sky, I could sense a darkness inside of me crying for all that had happened. *Don't you love me?* The man inside my head asked. I didn't know what this presence meant, so I didn't say yes or no.

Don't you love me anymore? The voice asked me again. I didn't know if it was God or the Devil or maybe some kind of trick my mind was playing on me. I could have said yes and maybe things would have been all right. Instead I pushed in the car lighter, stuck another cancer stick in my mouth, and when the lighter popped. I pulled it out and stared at the red burner and its swirling pattern—and then I knew what to do.

"Kiss my ass," I said to the voice. The presence was gone straight away. I knew it wouldn't bother me no more.

Do it. You know he deserves it. You going to let him do you that way, kid? Do it.

"I'm going to," I said. "Motherfucker."

Don't you just hate people? Especially adults! They're always hanging all their rules over your head. Tell you to do right when they don't. Why don't the rules to apply to them? Them mamas and daddys and rich people what run the stores down on the square and live up on Court Street all fat and sassy! Where do they get off? They can't make you do nothing. They're not the boss of you!

"I know that," I said.

Go do it then! But not because I'm telling you to--do it because every-one else is too chickenshit.

"Nobody's making me do nothing," I said. "Least of all you. You think you can tell me what I'm supposed to do? The hell with you. Get out of this car. Get out of my head. I'm running the show here! I don't care if I go to juvie or hell."

What about hell?

"I don't believe in it," I said.

I turned the key, revving up the Chevy to shut up the voices in my head. I flipped on the radio and turned it up loud. Some old Johnny Cash tune was playing. The rearend shimmied onto the road and I took off toward Vaughn's Hill. I didn't know what I would find. I figured every Vaughn would be out there with a gun lining up and down the road.

There was no choice, but Mama had to be saved. What Vaughn was doing with her and Arlene was not right. Some-one had to make it all right, even if I had to do something wrong, to put everything proper again. Mama did not have sense enough to straighten things out for herself. I could see it now. See it all so clear. Just like when I was baptized and coming up wet out of the water when everything was new again for about a second and a half before going back to square one.

It took me awhile to get my courage up. I kept driving the country roads. I quit drinking when I fishtailed in front of one of those old rusty one-ton bridges and straightened out just as the tires hit the wooden boards. It was like there were blinders like they put on horses and I was going down on a long thin tube with gnarled trees and ghouls in the ravines reaching out to slash at me with their pointed limbs like razor blades. The trees were growing out of the shrugging banks on the whitish roads, roots sticking out like veins, and the wind whispered down the natural tunnel just as I hit the fork in the road and turned down toward Vaughn Road. I sped up as I saw a long train about to block the lane. Just at a glance, I knew there were at least fifty cars on it maybe more. I was afraid if I didn't beat the train to the crossing, it would stop me long enough to make me think about what I was fixing to do.

It looked like it was going to be close so I mashed the pedal down to the floor and had to stand on it so I could still see through the space between the dash and the steering wheel with my ass up off the seat. There were no guard rails or flashing lights way out here in B.F.E. so I just hoped for the best.

The train whistle was blowing. I don't know if it was automatic for them to do it at crossings or if they could see the Chevy cruising at them. Maybe the conductor was cussing to himself, but if so he wasn't easing back off none.

Then I closed my eyes, held my breath, and the music on the radio seem to slur. The white edges returned to the outer reaches of what I could see. There was a blind blue light above me though the sun had about disappeared. The train was on top of me like a dragon screaming my name: *NATHAN. NATHAN. NATHAN.*

The car was in the air for what seemed like two days. Then it came crashing down on the washed out gravel road. The front end made a crunching sound. I think the hubcaps might have come off. I slammed on the brakes. The car swung across the road so that when she stopped the front end was in the ditch with her ass end hanging out in the road.

"Shit and goddamn," I said. The car engine died. I tried to turn her over.

She rattled, and then a loud screech. She started up again. "Thank God." Don't think I meant nothing by saying that. I wasn't trying to take God's name in vain. I just said it out of my bad habits.

When I came to the little rusted girder bridge over the creek at the foot of Vaughn's Hill, I had to shift down into second or I'd never make it up the steep grade. I didn't see anybody with guns on my way up. No one standing guard or trying to protect Elston.

The first house I passed, down in the dell, was Danny Vaughn's, but nobody appeared to be outside so I drove on by. I kept driving and passed Royal and Opal's falling down house that was old as Missouri; Claude and Nana's trailer; Earle and Corinne's place and their boy Rusty. There was no end to the Vaughns it seemed. I just named the ones I was familiar with, but where were they all?

Finally I came to Vaughn's Hill. I pulled onto Vaughn Road where I almost clipped a Nubian goat. I waited for the voice in my head to start up, but it never did. I flipped my cigarette out the window into the drive. Fireworks were going off in the air toward the city park in Fairmont. I could see them lighting up the sky: red, gold, and green. I wasn't sure if I would ever see another Fourth of July or watch the fireworks climb up and explode like tears down around the moon. There was that hateful gun calling to me from the glovebox. The smell of rotting flowers strong in my nose almost like blood. My hands were no longer shaking. I was ready for what had to be done. I found a spot where I could just pull into under a shade tree by the creek and waited for Vaughn.

When the evening sun went down, it hit me that Vaughn must have taken the old back way. It wouldn't have been easy, but he had four wheel drive.

I turned the ignition, and it groaned for a sec before it started. The Chevy had a transmission problem, because when I tried to put it into drive, it took a second to react. Life just ain't fair, I thought, for what good it did to complain. The lights were off at Mawmaw's. I drove by the shitty houses and trailers of all the Vaughns who lived there. Nobody seemed to be home still. It was almost as if they had heard about what happened in town and had left the country. A yellow dog was standing out in the road.

The rain had helped control the chalky dust a vehicle normally stirred up. I went up and down the hills with my heart in my stomach and the Glock laying there on the seat next to me. All the cigarette smoking had made me pukey too.

When I pulled into Vaughn's drive I was surprised to see Sonny's El Camino. Despite how I felt, I lit another Camel and let it dangle from my lip. The Dodge had almost as many bullet holes in it was Bonnie and Clyde's car in that movie. *Shit*, I said. I checked the Glock and then kicked the door open, and the car started to buzz since the keys were still in the ignition.

None of the dogs came running out from under the porch. The screen door had been yanked off it's hinges. The front door was standing open. Frogs were gulping down by the pond. The mosquitoes and cicadas were out in full force too. When I stepped onto the porch I turned and gave my cigarette a flip into the weedy yard.

Mama was sitting inside on the ugly brown and green sofa drinking coffee and smoking. She looked like she had been crying not too long ago. And it might sound like a strange thing to say in a situation like that, but she looked pretty.

"Honey," Mama said. "Put down that gun."

I sat the gun down on the coffee table in front of her. She threw her arms around me with her cigarette still burning in her hand. Her body was shaking with sobs and then that got me going too.

"I hope you didn't think I left you," Mama said, backing away from me to look me in the face. "Because I wasn't leaving you. I was trying to leave him. I had to get away from Vaughn, you know?"

"You left me, Lorene," I said. "What kind of mother does that?"

"Oh Honey, don't," she said.

"Don't," I said. "Don't? What the hell did I do to deserve that? When you left I thought you didn't love me anymore. It's not the first time you left me, but do you know how it feels? It hurts every time, but it hurts less each time. It hurts less because you quit feeling it as much, because a little part of you dies every time."

"I'm sorry, Honey," Mama said. "I love you."

"Great," I said. "I love you too, but what the hell does that change? Is Vaughn here? Where's Sonny?"

"Sonny's in the hallway by the back bedroom with Vaughn," Mama said. "But don't go back there . . ."

I snatched the Glock off the coffee table, turned on my heel, and goose-stepped down the hall.

"Don't!" Mama pulled at my T-shirt but I kept going.

When I found them, Sonny was hunched over Vaughn. There was a bullet hole almost in the center of Vaughn's chest. I could see where Red's bullet had chewed up his ear and traveled along his jawline.

His eyes were full with tears. He mouthed something to me, but I couldn't understand him. I had missed it. It was a relief. I took Vaughn's hand and held it to my chest. I was sorry, but it was right.

He gasped loudly. A gurgling sound. He turned his eyes on me opening his mouth as if he had something he wanted to tell me. I regretted everything I had done to help bring this on. He was my daddy and there wasn't no denying it. I hoped he said something like he knew I was his boy all along, maybe something about love, but his lips trembled without sound. His eyes lost focus. He breathed in once more and I noticed I was counting the seconds to his next breath, but it never came.

The way Vaughn was laying there I knew he was dead. Sonny was sitting on the carpet leaned against the wall and holding Vaughn's other hand and he sat there all cried out. I had never seen Sonny cry before, or ever even come close to it. I knelt down with Sonny and my daddy. I could feel my body trembling, but it was like someone was making my body work against its will. I hated Vaughn and refused to cry over him, but he was my own blood despite his wildness, his meanness, and his wrongness. I lay my head down across his chest and heard his heart still slowly beating and touched the rough fingers of his hand.

"He's dead," Sonny said more to himself than me. "He's dead. I shot him and he's dead. Why did he make me do it? Why did he have to go and make me do it?"

"If you hadn't," I placed Vaughn's hand down on the floor. "You don't understand. I wanted to be the one to do it." I stared at my daddy and imagined he would awaken any second and tell me to pull his truck around front. He was too tough to die and I could imagine the truthfulness of it, although I was looking straight at the fact. Vaughn was dead.

Sonny gaped at me with his mouth open. He was slunk up against the wall. He smacked my face for me. I could tell he didn't think about it—his hand did it without thinking. I could tell it tore him up, but I felt like I was guilty as hell and deserved it. I had murdered Vaughn in my heart where it counted like the good book said. I'd seen myself do it in my mind beforehand. Sonny's eyes were shocked as he looked at me and it went without saying that he and I were just the same and we were both just like Vaughn. I was a Vaughn in everything but legal name. No one had ever called me bastard, but I knew it anyway because I'd lived it. I didn't know then that no one would ever call me Honey Boy again or just how much I would miss it.

"I came back to kill him" Sonny tried to wipe the bloody mess off on his jeans. "I won't lie about that. I wanted Lorene. I wouldn't let him have her, no sir. She's too good for him."

Mama came over and took the gun from me and let it slide down on the carpet. She led me back to the couch in the living room. Sirens were howling in the distance. I heard some of the Vaughn's Hill dogs crying back at the sirens. Mama pulled me against her and kissed my temple and combed her fingers through my hair. Then I laid my head on her lap and just stayed down even when the police got there and the ambulance was waiting outside. I just stayed right there with my head on Mama's lap. It didn't embarrass me like it might some. A cigarette was burning in a green ashtray on the coffee table. A pack of Viceroys was next to the ashtray with a cheap red lighter pushed down into the cellophane. An old Creedence album was on the far end of the table.

A few minutes later, Sheriff Merrill walked through the front door big as life. I sat up slowly. He looked at Mama and tried to nod in a comforting way at her. He pretended not to see me until I opened up my mouth in defiance.

I rose up and said in a voice not my own, "Constable."

The sheriff's face went a deep oxblood. His ruined, bulging nose exploded with color like a flower shot with time-lapse photography. His hands went up to his hip, his right hand to his holstered .38, as if he knew he might need to use it on me, just by looking at the color of my eyes, and he stared hard until he turned and went down the hall with a new deputy following at his elbow wearing civilian clothes. Red Clearwater raised his chin at me and pointed in what was either a threat or a salute. I wasn't worried about his Chevy, but neither was he. Seeing him as a deputy was like being kicked in the face. He was here to get revenge for Rafe, if he could.

Corporal Stafford from the highway patrol came in. He took his hat off in his hands when he saw Mama and me. He knelt down on one knee in front of me and said softly, "You boys gave us a good run." I could tell there weren't any hard feelings now. He held out his big hand, and I shook it.

"You try to stay out of trouble there, Little Vaughn," Stafford said. "After all we've been through I'd hate to send you down to the Church Farm."

Stafford stood up and went down the hall with the others. There was a scuffle in the hallway. I didn't go back to look. It was in Sonny's nature to fight the law. They wrestled him through the house, slamming him into doorways and walls, him cussing them all the way until they put him in the back of the cop car. His head rested against the glass. He wouldn't even look at me.

I could feel Mama's heart beating loud in her chest, filling my ears with her fear, as I pushed myself up to a sitting position. The heat of her body burning away the worry I had carried around deep inside me where it would occasionally bubble up to the surface like a clogged drain. But I still didn't believe he was dead. You might as well try to kill an early summer thunderstorm with lightning striking all around. An act of God can't be shot or locked up in the penitentiary.

Sheriff Merrill came back through the door. There was a sheen of sweat on his forehead. He was no longer wearing his hat. "I hate like hell to do this, Lorene, but I guess you know."

"I know." She stood up then and turned around as Merrill cuffed her.

"What?" I said. "What's going on? Why are you doing that?"

"Now I'm sorry it's got to be thisaway," Merrill said.

"For helping Vaughn," she said like a whisper with her lips touching my ear. "Me and Arlene did some things we shouldn't have. We pointed guns at people. We helped him rob. I don't know what's going to happen. Call Aunt Oleta. She'll take care of you. I'll be back there soon as I can to get you."

"I'll have one of my guys stay with the boy." Sheriff Merrill squeezed the handcuffs around her wrists.

"Don't,"I said. "Don't take my mama."

"Don't cry." Mama's eyes leaked tears. Her nose was red and her mascara was smudged from crying. "I'll be back if I can. I won't never leave you again if they let me come home."

I prayed and hoped but who know how long they'd put her in jail for. She was sorry for what she done. Hell, Vaughn was the one who made her do it but she still done it. When I looked at her I could see that other person behind her face fighting to get away from everything and everyone she had ever known.

"Please." I threw my arms around her, but now she could no longer hug me back.

"Shhh, shhh," she leaned down a little and burrowed her face in my hair. "When they let me out, we'll run away together. Anywhere you want to go. How about Alaska? I always wanted to go there."

"Okay." I dried my tears on the back of my hand.

I wasn't sure how to tell her it had never been my dream to go anywhere. I would have been happy in Fairmont all these years even if I'd said I hated it before. There were problems here but at least these were the problems we knew. Out in the world, there were worse things like not knowing anybody and not having any relatives or friends to be with. She was looking for some magical person to take away all the problems, but I knew now that person did not exist and that we'd both have to do it for ourselves. I would have told her I didn't want to go anywhere, but now moving was in my blood. I wanted to stay long enough to see Vaughn buried, for one, but I knew if we stayed, everyone would expect me to be just like him. The Vaughns would want me to live up to his reputation. It was the one thing I knew I'd never be able to do. I couldn't be all bad like Vaughn or the good Christian boy that Aunt Oleta wanted either. I could only be what I was, and I still had to find that out.

I followed them out on the porch. It was hard to believe this was happening. I never dreamed this would happen to

Mama. The police radio squawked. The cherry lights were still flashing. I tried to catch a glimpse of Sonny but he was sitting with his head against the seat now, looking down.

They put Mama in Stafford's patrol car so she wouldn't be next to Sonny. What a hot mess this had all turned out to be. They were going to have to find Arlene now. Where was she and Sugarbaby? Was she on the run? Everyone was wondering. I heard the cops talking about it. They asked Mama but she didn't know. I imagined she could disappear back along the banks of the Osage river, where, it wouldn't surprise me none, she might take root, and turned herself into a bald cypress where the rest of her family was from. Vaughn had always called her a born river rat.

Sheriff Merrill made Red Clearwater stay with me until Aunt Oleta could get Luther to drive her and Clarence over. Red was not as bad as Rafe had been but his last name was Clearwater just the same.

I scratched at the scarred flesh from where Rafe had burned his cigarette into it. I sat down on one of the steps of the porch. Red sat down next to me and to my surprise threw an arm across my shoulders, but I shrugged it off after a minute. I got up to walk around. He gave me some shit about messing up his Chevy.

I picked up a battered Louisville Slugger and a few gravel rocks and hit them into the field across the road for a while just thinking about everything that had done happened. Adults didn't know it all. How was I going to grow up now? Where would I live? Who could a person count on in this life? Even the voice that sometimes talked to me in my head was quiet.

Now that the cops were gone, everyone who lived on Vaughn's Hill was walking down the road or pulling up and parking in the yard to witness what was happening. Mama Horne and Aunt Oleta pulled into the driveway in an old black Cadillac with a funky brown door. She held her head

high and hugged me to her bosom like her most prized pos-
session before stuffing me into the backseat with all my earth-
earthly things condensed to a battered army duffel bag. It was
plain how much they loved me. Tears welled up in their eyes.

"Am I coming home with you, Aunt Oleta?"

"You're darn right!" Aunt Oleta said.

"You poor thing," Mama Horne.

She called me a poor thing, but I didn't feel so poorly at
that moment. I missed Mama but I felt relieved and safe
knowing I was heading to Aunt Oleta's house again even if
she drove me nuts sometimes. It was where I needed to be
until Mama could come back to me if she ever did. A person
can be right beside you and still be far away at the same time
or they can be on the other side of the country and still be
locked up safely in your heart.

Lie Still, Sleep Becalmed

And then much later, as the sunlight died blood orange on the horizon at Aunt Oleta's house, everything was silent save for the murmuring voices of the old people keeping company in the sitting room. Aunt Oleta was quietly playing the piano and I could hear her singing in her falsetto voice: *"This is my story, this is my song, praising my Savior all the day long."*

It was like we had just been to a funeral. Bitter tears fell on my pillow, but I turned my face to the wall and cried silently so no one would know. I heard the red-winged blackbirds calling from the inky trees in the backyard making their peculiar noises like slow rain dripping into a standing pool of cistern water. It made me dream of roots growing deeper into the claybanked creeks, seedlings growing through the mire, creeper vine winding around a tight copse of river birch, Osage, and thorn in the heaving woods, bloodworms and beetles digging in the crowded earth until I fell into a restless sleep, the night sheets twisting around my legs becoming sycamore roots.

Acknowledgements

This book absolutely would not exist without the vision of Chris Tusa and his brainchild—Fiction Southeast Press! To have a friend and fellow writer who believes in your work so strongly is truly a blessing.

Much gratitude to those who inspired me with their love and friendship when it counted most: The Salmons clan, the Wolfmeiers, the Todds, Ted Lester, Rodean Sherwood, Malcolm Todd, Brett Williams, George Foster, Marty Newman, Beth Moore, Joe Moore, LeeAnne Ogletree, Mr. Jimmy and Ms. Hope, and Dave Kelsay.

Thanks to my fellow wordsmiths for support and advice: Eli Hastings, Dave Smith, Anthony Connolly, Jessica Smith, Dan Alamia, Lesley Parker Richardson, Angela Longerbeam, Andrea Quarracino, Jesse Waters, Margaux Fragoso, David Baker, Gladys Swan, Matt Dube, Jennifer Gravley, Michael Garriga, and Kent Wascom.

I couldn't have kept at it if it weren't for great teachers who encouraged me with their many gifts: Michael Pritchett, Marilyn Lake, Speer Morgan, Trudy Lewis, Frank Pisano, Nancy Hadfield, David Gessner, Rebecca Lee, and Clyde Edgerton.

My hats off to Evelyn Somers Rogers for her exquisite editing skills. Thanks to Nikki Waltz for online conferences. Also, I salute those who read and commented on the early pages of this novel at UNC Wilmington. A shoutout to all the Kickstarters! The encouragement of my SGI friends has been invaluable.

Thanks to my many talented students for reminding me what it's all about and to my fine colleagues in the English department at Louisiana State University.

ABOUT THE AUTHOR

Daren Dean's work has appeared in The Green Hills Literary Lantern, Missouri Life, The Oklahoma Review, Midwestern Gothic, Ecotone, Image, Chattahoochee Review, Fiction Southeast, StorySouth, and others. His story "Bring Your Sorrow Over Here" was selected as Runner-up by Judge George Singleton in Yemassee's William Richey Short Fiction contest and another story, "Affliction" was a Finalist in the Glimmer Train Short Fiction Contest for New Writers in 2012. He holds an MFA in Creative Writing from the University of North Carolina at Wilmington. Dean has also worked in scholarly publishing at the University of Missouri Press. Currently, he teaches writing and literature in the English department at Louisiana State University in Baton Rouge. Far Beyond the Pale is his first novel.

FAR BEYOND THE PALE

IN THIS DARKLY COMIC novel Nathan "Honey Boy" Kimbrough narrates a boy's search for a father and his mother's search for a "good man" in Missouri in the mid-1970s. Honey Boy is a thirteen year old, four letter spouting, pistol packing kid who is determined to learn something about the art of thieving swag from Kingdom County's own resident outlaw: Vaughn—a man so wicked that he is gone beyond the pale in his outrageous acts which include ransacking homes, stealing livestock, and intimidating anyone who gets in his way. Honey Boy watches as his mother Lorene is caught in a lover's triangle between brothers, Elson and Sonny Vaughn.

Dean sings a broken ballad with wit and tenderness about people too full of misunderstandings, rage, and an often destructive love. These are people who embrace their kin with fists and kiss one another with insults. It's a coming of age story about a boy in the seedy side of the adult world he longs to join but is too young to completely understand. Should he "be good" as his Aunt Oleta suggests or take up the life of a country outlaw?

Ultimately, he falls under the tutelage of Vaughn, a natural born killer with the conscience of a sociopath. What follows is a conclusion so violent that even Vaughn might wonder if he hasn't done his job too well. Vigilantes in Fairmont surround the outlaw at his favorite tavern with deer rifles and revolvers drawn in a modern grit lit novel with an explosive climax.

CPSIA information can be obtained at www.ICGtesting.com
Printed in the USA
LVOW10s0142190815

450691LV00006B/258/P